P9-DNO-708

Praise for *New York Times* bestselling author Diana Palmer

"Palmer proves that love and passion can be found even in the most dangerous situations."
—*Publishers Weekly* on *Untamed*

"You just can't do better than a Diana Palmer story to make your heart lighter and smile brighter."
—*Fresh Fiction* on *Wyoming Rugged*

"Diana Palmer is a mesmerizing storyteller who captures the essence of what a romance should be."
—*Affaire de Coeur*

"The popular Palmer has penned another winning novel, a perfect blend of romance and suspense."
—*Booklist* on *Lawman*

"Diana Palmer's characters leap off the page. She captures their emotions and scars beautifully and makes them come alive for readers."
—*RT Book Reviews* on *Lawless*

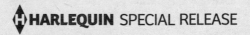

NEW YORK TIMES BESTSELLING AUTHOR

DIANA PALMER

A RANCHER'S CLAIM

Previously published as
The Rawhide Man and *Reluctant Father*

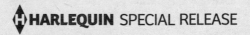

◆H HARLEQUIN SPECIAL RELEASE

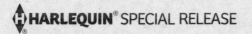 **HARLEQUIN**® SPECIAL RELEASE

ISBN-13: 978-1-335-55096-5

A Rancher's Claim

Copyright © 2021 by Harlequin Books S.A.

The Rawhide Man
First published as The Rawhide Man in 1984.
This edition published in 2021.
Copyright © 1984 by Diana Palmer

Reluctant Father
First published as Reluctant Father in 1988.
This edition published in 2021.
Copyright © 1988 by Diana Palmer

Recycling programs
for this product may
not exist in your area.

This edition published by arrangement with Harlequin Books S.A.

For questions and comments about the quality of this book, please contact us at CustomerService@Harlequin.com.

Harlequin Enterprises ULC
22 Adelaide St. West, 40th Floor
Toronto, Ontario M5H 4E3, Canada
www.Harlequin.com

Printed in U.S.A.

CONTENTS

A prolific author of more than one hundred books, **Diana Palmer** got her start as a newspaper reporter. A *New York Times* bestselling author and voted one of the top ten romance writers in America, she has a gift for telling the most sensual tales with charm and humor. Diana lives with her family in Cornelia, Georgia. Visit her website at www.dianapalmer.com.

Visit the Author Profile page at Harlequin.com for more titles.

THE RAWHIDE MAN

To Doris, Kay, Kathleen, June, Mary, Cindy, Sharalee
and all those lovely San Antonio ladies

CHAPTER ONE

THUNDER WAS CRASHING wildly outside the elegant middle Georgia house, but the poised young woman standing in the parlor was too numb to be frightened of it. The ordeal of the past two days had stripped her nerves of all feeling.

Elizabeth Meriam White was twenty-two and felt fifty. Her mother's lingering illness had been torment enough, but she hadn't expected the loss to be so traumatic. Wishing only the peace of oblivion for her beloved parent, she hadn't realized how empty her own life was going to become. Now she had no one. Her stepsister had left that morning for Paris in a whirl of expensive perfume and chiffon, with her share of their mother's estate firmly in hand. They'd never been close, but Bess had hoped for something more after the ordeal. She should have known better. Crystal had never once offered to help nurse her dying stepmother. After all, she'd told Bess carelessly, there was plenty of money to hire someone to do that.

Plenty of money. Bess could have cried. Yes, there had been, until Bess's father died and her mother remarried to Jonathan Smythe and turned her father's business interests over to him. Carla had never bothered with finance, except to make sure that the Rawhide Man couldn't get his hands on that precious block of shares in the Texas oil corporation his father and Bess's had pioneered together.

Bess shivered at the thought of Jude Langston. She'd always thought of him as rawhide through and through, because he was like that—lean and tough and very nearly invulnerable. He hadn't been at the funeral, but Bess had seen her mother's will and she knew he'd be along. Even in death, Carla's obsession with besting Jude went on.

With a long sigh, Bess walked to the window and watched the rain beating down outside on the bleak, barren trees, whose autumn leaves had only just disappeared as cold December hovered overhead.

She leaned her forehead against the cold windowpane and closed her eyes. Oh, Mama, she thought miserably, I never knew what loneliness was until now. I never knew.

It had been a long year. A long two years. Carla had had a progressive kind of bone cancer that hadn't responded to any kind of treatment, not radiation or chemotherapy. And Carla herself had refused any discussion of bone marrow transplants. So her death had been by inches, while Bess had tried to be brave and nurse her and not go to pieces. It hadn't been easy. Her mother had been demanding and perverse and irritable and impatient. But Bess loved her. And she took care of her, up until the final hospital stay. She did it without any help from Crystal, too, because Crystal was having a mad fling with a French count and couldn't be bothered to come home. Except to grab her share of the pitiful amount of money that was left, of course. Bess had reminded her coldly that hospital and doctor bills had drained the family resources. And then Crystal had asked about the oil stock…

Bess rubbed the back of her neck where it felt strained to the limit. She was sick all over with grief and the lack of rest and food. The stock, Crystal had said, might pull Bess out of the hole.

"Even so, you'll have to sell the house, Bess," Crystal had said, oddly sympathetic. "It's mortgaged to the roots of the grass."

"The minute he hears from the attorneys, Jude Langston will come down on my head like judgment," Bess returned, "and you know it."

"That sexy man," Crystal said, nodding dreamily. "My God, what a waste, to look like that and be as hard as he is. He could have women by the barrelful, but all he wants to do is play around with oil and cattle and that baby of his."

"Katy's not a baby anymore," Bess reminded her. "She's almost ten."

"That's right, you go to the ranch every summer, don't you, to those reunions? But you didn't go this summer…" Crystal remarked.

Bess colored delicately and turned away. "I had to take care of Mother," she said shortly.

"Yes, I know it was hard. I'd have helped darling, really I would, but…" Her delicate features twisted. "What will you do about the stock?"

"I wish I didn't have it," Bess said levelly. "I don't

relish having to face Jude. I only wish Mother hadn't tied up the stock the way she did."

"Oh, she hated him, all right," Crystal said, laughing. "Even when she was able, she'd never go to the reunions, because she knew he'd be there. Why were they such enemies?"

"Because she was a society girl," Bess said bitterly, remembering. "And there's nothing in the world Jude hates more. Katy's mother was one, you know. She broke their engagement while he was in Vietnam and married someone else, even though she was carrying his child. He still takes that hatred out on anyone handy. Mother. Or me. I just wish the battle had died with her."

"I think you'll manage, sweet," Crystal told her, sizing up her stepsister's tall, elegant carriage. Bess wasn't exactly pretty, but she was a lady and she had class, and it stuck out all over her, from her silver blond hair to her soft brown eyes and creamy complexion.

"Against Jude?" Bess smiled sadly. "I watched him back down an armed cowboy once, when I was with Dad at the Langston ranch. I was about fourteen, and one of the hands got mad at Jude for something. He took a couple of drinks and went at Jude with a loaded gun. Jude didn't even flinch. He walked straight into the gun, took it away from the cowboy and beat him to his knees."

"Your eyes flash when you talk about him," Crystal observed, watching Bess. "He excites you, doesn't he?"

"He frightens me." The older girl laughed nervously.

Crystal shook her head slowly. "You're awfully naive for a woman your age. It isn't fear, but you aren't experienced enough to know that, are you?" she asked absently. Then she shrugged and whirled away. "Have to run, pet. Jacques is meeting me at the airport. Let me know how things work out, won't you?"

And that was that. Bess was left alone in the house, and it was getting dark. She had no family, no close friends—there hadn't been the opportunity to make friends, with an invalid mother who needed constant care. So she was alone.

Involuntarily her mind went wandering back to Jude like a puppy that wouldn't mind. He'd be along, all right. As soon as he realized that Bess had control of his precious stock, he'd be at her throat. He hadn't managed to run over Carla, though, and he wasn't going to run over Bess, either. She had the shares and she was keeping them. They were all that stood between her and starvation, and they paid a high dividend.

She let the curtain fall and turned away from the window too quickly to catch the flash of car lights against the glass. The force of the rain muffled the sound of a purring engine coming closer.

Bess went into the bare hall and sat down on the steps, ruffling her disheveled blond hair. She touched her face lightly, mentally comparing it with Crystal's. Her nose was arrow straight; her mouth had a bee-stung appearance, full and red and soft. Her brown eyes were wide spaced and appealing. She wasn't beautiful like her stepsister, but she wasn't ugly, at least. Of course, she was very thin and small breasted—not voluptuous like Crystal. But someday she might find a man and get married. And again she thought of Jude and cursed her stubborn, stupid mind. Jude would never marry. For heaven's sake, he'd never even bothered to marry Katy's mother!

Bess stared around her at the opulent home, which had been part of the White estate for over a hundred years, surviving even the Civil War. How sad that it hadn't been able to survive the Smythes, she thought with a surge of humor. Crystal was right, of course. It would have to be sold. Dividends from her stocks would provide enough to support her if she was frugal, but not to maintain the house as well.

With a weary groan she got to her feet. She might as well get busy and clean out some drawers or something. It would have been a blessing if she'd had a job to go to, but she'd been trained for nothing except managing this monstrous house. And soon she wouldn't have even that. She laughed almost hysterically at the thought. She'd have to get a job.

The sudden clang of the doorbell made her jump. She hadn't expected visitors in this wild rain.

She glanced at her hair in the mirror. It looked as if it had been caught in a windmill, but there was no time to fix it, and she wasn't wearing makeup at all. She looked pale and plain and sickly. She hoped this wasn't going to be another bill collector; she had enough trouble already, and the phone calls and demands for payment were growing hourly since the news of her mother's death had been made public. When it rained it poured, she thought desperately.

A wild shudder went through her when she opened the door. The man outside was the image of every woman's secret dream. Tall, broad shouldered and long legged, dressed in an expensive gray pin-striped suit with matching Stetson and boots, he looked like something out of a smart men's magazine. But his face, deeply tanned, was as inscrutable as a stone carving. His mouth was rigid, as firm as his jaw. His eyes were deeply set under thick black lashes and they were a glittering pale green. His scowling eyebrows were the same jet black as the hair she glimpsed under his hat. And the whole portrait was so formidable that she instinctively stepped back.

"You've been expecting me, I imagine," Jude Langston said curtly, just a trace of a Texas accent in his deep, measured voice.

"Oh, yes, along with flood, earthquake and volcanic eruptions," she agreed, using the protective guise of humor that had always saved her nerves when she had to deal with him. "I won't even bother asking why you're here. Obviously, you've seen the will."

He moved forward, and she knew him too well to stand her ground. He closed the door roughly behind him, and rain dripped from the wide brim of the gray hat that shadowed part of his face.

"Where can we talk?"

She turned, remembering that she was still Miss White of Oakgrove, and led him into the shabby parlor.

"Still the society girl, I see," he taunted, dropping down onto the sofa. "Do I get coffee, Miss White, or aren't the servants working today?"

She blanched, but her chin lifted and her brown eyes accused. "My mother died two days ago," she said pointedly, "so could you save your sarcasm for a special occasion? Yes, there's coffee, and no, there aren't any servants. There haven't been for a number of years. Or don't you know yet that the only thing standing between me and imminent starvation is that block of oil shares you're so hot to get your hands on?"

He looked as if she'd actually surprised him, but she turned away. "I'll get the coffee," she said curtly.

While she was gone, she cooled down her hot temper. It wouldn't do her any good with Jude; the only chance she had was to keep her head and not go for his throat. By the time she carried the worn silver service into the living room, he'd discarded his topcoat and hat and was wandering around the room, glancing distastefully at the portrait of Carla and Bess above the mantel.

He turned and watched her set the heavy service on the coffee table without offering to help. That was like him, the original chauvinist who had no time for women.

"Thank you," she said elegantly, "for your kind offer of assistance."

"Is the damned thing heavy?" he asked carelessly.

She almost laughed. The situation was unbelievable. She sat down and poured out the coffee, handing him his black without realizing what that little slip gave away.

"Should I be flattered that you remember how I take my coffee?" he asked, leaning back to study her insolently, running his eyes over every curve outlined by the simple gray jersey dress she was wearing.

"Don't put on your cowboy drawl for me, mister," she replied quietly, lifting her cup to her lips. "I know you."

"You think you do," he agreed, his green eyes narrowing.

"How's Katy?" she asked.

He shrugged. "Growing up fast." His gaze focused on her. "She asked about you when the family got together this summer."

"I'm sorry I missed it," she said. "I couldn't leave Mother."

He flexed his broad shoulders and leaned forward. The action stretched the fabric of his pants over his powerful thighs and Bess had to look away.

"That's enough small talk," he said suddenly, piercing her eyes with his. "You're coming back to San Antonio with me."

She hardly had time to catch her breath. "I'm what?"

"You heard me." He set down his cup. "The only way I can control that stock is by marrying you. So that's how we'll do it."

Her body jerked as if he'd hit her, and she stared at him uncomprehendingly. She might have thought of this before—it was so like Jude to take the direct approach.

"No," she said shortly.

"Yes," he replied. "I've waited years to get my hands on those shares, and I'm having them. If you come along with the deal, I'll just have to make the best of it."

She went red in the face and sat up straight. "What makes you think you're any prize?" she asked in her coldest tone. "You're cold and hard and you don't care about anybody in the world except Katy!"

"That's absolutely gospel," he agreed, staring at her unblinkingly. "But you'll go to the altar with me if I have to tie you up and gag you, except for the part where you say, 'I do.'"

"I do not," she corrected. "You can't force me to marry you."

"Think not?" He stood up, his green eyes glittering with cold humor, his face confident and frighteningly hard.

He left the room, and Bess stood up, staring helplessly around. What in the world was he doing!

Minutes later he was back, with her coat in one hand and her purse dangling from his fingers. He slung them at her. "I've undone the fuse box. You can call a real estate agent from San Antonio and put the house on the auction block. Any little things you want can be shipped out. Now put on that coat."

She couldn't believe this was happening. It must be a hallucination brought on by the strain, she told herself. But a minute later, always impatient, he was stuffing her into the coat. He jerked the hood up and thrust the purse into her hands.

"I won't go!" she cried out.

"Like hell you won't go." He bent and swung her up into his arms like a sack of feathers and carried her out into the rain.

CHAPTER TWO

THIS ISN'T HAPPENING, Bess told herself an hour later as she sat beside Jude in the cockpit of his big Cessna. It simply isn't happening!

But the sound of the engine was very real, and so was Jude's set, humorless face as he concentrated on flying the plane.

Characteristically, he wasn't trusting his life to another pilot. He liked having total control—in everything. That was why he was flying himself and that was why he wanted the block of shares that Bess now owned. It was also, Bess suspected, why no woman had ever managed to get him to the altar in a conventional way. Falling in love would be giving a measure of control to someone else, too.

She leaned back in the seat, staring blankly at the clouds ahead, and wondered how she was going to get herself out of this predicament. Surely some other way could be found to give him the stock, if he reimbursed her. She brightened. Until she remembered the exact wording of the will. She muttered under her breath. Carla had taken care of that angle, too. The only way Jude could possibly get the stock was to marry Bess. And that, Carla had smugly thought, he'd never do.

He disliked Bess. Everyone knew it, too. They fought like cats and dogs, and people moved out of the way at Langston family get-togethers when they were both present.

The reunion two summers ago was the reason Bess had stayed away from the most recent gathering. She and Jude had gotten into a horrible fight about Katy. She could still blush at the language he'd used; the fact that there had been bystanders present hadn't slowed him down one iota.

Katy had told Bess about a fight she'd been in at school, stating proudly that she'd done just like Daddy, she'd pounded the hell out of a boy twice her size, and wasn't that super? "Super" had been Katy's latest word; it described everything from her dog, Pal, to the calf Jude had given her to raise for 4-H.

Bess hadn't thought it was super now that Katy was eight. She'd thought it was terrible, and she'd told Jude so later as they were sitting together having dinner with some of the other family members at a restaurant on the Paseo del Rio. Traditionally, they always concluded the annual picnic and rodeo at the restaurant, which Jude would book for an arm and a leg and the family would fill.

"What's wrong with Katy sticking up for herself?" he'd demanded. "The damned boy hit her first."

"She's a girl," Bess had burst out, exasperated with him. "For heaven's sake, she already dresses and talks like a boy. What are you trying to do to her?"

"Teach her to stand up for herself," he'd replied coolly, and had gone back to sipping his whiskey, raising his hand as another male member of the family entered the restaurant.

"Teaching her to be a freak," Bess had said under her breath.

That had set him off. She could still see him rising, as slowly as a rattlesnake coiling, his eyes glittering and dangerous, his face taut.

"Katy is my daughter," he'd said with a cold smile. "I decide what's good or bad for her, and I don't need help from some dainty little society lady who couldn't fight her way out of an eclair! Who the hell do you think you are to tell me how to raise my daughter? What qualifies you to be anybody's mother?" His voice was raised just enough to carry to the other tables, and there was a sudden hush, broken only by the sound of the river and the muffled voices of strolling passersby on the river walk. Bess had wanted to cringe.

"People are staring," Bess had said under her breath.

"Well, my God, let them stare!" he'd boomed, scowling down at her. "If you're so free with your damned advice on child raising, let's tell everybody. Go ahead, Miss White, do advise me on the behavior of my child!"

Her face was white with embarrassment and humiliation, but she held her head up and stared back at him. "I don't think I need to repeat it," she said very calmly.

It made him even angrier that he couldn't make her lose her composure entirely. That was when he'd started cursing. "You damned little prig," he'd tacked on at the end, and by that time her face was as red as it had been white earlier. "Why don't you get married and have kids of your own? Can't you find a man good enough?" He'd laughed coldly and looked over her body with contempt. "Or can't you find a man?"

And he'd turned and walked away, leaving her sitting there with tears stinging her eyes. The family had lost interest then and gone on to other topics. Bess had gone back to her hotel and packed. It was the last time she'd had any contact with Jude, until now.

"So quiet, Miss White," he taunted, jerking her out of her reveries. "So ladylike. You didn't even kick and scream. Is that kind of behavior too human for you?"

She lifted her chin, her perfect composure intact, and looked at him. "Look who's talking about being human," she said with a cool smile.

One of his thick eyebrows jerked. "But, then, I never claimed to be, did I?"

She averted her eyes. "If I'd had any doubts about it, you quelled them two summers ago."

He made a sound deep in his throat. "You ran," he recalled curtly. "Somehow, I didn't expect that. You've never run from me before."

The wording was unusual and it made her curious, but she wasn't in the mood to start trying to unravel Jude again.

"I didn't run," she replied, telling the lie very calmly. "I simply didn't see any reason to stay an extra day and give you any more free shots at me."

He glanced at her. "I meant what I said about Katy," he said darkly. "I don't want her made into a miniature debutante, is that clear? You lay one hand on her wardrobe and you'll wish you hadn't."

There was no arguing with him when he was in that

mood; she knew the look from memory. She turned her face away. "Don't worry, I won't be around long enough to do any damage."

"You'll be around. Now shut up," he added, glaring her way. "I don't like conversation when I'm flying this thing. You wouldn't want to crash, would you?"

"The airplane wouldn't dare," she muttered angrily, glancing at him. "Like most everything else around you, it's too intimidated to take the chance!"

Surprisingly, he laughed. But it was brief, and then his face was the familiar hard one she was accustomed to.

They landed at the San Antonio airport late that night, and Bess was exhausted. She barely noticed her surroundings until they were heading toward the exit and she got a good look at the walls. They were hung with paintings, all for sale, all exquisite, and most of Western subject matter.

"Oh, how beautiful!" she exclaimed over one, which showed a ranch house and a windmill overlooking a vast expanse of desert land. It looked like West Texas might have looked a hundred years ago, and she was instantly in love with it.

"Come on, for God's sake," Jude muttered, dragging her away with a steely hand on her arm. The touch went through her like fire.

"Could you stop grumbling for one minute?" she asked him, glaring up, and it was a long way despite her two-inch heels and her five feet, seven inches of height. "And glaring and scowling…"

He lifted an eyebrow and looked down his nose at

her. "Why don't you stop criticizing everybody around you and take a look at yourself, society girl?" he taunted. "What makes you think you're perfect?"

She knew she wasn't, but it hurt, coming from him. "I won't marry you," she said with controlled ferocity. "Not if you kill me first."

"If I killed you first, there wouldn't be much point in marrying you," he said conversationally. He pulled her along with him. "And you might as well stop arguing. You're going to marry me and that's the end of it."

They stepped out into the nippy air and she tugged her coat closer. It wasn't raining here, but it was cold all the same. The palm trees looked chilly, and the mesquite and oak trees they drove past in Jude's black Mercedes had no leaves on them. They looked as stark as the pecan trees back home.

Pecans reminded her of food, which reminded her that she hadn't had anything to eat since breakfast, and then she remembered what he'd said about turning off the power.

"My gosh, you idiot!" she burst out, turning in the seat. "You cut off the power to the refrigerator!"

He glanced at her. "Don't start name-calling. I've got an edge on you in that department. So what if it spoils? You won't be there to eat it."

"It will smell up the whole house!"

"I'll take care of it," he said calmly. "You can give me the name of a realtor."

"You can't order me to sell Oakgrove!" she burst out irrationally, though earlier she'd made up her mind to do just that. "It's been in my family for over a hundred years!"

"You'll sell it if I say so," he returned, giving her a hard glare. "Shades of Scarlett O'Hara. It's just a piece of land and an old house."

She thought back to all the family picnics, the rides through the woods, the beautiful springs and summers and the loving care that each generation had lavished on the estate. Suddenly it was clear to her that she wouldn't sell it, after all. "No," she said. "It's a legacy. If land is so unimportant, why do you hold on to Big Mesquite?"

"That's different," he said. "It's mine."

"Oakgrove is mine."

"God, you're stubborn," he growled, glaring across the passenger seat at her. "What do you want the place for?"

"It's my home," she told him. "When you come to your senses, I'm going back there to live." *And I'll figure out some way to maintain it,* she added to herself.

He turned his attention back to the road. "I need those damned shares. Your mother," he added curtly, "has very nearly cost me the corporation I've worked all my life to build up. By denying me the shares that were rightfully mine, she's tied me up in a proxy fight that I've almost lost."

"A proxy fight?" she asked dully.

"I have an enemy on my board of directors," he said shortly, as if it irritated him to have to tell her even that much. "He's shrewd and cunning, and he can sway votes. We're almost even right now. I've got to have that block of shares you own or I'll lose control of the corporation."

"Can't you find some other way to get them?" she asked bitterly.

He sighed. "I've got my attorneys working on it right now, going over your mother's will with a fine-tooth comb. But they aren't optimistic, and neither am I. She's made sure that I can't buy those shares from you. Under the terms of the will, you can't give them to me, either. It looks as if the only way I can control them is to marry you." He glanced sideways, his eyes hot and angry. "It would almost be worth losing the corporation," he muttered, "to send you home."

She drew in a weary breath. "The corporation is your problem. If you can find a way to get the stocks, well and good, but I'm not marrying you. I'd rather starve."

"The feeling is mutual, but neither of us may have any choice."

"I have," she returned.

"Not with me," he replied calmly. "Not a chance in hell. If it takes marriage, you'll marry me."

"I hate you!" she burst out, remembering graphically the humiliation she'd suffered from him. "Give me one good reason why I should even consider being tied to you?"

"Katy," he said simply.

She leaned back against the seat, feeling utterly defeated, and closed her eyes. "You don't want me around Katy, you've said so often enough. I'll corrupt her."

He lit a cigarette as he drove, staring ahead at the streetlit expanse of the sprawling city of San Antonio.

"She needs a mother," he said finally. "I've done some thinking about what you said at that reunion. I'm not agreeing that you were right," he added with a glare. "But I'm willing to concede that you weren't totally off base. She's growing up tough. Maybe too tough. A softening influence wouldn't be such a bad idea. And she likes you," he growled, as if that was totally incomprehensible.

"I like her, too," she said quietly, and let him chew on that. "But what are you offering me? You'd be getting control of my shares and a mother for Katy, but what would I get?"

His eyebrows went up. "What do you want? To sleep with me?" He let his eyes wander over her wildly flushed face. "I suppose I could force myself…"

"Damn you!" she burst out, hurt by the sarcastic way he'd said it.

He turned his attention back to the road. "Come on, wildcat, tell me what you want."

She shifted restlessly. "Not to be forced into marrying you."

"That's a foregone conclusion." He puffed away on his cigarette. "Tell you what, society girl. If worse comes to worst and we have to go through with it, I'll maintain that antebellum disaster for you, and you and Katy can spend summers there."

She turned her head and studied his unyielding profile. "You would?"

"I would." And he meant it, she knew. When he gave his word, he kept it.

She pursed her lips. "We couldn't just have a quick

marriage and a quicker annulment? To satisfy the terms of the will?"

"What would that do to Katy?" he asked suddenly.

She drew in a slow breath and let it out. "Oh."

"Yes, oh. She's so damned excited about having you here, she's half crazy," he said. "I told her," he added with a cold stare, "that you were coming out here so that we could decide whether or not we wanted to get married."

"She'll never believe you want to marry me," she replied tersely.

"Won't she?" A mocking smile curled his lips. "I told her I was nursing a secret passion for you and hoped to win you over."

"You bas—!"

"Uh, uh, uh," he cautioned. "None of those unlady-like words, if you please. You'll embarrass me."

"Satan himself couldn't do that," she shot back. "Oh, Jude, let me go home," she moaned. "I can't fight you. I'm too tired."

"Then stop trying. You won't win."

She laughed bitterly. "Don't I know it?" She turned away and looked out the window at the flat horizon as they headed south out of San Antonio. Tears pricked at her eyes as she thought how far away from home she was. From her mother. A sob caught in her throat and tears burst from her eyes as the control she'd maintained so valiantly slipped and broke.

"My God, you don't even cry like a normal woman," he ground out. "Stop that!"

She shook her head and dabbed at the tears. "I loved

her," she managed shakily. "It's only been two days, for God's sake, Jude…!"

"Well, all the tears in the world won't bring her back, will they?" he asked irritably. "And in the shape she was in, would you really want to?"

She shifted on the seat. He couldn't understand grief, she supposed, never having felt it. His mother had died when he was an infant, and his father had never been demonstrative. He had been even more unapproachable than Jude, worlds harder. Which was saying a lot, because the Rawhide Man was like steel.

She dashed the tears away and took a deep breath. "I don't want to live with a coldhearted statue like you," she said. "You're…you're like rawhide."

"But you'll do it, if it comes to that. You'll do it for Katy's sake." He turned onto the long road that led to the ranch.

"I'll run away!" she said dramatically.

"I'll come after you and bring you back," he said carelessly.

"Jude!" she ground out, exasperated.

"Remember that summer when you were fifteen?" he recalled with a chuckle. "You went out into the brush with Jess Bowman, and I rode all night to find you. You were huddled up in his coat with a twisted ankle, and he was walking down the road trying to flag down a car."

"I remember," she said, shuddering. "You broke his nose."

"I hit when I get mad," he said. "He riled me plenty, leaving you out there alone at night with rattlers crawling and cougars on the loose."

"He couldn't have carried me," she protested.

"I did," he reminded her. "And I wasn't as heavy in those days as I am now."

No, he'd filled out and firmed up and he was devastating. All man. She remembered that brief walk in his hard arms, the strength and power of his frame as he strode along. It was the safest she'd ever felt in her life—and the most afraid.

"That was the summer after Elise died, before I got Katy away from her stepfather. The last summer, too, that you ever spent any length of time at the ranch," he recalled. "That was when you started avoiding me."

She felt her cheeks go hot at the memory. She'd felt something that long-ago night that had haunted her ever since. And because it had frightened her, she'd avoided the ranch whenever possible, except for flying visits to see Katy. And the family reunions, of course, which came frequently during the year. Not that they were really family, but because of the partnership of her father and his, she was always included and expected to take part.

"Why did you stay away?" he asked quietly. "We've had our disagreements over the years, God knows, but I've never hurt you."

That was true enough. She stared down at her hands, folded in her lap. "I don't know," she lied.

He lifted a careless eyebrow. "Were you afraid I'd make a pass?"

She flushed, and he threw back his head and laughed deeply.

"You were fifteen," he reminded her with a chuckle.

"And you had even less to draw a man's eye than you do now." His eyes were on her small breasts, and she wanted to dive through the window.

Defensively she folded her arms over her chest and lowered her eye to the floorboard, so embarrassed that she wanted to cry.

"For God's sake, stop that," he growled. "You'd appeal to some men, I suppose. You just don't appeal to me."

Was that conscience, she wondered numbly? If it was, it didn't console her much.

"I'll get down on my knees and give thanks for that small blessing," she said coldly.

"You're the one with the small blessings, all right," he murmured wickedly.

She half turned in the seat to glare at him, and he chuckled at her fury.

"God, you're something when you get mad," he said with rare mischief. "All dark eyes and wild hair and teeth and claws. It sure as hell beats that so-elegant coolness you wear around you most of the time."

She regained her composure with an effort and stared at him calmly. "My mother raised me to be a lady," she told him.

"You're that," he agreed coldly. "But you'd be a hell of a lot more exciting if she'd raised you to be a woman, instead."

There was no reply to a blatant remark like that, so she turned her attention back to the darkened landscape and ignored him. Which seemed to be exactly what he wanted.

CHAPTER THREE

AGGIE LOPEZ, JUDE'S HOUSEKEEPER, met them in her dressing gown, yawning.

"Is Bess's room ready?" Jude asked curtly.

"Yes, Señor Langston," Aggie said agreeably, giving Bess a brief but thorough appraisal. Then she grinned. "You need some feeding up, *señorita*. A few weeks of *refritos* and enchiladas and my good Texas chili will put meat on those bones, I promise you. Come, I will take you up to your room and then I'll bring you some food. The little one has only just gone to sleep. She was so excited…!"

"But it's after midnight," Bess exclaimed.

"Go ahead," Jude growled, glaring at her with piercing green eyes, "say something about her bedtime hour. You've managed to disapprove of every other damned thing, why not that as well?"

She glared back at him, her chin lifted. "Children need their rest just like adults do," she threw at him. "And speaking of rest, look at you!"

"What's wrong with me?" he asked pugnaciously.

"Oh, Lord, just give me a full day with no interruptions and I'll be glad to give you an itemized list!"

Aggie was staring at them with her jaw in a slightly

drooping posture, her small, plump figure glued to the banister of the long staircase that ran up to the second story.

Jude glanced at Aggie. "Well, what the hell are you gaping at? Are you going to show her upstairs or not?"

"You are…really getting married?" the older woman asked, lifting her eyebrows until they almost touched the salt-and-pepper hair that was drawn into a tight bun.

"It's a love match, too," Bess assured her with a tight smile at Jude. "He loves my stocks and I love his daughter."

Jude said something rude under his breath and turned on his heel to stomp off into his study. He slammed the door with hurricane force behind him.

Aggie flinched. "Someday he will break all the windows," she said, sighing. "Ay, ay, life is so exciting since I came to work here." She eyed Bess. "It is none of my affair, you understand, but you are not the picture of a happy bride."

"I don't want to be a bride," she muttered. "He's trying to make me."

"As I thought," Aggie said. She shook her head. "I will not ask why you do not refuse him. Six months I have worked for Mr. Langston. In that time, I have never known him not to get his own way. Have you known him long, *señorita?*"

"I've known him most of my life," Bess grumbled as she followed the older woman up the staircase.

"Then I do not need to tell you anything about him," Aggie said quietly. She glanced at Bess as she stopped in front of the room where Bess always stayed when she visited the ranch. "He said that you have lost your mother. I am very sorry."

Tears welled up in Bess's eyes and her lower lip trembled precariously. "Yes."

Impulsively, Aggie put an arm around her. "*Señorita,* grief passes. I, too, lost my mother many years ago. I do not forget the hurt, but time is kind."

Bess nodded jerkily and tried to smile.

"Here, now. Katy insisted on redecorating the room when she heard you were coming." Aggie led Bess into the spacious room, which boasted a new bedspread and matching curtains of cream with beige and blue flowers, a deep blue carpet and elegant wallpaper. There were fresh flowers, mums, in a vase on the chest of drawers.

"It's beautiful!" Bess burst out.

"Oh, I hoped you'd like it!" came a joyous voice from the connecting door across the room.

Bess's eyes lit up. "Katy!" she exclaimed, and held out her arms.

Katy ran into them, laughing. She was the image of her father—pale green eyes framed by black hair and a stubborn square jaw. She was going to be tall, too. She already came up almost to Bess's shoulders.

"You smell nice," Katy remarked as she drew back to look at the older woman. "Like flowers. You always smell so good, Bess!"

"I'm glad you think so," Bess said with a grin. "How's school?"

Katy made a face. "I hate math and English grammar. But band is great. I play the flute! And I like chorus pretty well, and art class is neat."

"I'd love to hear you play," Bess said. She ruffled the short dark hair. "You're the nicest welcome I've had so far."

"Been at it with Dad again, huh?" Katy murmured with a wicked smile. "I heard," she confessed.

Bess colored delicately. "We, uh, had a slight disagreement."

"They have slight disagreements over the color of the sky," Katy told Aggie without blinking an eye, and she laughed. "Dad likes to give orders and Bess doesn't like to take them."

"Now, Katy…" Bess began.

"I know. 'Now, Katy, mind your own business.'" Katy sighed. She arched her eyebrows. "But you're going to be my mom, so it is kind of my business, isn't it?"

At the sound of the word, Bess's eyes glittered again with unshed tears. She was going to have to stop this!

"Oh, I'm sorry," Katy said quickly, after a speaking glare from Aggie. "I'm very sorry, I forgot!"

"It's all right," Bess said, brushing away the tears. "It's just so fresh, you know. I loved her very much."

"I never knew my mother," Katy said, "but Dad said she was a first-class bit—"

"No!" Aggie burst out, horrified. "You must not say such things!"

Katy's lips pouted. "Dad does."

"Yes, but you shouldn't speak that way of your mother," Bess said gently. "Besides, ladies don't use language like that."

Katy just stared at her blankly. "Huh?"

"You'll have to show me around the ranch tomorrow," Bess said quickly, deciding to let it drop for the time being. "It's more than a year since I visited. I'm sure there are a lot of changes."

That brought the smile back to Katy's young face. "You bet! Unless…you wouldn't rather Dad showed you around?" she asked with a calculating look, and Bess knew she was thinking about that dreadful lie Jude had told her.

"He can show me around later," Bess promised the young girl. "Now, how about bed? I'm so sleepy I can hardly stand up."

"Where are your things, *señorita,* and I will unpack," Aggie volunteered.

"I'm wearing them," Bess said gaily, opening her coat to disclose the dress underneath. "Jude decided that I could do without clothes, makeup and all those other frivolous things."

Aggie scowled. "I will lend you one of my gowns," she said. "Men, they never think about these things," she muttered as she went out the door.

Katy was watching her closely. "Why didn't you pack a suitcase?" she asked slowly.

"Because your father picked me up in what I have on and carried me bodily out the door, that's why," she said.

Katy tried to stifle a laugh, but it burst out anyway. "Good night, Bess!" she said, and beat a hasty retreat back to her own room, closing the door quickly. Behind it, there was hysterical laughter.

BESS HAD FORGOTTEN just how big Big Mesquite really was until she walked around the grounds with Katy the next day. The house, which she'd always loved, was very old and very Victorian, with a turret and exquisite gingerbread woodwork. Jude had obviously had it painted not too many months ago, because it was blistering white.

"I remember summers long ago when I used to swing in that front porch swing," Bess recalled dreamily, hanging on to a small mimosa tree in the front yard as she stared toward the house. "And your grandmother would make iced tea and big, thick tomato sandwiches and I'd swing and munch."

"Did you and Dad used to play together?" Katy asked, all eyes.

"No, darling," Bess said, laughing. "Your father was already a grown man when I was barely in my teens. I hardly ever saw him in those days. He was away at college, and then in Vietnam."

"Oh, yes, I know all about the war," Katy said seriously. "Dad's got an awful—"

"Katy!" Aggie called out the door. "Deanne wants to talk to you on the telephone!"

"Okay, Aggie!" Katy moved away from the tree. "Deanne's my best friend," she explained. "I won't be long."

"Don't hurry on my account," Bess told her. "I'll just ramble around and look at the stock."

"Don't go close to the corral. Dad's got Blanket in there," the young girl cautioned.

"What a name. Does it belong to a bull?"

"No, a horse." Katy laughed. "They call her that because she likes to fall on people—like a blanket."

"I'll watch my step," Bess promised.

Katy ran into the house and Bess wandered quietly around the yard in the same jersey dress she'd worn the day before. She had one of Jude's Windbreakers wrapped around herself to keep out the cold, and she hated the pleasure it gave her to wear something of his. She was really going to have to stop feeling that way. If he ever found out how he affected her, it could be a disaster, in more ways than one.

As she was thinking about him, he came out of the barn with a halter in his hand, heading straight for Blanket.

Bess climbed up on the fence and leaned her arms over the top rail. "Going to bounce around a little?" she asked. "Don't fall off, now."

"No, I'm not going to bounce around," he said curtly. "I'm going to put her on a halter so Bandy can work her."

She watched him approach the horse, talking softly and gently to it in a tone she'd never heard him use except, infrequently, with Katy. He moved closer inch by inch, soothing the horse, until he was near enough to ease the halter over the jet black muzzle and lock it in place. He continued to stroke the silky black mane while the horse trembled in the chill air, not from cold but from nervousness.

Bess didn't speak. She didn't dare. Jude would climb all over her if she spooked the horse. But he glanced at her warily when the little bowlegged cowboy named Bandy came out of the barn with a lunging rein to attach to the halter.

Jude said something to the cowboy and then climbed

over the fence, perching himself on the top rail near Bess. He was wearing denims and the old battered gray Stetson he used on the rare occasions when he was around the ranch. He looked good in denim. He looked good in anything, that long, muscular body sheer elegance when he moved.

"Don't trust her too far, Bandy," Jude said as he lit a cigarette. He glanced at Bess. "She's a lot like some women. All long legs and nerves."

Her chin lifted. She'd put up her hair to keep it out of her face, and she looked chic and elegant even in his leather jacket.

"Where did you get that?" he asked, indicating the jacket.

"Aggie got it out for me," she said defensively. "You wouldn't let me pack," she reminded him.

"It doesn't do much for you," he remarked derisively.

"It keeps me warm," she returned. "But if you want it back…"

"Oh, hell, stop playing Joan of Arc," he growled, his green eyes glittering at her over a wisp of cigarette smoke. "It's an old jacket. I had it when I was in Vietnam."

And probably it brought back memories he'd rather not dredge up, she thought, feeling guilty. She averted her eyes to the cowboy working the young filly on the leading rein in a long, wide circle.

"You didn't hit the floor screaming bloody murder this morning," he remarked. "Does that mean you've stopped fighting the idea of marriage?"

She drew one long, polished fingernail across the

top rail of the fence and watched it scar the old wood. "Katy was so excited," she said quietly.

"Yes, I told you that."

Her dark eyes pinned him. "I don't like you very much, Judah Barnett Langston," she said.

He took a long draw from the cigarette and pursed his chiseled lips. "What a disappointment," he said after a minute, and his eyes were mocking. "I thought you might be harboring a secret passion for me."

"Sorry to dash your dreams," she replied. "I'd rather lust after a rattlesnake."

He chuckled softly, and his cold green eyes wandered over her slimness slowly. "You'd have better luck there, all right," he remarked. "Hell, you're too fragile for sex."

She gasped at the unexpectedly intimate remark and felt her face go hot.

His eyebrows lifted at her expression. "Well, my God, I do know what sex is," he said.

"I didn't say a word," she chewed off.

"You were thinking it," he said. He smiled tauntingly. "I didn't find Katy under a cabbage leaf."

Her eyes fell away from his. The discussion was getting far too intimate for her taste. She knew hardly anything about intimacy except for what she'd read. And the last person she wanted to learn that kind of lesson from was Jude Langston. She couldn't picture him being either patient or tender with a woman.

"Is Katy matchmaking?" he asked after a minute. "She deserted you."

"Her friend Deanne called," she murmured.

He scowled. "Deanne is a city kid. Very sophisticated for her age. I don't like Katy associating with her."

"Why, because she wears dresses?" she asked. "Is Katy going to run the ranch for you when she grows up, bullwhip and all?"

He just stared at her until she dropped her eyes. She'd never been able to outglare him, not ever, and it rankled.

"I wish she'd been a boy sometimes," he said, surprising her. "But that wasn't her fault."

"She's going on ten," she said quietly. "The age of parties and pretty dresses and boys is coming along down the road. It would be sad if she was excluded from all those things because she was too tough to fit in. Wouldn't it?"

He glared at her and threw down his cigarette. "Why don't you mind your own damned business? Go arrange some flowers or something. That's all you're good for!"

He got down off the fence, and tears stung her eyes as she did likewise. She turned on her heel and stomped back off toward the house.

A piercing whistle split the air and she stopped and whirled. "What!" she yelled.

"Go into town and get some clothes. I've opened an account for you at Joske's."

She caught her breath. Things were moving fast. Too fast. "I don't want any, thanks."

"Suit yourself," he said carelessly. "If you want to be married in your slip, it's your business." He turned back to Bandy.

"I'm not going to marry you!" she yelled at him.

"You are if I can't find another way to get those

shares!" At that, she almost scooped up a rock and threw it at him. But she knew Jude too well, so she didn't.

BY THE END of the week, it was sadly apparent that there were no loopholes in Bess's mother's will. Jude came in Friday afternoon looking as if he'd like to tie her to a stake and roast her. Instead, he ordered her into the living room and closed the door behind them.

"There's no way out except marriage," he said without dressing it up. "We can't break the will unless we can prove mental incompetence, and your family attorney assures me that we can't."

"No," Bess said, "she was in her right mind up until the very end."

He picked up a book on the table by the window and abruptly slammed it down on the highly polished surface. "Damn it, I don't want marriage!" he cursed, glaring at Bess.

"Well, don't blame me," she shot back. "I didn't drag you off out here and try to force you into it. I'd just as soon forget the whole thing!"

"So would I, but I've got to have those damned shares, and soon. It's no use fighting me, Bess." He rammed his hands in the pockets of his gray slacks. "I'll talk to a minister about the ceremony. We can have it at San Jose, if you like."

"At the mission?" she asked. Her eyes brightened a little. "That sounds nice."

"Then you'll agree to the marriage?" he asked quietly, and she knew he was in deadly earnest.

"I don't seem to have much choice," she replied.

"And you're right—Katy does need a woman's touch. And I need her. I don't have anyone else to love now that Mother's…" She broke off, trying desperately to keep the tears from falling. "She was all the family I had in the world."

He turned away, obviously uncomfortable at her show of emotion. "You'd better go to the printer and get some invitations sent out. I'll have my secretary make you a list of people to invite." He glanced at her. "Do you want your stepsister to come?"

"No," she said without thinking.

He laughed shortly. "Somehow, I didn't think you would. But you owe her the courtesy of telling her about the marriage. She is your only living relative."

"I will." Several weeks from now, she added silently.

He studied her. "You don't like Crystal, do you?"

"Neither would you, if she didn't worship the ground you walk on," she said with bitter sarcasm. "Crystal's main ambition in life is to keep Crystal happy and comfortable. But men don't notice that very often."

"No," he agreed, "they're too busy noticing how much woman she is." His eyes went up and down Bess's slender figure. "She puts you in the shade, doesn't she?"

Not for the world would she have let him see how much that hurt. She smiled coolly and turned to leave the room.

"So proud," he chided. "So poised. Does anything ever ruffle you, society girl? I'll bet you'd be that way in bed with a man, all cool discipline and—"

"Stop that," she bit out, glaring at him. "How I'd be is none of your business." She stopped, her eyes uncertain.

He laughed shortly as he read the fear in them. "Don't get your hopes up, Bess. You don't turn me on. It won't be a marriage in that respect."

"Thank God," she muttered, opening the door with her back to him so he couldn't see her hot cheeks.

"I can't imagine you blazing with passion," he said thoughtfully. "Some women are born cold, I expect."

She closed the door sharply behind her and went to her room before he could see the tears that refused to be held at bay any longer.

Two DAYS LATER Bess and Katy made a trip into San Antonio. Joske's, where Jude had set up an account, was one of the biggest department stores in town, crammed full of delicious clothes and accessories. Bess, determined to make the best of the situation, threw herself into trying to decide what she wanted. Katy looked bored with the whole thing, and wanted to stay out in the parking lot across the street with Bandy, who'd been volunteered to drive them to town.

"But I have to have help," Bess had protested. "It's partly your wedding, too. After all, you're going to be bridesmaid."

That had caught the young girl's interest momentarily, but after Bess had worked her way through half the dress department, Katy was getting restless.

One of the salesladies finally suggested a dress with a Mexican flavor, a gauzy white creation with hand-crocheted lace around the neck and the short puffy sleeves and around the bottom. It was like a peasant dress, but exquisite. Perfect. When Bess tried it on and posed for Katy, the young girl caught her breath.

"Blondes sure look good in white," Katy said with a smile. "Gosh, you're pretty, Bess!"

"Thank you, darling. Now," she said, "next we've got to find something for you."

Katy protested loudly, but Bess was stubborn. Finally, more to get out of the store than for any other reason, Katy decided on a frilly blue dress. Bess bought her a pale blue velvet ribbon to wear with it, and white shoes and a dainty bag and gloves.

"Everybody will laugh at me," Katy wailed.

"Not in church," Bess assured her. "Besides, it's going to be in one of the old missions."

Katy frowned slightly. "It is?"

"Your father said so."

"Well." Katy brightened. "It might not be too bad after all."

I hope, Bess said silently. She couldn't imagine herself and Jude ever getting along together. She wondered how Katy was going to react to living in a constant state of war. But oddly enough, the little girl seemed to be more amused than disturbed by the warring adults.

"What did you buy?" Jude asked that afternoon when he came back from a budget meeting at a college where he was a trustee.

"A white Mexican dress," Katy said before Bess could. "And I have to wear a blue one with—yuck—lace," she added miserably. "Gosh, couldn't I wear my boots and jeans?"

"Afraid not, tiger," Jude said. "But you can always put them on after it's over."

"I guess." She got up from the table. "Well, I'd better get my homework done, I guess. I hate school. Can't I quit?"

"Sure," Jude agreed. "When you're eighteen or get your diploma, whichever comes first."

Katy stuck out her tongue at him and went upstairs.

"Show me the dress," Jude said unexpectedly.

"I'll bring it down."

"Wear it."

She glared at him. "It's bad luck."

He drew in a deep breath. "I guess having to marry you is all I need of that," he replied.

She raised her hand and hesitated.

"Go ahead," he said with an insolent smile, staring at her. "But you won't like how I get even."

Her hand fell and she left. He was still drinking coffee when she came back down with the dress over one arm. She held it up to herself and let him scan it with cold, hard eyes.

"White?" he scoffed, his green eyes piercing.

Her chin rose. "I do realize that in this permissive age, anything goes. But I still have the right to a white wedding gown, and I'm wearing one."

He frowned slightly, searching her eyes. "You're a virgin?"

"Well, don't faint," she said curtly. "There are a few of us left!"

"I suppose I should have realized it." He sighed. "You're so damned controlled."

"Said the pot to the kettle," she agreed. Her eyes ran up and down him coldly. "Thank God I don't have to sleep with you."

She turned to leave the room, but he was on his feet before she completed the motion. He caught her arm and jerked her around with a grip hard enough to hurt, and pulled her so close that she could see the dark green circles around his pale green irises.

"Push a little harder, society girl," he said harshly, "and see what happens."

"You're hurting me," she whispered, shaken by the sudden, vicious motion of his fingers.

"You cut, too, in your own way," he replied. His nostrils were flared with anger, and his eyes were glittering in a way that was a little frightening.

"You started it," she said childishly, clutching the wedding dress in one hand.

He sighed heavily and the hand on her arm slackened a little. "I guess I did." He searched her face for a long time. "You set me off, Bess. You always have."

"I do realize that you'd rather die than have to marry me," she said tightly. "I hope you realize that the same thing goes for me, double. But it might be a good idea for Katy's sake to try and get along."

"I am," he said.

"With me!"

"That presents a problem." He noticed his hand on her upper arm and seemed fascinated with it. He drew his fingers softly down to her elbow, feeling the warmth of her skin, and he frowned. "My God, you're thin."

"It's fashionable," she said tightly, disturbed by that slow, caressing motion that he seemed hardly aware of.

"So is sex," he returned, catching her eyes. "But you haven't followed the crowd in that respect. If you're telling the truth." He dropped her arm. "Frankly, it doesn't matter to me one way or the other, since I'll never be concerned with your virtue—or your lack of it. This is a merger."

"So cold-blooded, Mr. Langston," she said under her breath, her pride stinging at what he'd said. "And so hard. You're a rawhide man."

"Sticks and stones, lady," he said carelessly. "By the way, Katy doesn't like going to bed at eight." He must have noticed the new hours Bess had implemented.

"She told me so."

He lifted an eyebrow. "But she's still doing it."

"As you said once, she likes me," she told him smugly.

He started to speak but she glared until he changed his mind. He jerked off his tie and opened the top button of his shirt with a hard sigh. "Want a drink, debutante?"

"I don't—"

"Drink," he said for her, glancing over his shoulder. "I should have remembered that. No booze, no sex, no bad habits…all the virtues of a saint." He wandered off into his study without another word and closed the door.

Without understanding her own actions, she picked up a small earthenware pot from a planter in the hall and threw it straight at the center of the door. It disintegrated with a pleasingly loud smash.

Jude jerked open the door and glared at her, his eyes falling to the polished wood floor. His eyebrows rose.

"Planting a garden? Aren't you a few months early and in the wrong spot?"

"I know something I'd like to plant," she returned, and her eyes measured him from head to toe. She draped the wedding gown across the banister and bent to pick up the shards of pottery.

He bent to help her and their heads collided. He caught her shoulders to stop her from pitching over backward and held her in front of him. She looked into his eyes at point-blank range and time exploded.

She could feel his breath on her mouth, he was so close; she could smell the expensive cologne he wore. It was like a dance. They both rose together to their feet, with his lean, hard hands gripping her shoulders. His eyes searched hers, and his thumbs made wild patterns on the insides of her shoulders as they moved involuntarily, finding the smooth skin under the beige top she'd bought to go with matching slacks.

His darkening eyes went slowly down to her mouth as hers went to his. His lips parted and she could see their chiseled perfection, the hard, firm lines of them with the faint darkness above the upper one where he needed a shave. It was exciting to feel his breath mingling with her own, to see his mouth so close to hers. For a long, long time she'd wondered how it would feel if he kissed her. Part of her had feared it, but another part was hungry for it.

His hand suddenly caught the thick bun of her hair and pulled her head back. His eyes glittered down at her; his nostrils flared. He was watching her mouth with an unblinking intensity, and his fingers on her shoulder and in her hair were hurting. But she could feel the long, hard line of his body against hers and it fired a hunger she'd never felt before. Just the touch of him made her weak and shaky, and she couldn't get her breath. He couldn't, either, if his raspy breathing was any indication. He muttered something and abruptly bent his head.

But even as his mouth was opening to take hard possession of her own, Katy's voice burst out from the top of the staircase. "Holy cow, what happened?"

Jude jerked as if he'd been hit, almost throwing Bess away from him. She turned and picked up her wedding gown, feeling shaken and confused and more than a little angry at her own responses.

"Your mother-to-be was planting flowers," Jude said curtly. He turned and went back into his study with a hard, dark glare at Bess. As if it were her fault, she thought wildly.

Aggie came in, and Bess ran for it, dress in hand and watched by a giggling Katy.

Bess kept out of Jude's way the next day, but he was at home and his eyes watched her accusingly. She knew he wasn't going to let her escape so easily, but she still wasn't quite prepared for what happened. Katy had gone out to groom her calf and Aggie was working on lunch when Jude strode angrily into the living room where she was busy addressing invitations for the wedding.

"There's something you and I need to get straight," he said, ramming his hands into the pockets of his slacks, looking so darkly handsome that she hated the sight of him. "I don't like having flowerpots flung at my head."

She felt the accusation all the way to her toes and her body tingled when she met his eyes.

"I beg your pardon?" she asked stiffly.

"Don't be haughty, it won't wash." He moved closer, so that he was looming over her. "You threw that pot deliberately."

"So what if I did?" she said curtly.

"I need your damned shares in my corporation. That's why we're getting married, remember?"

"That's why you're getting married," she said, straightening as pride came to her rescue. "I'm getting married for Katy."

He nodded slowly. "Okay. Let's leave it like that. No complications."

"I…" She dropped her eyes to his chest, where the gray patterned knit shirt he wore strained across his powerful muscles. Under it was a shadow, and she wondered absently if he was hairy or smooth there.

"You what?" he asked.

"I didn't mean that to happen, out in the hall. You just make me so mad, Jude," she said helplessly, looking up into his eyes.

"We've always made sparks together," he agreed. His eyes narrowed. "But it's got to stop."

"Then quit baiting me," she returned. "Treat me like a human being instead of some festering thorn."

"Is that how I treat you?" he asked. "I thought I was being kind. For me," he added with a hard laugh.

"I don't imagine you can help being the way you are," she said quietly, avoiding his eyes.

"Do you think you understand me, miss debutante?"

he asked with a mocking laugh. "By all means, tell me about myself."

Her eyes met his and went back to her list. "I wouldn't presume that far."

"I don't have much respect for women, if that's what you meant," he said, bending his head to light a cigarette. "Katy's mother taught me a lot about them."

"All the bad things and none of the good," Bess argued. "And how could you tell Katy that her mother was a…" She cleared her throat.

"Can't you say the word? Would it soil your elitist tongue to say it?" he taunted.

"Anyway, it was cruel to say it in front of Katy. A girl needs at least the illusion of a mother, and you've robbed her of hers," she returned. "She's dead, after all. She can't harm Katy."

"Her memory could," he said flatly, his eyes glittering. "I won't discuss Elise with you."

"I'm not asking you to," she said, avoiding his gaze. "But it would be kind if you could stop saying horrible things about her to Katy."

"I can't talk to you," he ground out. "Everything I say winds up being defensive."

"Pardon me for breathing," she said calmly.

"Damn you…!"

She jerked at the hot whip of his deep voice, and pushed herself back into the cushions, crushing the list she was following in one hand.

He took a deep drag from the cigarette. "You make my blood run hot," he said savagely. "I've never in my life wanted to hit a woman as much as I'd like to hit you, so don't press your luck!"

She didn't say a word. In that white-hot anger, he was more frightening than ever. She sat, stiff-backed, and tried not to back down.

He studied her pale face for a long time. "You're afraid of me, aren't you?" he asked suddenly. His eyes narrowed. "Yes, I think you are. That's why you're so much on the offensive with me. Offense is the best defense, is that how you see it?"

He saw altogether too much. He rattled her. She put the list aside and stood up, moving quickly out of his reach. "I need to help Aggie," she said nervously.

"No, you don't. You just need to run off and hide."

Her lower lip trembled betrayingly as she looked at him from the safety of the door. "I'll be careful to keep my thoughts to myself from now on," she said with dignity. "Will that satisfy you?"

He frowned and studied her. "You are afraid," he said, as if it shocked him.

She turned and ran out the door, slamming it quickly behind her.

After that, he was strangely quiet around her. But watchful, and faintly calculating. It made her more nervous than ever.

Meanwhile, she was reacquainting herself with the ranch and loving every mile of its awesome spread. Katy had told her that wildflowers bloomed profusely in the spring—Bess had never been there at that time of year—bluebells and Indian paintbrush and Indian blanket, prickly poppies on the cactus, and maypop and lantana. There would be beautiful yellow black-eyed Susans with black centers, and Mexican hats with their festive yellow-fringed red petals around tall black centers.

Right now, though, it was winter and nothing was blooming except Bess's growing but reluctant attraction to Jude. She found herself staring at him when he didn't see her, her eyes glued to his tall, powerful figure as he walked around the ranch and the house. It was growing increasingly harder not to stare at him over the dinner table. And all the time, he looked at her with that strange, calculating expression.

On their wedding day, she dressed in the white gown, but with all her uncertainties showing in her eyes. Was she doing the right thing? Was it sane to let him force her into a marriage that might destroy her? She was afraid of him, all right, but not for the reasons he thought. She was afraid because she wanted him. That wild encounter in the hall had shown her just how much she wanted him. But he didn't want anything from her except her shares. He'd made that perfectly clear. Could she risk living in such close proximity to him and go from day to day without letting everything she felt show? He was shrewd, and he could read rocks, much less Bess. And if he found out, every time they argued he would taunt her with her weakness for him.

She almost went downstairs and backed out of it. But it was far too late. The guests, friends of Jude's and members of the Langston family, were already waiting for them at the little Spanish mission outside San Antonio. So what could she do but go through with it and hope for the best?

But she felt empty in a way even her mother's death hadn't made her feel. To live with a man like Jude was going to be a daily ordeal. One she was already half dreading, half anticipating as she gathered the bouquet of white-and-pink silk roses Katy had chosen, and went down the staircase.

CHAPTER FOUR

THE MISSION SAN JOSE y San Miguel de Aguayo lived up
to its nickname, the Queen of Texas missions. The towering, imposing stone structure had a grace of design
and a sense of history that made Bess tingle as she entered it on the arm of Jude's neighbor Adam Teague, a
towering gray-headed man she'd known for years who'd
agreed to stand in for Bess's late father.

There were red-and-white poinsettias all around the
altar, and it was truly the season for them with Christmas only two weeks away. Bess had almost asked Jude
to postpone the ceremony until then, but he was impatient to gain control of the shares and she'd known
he'd only refuse.

He'd hired Mexican mariachis to provide an even
more Spanish flavor to the ceremony, and Bess thought
she'd never heard anything so beautiful as the "Wedding March" played on dozens of throbbing, romantic guitar strings. The music echoed harmonically in
the interior of the church as Bess walked stiffly beside
Teague to the altar, under the vaulted ceiling and dome.
The three vaults of the nave were outlined in beautiful, rich hues, but Bess's eyes never saw them, riveted
as they were to Jude's tall figure in a somber blue pin-

striped suit with a white carnation in the lapel. Her heart leaped wildly as his head turned and he stared at her with cold green eyes.

In spite of the romantic setting, he was hating every minute of this. His eyes told her so.

Teague left her beside Jude and sat down. Bess stood rigidly at Jude's side, trembling, and only half heard the brief ceremony. She was only vaguely aware of Katy standing up with them, of the faint movements of the guests in the pews. There was a smell of stone and dust and the days when this mission was a bastion of civilization in an uncivilized land. The words the minister spoke echoed around the interior of the church, as other vows must have echoed over the two centuries of the mission's existence.

Jude slipped a ring onto her finger. More words were spoken. She said two of them. Jude bent to touch his cold mouth to her lips in their first kiss as man and wife—so removed from the heated confrontation in the hall when he'd looked as if he'd kill for her mouth. And they were married.

She heard the mariachis begin to play as Jude led her out to the church steps where the guests were waiting with rice. The rice stung. She was cold because the beautiful white dress wasn't meant for warmth on a cool December day. But she laughed and pretended that it was the happiest moment of her life as she crawled into the black Mercedes with Jude and Katy. They drove toward home, and her eyes turned back for a last glimpse of the mission complex. Now that it was all over, she wished she could go back and really see the historic shrine.

"We'll come back again someday and you can see the rose window, Bess," Katy promised. She blushed. "I mean, Mother."

Bess caught her breath as she looked over the seat at Katy, whose face was radiant. "I like that," she told the young girl with affection. "Oh, I like that very much. It sounds just right."

"It sounds absurd," Jude snapped, glaring at both of them. "She isn't your mother."

Katy's lower lip trembled and she looked down. "Yes, sir." Her eyes went to Bess. "Congratulations anyway… Bess."

"Thank you," Bess said, ignoring Jude's deliberate cruelty. There would be plenty of time later to tell the sweet man what a crude, unbearable, insensitive ass he was.

BUT IN THE days that followed, Jude made a point of staying away from the house. If he saw Bess at all, it was rarely, and he made no attempt to come near her at night. Apparently he'd meant exactly what he'd said about their marriage. It was to be a merger, period, with no intimacy of any kind. Bess was almost relieved; it prevented any more of the horrible confrontations that had occurred before their wedding. With plenty of time on her hands, she concentrated on preparations for Christmas.

"We never have a tree or anything," Katy said sadly when Bess started talking about where to put one.

"There's no Santa Claus, so Daddy says it's just a bunch of nonsense."

Bess was horrified. She stood in the middle of the floor gaping at Katy. "But, darling, don't you know what Christmas means?"

Katy shifted uncomfortably. "The teacher tells us about it," she murmured.

"But don't you go to church on Christmas Eve and…?"

Katy looked even more uncomfortable. "Daddy says—"

"Daddy says entirely too much," Bess burst out, dark eyes flashing. "Now, Katy, we're going to have a tree and presents, at least from each other," she said firmly. "And you and I are going to the Christmas Eve service at church, whether or not your father goes with us. And Aggie and I are going to fix a turkey with all the trimmings, and we're going to have Christmas."

Katy's eyes sparkled and she burst out laughing. "Oh, Bess, you make it sound so wonderful." Then the smile faded and became bittersweet. "But Daddy won't let you, I'm afraid."

"We'll see," she said firmly. "Now." She turned her attention back to the living room and pursed her lips. It was a massive room, and there were double windows facing the porch, which in turn faced the road. "We'll put it right there," she decided, "so that it can be seen outside. Do you have ornaments or decorations?"

Katy shook her head.

Bess frowned. "Haven't you ever had a tree?"

Katy shook her head again.

She'd barbecue Jade, Bess decided. Over an open pit

on Christmas day with an apple in his mouth. "We'll go to the store, then," Bess said. "Get a sweater. After I speak to your father, I'll get one of the cowboys to drive us into town to get a tree and ornaments and things."

"You will?"

"I certainly will." Bess pulled on Jude's leather jacket and went out to find him.

She found him in the barn talking with one of his men, and Bess waited patiently until he finished, enjoying the nip in the air.

He came out a minute later, wearing dark slacks with a white pullover sweater and a sheepskin jacket that must have cost the earth. He stopped in the act of lighting a cigarette and stared at Bess.

"Did you want something, Mrs. Langston?" he asked with deliberate sarcasm, his green eyes alive with it.

"Yes, Mr. Langston, I did," she said imperturbably. "I want you to have someone drive us to town so that I can buy a Christmas tree and something to go on it."

"No," he said coldly. "Not in my house."

She had realized already that it was going to take a fight. She was prepared. She lifted her head with the blond hair coiled haughtily atop it and stared at him.

"Before we married, you agreed we should try to get along, didn't you?" she asked. "I haven't asked anything of you up until now. Not one single thing. But now I want half the living room. In fact, I want the half that faces the road. It has a double window. Then," she added, watching his eyebrows slowly go up in astonishment, "I want a tree—something bushy, I don't care what kind—and some ornaments and a turkey and a ham."

"Are you going to put the turkey and ham on the tree?" he asked.

She glared at him. "I also want you to buy something for Katy to go under the tree. A present that you pick out yourself, not that your secretary runs out to get on her lunch hour."

He took off his hat and idly brushed it against his leg while he looked at her. "Anything else?"

"No. That's all."

He searched her eyes and laughed shortly. "You've said your piece, now I'll say mine. Christmas is for featherbrains who haven't anything better to do…"

"You hush!" she said under her breath. "You know very well what Christmas is and why we celebrate it, and shame on you for spoiling it for Katy! How do you think she feels when all the other children are telling her about their Christmases and all their presents and going to church together to thank God for them? What do you suppose she says?"

He looked stunned for an instant. "It's only another day," he said defensively.

"Not to a little girl without a mother," she said quietly, and felt her own loss keenly at that moment.

He drew in a heavy breath. "All right, damn it," he bit off. "Have a tree. Have a turkey. But don't expect to drag me to church, because I won't go."

"Don't worry," she returned hotly, "I wouldn't want to have to be seen with you anyway!"

She was turning on her heel when he caught her arm and jerked her back.

"Where are you going for the tree?"

She swallowed. He was much too close. "I don't know."

His hand loosened, became slowly caressing on the leather sleeve. "You've got Katy all het up about this, I suppose," he growled.

"She only wants what other children have."

"All right. I'll drive you to town."

She turned, gaping up at him. "I… I thought I'd ask one of the boys. I didn't expect you to go."

His eyes searched hers slowly. "Don't you want me to?"

She couldn't answer him. Her gaze caught in his and couldn't free itself. For a long, hot moment they stood in the cold and just looked at each other.

"Hell, if we're going, let's go," he said irritably, throwing her arm away. "Get Katy." He slammed his hat over his eyes and stalked off toward the garage.

It was astonishing that he'd agreed to it. All the way to town, Bess cast curious glances his way.

"I need to run by the office for a few minutes," he said after the silent drive into town. "I'll leave you both downtown and let you shop. Meet me in front of the Menger Hotel at three."

"Yes, sir," Bess said smartly.

He glared at her as she clambered out with a giggling Katy, and his eyes promised retribution in the near future. Bess gave him her sweetest smile and blew him a kiss. That really set him off; he left rubber behind when he accelerated.

"The police will get him if he does much of that," Bess said smugly.

"He never has before," Katy murmured with a teasing smile. "My, my, he sure is strange since you came."

Bess laughed, impulsively freeing her hair from its bun and letting it fall around her shoulders. "It's nice out today, kind of like autumn." She frowned. "What am I saying, it is autumn until the twentieth, isn't it?"

"Everybody thinks of December as winter," Katy said. "Bess, is he really going to let us have a tree?" she added excitedly.

"Yes, he is," Bess said, without adding what a fight it had been. "Now. Let's get busy."

She and Katy bought boxes of ornaments and tinsel and a tree stand and skirt with the wad of bills Jude had pushed into her purse. She sent Katy into a bakery to get breads and cookies, and while she was gone Bess quickly bought some items that the little girl had expressed a desire for. Before she could regret it, she added a new model of pocket computer that Jude had been muttering about, along with a nasty-looking tie that he was sure to hate. On Christmas morning she'd decide which of the presents to give him, she promised herself.

Jude picked them up in front of the historic old hotel near the Alamo at three, and Bess glanced hopefully down the street toward the building.

"Not today," he said flatly. "I've got a budget meeting tonight. We'll only have time to buy the damned tree and go home."

Katy looked sad, but Bess smiled over the seat at her. "You and I will go another time, okay?"

The car jerked suddenly and he gave her a look that would have stopped traffic, but she turned away and ignored it.

"So brave, aren't we?" he murmured as he flicked on the radio.

It was playing a particularly mournful song about lost love, with a line that was repeated to the point of madness: "I feeeyul sooo sick in mah heart for you."

Bess lifted her eyebrows and smiled at Jude.

"What are you grinning about?" he challenged.

"I feeyul sooo sick in mah heart for you," she drawled off-key, and Katy rolled over in the back seat, muffling her laughter.

One corner of Jude's mouth actually curled up as he glanced at Bess. He'd stopped at a traffic light, and his lean hand shot out to catch a strand of her loosened hair and jerk it roughly.

"Thorn in my flesh," he muttered, letting go when she squealed. "Life was so peaceful until I got tangled up with you."

She pushed back the long hair that he'd tugged. "Is that what you call it? I was thinking you were probably just bogged down in bad temper."

"Careful, lady," he cautioned as he lit a cigarette. "Eventually, you'll be unprotected."

She knew what he meant, but there was a wild sweet recklessness in taunting him.

"You don't scare me, masked man," she replied. "My ancestors survived carpetbaggers and reconstruction. I reckon I can survive you."

"Out here we had Apaches and Comanches," he said, glancing at her. "As a matter of fact, my grandmother was a full-blooded Apache woman."

That explained his black hair, dark complexion and high cheekbones, she thought, studying him.

"Yes, it shows, doesn't it?" he asked. "We've got photographs of some distant cousins. Get Katy to show them to you."

"Oh, yes," Katy agreed, all eyes, "and there's a bow and arrow, and a skinning knife and a buffalo robe!"

"I used to read a lot about Cochise and the Chiricahua Apaches," Bess volunteered. "Western history was Dad's passion. He had books full of old photos of the war chiefs. Some of them were beautiful," she recalled, memories of those sculpted, proud features flashing through her mind. Involuntarily her eyes were drawn to the smooth skin of Jude's face, with the faint shadow of new beard around his mouth and chin.

He lifted an eyebrow at her. "Some Apache men took white women for their lodges, you know."

She turned back to her window. "There's a Christmas tree lot over there," she said quickly. "Could you stop?"

He pulled into the side street and parked the car. Katy ran ahead of the adults to the small dirt lot where pine and spruce trees were displayed.

"This is stupid," Jude growled, out of earshot of the civic club men who were operating the lot. "Why buy a tree when we've got thousands on the ranch?"

She looked up at him. "Because the money goes to provide Christmas for children who wouldn't have any otherwise," she said gently. "Suppose Katy lived like some of the families whose houses we drove past to get here, Jude?"

His eyes lowered to hers and that same odd, penetrating look was back in them again. It made her feel trembly all over.

"Money doesn't bring happiness," she continued, "I realize that all too well. But the lack of it can cause a lot of misery."

He shifted his broad shoulders uncomfortably and glanced toward Katy, who was signaling wildly. "She's found one she likes." He glared down at Bess. "You'll have to decorate the damned thing."

She beamed. "I like decorating trees. We bought all sorts of things to put on it."

"Yes, I know," he said with a rare smile. "A turkey and a ham."

She laughed gaily, and it changed her eyes. They were filled with warmth, and her creamy complexion glowed. She tossed her head, and her silver gold hair caught the sunlight and shone like metal. Jude stared at her for a long time before he moved abruptly and went to join Katy.

The tree the little girl wanted was a huge pine over eight feet tall. Jude tried to steer her toward something smaller, but it was the only tree she wanted and she wouldn't change her mind. So Jude gave in, growling a little, and handed the man with the cash box a large bill. Bess and Katy had gone back to the car because the wind was coming up and it was cold. But Bess glanced back in time to see Jude refusing any change, and she wanted to cry. It was just a little victory, but it was solid gold.

JUDE PUT THE tree into the stand for them and set it up; then he glared at both of them and went into town for his meeting, announcing that he'd have dinner there before it started.

Bess giggled, and Aggie came in with a puzzled frown. "He never eats in town," she said. "I do not understand."

"He's in a snit," Bess explained, laughing at the older woman's puzzled expression. "He's furious because he had to buy us a tree."

Aggie laughed. "But such a magnificent tree!" she exclaimed, sighing over it as she dried her hands on her apron. "Of course, at home we always made a *nacimiento*—a nativity scene. But the tree is lovely, too."

"We bought a little nativity scene, though, Aggie," Katy told her excitedly. "And we got lights, and all sorts of stuff! I have to call Deanne and tell her!"

She ran off and Bess sighed, smiling, as she studied the huge tree. "She's been like that all afternoon," she confided. "So happy and excited. I could have cried."

"The men tell me the *señor* has never liked to see celebrations, *señora,*" Aggie said sadly.

"Well, we're having one this year," Bess said shortly. "I insisted. We're even going to have turkey. And a ham, and all sort of trimmings. I have a recipe book— I had a recipe book," she added on a sigh. "I know, I'll call the caretaker and have him send it out here express mail!"

"You have sold your home?" Aggie asked.

"Oh, no. I had Jude hire a caretaker for it," she said. "It's been in my family for a hundred years. I just couldn't sell it. It was part of the marriage contract. I gave him his blessed shares, and I got my home. And part of the living room," she added, glancing toward the tree. "He said he wouldn't have it in his house. I figure part of the house belongs to me now that we're married, so I told him I wanted half the living room."

Aggie laughed. "*Señora,* you have him on his head. I have never seen him so confused. He curses all the time. But I have seen him smile when he looks at you. A true smile, that of a man who is pleased with what he has."

That was shocking. Bess had to restrain herself from pumping Aggie about her remark. But she didn't dare hope. Jude was determined to keep her at a distance, so she'd better not expect very much from him.

She and Katy decorated the tree, finishing just before Katy's bedtime. When Bess plugged in the lights, the young girl stared at it as if she'd never seen anything so beautiful. She hugged Bess hard.

"I love you," she choked out, and then ran away before Bess could reply.

She stood watching the tree with tears in her eyes. Who'd have thought it would mean so much to the little girl? She thought about Christmases when she was a child, and the trouble her mother and father had gone to to make them special for her. The tears rolled slowly down her cheeks. They'd been such a happy family, so happy. Then her father had died and her mother had married Crystal's father, and Bess's fragile happiness had collapsed. She couldn't help feeling sad about the past. It had been so lovely to have a family, to be part of that warmth. That was why she wanted to make it beautiful for Katy. A little girl should have some sweet memories to look back on when she grew up.

It was midnight when Bess went up to bed, and Jude hadn't yet come home. She was still amazed that he'd agreed to her demands. But, then, he was full of surprises, and she wasn't certain yet that he wouldn't get even with her for forcing his hand. Maybe Katy's expression on Christmas morning would be enough to stall him.

AS IT TURNED OUT, Jude didn't make any snide remarks about the tree; in fact, he pretended it wasn't there at all. But she saw him bring in a big, bulky package one night before Christmas and take it upstairs without saying a word about it to anyone. And suddenly her heart soared with happiness for Katy.

The only unpleasant note in the week before Christmas was a card from Crystal, saying that she'd only just gotten Bess's note about the wedding and would come to spend the holidays with her and Jude. That was enough to spoil the spirit of anticipation that was building inside Bess. Crystal was all she needed right now, to shatter the delicate truce she was establishing with Jude.

She could have cried. Crystal had always taken things from her. Crystal, who was beautiful and fragile and spoiled. But Bess had never minded losing before.

Now it was a different story. She had Katy and at least the hope of some kind of relationship with Jude if she was patient. What if Crystal decided she wanted Bess's new husband? A black cloud settled over the holiday preparations, like the despair of the days before Bess's mother had died. She felt old suddenly, and afraid.

CHAPTER FIVE

"WHAT IN THE hell is this supposed to be?" Jude asked Bess as she was setting the table for supper on Christmas Eve.

She glanced at the gracefully folded napkin beside his plate. "It's a napkin," she told him.

He glowered at it, and abruptly lifted it in his lean hand and shook it out. "If it's a napkin, suppose you let it look like one! This isn't your plantation, little Georgia peach."

She glared at him. "You'll find napkins done that way in elegant restaurants all over the country," she said with deliberate sarcasm. "If you'd rather wipe your mouth on your sleeve…"

His eyes flickered with a burst of emotion. "Like a savage?" he taunted. He threw the napkin down onto his plate. "That's what you've always considered me, Bess. From the early days."

"That's not at all true," she said quietly. She stopped lining up silverware and stood erect, her hair long and soft, floating around the shoulders of the white Victorian dress she was wearing.

"Isn't it?" He laughed shortly. He bent to crush out his cigarette in the big ceramic ashtray she'd put out for him. "Then why do you throw pots at me, and try to slap my face, and…"

"Jude…" she said beseechingly. "Why can't we let bygones be bygones?"

"Do you really think we can ignore the way we react to each other?" he said in surprise, and even smiled a little. "My God, I can't remember the last time a woman fought me like you have."

The remark brought embarrassing pictures to mind— Jude with a woman. She'd never thought about him in bed with a woman before, and it shocked her. Unfortunately, the shock was quite visible to his piercing eyes.

"That isn't what I meant," he murmured softly.

"Don't read my mind," she grumbled, turning back to her chore with fingers that trembled.

"Was I? What were you seeing in that suspicious little mind of yours? I didn't think ladies ever dwelled on such sordid subjects as sex."

She ignored the deliberate taunting. "Katy should be down any minute," she said quietly. "Please don't make fun of the dress I bought her to wear to the Christmas Eve service at church tonight."

He looked frankly insulted. "I never make fun of my daughter."

"Our daughter," she said coolly, staring at him.

A corner of his chiseled mouth curled upward. "Excuse me. *Our* daughter."

She finished arranging the silverware. "And would you say something nice about the way she looks?"

"Hold it, honey," he said silkily, noticing the way her head jerked up at the careless endearment that he'd just used for the first time in their stormy relationship. "I've let you get away with murder for the past week, but there's a limit to my patience."

"Do you have any?" she asked conversationally.

His chin lifted and his eyes narrowed. "Given the right circumstances, I have quite a lot," he said, in a tone that rippled along her nerves like a teasing finger.

She hated the hot surge in her cheeks and lowered her hands to rearrange one of the place settings. "That's something I'll never know about," she said.

He didn't reply, and she looked up straight into his unblinking stare.

It was like lightning striking. She couldn't have dragged her eyes away from his to save her life, and the intensity of the look they were exchanging made her tingle all the way to her toes. Jude's nostrils flared with a harsh breath and he moved abruptly, coming so close that she could smell his tangy cologne and feel the heat of him.

He slid one hand into the small of her back. The other pressed against her cheek, and he watched her curiously while his thumb began to move slowly, sensuously, across her lips, back and forth in a rough caress that had the oddest effect on her pulse.

"Cool," he breathed, "like ice to the touch, even your mouth. I've wondered for years what it would take to unstarch you."

"Don't think…you could do it," she whispered shakily.

But he could see the effect his hard thumb was having on her, he could see her lips parting helplessly, feel the in and out of her breath on his chin.

"I'm a man," he said quietly. "That's something you seem to have overlooked for a long time. I have all the usual needs, and I'm no virgin."

She felt her heart beating wildly and she wanted to move away, but when she tried, that steely hand behind her brought her legs against the powerful muscles of his own.

"Stop running, I won't hurt you," he growled, watching her mouth. "Not this time, at least. I'm curious about you. I want to know why you're so damned cold with me."

"You make my life miserable," she said jerkily, "you carry me off from my home and force me into a marriage I don't want, you insult me…and then you have the audacity to wonder why I back away when you come toward me!"

His eyebrows lifted. "You were backing away from me long before I brought you here. Two summers ago. The summer before that."

Her eyes fell to his chiseled mouth and she tried not to want it. "I've only tried to defend myself."

"After you attacked and set me off," he agreed. He sighed quietly. "I guess I am pretty hard on you sometimes."

That admission was startling, because he'd never admitted any such thing before. She glanced up, curious.

"You don't know why, do you?" he asked, searching her eyes.

She nodded. "Because you dislike me."

He laughed shortly. "God, you're green," he murmured. "Grass green and as out of place here as hot-house orchids." He caught her chin and tilted it. "That reminds me. I want you to stop putting those damned flowers in my study. Bandy made a remark about it this morning—and about the damned tree you put in the living room. Said you were softening me up."

She gave him her most belligerent glare. "And what's wrong with that, Rawhide Man? You're so hard you can't enjoy the simple pleasures of life."

That made him angry. "We don't need all that," he said gruffly. "Christmas trees and wreaths on the damned door...next, I'll find lace sewn on the edges of my damned underwear!"

The thought of it made her giggle. She put up a hand to muffle her laughter, but he caught it savagely and pressed it against his chest.

Her fingers felt the heavy rise and fall of his breathing. The hand at her back involuntarily drew her closer, and with a shock she realized that the closeness of her body was beginning to have a noticeable effect on him.

Apparently he wasn't anxious to have her know that, because he immediately loosened his hold so that several inches separated them.

His eyes went down to the slender hand resting on his white shirtfront. His own hand touched it lightly, tracing the pale blue veins on its back, running over her long fingers.

"You play something, don't you?" he asked in a deep, slow drawl. "The piano?"

"Yes," she whispered.

"You have...lovely hands," he murmured. His breathing was growing more ragged by the second. Slowly, almost absently, he flicked open two of the top buttons of his open-necked shirt and drew her fingers inside.

She went rigid at the feel of him, at the hair-roughened warmth and strength of the hard muscles of his chest, just below his collarbone.

His lips parted as he watched her hand against his body. He opened another button and guided her hand from one side of his chest to the other, letting her fingers rest finally on one rigid male nipple.

She hadn't realized that it happened to men the way it happened to women, and she looked up with the discovery in her eyes.

His eyes held hers for a long, static moment. He bent his head just enough for her lips to come within reach of his, and she could feel the banked-down fire in him like an imminent explosion.

"Open your mouth, and fit it to mine," he whispered in a deep tone that hypnotized her.

She obeyed him in silence, a thick silence that throbbed with new emotions, new knowledge. She stood up on her tiptoes, staring at his mouth, and opened hers very slowly.

Holding her breath, she fitted her lips exactly to his hard, open mouth, and a gasp caught in her throat at the exquisite sensations that rippled through her body.

His breath mingled with hers, coming quick and harsh. Both his hands moved to her waist and lifted her gently up against his hard body while his mouth slowly increased its intimate pressure.

Her hands, both of them exploring his hard chest now, tangled in the thick mat of hair over the warm muscles and pulled, like a kitten kneading a soft cover in pure pleasure. He moaned sharply, and his mouth was suddenly demanding, hungry and relentless, forcing hers into a deeper union that drew a moan from her own mouth. She slid her hands up around his neck and pressed her breasts hard against his chest. She felt as though she were drowning in new and exquisite pleasures.

All at once he set her back down on her feet and stood glaring at her, his face showing mingled anger and reluctant satisfaction.

She drew away from him, surprised that he let her, and turned back to the table. "Katy...and I are going to services in a few minutes," she said, shaken. "Would you like to go with us?"

"No, I would not."

If she hadn't been so shaken, she might have noticed the rasping sound of his voice, the quickness of his breath, which betrayed how moved he'd been. But she didn't, and he turned away.

"I'm going out for dinner," he said coldly. "You can gush over Katy all by yourself!"

"She's your daughter, Jude," she said, her voice soft and hurt and shaking.

He stopped, his back to her, and said something rough. "I can't stay here with you," he ground out after a minute.

That was deliberately cruel, but she didn't react.

"Don't worry, Katy and I will be out of the house for at least two hours," she retorted.

"I'd still rather go to town. I've had about all the

high society I can stand," he added before he slammed out the door.

She turned her back and went toward the kitchen to see how Aggie was coming with supper. But she hesitated outside the door and dried the tears that insisted on falling, no matter how hard she tried to stop them.

She put on a happy face for Katy, making some excuse about an unexpected business meeting that Jude had to attend. It pacified the little girl, but her disappointment showed. She had her long hair brushed around her shoulders, and she was wearing the ruffled pink dress Bess had bought for her. She looked so lovely. And Jude didn't even care enough to stay and see her. Bess could have shaken him.

Later, when it was bedtime, Katy came into Bess's room and they sat in their nightgowns on Bess's bed while the older woman told her about Christmases at the Georgia estate where she grew up.

"Do you miss your mother a lot?" Katy asked.

"Yes," she said. "I miss her terribly. But she was very sick and she's so much better off."

"She's in heaven," Katy said, understanding. She held Bess's hand. "You aren't sorry you came here, are you? You aren't sorry you married Daddy?"

"No, I'm not sorry," Bess said softly, and smiled. "Look what a beautiful daughter I got."

Katy blushed and grinned. "Bess, did you have parties at Christmas when you were a little girl?"

"Not a lot of them," Bess said, sighing. "But when my stepsister got big enough, her father insisted that she have them. She had lots of boyfriends."

"Did you?"

Bess shook her head. "No, darling. I'm very plain, you know."

"Daddy doesn't think so," Katy said. "I heard him tell Mr. Teague that you were a vision. Doesn't that mean pretty?"

"There are different kinds of vision," Bess said sadly, thinking Jude probably meant she was a nightmare. Remembering the way he'd kissed her downstairs, she went hot all over. Why had he done that?

She stretched, bringing the elasticized bodice of her nightgown precariously low, but she didn't notice. "Darling, I'm tired, and tomorrow is Christmas. Let's get some sleep," she told Katy. "Tomorrow we'll make some roasted pecans to snack on, all right?"

"All right," Katy said, getting up. "Bess, I'm so glad you came to live with us."

"So am I," Bess said, and was about to elaborate when Jude walked in.

He hadn't even bothered to knock, and he looked a little wild. His black hair was hanging untidily down on his forehead and his green eyes were hard and glittering.

"Have a party?" he asked, his voice slightly slurred.

"Just saying good night to each other," Bess said, sitting up straighter even though the action brought her bodice still lower. She felt a sense of power at the expression that went over his hard features, and she didn't follow her first impulse, which had been to pull up the slipping fabric.

"Good night, Daddy," Katy said, standing on tiptoe as he lowered his cheek so she could kiss him. "You should have come to church with us, it was lovely. The minister said I looked pretty," she added, grinning. "'Night, Bess."

"'Night, darling," Bess said, cringing inside when Katy went out with a wicked smile and deliberately closed the door behind her.

"Church," Jude growled. "And Christmas trees and turkeys and turning my damn house and my life upside down." He was breathing roughly, and Bess suddenly realized that he'd been drinking.

Her lips parted on a rush of breath. "The service was very nice," she said after a minute. "And Katy did... look lovely."

"So did you," he ground out, staring pointedly at her bodice. "All lace and ruffles...did you wear that thing deliberately?"

She swallowed nervously. "What thing?"

"That gown," he said, moving closer to the bed with a little less than his usual elegance of movement. He sat down heavily beside her, still staring at the gown.

"I...couldn't have known...you'd come in here," she managed through tight lips.

"Oh, of course not," he muttered, glaring at her. "But you let it slip deliberately, honey," he added with a glittering smile. "You saw my eyes on you and you liked it."

He caught both her nervous hands in one of his and locked them together over her waist, pressing her back in a sitting position against the pillows. The other hand went to the elasticized bodice, and his eyes were suddenly cruel. "If you want me to look at you, Bess, you don't have to play teenage games. Just tell me."

As he spoke, he ripped the bodice down to her waist, baring her small, taut breasts to his hot eyes.

He stared down at them as if he had every right, letting his eyes take in each line, each soft curve, each contrast of color from soft pink to mauve.

The hand holding hers tightened as he studied her, and his face went curiously rigid, leaving only his eyes to express his churning emotions.

Bess couldn't move. His intent stare kept her still. He was looking at her in a way no man ever had before, and there was an expression in his eyes that puzzled, excited. Her breath came in unsteady gasps while sensation after sensation washed over her like flames.

Finally, finally, his eyes wandered back up to hers, to read the wonder and faint embarrassment in them.

"Yes, you do like it, don't you?" he asked curtly. "Haven't you ever been like this with a man?"

She shook her head slowly, but words were beyond her.

His eyebrows rose slightly. "Never?" he asked, as if that were incomprehensible.

"As you, yourself, said…my blessings are small," she said in a whisper, turning her face away.

"Don't," he breathed. He freed her hands and drew her face back to his eyes. "Don't. You're exquisitely formed, as delicate as the inside of a seashell, pink and cream…" He caught his breath as he looked back down at her body, his eyes fiercely possessive. "My God, I've never seen anything so sweet as this!"

He'd been drinking, of course, she told herself as she watched him. But he was making her feel things she'd never experienced, and she loved having his eyes on her. She wanted him to bend down and put his mouth there, *there*.

Her thoughts shocked her and she caught her breath.

His eyes came back up to hold hers. "We're married," he reminded her quietly. "There's no shame in this."

Her breath stopped in her throat. "Yes, I... I know," she said.

He reached out a gentle hand and touched her cheek, then eased his fingers into her hair. "You're so young," he said in the tenderest voice she'd ever heard him use. "So untouched by ugliness and pain. I should have had enough humanity left to keep you away from me." He drew in an angry breath and stood up, standing rigidly with his back to her as he lit a cigarette.

She lay there helpless, puzzled by words she didn't understand. "Jude?" she asked softly.

He turned, his eyes going helplessly to her soft bareness. They closed, almost painfully. "Oh, God, will you cover yourself up?" he asked under his breath as he turned away again. "I've had three neat whiskeys, Bess, and it's been months since I've had a woman."

She tugged her bodice back in place with trembling hands. "And you don't want me. You needn't bother repeating it," she said in a cool tone that hid her wounded pride.

He actually laughed, but bitterly. "You might be surprised at the things I want, but I'm a realist these days. I know my own limitations."

"You, with limitations?" she scoffed, dragging the coverlet over herself. "How shocking."

He glanced back and then turned around, lifting the cigarette to his mouth as he studied her flushed face. He looked so masculine and sensuous that she wanted to climb out of the bed and throw herself at him. The way he'd looked at her body had been unspeakably beautiful, and she knew that despite the fact that he'd been drinking, she'd treasure the memory of this night forever. A kiss and then this… It was like having her secret longings all fulfilled at once.

"You aren't really cool at all, are you?" he asked quietly. "It's a kind of armor you wear, a form of protection."

She flushed wildly. "Stop taking me apart."

He shook his head. "I'm not doing that. You're much too complex. But, downstairs—" he watched her flush with the memory of it "—you were with me every step of the way. I hadn't expected you to kiss me, even when I told you to. I was…teasing."

Oh, God, she thought miserably. She closed her eyes and drew in a steadying breath. Please, please don't let me give myself away, she pleaded silently.

"Would you mind finding some other method of torture in the future?" she asked unsteadily. "As you said yourself, I'm too green to know the difference."

"Did it hurt?" he asked, as if it mattered.

She laughed bitterly. "I wouldn't let you hurt me. Not in a million years."

He made a rough sound in his throat and crushed out his cigarette, even though he'd only finished half of it. "Damn it, what I had in mind for us was a simple merger, a marriage based on business concerns, not emotion. I haven't changed my mind. I wanted the shares, not complications."

Her eyes fell to the coverlet, which her fingers were worrying. "Then stop creating them," she said.

"Stop helping me," he shot back, glaring at her. "I'm human. I respond to temptation just like any other damned man."

"I wasn't—"

"Try again." His eyes darkened as he studied her, and she looked away because she couldn't outstare him.

"I won't forget," she said on a sigh.

"See that you don't." He paced the room angrily.

She studied the coverlet as if it fascinated her. "Jude, why haven't you ever had a Christmas tree before?"

He glanced at her briefly. "Because I never realized how much it meant to Katy until now." He laughed shortly. "All this time she pretended that she didn't care. And I was too damned busy." He lifted his chin and studied her thoughtfully. "She shines like a new penny these days. You've got her heart in your pocket. Just don't set your cap at mine, lady."

"That frozen thing?" she asked with a calm she didn't feel. "Why should I want it? Anyway, you don't want me," she added quietly.

His eyes pinned her to the bed. "I wanted you downstairs," he said, shocking her.

Her face went bloodred, and he watched it with lifted eyebrows.

"My, my, what an interesting reaction," he said. "Very virginal."

"Not exactly by choice," she said coldly. "There was

little opportunity for me to attract men as long as Crystal lived at home."

"Tinsel usually overshadows gold," he said thoughtfully, looking at her. "Your stepsister is beautiful, all right. Did she steal all your boyfriends?"

"Every last one."

"Then they couldn't have cared very much," he said. "It's probably better that you kept your chastity."

"It will be a great comfort to me in my old age," she agreed.

His eyes searched hers. "You won't change a lot with age, I don't think," he mused. "You have beautiful bone structure."

She returned the long, searching glance and slowly, poignantly, an idea began to form in her mind. He wasn't quite as unapproachable as he usually was. If she could find a way to capture his attention before Crystal showed up, if she could…

Her lips parted nervously. "Jude…are you…very tired?" she asked hesitantly.

His darkening eyes wandered slowly over her. "Are you offering me your body?"

She swallowed down a quick denial and caught her nervous fingers in the coverlet. "Do…do you want it?"

His chest rose and fell roughly. "Oh, yes," he said with self-contempt. "I want you."

She stood up, feeling wildly reckless and inhibited at the same time. She forced herself to face him. Her fingers went to the gown and slowly, deliberately, eased it down her waist, over her smooth hips and onto the floor.

Jude stared at her as if he'd never seen a woman in

his life. His face flushed slightly, and his eyes exploded with a desire that darkened them almost to black.

"Grace and elegance," he breathed. "I imagined you'd be proud even when you offered yourself. You are so lovely, Bess," he added with deep emotion. "So lovely. Don't tempt me, honey. I'm hungry and it's been a long time."

He started to turn away, but she touched his arm, daring everything.

"Would...would it be so hard?" she whispered, her voice shaking with embarrassment.

"No." He shook his head. "Quite the contrary. But if you got pregnant..."

Her face brightened, changed, and her eyes softened. "Oh, I'd like that," she breathed. "I'd like being pregnant with your baby."

He actually trembled. "Bess..."

"Don't you want a son, Jude?" she asked, looking up with her whole heart in her eyes.

He reached for her, crushing her bareness to every hard line of his body, burying his face in her soft hair.

"Yes," he ground out achingly. "I want a son. I want you. But..."

"But what?"

His fingers tightened at her back. "Bess, you know that I served in Vietnam, that I saw combat?"

"Yes."

He sighed heavily. "My unit ran into an ambush, and I caught a lot of shrapnel. My right hip and thigh look like a road map of the moon. The scars have faded some over the years, but I've had women ask me to put out the light…"

He laughed when he said it, but Bess ached for his pride. How it must have hurt!

"I won't ask you to put out the light," she said into his ear. "I wouldn't care if you were missing an arm or a leg…you'd still be Jude!"

He caught his breath at the admission and she felt a shudder work its way through him. "You may regret this in the morning," he ground out.

"I'll worry about it in the morning. Jude, please…?"

"Good God, you don't have to beg. Can't you feel how much I want it?" He bent and took her mouth roughly, possessively, and she gave herself up to the wild arousal.

She felt him lift her onto the bed and she lay watching him as he undressed with jerky, urgent movements. She knew he wasn't quite sober, but at last some of the barriers were down and she was going to take full advantage of it. Her eyes didn't waver when he turned back to her; she let them linger on the white scars across his hip and thigh. He was pale there, probably because he never went swimming or wore shorts, and she could see why. It wasn't pretty, but it wasn't as horrible as he seemed to think it was. The rest of him was all hard muscle when he moved. He was broad chested, narrow hipped, as graceful as a cat.

"No comment?" he asked as he slid onto the bed beside her.

"Did you expect me to faint?" she asked with a tiny smile. "I almost did, but it wasn't because of the scars."

His eyebrows arched and he made a tiny, amused sound. "Haven't you ever seen a man undressed before?"

She shook her head.

His fingers touched her mouth, her cheek. "I'll try to be careful," he said, bending to kiss her softly. "But I'm pretty rusty, Mrs. Langston. It's been a long, long time since I had a woman in my bed."

Amazingly uninhibited with him, she reached up with loving arms to hold him while he teased her mouth. She felt as if she were seeing for the first time the man beneath the hard veneer.

"I didn't think you felt...like this," she whispered, tautening when he touched her unexpectedly.

He lifted his head, frowning. "Why not?"

She flushed, lowering her eyes to his hairy chest. "You're always sniping at me."

"Don't get any ideas about it," he said coolly, hesitating. "I don't love you, Bess. I want you, but that's it."

She felt a cold sickness well up inside her and almost jerked away from him. But there was something different in his manner, in his eyes. She knew she wasn't going to change him overnight. She'd just have to be patient. And at least he wanted her. A child might soften him, just a little, if he could watch her grow big with it and be there in its early years—things he'd missed when Katy was born.

"I'm not asking for miracles," she said softly. "I... I'll try to please you if you'll tell me what to do."

His eyes closed for an instant and his lips compressed. "Damn, Bess!"

"What is it?" she asked, reaching up to smooth her fingers over his broad chest as she had done in the dining room.

Surprisingly, he turned over on his back. "Don't stop now," he said quietly.

Her hands, shy at first, smoothed over his shoulders and chest, rediscovering the different textures of skin and hair and muscle and bone. He watched her, lying back on the pillows, faintly smiling.

When her hands stopped at the powerful muscles of his stomach, just below his waist, he actually grinned at her embarrassment.

"Coward," he taunted.

She smiled back. "I'm new at this."

"You'll learn." He sat up, bringing her body against his, watching her breasts vanish in the thick hair over his chest. "Now, it's my turn," he breathed, bending to kiss a shocked gasp from her parted lips. "My turn," he growled again, easing her down onto the mattress.

She felt her body blaze up with sensation. His strolling fingers learned every silken inch of her, his lips soon following the same path. The room was utterly quiet except for the reckless sounds they made together.

Once, her eyes opened and looked straight up into his as his powerful body eased down totally against her.

"Afraid?" he whispered.

"Yes," she agreed unsteadily.

His body moved and she gasped.

"It won't ever hurt again after this," he whispered gently, controlling the motion of his powerful body with an effort that showed in every strained line of his hard face. "Is it bad?"

It was, but she shook her head, and a minute later the lie became truth. She arched helplessly and there was a sudden tenderness in his eyes as his motions grew deep and urgent and his hands taught her the strange new rhythm.

She lost track of time and place in the grip of something so exquisitely torturous that she felt as if she were dying of a particularly vicious fever. Her body burned with it, and there was no relief. She was slowly, agonizingly being stretched in a tension that would surely kill her.

"No," she whispered urgently, her fingernails clutching wildly, her teeth against his shoulder. "No, I can't!"

He was laughing triumphantly…laughing! His hands controlled her wild body, forcing it to comply with the demands he was imposing. And then it was all sweet explosion and consuming flames, snapping the tension, and she fell and fell and fell…

It seemed like hours before she could breathe again, before her eyes stopped melting in hot tears that fell onto his damp chest. She was trembling, and so was he in the aftermath of something so volcanic that she blushed just remembering it.

His hand brought her eyes up to his and he caught his breath as he watched her. "Not what you expected, honey?" he asked softly.

"I…thought it would…hurt," she whispered.

His eyes wandered slowly down the length of her body. "Didn't it? You cried out."

She blushed wildly and hid her eyes, and he laughed again, softly. He bore her down onto the mattress with a glittering wildness in his eyes that she'd never seen in them. His nostrils flared as he breathed.

"Last time was for you," he said under his breath as his fingers moved in slow exploration. "This time," he whispered, bending to her mouth, "is for me…"

The night was at once the longest and shortest she'd ever spent, and as dawn slowly erased the blackness outside the window, she ached pleasantly from head to toe. She was astounded at Jude's inexhaustible ardor. She flushed at just the memory of it and wondered at his stamina—and her own.

But the tender, hungry lover of the night was sadly lacking in the bitter-faced man who dragged himself out of bed and dressed in the dim light. She didn't remember when he'd turned the lights out.

He dragged on his shirt and flicked the light on, standing quietly in his jeans and staring at her with eyes she couldn't read.

Self-consciously, she tugged the sheet over her breasts and flushed at the intensity of his gaze.

"And now you know, don't you?" he asked with a mocking laugh. "You know that I want you to the point of obsession. But don't think you're going to put a ring through my nose because of it, honey. You won't own me. Not even if you give me a child out of last night. I hope you meant what you said about wanting that baby, Bess, because I'm through keeping my distance from you. I'll have Aggie move your things into my room in the morning and you can sleep with me from now on."

She stared at him with slow comprehension. "But… you said you…wanted a child, too," she reminded him.

"My God, I wanted you, you stupid woman," he ground out, glaring down at her. "I'd have agreed with anything to get…" He sighed and turned away, running a restless hand through his hair. "It had been months, and I was hungry for something female in my arms. All that whiskey and all the lonely nights caught up with me." His eyes glittered at her. "And you stripped off that damned gown and came at me like Venus rising. I'm human, damn you!"

She turned her head away on the pillow, her eyes closed as the tears ran freely down her cheeks. For just a few hours she'd thought he was as involved as she was, as full of wonder about what they'd shared. But it had all been a sham, like their marriage.

"Regretting it won't help now," he said coldly. "Just remember, lady, it was all your idea."

But she didn't answer him. She couldn't. Her heart was breaking in half.

He stood by the bed for a minute, and she felt that he wanted to say something. But the moment passed and he left her, slamming the door behind him.

CHAPTER SIX

GETTING UP AND pretending that everything was fine was the hardest thing Bess had ever done. She put on the soft beige jersey dress that she'd come from Georgia in, and rolled her hair into a French twist at her nape. She hardly bothered with makeup because no one would see her except Jude and she didn't care how she looked anymore. She'd wanted him so much, loved him so much. She'd thought he cared a little…and it had all been sex.

She laughed at her own naiveté. And tonight she'd sleep in his arms and it would all happen again. But her response wouldn't be as uninhibited, she promised herself. He wouldn't wring that madness from her twice, not when she knew he was hating her for "tempting" him. She picked up her brush and almost flung it into the mirror in pure fury. If only she hadn't been so stupid, so trusting. She straightened. For Katy's sake, she was going to have to put on her brightest face and pretend everything was just fine.

She went to Katy's room and knocked on the door. She peeked her head inside and smiled at the head under the covers.

"Hey," she called softly. "Santa Claus has come by now, I imagine. Want to go downstairs and see?"

Katy was instantly awake and all eyes. "Oh, let's!" she agreed, bounding out of bed to grab her quilted pink robe and slippers.

Bess put an arm around her as they went to the staircase, dreading the confrontation that would undoubtedly come with Jude.

The presents she'd put under the tree last night after she'd sent Katy upstairs were where she'd left them, but some more had been added. She frowned at the size of one of them, a big rectangular thing wrapped in brown paper with a frilly bow stuck to one corner. Perhaps Aggie had put it there.

"Shouldn't we get Daddy?" Katy asked at the foot of the stairs.

"Yes, I suppose so," Bess said halfheartedly. "Why don't you go upstairs and knock on his door, darling?"

"No need," Jude said from the hall. "I woke early."

He had a coffee cup in one hand and he was wearing jeans and nothing else. His broad, hair-covered chest was bare and so were his feet, and he looked…odd.

Bess couldn't meet his eyes. She went into the living room behind Katy, aware of Jude near her. It must be some sort of radar, she thought hysterically. She always knew where he was.

"I knew you'd come to watch me open my presents," Katy said, laughing, dragging her father to the tree. "Here, this one is yours. I hope you like it!"

Jude sprawled on the carpet and opened the package, murmuring appropriately at the special cigarette case Katy had bought him with her own money. Bess knew it was something he'd never use, but Katy had insisted.

"Oh, Dad, thank you!" Katy was cooing, as she opened a present that contained an automatic camera with film and flashcubes. "You remembered!"

"It was hard to forget," he murmured drily, and Bess almost laughed as she recalled Katy's repeated hints every morning at breakfast.

"Aren't you going to open yours?" Jude asked Bess, glancing in her direction without actually looking at her.

"Yes, here it is, Bess!" Katy said, handing her a small present.

"That wasn't the one I meant, but go ahead and open it," he said.

Bess tore the ribbons and paper and found a bottle of her favorite cologne. She leaned forward and kissed Katy. "Thank you, darling," she said softly. "It's my very favorite."

"I hoped you'd like it. Thank you for mine," she added, hugging the musical computer that Bess had given her.

Jude reached out and tugged the big, rectangular package from its perch against the wall and handed it to Bess.

"I... I didn't expect anything," she said, avoiding his eyes.

"Neither did I," he said, holding up the as yet unopened package that contained the nasty tie.

She tore open the paper, and when she saw what he'd given her she couldn't say a word. Her eyes filled with tears and she chewed hard on her lower lip to keep from crying. There, in the torn folds of the wrapping paper, was the painting she'd admired that first day at the San

Antonio airport—with the windmill and ranch house against the flat horizon.

"Cat got your tongue?" he taunted.

She took a slow breath. "Thank you," she said in a subdued tone, touching the painting lightly, lovingly. "I… I wanted it very much."

He didn't say a word, but when he started to open his gift she touched his hand lightly.

"No," she said. "That's just a tie. I have another…"

She jumped up and ran all the way up the stairs to take the pocket computer out of her chest of drawers. She was breathless when she got back and thrust the small package into his hands.

Puzzled, he unwrapped it with slow, deliberate movements of his lean hands, and when he saw what it was he just stared at Bess.

"How did you know I wanted this?"

She shifted uncomfortably. "The same way you knew I wanted this, I guess," she said, touching the painting.

He was leaning back against the armchair with one leg propped up, and his eyes were calculating. Half dressed as he was, he looked devastating.

"Well?" he said curtly.

"Well what?"

"Don't I get a kiss?" he asked with raised eyebrows. "You gave Katy one."

"You must, Bess!" Katy insisted, his willing co-conspirator, both of them ignoring the older woman's blush. "It's Christmas."

"She's shy," he told Katy. "Why don't you go get Aggie and tell her to come and open her presents?"

"Sure!" Katy laughed, leaping up to go in search of the housekeeper.

Bess flushed wildly, lowering her eyes to the carpet when they were alone.

"Shy?" he taunted. "There isn't an inch of you I don't know now."

"Oh, yes, there is," she replied, lifting her eyes. "My mind. And my heart. You don't know the first thing about either one."

"And I don't care to," he said flatly. "Your body is the only thing about you that interests me. Come here."

"Go to hell."

"It's Christmas," he reminded her, lifting his arrogant chin and smiling, but it wasn't a friendly smile. "Come here, Bess, or I'll tell Katy you don't like me."

"Go ahead, it's the truth," she said, hating him.

He leaned forward and caught her wrist, propelling her across his powerful legs and into his arms. He levered her down to the carpet, looming over her and pinning her there with his hands on her wrists.

"Fight me," he whispered with a husky laugh. "Fight me, Bess, and we'll see who wins."

She drew in an angry breath and let her eyes tell him how furious she was with him. But she stopped struggling. He seemed to like subduing her. But that was like him, too.

"That's more like it," he murmured as he bent his head. His lips were poised just above hers, so that she could feel and taste his smoky breath. "Now open your mouth the way you did last night, and let's get drunk on the taste of each other all over again…"

Her mind rebelled even as her body obeyed him. She tried to be cool, not to respond, but he was hungry and she liked the roughness and power of his embrace; she liked the way it made her feel to know that he was aroused.

"Oh, yes," he breathed as he felt her shy response. "Yes, like that. Hold me, Bess."

Her arms went up around him and she felt with a sense of awe the full weight of his body on hers.

"Katy…" she whispered shakily.

"I'll hear them," he whispered back. "Bess," he breathed, and she felt his hand brush from her waist up over one taut, full breast to cup and caress it while his mouth made her want to scream with its slow, taunting arousal.

His thumb was stroking her, driving her mad, and she twisted to escape it, but it followed, easing under her bra, taking fabric with it, to find the softness of her.

His eyes were wild when he drew away, glittering like green fireworks in his taut face. "We'll sleep together tonight," he breathed huskily. "I'll have you again. And again." His mouth crushed down onto hers. "Oh, God, I want you!" he groaned.

He moved, making her aware of the force of his passion, and she gasped.

"You can feel it, can't you?" he asked roughly. "A man can't hide his hungers the way a woman can. I've tasted you and now I want more, I want to make a banquet of you. You knew I would, damn you. You're just like every other damned woman…"

She turned her head weakly away, closing her eyes. Would he never tire of hurting her?

He rolled away abruptly and propped himself back up against the chair. He pulled a cigarette and matches down from the coffee table and lit one with fingers that weren't quite steady.

Bess sat up, straightening her hair.

"You look tidy enough," he said curtly, glaring at her. "Nothing ruffles you very much, society girl, not even rolling around on the floor with me."

She got to her feet with exquisite grace and turned away to pick up the wrapping paper and stuff it into one of the boxes Katy's presents had come in.

"No comment?" he taunted, his voice cold and hard.

"What would you like me to say, Jude?" she asked quietly, turning to face him. "I'm vulnerable with you. I can't help it. I don't have the experience to pretend I don't like what you do to me. But it isn't kind of you to make fun of me."

He laughed shortly and averted his eyes. "But then, I'm not a kind man. I never pretended to be."

"If you hate me so much, then file for divorce," she said proudly.

"What kind of settlement would you like?" he asked with pursed lips and biting sarcasm. "An oil well or two? A new mink and a Ferrari every year?"

"I don't want money," she said, bending to pick up a stray ribbon. "I never did. I can work for what I want."

"I can see you now, waiting tables," he chided.

She stood up, regal and cool. "There's no disgrace about honest work. I could wait tables as well as anyone else. I'm not trained to do much, but I'm not afraid of hard work. Keep your money, Jude," she added with a faint smile. "I don't need it, or you."

His eyes began to glitter and he got to his feet slowly, menacingly. "Don't you? I could make you beg for me."

She straightened. "Yes," she agreed in a small voice. "I know you could."

His hand sliced through the air, making the cigarette tip glow wildly. "Damn you! So cool and untouchable!"

"Here's Aggie," Katy called as she and the housekeeper joined them. She paused, glancing from Bess's white face to Jude's red-tinged one.

"I...was just telling Jude that my sister is coming to spend some of the holidays with us," Bess blurted out, flushing.

Jude's eyes widened. "Crystal?"

"Yes," she said with a nervous smile. "I meant to tell you sooner, really I did, but I kept wondering how to do it."

"I don't mind having her here," he said with a smile that only Bess saw. "She'll be a nice decoration. How long is she staying?"

"She didn't say," Bess managed.

His eyes wandered over her face. "Afraid of the competition?" he chided.

She turned away. "I've never been any competition for Crystal," she said with quiet dignity. "She takes what she likes."

Jude scowled at her, his eyes strange and intent. But he didn't say a word. He only lifted the cigarette to his lips and turned back to Katy and Aggie, who were exclaiming over the scarf Aggie had gotten from Bess and the hand-crocheted shawl she'd gotten from Jude and Katy.

Later, Jude went upstairs to dress for dinner and Katy and Bess helped Aggie set the table. It was overflowing with everything from Sally Lunn bread, which Bess had made from the old home recipe, to ambrosia and ham and turkey and dressing and giblet gravy with home-made potato rolls and Southern cornbread, cranberry sauce, green beans and mashed potatoes and sweet potato soufflé. For dessert there was fruitcake, and apple pie, and hand-dipped chocolates.

Bess forced herself to eat, even though she'd long since lost her appetite. Jude managed to put away a filled plate, but his eyes kept lancing toward Bess, and she couldn't meet them. He hated her, and she knew it. But there was nothing she could do or say in her own defense. She'd tempted him, all right. She'd wanted him desperately. She loved the horrible man, and he wanted no part of her.

Her eyes drifted down to her black coffee in its delicate china cup. Why had he bothered to buy her the painting? she wondered. Had it been for Katy's sake? To keep peace? She sighed, sounding so lonely and forlorn that everyone looked at her.

"Bess, why are you so sad?" Katy asked gently.

"*Niña,* the *señora* has no mother to celebrate this Christmas with," Aggie said gently. "We must not mind if she feels a sadness."

Bess looked at Aggie and smiled. "Thank you, but

I'm coping very well. I have another family now to celebrate with."

Jude abruptly threw down his napkin and got up from the table, strode away toward his study and slammed the door behind him.

"What's the matter with Daddy?" Katy asked, shocked.

Bess shook her head. "He doesn't like—" She almost said "me," but caught herself in time. "Christmas," she said instead. "I'm afraid it's all caught up with him."

"But he said he liked the tree," Katy told her. She grinned. "And he told me how long it took him to find the painting you wanted. It had been sold and he had to find the man who bought it to get it back."

How strange that he'd gone to so much trouble for someone he disliked. But before Bess had time to reflect on Jude's odd behavior, the phone rang. Aggie was back in a minute to get Bess.

Bess picked up the receiver, feeling a sense of impending doom because there was only one person who might be calling her today.

"Hello?" she said.

"Hello, Merry Christmas!" Crystal's bubbly voice was instantly recognizable. "Send someone to the airport to fetch me, love. I've come to cheer up your dreary holidays!"

CHAPTER SEVEN

THE AIRPORT WAS bustling when Jude and Bess got there, but it only took a minute for them to spot Crystal. She would have stood out anywhere in the white satin blouse and black skirt she wore. With her exquisite face and figure and her tumble of long, straight blond hair, she was absolutely stunning.

"Darling!" she called, running straight toward Bess and Jude.

But it was Jude whose arms she ran into, and while Bess watched, horrified, Crystal kissed him on the mouth, her ardor real and sickening to watch. Worse, Jude didn't seem to mind at all. His arms contracted and he laughed as he let her go.

"Hello, bubbles," he said, grinning at the younger woman. "How long can we keep you?"

Crystal looked ecstatic, Bess thought. Already she had a captive male. And who cared that it was dry old Bess's husband anyway? "As long as you'll let me," she told Jude, grinning gaily. "I've had a tiff with my count, and I may never leave Big Mesquite. How's that?"

Bess stood rigidly while Crystal hugged her. She was certain Crystal's affection was all for show.

"Hi, love," Crystal murmured. "Bad Christmas for you this year, isn't it, with Carla dead?"

Bess's eyes began to water and she turned away. "I'm glad you could come to visit," Bess said tautly.

Jude was glaring at her, but she didn't look his way. "You just missed Christmas dinner, but Aggie can fix you a plate," Bess said graciously, remembering her manners.

"Lord, I couldn't eat a bite!" Crystal said. "I had dinner on the plane, you know. Cardboard and all that, but it was filling, at least. And I never eat much. Have to watch my figure!"

So did everyone else, Bess thought uncharitably, seeing the way male eyes followed her flamboyant stepsister as they weaved through the travelers on their way to the parking lot.

"You're very quiet today, Bess," Crystal remarked when they were settled in the Mercedes—with Crystal, as Bess had expected, in the front seat and Bess in the back.

"She had a bad night," Jude said, straight-faced, and fortunately Crystal turned around before she saw Bess's wild flush.

"Well, I could have died when I read that note about the two of you getting married," Crystal told Jude. "You used to swear you'd never let any woman get a hold on you."

"I meant it, too," he said imperturbably, lighting a cigarette. "I married Bess because of those damned shares. I couldn't get them any other way, thanks to Carla."

"Lord, she did hate you, didn't she?" Crystal laughed. "Poor Jude. Is marriage awful?"

Bess, sitting ignored in the back seat, could have shot them both. If only Jude had allowed Katy to come with them so she could have had someone to talk to!

"It has its compensations," Jude murmured, glancing in the rearview mirror. "Doesn't it, Bess?"

"Yes," she said sweetly. "Katy is one of them."

He didn't like that. His eyes glared at her. But Crystal laughed.

"That sounds like you, darling," she told her stepsister. "You always did love kids. Are you going to have some of your own?"

"Yes," Bess said curtly, and her eyes dared Jude to argue. He didn't seem to want to.

"Bess is good with Katy," he said as he turned onto the main highway. "They're already pals."

"I can't wait to see Katy again," Crystal said with a lazy smile. "She was just a baby the last time at that family get-together."

"You've missed them all for years," Jude reminded her.

"Oh, I've been busy." Crystal sighed. "Traveling, you know."

And sleeping around and such, Bess thought venomously, but she didn't say anything. She just stared out the window.

When they reached the ranch, Bess showed Crystal up to the guest room. Hoping to take advantage of the moment of privacy, she lingered while Crystal unpacked.

"Seriously," Bess asked as Crystal dropped her cosmetic bag carelessly on the bed, "how long are you staying?"

"Just a little while," came the sunny reply. "You don't mind, do you? I...need someplace to stay, just until I can get my life and my finances in order again."

Is that it, or are you after my husband? Bess wondered bitterly, but she was geared to keeping her worries deep inside. She fingered the door facing.

"You're welcome, of course," she said.

Crystal turned from the window and gazed at her. She made an odd little gesture with one manicured hand. "Marriage not going well?" she asked with faint humor. "Most relationships have rocky starts, darling."

Bess only stared at her. "How was Paris?"

Crystal looked haunted. "Beautiful, of course," she said, laughing nervously. She stared at the coverlet. "Bess, I wish..." She glanced toward her stepsister hopefully, but there was no softening. She shrugged. "Thanks for letting me come."

Bess turned. "Come on down when you've unpacked. Katy will be glad to see you."

"I wish you were," Crystal murmured, but her stepsister was already out of earshot.

KATY HAD BEEN courteous to Crystal, but Bess sensed that the young girl really didn't like her very much.

"She's not like you at all, is she?" Katy asked later that afternoon, when the two of them were walking around the ranch yard. Crystal had pleaded with Jude to explain his computer system to her, and she'd managed to get him all to herself.

"No," Bess said, tugging her leather jacket closer. "We were never really close. We had nothing in common."

Katy sighed, snuggling closer as the wind whipped around them. "Bess, are you going to have some babies?"

"I hope so," she replied. She glanced down. "Will you mind?"

"Oh, no," Katy said honestly. "I'd like to have a baby to help take care of. I like babies. They smell nice."

Bess laughed, daydreaming about how it would be to have a little pink baby to hold and kiss and share with Katy and… The smile faded. Jude hadn't really meant it about wanting one. He'd only wanted Bess and had been ready to say anything to get her.

"Want to go watch Blanket eat?" Katy asked. "She's working out real well, Bandy says. She's going to be a good saddle horse."

"If she ever stops falling on people," Bess said, smiling. "Sure, let's go look."

Blanket was munching oats when they walked down the long, wide aisle between the hay-filled stalls. She tossed her mane and stared at them with her big soft eyes as they approached the stall warily. Bess reached out a hand to her.

"Careful," Katy cautioned. "She bites."

"I know. But she's got other things to eat besides me right now." Bess laughed. She stroked the silky muzzle gently. "Oh, Blanket, you're so pretty. I always wanted a horse, but I never had the time. Mama was sick for so long, and I had to take care of her."

"What was it like where you grew up?" Katy asked.

Bess's eyes were dreamy. "Green, darling," she said wistfully. "With groves of big pecan trees and wisteria and Spanish moss hanging from the trees by the river, and fields of peanuts and soybeans. Our house was two-storied with columns, and a river-rock patio in the back. My great-grandmother was born in the front bedroom."

Katy was watching her, smiling. "Did you go to a school like I do?"

Bess shook her head. "I went to a boarding school up north. I didn't like it very much, but it was fashionable. I'd much rather have gone to a public school in town and been able to stay with my parents."

"I'm glad I go to my school," Katy said. "I like going with all my friends."

"I never had friends," Bess confided. "Except one. She died when we were in the eighth grade, and I mourned her for a long time. I...don't get close to people easily."

"You're close to me."

"You're different." Bess smiled. "You're very special."

The young girl hugged her. "So are you. I'm glad you're my mother."

"Darling, so am I." Bess kissed the black hair that was so like Jude's, and then reached out to stroke Blanket's nose again.

"Would you like to go riding?" Katy asked. "We've got a lot of saddle horses, and Benny's as gentle as a lamb."

Bess's eyes lit up. "Yes!"

"Come on."

Minutes later, Bess was riding the old gelding beside Katy's little buckskin mare, heading down one of the trails on the property. The air was nippy, but it felt good.

"I should have worn boots, I guess," Bess said, glancing down at her low-heeled walking shoes. "Not to mention jeans. This is insane, riding around in a dress. What if someone sees us?"

Katy laughed at Bess's bare legs. "Nobody will, I promise."

They rode through the woods where pines and leafless oaks and mesquite sheltered the trail, and Bess thought she'd never felt so alive. She forgot Crystal and Jude in his study; she forgot everything but the joy of being alive, and gloried in the stark beauty of the landscape.

"The cattle look cold," Bess murmured, watching them as they paused beside a barbed-wire fence where cactus grew in a line paralleling it. "And so am I," she added, glancing at her bare, chilly legs. "We'd better go—"

"So there you are," Jude growled, riding up on his big chestnut gelding. He looked ferocious with his hat pulled low over his eyes; his very posture spelled trouble. His eyes went to Bess's bare legs and he caught his breath. "Are you crazy?"

"Don't be mad, please, Daddy," Katy asked gently. "We just wanted to go riding, and Bess didn't want to go all the way back to the house to change."

"No, she'd rather catch pneumonia and be waited on," he growled.

"We'll go back now," Bess said quietly, turning her mount. All the sweet pleasure of the day had gone, and the excited, happy radiance of her face had paled to numb disillusionment.

"Go ahead, Katy. It's getting cold. Go play in the house," Jude said tautly.

"Yes, sir." Katy tossed an apologetic glance at the older woman and reluctantly turned back toward the barn.

Bess sat straight in the saddle and met Jude's hard eyes. "Where's Crystal?"

"Back at the house, wondering why her damned stepsister can't spare a few minutes to talk to her," he said coldly.

"You took her into your study and closed the door," she reminded him. "I assumed that meant you wanted privacy, and Katy wanted to go riding."

"Didn't you mind that I closed the door?" he asked with a watchful expression.

She had, but she wasn't going to let him know that. She shook her head. "Do what you please, Jude. I don't have the right to say anything."

He looked as if she'd hit him. She coaxed her mount forward, but his lean hand shot out and jerked the bridle, halting her.

"For God's sake, stop looking like a lost orphan," he said harshly.

"I am an orphan," she said quietly, searching his hard, shadowed eyes. "And I feel lost."

"Bess...damn you!"

He was out of the saddle before she could blink,

reaching up to pull her down with him. And even as she looked up, stunned, his mouth went down to take total, absolute possession of hers.

"No, don't fight me," he whispered urgently when she put her hands against his chest. His mouth softened on hers, coaxing, teasing.

"I wasn't going to," she confessed. Her fingers unbuttoned his shirt, very slowly, while his mouth teased her lips and his breath rasped against them.

The shirt came open and her hands went inside it, against his warm body, spearing through cool, thick hair to find smooth, hard muscles.

His mouth grew harder with the rough caress of her hands, and she felt him shudder.

He picked her up and carried her off the trail to an open space under a huge live oak, where leaves carpeted the ground, and he laid her down.

His hands slid under her to find the zipper at her back while his mouth brushed over hers.

"I'll... I'll catch cold," she whispered shakily as he drew the dress down her arms and removed her bra.

"I'll keep you warm," he whispered back, and moved so that his bare chest eased down over her own bareness, his hands going under her again to bring her body up against his in a wild, hungry rhythm.

It was because of Crystal, she thought wildly, because he wanted her but couldn't forget his marriage vows, so he was venting his passion on Bess.

But even as she was thinking, her hands were twining through his black hair, dislodging his hat to give her access to it. Her body moved wildly against his.

"Please," she whimpered against his devouring mouth, her hips arching under his in helpless invitation.

"Keep that up and I'll have to," he bit off. His hands went down to her hips, grinding them into his. "Feel me?" he whispered roughly.

"I want you, too," she whispered back, her hands feverish as they tugged his shirt loose from his jeans and went under it to find the hard, smooth muscles of his back. "Oh, Jude, I want you, I want you…!"

"All that fire," he breathed unsteadily, lifting his head so that his mouth could reach her high, trembling breasts. "That's it, honey, that's it," he murmured when her body leaned toward him, helping him, as his lips drew slowly back and forth over soft curves, open and moist and rough in their hunger. "You're burning me alive, Bess, do you know it? I look at you and start aching. Ever since last night, when you let me see all of you and I went crazy and took you… I want you, right here, Bess. Right now."

He was out of control. Totally, wildly, helplessly out of control, and so was she. It was insane; Katy might come back; any one of the men might ride past…!

But minutes later their clothes were out of the way; it was bitterly cold but neither of them felt it, they were so hungry for each other.

He lifted her as his body overwhelmed hers in the cool silence of afternoon, and she gasped, her tiny cry merging with birdcalls from the distant meadow.

He watched her intently, his eyes blazing, cloudy with desire and recklessness, his hands hurting her as they held her narrow hips to his, his heartbeat pounding as the world seemed to catch fire around them.

She heard his voice repeating her name in a feverish rush until it splintered over her, and she felt him lose control, completely lose it, while her own body tautened and tautened and finally snapped in a glorious fury.

He fought to catch his breath, his face buried in the damp hair at her throat.

"My God, we're both crazy," he said in a voice that shook. "It's damned near freezing…"

Her eyes were closed, her hands delicately stroking the hair at the nape of his neck while she savored this one moment of closeness, loving him with all her heart, delighting in his insanity, and her own.

He pulled himself away and rearranged his clothing, keeping his back to her while she got back into her own things. She was shaking so much she could hardly do it, and he had to zip the dress back into place for her.

"Here," he said gently, helping her into the leather jacket. "You're trembling."

She was, but it wasn't from cold. "Thank you," she said softly. She forced her eyes up to his, shy with him all at once.

His lean fingers brushed her cheek and he looked at her strangely, quietly. He bent and his mouth brushed hers in a kiss so tender that it turned her heart over.

"Every man's dream," he whispered. "A lady in public and a wildcat in bed."

She blushed, and he smiled, but it was a different kind of smile than it had been before. But only for an instant. He got to his feet and pulled her up with him.

"In the middle of the bridle path," he mused, glancing down at the disordered leaves where they'd been together. "My God."

She was pulling leaves out of her hair with trembling hands. "They'll miss us," she said shakily.

"You were the one who wanted a baby," he said, all the old sarcasm back as he stared at her. "I'm only trying to oblige."

She turned away, feeling empty all over again at the sarcasm in his voice. "Was that why?" she asked coolly. "I thought you might have gone wild over Crystal and were looking for relief."

The look on his face was a revelation. He glared at her back. "And why do you think I wouldn't look for it with Crystal?" he taunted. "She might not mind the scars in the dark, you know, and she's not inhibited, either."

Her face blazed wildly. She whirled. "Then why don't you try your luck, Rawhide Man?" she challenged with burning eyes and a cool smile. "She likes men with money."

"All the better, if she gives full value for it," he returned. He moved toward his horse. "Never mind what I said about moving into my room and sleeping with me," he said when he was mounted and his hat was back in place. "You might cramp my style."

She felt as if she might explode. But with an effort she controlled herself and got back into the saddle, gripping the reins tightly.

"It's just as well," she said. "You probably snore."

He looked as if she'd surprised him, and he laughed

unexpectedly. But before he could say anything she turned the horse and coaxed it into a canter. She couldn't handle any more sarcasm from him right now, or any more threats about Crystal. She was hurting too much.

CHAPTER EIGHT

THAT EVENING AT the dinner table it was like old times for Bess as she sat quietly, picking at her food, while Crystal held court.

Her stepsister was charming, there was no doubt about that, she thought miserably as she watched her. And Jude was responding to all that blond charm like a blind man just able to see.

"Want some more corn, Bess?" Katy asked, sounding concerned.

She shook her head and even managed a convincing smile. "No, thank you, darling."

"Daddy wasn't mad at you for going riding in your dress, was he?" Katy asked under her breath.

Remembering how it had been in the woods, Bess flushed to the roots of her hair. "Uh, no," she whispered, and turned her total attention to her plate.

"Bess, I said, 'Do you remember the Cochrans?'" Crystal repeated. "I ran into them on the coast of France early in the year. Bert's in college, can you imagine?"

"That's very nice," Bess said, refusing to be drawn into the conversation. What was the use anyway? It was Jude Crystal wanted to talk to, not her.

She excused herself as soon as she could and went

upstairs with Katy, while Jude watched her from his chair with an intent stare.

That night set the pattern for the next few weeks, as Crystal settled in and enlisted Jude's aid in getting her affairs in order. Apparently she'd invested some of her small inheritance from Carla and needed advice on how to play the market. It was a nice excuse, Bess thought angrily, for her to get Jude's attention as she asked him question after question about finance and investments.

For his part, Jude seemed to spend most of his time away from home on business, and if he spoke to Bess at all, it was curtly, reluctantly. He hardly ever looked at her these days, while he laughed and teased Crystal as if…as if she were his real wife.

"What is it like, living with Jude?" Crystal asked unexpectedly one afternoon during a rare few minutes together.

Bess glanced at her warily. "Why do you ask?"

"I'm just making conversation. Or trying to," came the exasperated reply. "Bess, I've been here just shy of a month, and we haven't really talked yet! Can't we communicate with each other? If it's because of Carla, I realize I should have shouldered more responsibility, but it's ages too late now. I can't help it that I was spoiled my whole life, can I?"

Bess looked away. She'd have loved a little of the spoiling that had always gone to Crystal, with her finely honed beauty. "Being beautiful has its advantages," she murmured.

"And its disadvantages," came the bitter reply. "Has it ever occurred to you that I never know where I am with men? Whether they want me because of me, or because of how I look? Beauty doesn't last, Bess. It's gone in such a short time. And I don't have anything to show for all mine. Not a husband or children or a future I want to look forward to."

Do you want my husband? Bess almost asked. She sighed wearily. "What about your French count?"

Crystal looked away, her features going rigid. "I hate him."

Bess almost asked what had gone wrong. She almost did, but the reticence of years made it impossible for her to go that one step toward camaraderie. She didn't know how to approach Crystal. She'd never tried.

"You'll find someone else," Bess said instead. "Would you like some coffee?"

Crystal looked at her as if she desperately wanted to say something, but Bess's practiced coolness wasn't encouraging. She laughed shortly. "Sure, I'd love some. When is Jude coming home, by the way?"

Bess froze. "In a few days, I suppose. I'll have Aggie fix a tray," she murmured as she left the room.

"What did I say now?" Crystal asked the coffee table with a sad smile.

Bess paused in the hall to get herself back together. Why didn't Crystal just go with Jude if she wanted his company so much? He'd let her. She laughed until tears rolled down her cheeks. He'd let Crystal go anywhere with him, and at the same time, he wouldn't notice Bess if she dropped dead at his feet!

"Bess?" Crystal, hearing the unfamiliar sound of

weeping, had come to the door and was standing aghast at the sight of her normally composed stepsister in tears.

Bess dried the tears with the hem of her blouse. "Sorry," she muttered, "I...think about Carla sometimes," she lied, letting it go at that.

"I know you miss her, darling," Crystal said gently. "I miss her, too. I don't suppose I realized just how much I cared until it was too late to tell her." She reached out toward Bess, but drew back before her fingers could make contact. "Say, you don't really mind my staying, do you? Or getting Jude to help me with this financial tangle I'm in?"

"Of course not," Bess said with magnificent carelessness.

Crystal, taking the statement at face value, relaxed. "Thank goodness. I mean, I hoped you weren't jealous or anything."

Which intimated that she had reason to be. Crystal couldn't have missed the coolness between husband and wife, the pointed way they had avoided each other ever since that wild afternoon in the woods.

"I'll get the coffee," Bess said tautly.

Crystal stared after her quietly. Her lovely face was strained.

THE DAY JUDE came home Katy and Aggie had gone with Crystal to shop in San Antonio. Bess was sitting in the porch swing alone when he drove up, and her stupid heart went wild at the sight of him.

He walked up the steps as if he was bone tired, his attaché case held firmly in one lean hand.

"Isn't it a little early in the year for swinging?" he asked curtly.

She was wearing his leather jacket with jeans that, strangely enough, wouldn't fasten at the waist, and a pale yellow sweater. Her hair was in a French twist. She hadn't noticed the cold.

"I like swinging," she returned.

"Yes, I remember," he murmured, watching her closely. "Where's Crystal?"

Her face closed up and she stared out over the bleak landscape. "Gone shopping with Aggie and Katy."

His fingers contracted on the handle of the case. "Damn it, why do you do that?" he ground out.

She glanced up at him, startled. "Do what?"

"Close up like a flower whenever I come close," he said. His eyes swept over her face. "Do you think I haven't noticed? I can walk into a room when you're playing and laughing with Katy, and the color drains out of you the second you catch sight of me."

She lowered her eyes to his chest. "What do you expect me to do, run to you?"

He was rigid for an instant, his eyes narrowed. "I can't imagine you doing that," he said heavily. He set the case down on the settee and eased himself down beside Bess, lighting a cigarette on the way.

The feel of him so close was unnerving. It had been weeks since he'd touched her, since she'd been near him physically. She had to clench her hands in her lap to hide her nervousness.

"You used to spend quite a lot of time out here in the summer," he remarked, leaning back to rock the swing back into motion. "God, you were a pretty little thing, all long tanned legs and smiles." He looked down at her assessingly. "Away from your stepsister, you blossomed. But the minute you got in the same room with her, you turned it all off. You're still doing it."

"How can I compete with someone who looks like Crystal?" she asked, as if she didn't mind. Her eyes studied her folded hands. "She could charm a dragon."

"I suppose she could. But it isn't because she's beautiful, Bess," he said. "It's because she has a bubbly personality. She reaches out."

"Is that a dig at me?" she asked curtly, glancing up.

"You don't reach out at all," he returned. "You never have. Is that why you're so eaten up with envy that you can't even stay in the same room with Crystal? Because she can communicate and you can't?"

She hated that mocking smile. She hated what he was saying. Her hand lifted toward his face without her being aware that it had moved.

He caught her wrist, and a fierce heat blazed in his green eyes, in the half-amused smile on his dark face.

"Did it hurt?" he asked curtly.

"Let go of me, you savage," she breathed furiously, her eyes glittering, her face bright with anger and frustration.

He laughed harshly as he jerked her across his lap and held her there despite her struggles. He pitched the unfinished cigarette off the edge of the porch and wrapped her tightly in his arms.

"Jude!" she protested, wriggling.

"Keep that up, honey," he breathed unsteadily in her

ear, "and we'll wind up the way we were in the woods that day. Can't you feel what's happening to me?"

She was still instantly as the feel of his body got through to her. She lay quietly in his arms, aware of the sharp tang of his cologne, the clean smell of him, the warmth of his body as he held her. The hand curled around her wrist was strong and bruising. The arm at her back was just as steely. And she was awash in sensation.

He laughed softly at her embarrassment, and he released her wrist to tilt her face up to his hard eyes.

"Society girl," he growled, studying her quiet body in his arms. "Do you hate it here? Do you hate living with a man who can't recite Shakespeare and discuss the latest bestseller with you?"

She gaped at him, stunned. "You're college educated," she managed.

"I took my degree in business, with a minor in economics," he reminded her. "I didn't have time for the arts."

She searched his eyes in dead silence. "I... I don't have much time for reading these days, and I can't... recite Shakespeare, either."

He seemed to hesitate, and the fingers holding her chin relaxed, became caressing. "Do I know you at all?" he wondered quietly.

Her lips parted on a rush of breath. "Probably not, and what difference does it make? You wanted a mother for Katy and my share of the stock. Isn't that enough?"

"Apparently it is for you," he said, his voice cutting.

He searched her eyes. "You can do without me very well, can't you, honey?"

Her eyes fell to his jutting chin. "You've been avoiding me just as hard," she said curtly.

"Do you miss me when I go away?" he challenged. He tilted her chin back up and searched her shadowy eyes. "No, hell, no, you don't."

"Why should I?" she demanded, her voice breaking.

His face hardened and a curtain fell over his darkening eyes. "I haven't been particularly kind to you, have I, Bess?" he asked after a minute. "Dragging you out here, forcing you into a marriage you didn't want, and for all the wrong reasons." His fingers touched her lips gently, softly, and he looked at her as if he'd never taken the trouble to really see her before. "Married, but not married."

"And with no way out," she said with a weary sigh.

"Yes." His voice was curt, as if he didn't like admitting that. "And up until now neither of us has made any effort to live up to our vows, have we?"

She studied him warily.

"I haven't cheated on you," he said coldly, "if that's what that searching little look was all about. The only woman I've had since we married was you."

She blushed and looked away.

His hand moved into the thickness of hair at her nape and stroked it gently. "Even that wasn't much to look back on, was it?" he asked bitterly. "Both times, I gave you hell afterwards."

"I'm sorry I was such a disappointment," she said coldly.

"You've never disappointed me," he said under his breath. "Not ever."

That brought her eyes wavering up to his and held them.

"I was like a boy with you," he breathed, grinding out the words. "I couldn't stop, I couldn't control what I felt. You…made me vulnerable, and I hated you for it."

Her eyes searched his, and she could hardly believe what he was admitting. "Me?"

"You." His hand stroked her throat, then moved down over the softness of the sweater, touching her hesitantly with fingers that were unexpectedly gentle. "It's been like this since I carried you out of the darkness that night you were fifteen, Bess," he said quietly, holding her eyes. "If I'd kissed you that night, we'd have gone for each other like starving wolves. We start burning up the minute we touch. You see?" he breathed, running his fingers lightly over the taut thrust of her breasts, dropping his eyes to them. "In broad daylight…"

Yes, she knew. Something inside her had always known how much he wanted her. But it was only desire, and that wasn't what she wanted. She wanted love.

His fingers were under the sweater now, on bare flesh, and he was watching her as they moved up.

"No bra, Bess?" he asked as his hand brushed lightly over warm, swollen flesh.

Her bras were too tight, and she hadn't had time to replace them, but she wasn't going to tell him that. She caught his wrist as the old familiar weakness began to smother her.

"Jude, don't," she pleaded, removing his hand.

"You're mine," he said curtly. "All of you. Why shouldn't I touch you when I want to?"

Her lower lip trembled. "What's the matter, Jude, have you been missing Crystal's company so much that even I can stand in for her?" she burst out.

He froze. A black scowl darkened his face. "What did you say?"

"You want her, don't you?" she whispered. "Even if you haven't made love to her yet."

His chiseled lips parted. "Are you jealous of me?" he asked slowly.

Her eyes fell to his chin. "Let me go, please."

"No, not yet. Answer me. Are you jealous?"

Her long eyelashes swept down over her cheeks and she relaxed against him with a weary sigh. Her hand rested against the vest beneath his jacket, and he was pleasantly warm against the chill.

"Ask me why I spend time with Crystal and I'll tell you," he said over her head.

But she didn't want the answer. She didn't want to know. Impulsively, uncharacteristically, she let her head slide back onto his shoulder and curved an arm up around his neck. He looked as if she'd hit him.

She felt the advantage and took it, smiling breathlessly at the look in his glittering eyes. Her lips parted and she ran her fingers through his thick hair, carelessly dislodging the hat as she did.

The recklessness she felt was mirrored in his hard face. "Is this what you felt?" he asked curtly, winding his own hand into her hair to jerk her head back. "This, Bess?"

His mouth opened on hers, forcing her lips apart, penetrating deeply in an assault that was all wild tenderness. She arched in his arms, both hands in his hair now, her mouth answering his, demanding, needing.

The swing stopped and was still. His hands slid under the sweater again and took the warm, swollen weight of her breasts. She trembled and moaned sharply.

He lifted his dark head slowly, staring down into her hungry eyes. His thumbs edged over the taut peaks in a lazy, maddening rhythm, and all the time he looked at her, watching her helpless reaction to him.

"When are they coming back?" he asked in a voice that sounded unusually thick.

She licked her lips. "I don't know."

He bent and brushed her open mouth with his. "We could lock the bedroom door," he whispered.

"Yes." She arched again, crying out, as the pressure of his hands increased. She was unusually sore, and he drew back instantly.

"Did I hurt you?" he asked tenderly.

"I… I'm sore," she said, and laughed nervously. "I don't know why."

"I'll be careful with you," he said, studying her eyes. "I'll be gentle this time, I'll take longer. I'll treat you like the virgin you were that first time, Bess."

She trembled softly in his arms as he slowly got up from the swing, cradling her against him.

"You…laughed the first time," she remembered shakily.

"You were wildfire in my arms, blazing with the pleasure that I was giving you," he said quietly. "My

God, I was so proud…you were a virgin, and I was making you feel that way."

She caught her breath. "I didn't know."

"I couldn't tell you." He bent and kissed her softly. "Do you really want me this time?"

Her lips parted on a wild breath. "Oh, yes, I want you," she whispered feverishly. Her arms locked around his neck and she trembled. "Jude," she moaned, arching up.

His eyes flashed as he walked into the house with her. Inside the doorway he bent, his open mouth pressing down on the high mounds of her breasts even through the fabric, and she cried out.

His heart was thundering as he walked with her toward the staircase, and she felt the same wildness they'd shared that day in the woods. He might not love her, but he wanted her. He wanted her! And, God, she wanted him!

But even as his boot touched the first step, the loud sound of a car approaching burst into the silence, and Jude cursed roughly.

"Not now," he ground out, burying his face against Bess. "Oh, God, not now!"

Her hands cradled his head and she struggled to regain her lost composure. Slowly he put her down, regret and bitterness mingling in the expression on his hard face.

She turned away, tidying her hair as best she could with her back to him.

"Bess?" he asked softly.

But before she could answer him, the door burst open

and Katy and Crystal descended on them in a swirl of skirts and laughter.

"So you're finally back," Crystal called, following Katy's example as she ran into his arms and kissed his tanned cheek soundly. "About time, too. We've missed you, haven't we, girls?"

"*Si,* we miss the sound of yelling from the study, all right," Aggie murmured with a grin as she carried packages into the living room.

"Welcome home, Daddy!" Katy laughed.

Jude, caught up in it, was laughing, too, his face more relaxed than Bess had ever seen it, and she mourned the little taste of happiness she'd just lost. She turned and walked off toward the kitchen as Jude was coaxed into the living room to look at the purchases.

"Don't you want to see what they bought?" Jude asked Bess.

She stopped with her back to them, blind to the hopeful look on his face, the almost pleading one on Crystal's.

"I need some coffee. I'll make a pot, shall I?" she asked brightly, and walked away before they could question the quaver in her voice.

Bess didn't look at Jude for the rest of the night; she couldn't bear to remember how she'd tempted him. He was going to be furious about that. He always was when his fiery ardor cooled. She kept carefully out of his way until she could sneak upstairs and go to bed.

"Why didn't you go with us today?" Katy asked as Bess tucked her into bed. "We missed you. Crystal said we should have dragged you along and made you come."

"I had things to do here, darling," Bess said with a smile. "I'm glad you had fun, though."

"I didn't. Not really," Katy admitted. She reached up and kissed Bess's cool cheek. "Crystal is fun to be with, but she just talks all the time, like she's afraid to stop, so nobody else ever gets to. You know? You listen."

Bess's eyes clouded. She kissed the young girl back. "I love you," she whispered.

Katy beamed. "I love you, too. Good night, Bess. Isn't it nice that Daddy's home?"

"Lovely, darling."

"He said he'd be up to tuck me in later. He had to talk to Crystal."

Bess nodded, turning away before Katy could see her hurt expression. "Good night, darling."

"'Night, Bess, sleep well."

Back in her own room, Bess put on her flannel gown and crawled wearily into bed. She felt vaguely nauseated, and the swelling in her breasts was beginning to be uncomfortable. Something that should have happened three weeks ago hadn't, and she felt frankly nervous. It was too soon to tell, of course, but she had an odd feeling that she was carrying Jude's baby.

Her hands went unconsciously to her flat stomach. A baby. A little boy with green eyes and black hair, or a little girl who might look a lot like Katy. She smiled. Even if she lost Jude, at least she'd have the baby to love. She could give it all the warmth and adoration she longed to give to him. Except that he didn't want it. He only wanted her body, and not even that when Crystal was around.

What if Crystal did want him? She was playing her cards close, and Bess couldn't figure out why she was staying at Big Mesquite so long. Why wouldn't she go back to Oakgrove, or to France, or somewhere? But it would be impolite to ask her to leave. She laughed shortly. Jude would never let her go anyway. He…cared about her. He laughed with her. She hit the pillow with an angry fist. Why couldn't he laugh with Bess like that?

Even as she was silently asking the question, the door opened and Jude walked in. He was wearing his suit slacks, but only a partially unbuttoned white shirt with them. And he looked oddly tired. Worn-out.

"Yes?" she asked coldly.

He laughed shortly. "So we're back to that, are we?" he asked quietly. "The mask is in place, the barriers are up. I can't get near you."

"Can't you?" she asked bitterly.

"Physically, yes," he agreed. He rammed his hands into his pockets and went to stand beside the bed, looking down at her tousled hair and flushed face with strange, lingering eyes.

"That was all you wanted, wasn't it?" she asked.

"At first." His eyes searched her face. "I must have hurt you a hell of a lot those first few weeks."

"Don't worry, Jude, I'm a survivor," she replied, lowering her eyes to the coverlet.

He sat down on the bed, tilting the mattress with his weight, and she cringed away from him.

"Oh, God, don't do that," he ground out, wincing.

"Bess, I won't hurt you. I won't even touch you if you don't want it."

She relaxed a little, but she was still tense, and it showed.

"What do you want?" she asked unsteadily.

"What a question." He pulled a cigarette from his pocket and glanced at her. "Do you mind?"

She shook her head. He lit it and rose to produce an ashtray from the dresser before he sat down again. "Bess, we can't go on like this."

Cold sensations worked down her backbone. "You want a divorce?" she asked.

"No!" he burst out, scowling. "For God's sake, I told you at the beginning that it wasn't going to be a fly-by-night marriage."

"Yes, of course," she whispered.

He drew on the cigarette. "I meant, we've got to start trying. Both of us. Doing things together, living like married people. We've got to stop making our lives and Katy's a battleground."

Katy. Of course. He was worrying about Katy, as usual. She folded her hands and stared at them. "What do you suggest?"

He looked down at her. "You could start sleeping with me."

"Will your bed hold all three of us?" she asked venomously.

His eyes flashed. "I'll tell you one more time. I am not sleeping with your sister," he said coldly.

"My stepsister," she corrected.

He ran an angry hand through his thick hair. "My God, can't we even talk without arguing?"

Her face was icy, but she kept her mouth shut.

"Bess, meet me halfway," he said softly, glancing at her. "You can't know how hard this is for me. I'm painfully aware of how I've treated you. But at least make the effort, can't you?"

She watched him curiously. She wondered at this change in him. Or was it just another trick, another way to make her pay for forcing him into a marriage he didn't want?

"You don't trust me, do you?" he asked levelly.

"How can I?" she asked honestly. "Every time you let me get close, you find some nasty way of getting at me, of making me pay for what you consider your weakness."

He bent his head and smoked his cigarette quietly. "Yes," he said finally. "I suppose I do. Next to Katy, you're the only weakness I've ever discovered, society girl." He laughed bitterly.

"And you hate that," she muttered. "You hate being out of control in any way."

"Don't you?" He lifted his head, watching her. "You fought every inch of the way that first time with me, not to give in, not to let me please you. But it happened anyway, and you were angry, just as I was."

She lowered her eyes to his chest. "I was the one who paid for it," she murmured.

"Yes," he said curtly. "I hurt you. I meant to. But it backfired, in ways you can't imagine." He bent over her, holding her eyes. "But all that aside, we can't go on like this. Avoiding each other, cutting at each other. We're married, Bess, for good. We've got to pick up the pieces and make a go of it."

"Then send Crystal away," she said coldly.

He lifted his chin. "Is that an ultimatum?" he asked. "Have you reached the stage where you think you can give me orders because you know I want you?"

She swallowed. "I'm not trying to do that."

"It sure as hell sounds like it." He got to his feet, glaring down at her. "I'll go halfway, lady. But I won't go the distance. When you're ready to talk sense, you know where to find me."

"Sure," she agreed. "Wherever my stepsister is."

He gave her a hot glare before he walked out the door, slamming it behind him. Bess lay there with tears running silently down her cheeks. Why hadn't she agreed to try, at least? Why were her emotions so haywire that she couldn't even talk rationally? She turned her face into the pillow. It was probably all just tension. Just tension. Her body would resume its natural rhythm in no time. She wasn't pregnant, she wasn't! It was all just her own imagination.

As the days passed, Jude invited her to go places with him: into town to buy wire, on brief trips to neighboring ranches, to social affairs. And she turned down every invitation abruptly and without explanation.

"My God, Bess, won't you even try?" he growled one night in exasperation.

"I am trying. To be left alone," she returned.

He sighed wearily, watching her in an increasingly familiar way, one that turned her weak. "One day I'm going to take the choice right out of your hands, honey," he said in a menacingly soft tone. "I'm going to carry you up to my bed and love you out of your mind. Then we'll talk."

She flushed and got up out of her chair. "About what? About how you hate wanting me?" she asked. "Well, I don't want you, Jude. Not anymore."

He made a sudden move toward her, and she backed up against the door, wide-eyed and frightened.

He scowled darkly at that look and hesitated. "I could make you beg," he said harshly.

Didn't she know it. Her eyes closed. "What would be the point?" she said gently. "I haven't made any trouble lately, have I? I've been polite and sweet to Crystal, and you and I have put on a grand front. Katy thinks everything is just fine."

He sighed wearily. "Bess, do you hate me?" he asked quietly.

She studied his face, noticing how tired and worn he looked, how sad. "No," she said. "I don't hate you."

He moved toward her slowly. "We could sleep together," he said. "No sex. Just sleep. We could try to get used to each other."

But she couldn't bear that. Especially now. Because she was beginning to lose her breakfast each morning, and Jude wasn't stupid. He'd know.

She swallowed. "I...like sleeping alone," she whispered.

"That's the whole damned problem with our marriage," he said curtly. "You like doing everything alone!"

"Well, I didn't drag you out here and force you to marry me!" she burst out, tears welling up in her eyes.

He reached out and dragged her into his arms, holding her close, rocking her like a child. "Hush, honey," he whispered. "Hush, now, don't cry. Don't. Please don't." His hand soothed her cheek, her hair. His lips touched her forehead, her cheeks, the corner of her tear-washed mouth. "Don't cry, honey, I can't stand it."

He was so tender. Tender in a way he never had been before, and she reacted to it helplessly, letting him dry her tears with his handkerchief.

"So trusting," he breathed, studying her eyes. "You used to look at me like that once. In the very beginning. And I cut you like a whip, didn't I?"

She dropped her eyes to his chest. "You didn't want to marry me. I understood."

His hands caught her shoulders and held them bruisingly tight. "I didn't want to marry anyone. But I wanted you so damned much. I'd wanted you for years. And once I had you, all I could think about was having you again." He leaned his forehead against hers with a weary sigh. "Bess, I get up wanting you in the morning and I go to bed wanting you at night. Isn't that revenge enough for you?"

It was. Oh, yes, it was. But she didn't think she could bear to be intimate with him again when he didn't love her.

"I'm so tired, Jude," she whispered. "I need to sleep."

He drew away, studying her. "You really don't want me anymore?" he asked quietly.

Gritting her teeth, she slowly shook her head.

He let her go finally with a rough laugh and turned away. "I'm not even surprised. Women haven't made a habit of wanting me."

He was at the door when she remembered Elise and the scars and all the torment he'd sustained at the hands of women who didn't want him.

"Jude!" she cried.

But he wouldn't look at her. "Go to sleep, Bess. I won't bother you again."

And with that mocking remark, he went out and closed the door between them.

CHAPTER NINE

THE NEXT MORNING Crystal was at the breakfast table when Bess got there, sitting next to Jude and apparently flirting for all she was worth.

"There you are, finally," Crystal chided. "I thought you were going to spend the day in bed."

Actually, she'd been in the bathroom, not in bed, feeling sicker than usual first thing in the morning. But it wouldn't do to let that out, so she smiled instead.

"I was sleepy," she told her stepsister. "Hi, Katy," she added, winking at the young girl. Jude, she ignored.

"Crystal wants to go and see the Alamo this morning," he said, forcing her to look at him.

"You'll have fun, I'm sure," she replied coolly.

"You and Katy are coming, too," he continued, finishing his eggs.

"No, I'm not," Bess replied. "I don't feel like hiking around downtown."

His eyes narrowed. "I said, you're coming."

"Now, Bess, don't spoil the day for the rest of us," Crystal coaxed, and shook back her glorious hair. "You were telling Katy the other day that you wanted to see it. Why not today?"

Bess could have told her stepsister why not, but she

bit her tongue and sipped her coffee instead. "All right," she said finally.

"You'll like it, honest you will," Katy promised. "You and I will go around the grounds and I'll show you this neat old squirrel who poses for pictures."

"She isn't kidding," Jude said with a quiet smile. "He's an old squirrel, and he actually will stand still when he's photographed."

"Have you taken his photo, Jude?" Crystal asked.

"No, but my office is near the Alamo grounds. Sometimes, in the spring, I walk around there at lunchtime on my way to a restaurant."

Bess studied his hard face as he smiled back at Crystal, and she wished that he'd smile at her like that. But it wasn't good to live in a dreamworld, she told herself, and finished her breakfast.

The Alamo Plaza was located near the historic Menger Hotel, and Bess was surprised by the immensity of its grounds, which included paved walkways and benches and tables as well as buildings, all dedicated to the preservation of the old mission's history.

The second stone church of Mission San Antonio de Valero stood with ancient dignity, flanked by gates on either side, which led to the rest of the compound. Bess touched the scarred stone with fingers that trembled as she felt the bravery and torment of the 180-odd men who had died there one cold March day in 1836. Her eyes moved up and down it with quiet awe as she tried to imagine what it would have been like to face certain death at the hands of Santa Anna's overwhelming Mexican forces.

"Six of the men who died here were Georgians, including Bowie, though some people say he was actually from Kentucky," Jude told her, moving to her side.

She glanced up. "Really?"

"Some were from Ireland and England and Germany. Travis was from South Carolina, Crockett from Tennessee." His own lean hand touched the surface of the building. "They left us quite a legacy. It takes a special kind of courage to face death in the way they faced it."

"They were special men," she murmured.

"And used to seeing death," he added. "They lived in hard times, without any of the luxuries we take for granted today. They were veteran fighters for the most part."

"I've read several books about the siege," she mentioned. "Most of them disagree on how many men died here," she added.

"There were eyewitness accounts by those who survived it," he reminded her. "They give the best chronology. Come here."

He led her inside and pointed out the room where the powder and shot had been kept and where Jim Bowie had lain on his cot when the enemy broke in. Another large room was railed off with wrought iron, and flags were placed inside.

"Some of that graffiti on the wall is very old," he explained, while she tried to decipher the aged scribbling.

There were paintings on the wall depicting the two-hour battle when Mexican troops had overrun the walls, and weapons under glass cases, along with other memorabilia. The stone floor, he added, was a later addition. The floor of the Alamo had been dirt at the time of the actual battle.

She stood by the rear exit and shivered, looking up at the ceiling, listening silently to the echo as a tour guide outlined the days of the siege and the final battle.

"Cold?" Jude asked gently.

She shook her head. "It's just…" She looked at him helplessly. "I've read about the Alamo, you know, but actually being here…it's very different. It's more than pages in a book now. I feel strange."

He slid an arm around her and drew her close against his side. "They knew what they were doing," he said, glancing around. "And why they were doing it. It was what happened here, and at Goliad, that united Texans into the force that won victory with Sam Houston at San Jacinto. And that led to Texas independence and statehood. All because a handful of men wouldn't raise a white flag." He glanced down at her. "Even the women had spirit."

She looked up at him and smiled slowly, softly. Her dark eyes searched his pale green ones. "Did they?"

His breath came quickly. His jaw tautened. "Bess—"

"There you are," Crystal interrupted. "Come on, you two. Let's go see the souvenirs."

There was a huge live oak outside the Alamo, its limbs held aloft with chains, just in front of the ruins of the Long Barracks, where the last stand had been made. Jude still had his arm around Bess and she pressed closer unconsciously as she stared at the darkened doorways.

"I don't want to go in there," she said quietly.

"Me, neither," Katy said firmly. "Let's go see the squirrel, please."

Crystal only shrugged. "I think I'd rather go to the museum. Have they got turquoise in the museum shop? I love turquoise."

She led the way, and Bess didn't argue about going there first. She was in heaven so close to Jude, and he didn't seem in the least anxious to let her go, either.

But once they were inside, there was so much to see that the two of them became separated. Bess wandered around looking at the manuscripts and coins and historical portraits and guns displayed in the building, while Crystal and Katy hung around the gemstones and souvenirs.

Crystal talked Jude into buying her a ridiculously expensive turquoise bracelet. Katy he bought a "coonskin" cap.

"What do you want, Mrs. Langston?" he asked Bess, his eyes twinkling, and she realized suddenly that he was happy, and that she hadn't seen him that way before.

Her lips parted, and she tried to think. What would she like if she had only one tiny memento of their time together? Something…

"I'd like… I'd like a ring," she said.

His face brightened, and his eyes glimmered down at her. "A ring?"

"A gemstone one."

He led her over to the counter and let her look. She picked out a silver band with inlaid turquoise which, when the saleslady took it out of the glass case, fit her ring finger exactly. She put her simple gold wedding band on after it and stared at it lovingly.

Jude paid for it—it wasn't a tenth as expensive as Crystal's—with a curious frown.

"Is that all you want?" he asked, as Crystal and Bess went out the door toward the wishing well in the court-yard.

"Yes," she said, staring at the new ring. "Thank you, Jude."

"You could have had a silver wedding band," he said. "I…didn't think to ask you."

"It didn't matter," she said quietly. "I like this ring. It's simple, but it has a grace and dignity that I don't associate with diamonds."

"You're a strange lady."

"What does that make you?" she asked, glancing up. "You married me."

"Yes," he said absently, watching her. "I married you."

"But not out of choice." She dropped her eyes.

"About the marriage, Bess…" he began slowly.

"Don't bother," she said quickly. "We've been over it and over it, and nothing ever changes. We only argue."

"We might not, if you'd meet me halfway. You might run toward me for a change, instead of from me."

"It's safer running from you," she said sharply, glaring up at him. "It hurts less!"

His face paled and he looked bitter. "I realize I haven't been particularly kind to you. In case it's escaped your notice, I'm trying damned hard not to hurt you these days, but you're determined not to make it easy for me."

She gaped at him. "Are you trying? I wouldn't call hanging around Crystal's neck trying very damned hard!"

"Are you jealous? Answer me this time."

She turned away. "I am not. And if I were, I'd die before I'd let you know it. I don't give away troop movements to the enemy, Mr. Langston," she added, glaring back at him.

"Am I the enemy these days?" he asked.

"What do you think?"

He sighed heavily. "I try not to think anymore, Bess."

Katy came running back toward them, her eyes aglow. "It's the squirrel. Hurry, Bess, there's a man feeding him nuts!"

The man was still feeding him nuts when Bess arrived, and the grizzled old squirrel was taking them right from his hand.

"Ain't he a character?" the elderly man said, chuckling as the rodent took the nut from his fingers. "Sure is a hit with the tourists. They can't get over how tame he is."

"I wish I had my camera," Bess said enthusiastically. "What a picture he'd make."

Obviously another tourist felt the same way, because she moved forward with a 35-mm camera and clicked away.

Bess had thought that everyone would want to go home after their excursion, but they wound around through the downtown area, through La Villita with its arts and crafts, and on to the Paseo del Rio, the River Walk. They saw the Arneson River Theatre, with its seats carved into the bank, and the dozens of restaurants and pubs along the way where in the spring and summer tourists could sit outside and watch the river run. Bess sighed as she strolled alongside it, wishing that the weather were warm and she could sit and daydream by its banks. She was already getting tired, feeling her pregnancy in a new way.

Jude caught her arm. "Want to rest a few minutes?" he asked gently.

She looked up, surprised by his courtesy. "Yes, I would," she confessed.

He smiled at her. "Just a few more feet and up the steps."

He led them into a restaurant overlooking the river, the same one in which they'd once argued so fiercely. They were seated and handed long, impressive menus by a courteous waiter. Bess was feeling strangely hungry, so she ordered prime rib.

Jude watched her, his eyes oddly protective, while Crystal, as usual, kept up an animated flow of conversation. She continued it all through the meal, but when they started back toward Joske's, near which they had parked the car, it was Bess's arm Jude took, not Crystal's. It was as if he were afraid she might get away from him.

When they got back to the house Bess went immediately to her room and lay down. She felt tired to the bone, and a little nauseated. But most of all, she was confused. Confused as to what Jude wanted of her... what she wanted herself.

CHAPTER TEN

BESS FELL ASLEEP and when she awoke again it was dark outside. She rolled over onto her back, feeling oddly cool, and suddenly realized that she was wearing a nightgown. She blinked, staring at the ceiling. Had she taken the time to put it on?

The door opened while she was getting oriented again, and Jude came in with a tray.

"Awake at last," he murmured, putting it down on the bedside table. "Aggie thought you needed feeding."

She propped herself up against the pillows with a soft smile. "I'm starved," she admitted. Shyly she glanced at him. "Did you put this on me?" she asked, picking at the soft white lacy gown.

"You were sound asleep in your jeans and shirt," he remarked, studying her. "I thought you'd be more comfortable this way."

"I am. Thank you."

"Here," he said, offering her a spoonful of Aggie's special chicken and broccoli crepe.

She took it, savoring the creamy taste, and smiled. "Delicious!" She started to take the spoon from him, but he ignored her and kept on until he'd fed her every bite.

"Want some dessert?" he asked. "Aggie made an apple pie."

She shook her head. "I couldn't eat another bite!"

"You look as if you've gained a little weight," he murmured as he put the plate aside. "Your jeans weren't buttoned. Only zipped."

She kept her nerve, but barely. "I've been eating more lately," she lied. "Besides, what do you care if I gain weight? You never notice."

His head turned back, and against his thick black lashes his eyes were unusually green. "I notice everything about you," he said quietly. "Everything."

"Do you?" She dropped her eyes to his shirt. "But you notice Crystal more."

His lean hand moved to her cheek, turning her face toward his. "Crystal knows how to flirt, honey. You've never bothered to learn."

"Meaning I should learn from her?" Her eyes glared accusingly at him. "What could she possibly teach me except how to be promiscuous?"

"You do hate her, don't you?" he asked with narrowing eyes. "Is it really because she sleeps around? Or because you're jealous of her success with men?"

"Damn you!"

His eyes searched hers. "How unladylike, Mrs. Langston," he said with amusement. "You know, you've lost a lot of your starch since you've been here. You're still a lady, but you're more human."

"Look who's talking about being human," she threw back. "What would you know about that?"

"Is that a question or a dare?" he murmured. He

leaned down, resting his weight on his hands on either side of her. "I asked you once to sleep with me and you turned me down. Suppose I take the choice away from you, the way I did before?"

She felt herself panic. She was all too vulnerable to him. She still needed time to straighten out her feelings about their marriage.

"Please don't," she whispered.

He looked calculating, not angry or particularly disappointed. "If I promised to be very gentle?" he whispered, searching her eyes quietly. "Not to hurt?"

She could feel herself weakening, because the way he was looking at her was different from any way he'd looked at her before. She could hardly breathe for the wild beating of her heart. But she couldn't do what he wanted her to do. Not yet.

She lowered her eyes. "I…don't feel that way anymore, I told you last night," she bit off.

"You told me. I just didn't quite believe you." He stood up, and his look was unnerving. "Is it just me, or are you frozen clean through? Damn it, you wanted me when we married."

"Yes, I did," she said. "And you threw it in my face until I choked on it!"

He turned away. "I suppose I did," he said wearily. He ran a hand through his hair. "But on the front porch, when you were sitting in the swing…and that hasn't been so long ago, lady."

She avoided his accusing gaze. "That was then. This is now."

"What's changed?"

"You!" she burst out, glaring at him. "I don't know what to make of you. And I just don't dare trust what you say. First you force me into marrying you, but you don't want anything to do with me. Then you want me in bed, but you go out of your way to hurt me. Now you say you want to make the marriage work. Sometimes I think you enjoy torturing me!"

"Is that what it seems like?" He moved back to the bed with a weary sigh. "Bess, must we fight? I'll be the first to admit that I've given you plenty of reason not to trust me. But there has to be a common ground."

"Does there?" She stared at the coverlet blankly.

He tilted her chin up. "You look different lately," he murmured, changing the subject. "Your face is rounder, your breasts are bigger." His eyes went down to them and she flushed.

"Thank you for bringing up my supper," she said.

"Thank you and good night?" he asked. He stood up and laughed curtly. "I had you in the palm of my hand once upon a time, Bess. What a pity that I was too damned stupid to realize what I was holding until it was too late." He picked up the tray. "Get some rest, honey. Maybe we'll eventually be able to sort things out."

"Is Crystal still up?" she asked as he started toward the door.

He glanced back at her, looking strangely pleased. "Yes, as a matter of fact, she is. Jealous, honey?"

She was getting tired of having him ask that. Her eyes flashed wildly. "Go away! I hate men. I hate you. I hate Crystal. I hate the whole world!"

He only laughed, moving gracefully toward the door.

"When you get tired of brooding, come and get me. You might discover that it's easier than you think."

But Bess only half heard him. She was too busy trying not to cry. How could he, how could he!

She tossed and turned all night, her mind overwhelmed with images of Crystal with Jude, dark and light, in bed together. She'd kill him. She'd kill Crystal. She'd leave and go home to Georgia. She'd do something! But when she awoke, worn-out and feeling deathly ill, revenge was the last thought on her mind.

She glanced at the clock and realized that it was already past time for church and she'd never make it before services were over. With a weary sigh, she pulled on a loose gray dress and brushed her hair, leaving it long.

She went downstairs, but the house was oddly quiet. There was a muffled sound in the den, where the door was ajar.

Her hand reached out and pushed the door gently open. Her face went paper white. Crystal was wrapped tight in Jude's arms and they were kissing. Bess stood there gaping at them, her whole life flashing in front of her, hating them, hating them!

At that moment Jude lifted his head, laughing, and saw Bess. The look on his face would have been, in another time and place, utterly comical. But to Bess, whose whole world had just gone down in ashes, it was only confirmation of her worst suspicions.

Crystal stared at her with her mouth open. "Now, Bess," she began hesitantly. "Darling, let me…"

"It isn't what you think," Jude added slowly, his own face oddly pale under his deep tan.

"Of course not," Bess said. Her lower lip trembled and all the years of control, all the years of cool acceptance went flaming up in the grip of the worst fury she'd ever felt.

"Damn you," she threw at Crystal, her brown eyes blazing, her face lined with anger. "You tramp! It isn't enough that you spent the past ten years taking everything of mine you could lay your hands on, or that you went flying off to Europe and left me alone to take care of Mother all those long years. No, you had to come out here and make a grab for my family."

Crystal was slowly turning pale herself. "Bess, wait—"

"Wait, hell!" she shot back. Her fists clenched by her sides. "All the years I dated, you stole every single beau I had. You coaxed Carla into giving you my grandmother's jewels, the heirlooms I would have passed to my children, and you hocked them to get money! You even had the gall to question the will that left Oakgrove to me. Oakgrove, for God's sake, that had been in my family for a hundred years! And now you want Jude."

"Darling, Bess, please…!" Crystal pleaded, moving toward her.

But Bess backed away, hating them both. She tore the wedding bands from her hand—the gold one Jude had reluctantly slid on to her finger, and the silver one he'd bought her at the Alamo.

"You might as well have it all," she said harshly, and

flung the rings at Crystal. "All of it! Finally, this time, you've taken something I didn't want to begin with!"

Jude looked as if she'd slapped him. He didn't even move.

"I'm going home," Bess wept, brushing wildly at the tears on her cheeks. "If I have to walk every step of the way. And I never want to see either of you, ever again!"

Blindly she turned and rushed out of the study, deaf to Crystal's harsh plea. Without any particular course in mind, she threw open the front door and ran for the steps. But, blinded by her own tears, she didn't see the first one. She lost her footing and tumbled headfirst down the long wooden row of steps, feeling at first a sudden, sharp pain, and then a quiet black oblivion.

THE DREAMS WERE wild and strange. She was drowning as she reached out toward Jude, but he was dancing with Crystal, and she couldn't make him hear her. She was drowning, drowning...

"Wake up now, wake up, that's it," came a slow, soothing voice.

She opened her heavy eyelids and looked up into a round face with glasses behind an optical tool with a light in its center.

"Hello," she murmured drowsily.

"Hello, yourself," he murmured back. He looked in her other eye and stood up. "Well, that doesn't look too bad. You were lucky."

She swallowed, looking around the room. It was empty except for a nurse hovering in the background. "The baby?" she whispered, frightened as she remembered the long fall. Her eyes looked up into his for reassurance. "What about my baby?"

He frowned. "Are you pregnant?"

"Yes, I think so," she whispered unsteadily, and proceeded to tell him about her symptoms.

He examined her again, very carefully, and ordered tests. "You'll need to stay overnight," he said. "I don't think you've done any damage, but we'll have to make sure." He patted her on the shoulder. "Don't worry, now. We'll take good care of you."

"Doctor, please, if my husband and family are out there, don't tell them about the baby just yet," she asked pleadingly.

He lifted an eyebrow and grinned. "Don't steal your thunder, huh? Okay. But if I don't let that husband of yours in here pretty quick, I won't have any staff left. He's been chewing them out ever since he brought you in here. I'll get him."

Not Jude, she wanted to say. Not now, please, when I'm too weak to fight. But that would have sounded strange, and she wasn't up to explanations, either.

She closed her eyes, and when she opened them Jude was standing over her, white as paste and with eyes that frightened her.

"How do you feel?" he asked tautly.

She licked her dry lips and tried to breathe normally. They'd given her something for the pain and she was already feeling foggy.

"I feel sort of numb," she whispered.

He reached down and touched her hand very lightly, as if he expected her to jerk away from him, and she saw that her wedding bands had been replaced on it. "He said you weren't hurt. Why are they keeping you?" he asked in an odd tone.

"Just…to do some…tests," she said. "I'm okay."

His fingers curled around hers and tightened. His jaw clenched. "Oh, God, honey…" he ground out, closing his eyes. "Bess!"

He sounded terrified. If only she weren't so sleepy. She tried to get her hand away from his because she wanted to reach up and touch him. But he misunderstood the weak gesture and moved away.

"Shall I stay with you?" he asked tautly.

But she was already fading out and she didn't hear him. The pain was going away…

When she came to again it was dark. Very dark, and quiet. She opened her eyes just in time to see Crystal come in the door with a Coca-Cola in one hand.

Her eyes went cold and she started to speak, but Crystal moved toward the bed quickly.

"Please, don't get upset," Crystal pleaded gently, her face a mask of pure anguish. "Please, Bess. They'll make me leave, and I've got to stay with you. I promised Jude I wouldn't leave you alone for a second."

She lay back on the pillows with a bitter sigh and closed her eyes. Maybe she could pretend she wasn't conscious.

"Please listen," Crystal begged softly. "Please. Then if you want me to go, I'll call a nurse or somebody to stay with you instead of me. All right?"

"I can't go anywhere," Bess said weakly, turning her head away.

"No, you can't." Crystal sat down by the bed, putting her soft drink on the elevated tray nearby. "What you saw... I swear to God, it wasn't anything more than gratitude. Despite what you seem to think, I didn't come here to steal your husband. As if I could." She laughed. "Jude doesn't want me."

Bess stared at the wall, wishing her stepsister would just go away.

"I got a phone call this morning from Jacques, my Frenchman," she said softly. "He wants to marry me, Bess. Can you imagine? He actually wants to marry me!"

That drew Bess's attention for the first time. She turned her head on the pillow and stared at Crystal.

"I didn't dream that being away would make him miss me that much," Crystal continued quietly. "Even though Jude told me that if Jacques cared at all, it would happen. I wanted to leave weeks ago, but he asked me to stay. I thought maybe he was spending time with me to try and make you jealous. And I played up to him a little, to see if I could help." She smiled sadly. "But all I did was make things worse. Darling, you're so... withdrawn. You won't let any of us near enough to hurt you. I suppose I even understand." She reached out hesitantly and touched her stepsister's arm. "I've been pretty callous at times, haven't I? I knew you didn't want me here. But I kept telling myself that if I tried a little harder I might be able to reach you. I just wanted someone to talk to, Bess," she finished. "I had no one else, only you."

Bess's eyes felt wet. "Why didn't you tell me?" she burst out.

Crystal stared at her lap. "I didn't know how. It's all bluff with me, Bess. I laugh and tease and pretend that I'm always on a high. But I can't stop acting and be myself. Especially with the people who matter."

"Like Jacques?"

She nodded, smiling. "You see, he thought there was nothing under the fluff. He thought I was a shallow little flirt with no real feelings. He told me so. I came here hurting, but I hid it so well that nobody knew. Except Jude," she added quietly. "I suppose he's been hurt so much that he knew the signs."

Bess closed her eyes. She couldn't bear to think about that.

"Please don't hate me," Crystal said unsteadily. "I was thanking him in the only way I could. I wouldn't have hurt you for the world."

Bess reached out and gently touched Crystal's hand. "I'm sorry I didn't understand," she said softly. "I'm sorry for the things I said…"

"You had every right," Crystal returned. The hurt faded out of her eyes and she smiled. "Wow, what a temper!"

Bess laughed self-consciously. "I never knew I had one, except when Jude baited me."

"Poor old guy," she murmured. "He's paid today for sins he hasn't even bothered to commit."

Bess searched her stepsister's eyes. "Is he here?"

"All day long," came the quiet reply. "Up until just a

few minutes ago. I made him go get something to eat. He's sick about what happened. He feels responsible."

That was like Jude, to bear the brunt of responsibility for whatever happened to his possessions. Wasn't that what she was?

She smiled bitterly. "Well, I'm all right now. He can go home and…"

"And do what?" Crystal asked quietly. "Bess, the man loves you. I've never seen a man suffer the way he did when you fell down those steps. I had to call the ambulance. He wouldn't leave you even that long. And when the ambulance attendants came, they had to work around him because he wouldn't let go. He was terrified. Thank God Katy wasn't home when it happened."

"Katy!" Bess tried to sit up, but she held her head as it began to throb. She lay back down. "Poor Katy, have you called her?"

"Hours ago," Crystal said. "She and Aggie are at the house."

"I feel like such a fool," Bess moaned. "All this, because I was eaten up with jealousy and couldn't admit it." Her eyes searched Crystal's. "Can you forgive me?"

"If you can forgive me," came the soft reply. "Oh, Bess, don't you know that I'd never be able to compete with you? You're so gentle and caring, so giving with the people you do open up to. You're warm and generous, and you have a poise and sophistication I'll never have in a million years. Beauty fades. But character never does."

Bess held out her arms, crying as she embraced her stepsister.

"Are you really okay?" Crystal asked as she drew back, frowning.

Bess nodded. "Just a little whacked and bruised. But I'll be fine, now. Really I will."

"That's good. Because I have to catch a plane to France in the morning, before a certain count changes his mind about that emerald engagement ring he promised me." Crystal grinned. "Will you mind?"

"Not if I can come to the wedding," she replied, amazed at the ease with which they conversed now.

Crystal grinned. "You'll get the first invitation. Jude can bring you."

The smile faded. "Yes."

Crystal squeezed her hand. "Give him a chance," she said. "He hasn't had an easy time of it, either."

"He takes his responsibilities seriously," Bess agreed tiredly.

"You're more than that to him, darling. If you'd seen him the way I did, you'd realize that. Now get some rest. I'll sit here and sip my Coke and in the morning you'll be all better. Okay?"

"Okay." She smiled, clutching Crystal's slender hand as she drifted off to sleep peacefully for the first time.

When she opened her eyes again, the doctor was there and Crystal was blowing her a kiss from the doorway.

"I feel like Santa Claus," Dr. Barnes said with a grin after Crystal had left. "Which do you want, a boy or a girl?"

"I'm really pregnant?" she asked, rising.

"You're really pregnant," he answered. "Not bad news, I gather?"

"Oh, gosh," she breathed. She lay back down, grinning like a child. "Oh, gosh." Her hands went to her stomach and all of a sudden she felt wonderful.

"No sense talking to you any more tonight, I can see that," he murmured after he checked her over. "Baby's fine. So are you. I may let you out of here tomorrow. We'll see in the morning. Sleep tight!"

But she only smiled. What a wonderful, sweet secret. She closed her eyes and carried it off into the dark with her.

CHAPTER ELEVEN

SUNLIGHT STREAMED IN through the blinds and she moved restlessly. She felt bruised from head to toe, aching and miserable.

Her eyes opened and Jude was sitting rigidly in a chair by the bed. His eyes were bloodshot, staring straight ahead in a face like rawhide. His black hair was disheveled, and the pale blue silk shirt he was wearing with a blazer and dark slacks looked rumpled. It was unbuttoned halfway down, displaying bronzed muscles and curling dark hair, and she remembered with a shock of pleasure how it had felt to touch him there.

"Jude?" she whispered.

He sat up, his face alert, his eyes probing. "How are you?" he asked tautly.

"A little bruised," she said, avoiding that probing stare. "Where's Crystal?"

"On her way to Paris. She said she'd phone you tonight."

"Yes, I'd like that."

He studied her wan face. "She said you talked last night."

She nodded. Her eyes glanced off his. "Crystal told

me why she was kissing you. I'm sorry for the accusations I made," she said gruffly.

He caught her hand and pressed the palm hotly to his mouth, his eyes closing as he kissed the soft flesh hungrily. "Shut up, will you?" he asked on a harsh laugh. "My God, when I saw you pitch down those steps I wanted to put a gun to my temple!"

"It wasn't your fault," she managed shakily.

"The hell it wasn't." He kissed her palm again before he laid it back gently on the bed. He got to his feet, stretching as he went to the window and opened the blinds. "The doctor said you could go home today."

"I'd like that."

"If you feel like it," he emphasized. "I don't want you taking chances."

"I'm okay," she said, touched by the concern in his voice.

He turned from the window and moved back to the bed. "Bess," he said, oddly hesitant as he looked down at her, "Aggie said you were losing your breakfast lately."

She looked up at him through her lashes and her heart ran wild. "Did she?"

He sat beside her, touching her hand, feeling the rings that were back in place. His hand moved to the warm swell of her stomach and lingered there, pressing tenderly. "Are you going to give me a baby, honey?" he asked, looking into her eyes with a warm, questioning glance.

It was the wording as much as the deep velvet of his voice that made her flush with warmth. She hesitated a second, searching his hard face. Her fingers touched his tentatively. "Yes, I am," she said after a minute.

He studied her body in the shapeless gown, learning the new contours of her waistline and stomach, and he smiled gently. But when he looked up, the smile faded. "Couldn't you tell me?"

Her fingers lifted and brushed softly across the dark skin and hair on the back of that long-fingered hand. Amazingly, it trembled. "I was afraid," she said softly.

"Of me?" he asked, anguished.

"No!" She looked up, feeling his fingers lock into hers and draw them onto his broad, powerful thigh. "Of making you feel more tied than you already were. I… I thought you wanted Crystal, Jude."

"And I thought you didn't want me," he said quietly. "You even told me you didn't."

"Because I wasn't sure of you," she replied. Her eyes fell to their locked hands. "I never have been. You're so self-sufficient, so controlled. I never know what you're thinking or feeling."

"That makes two of us." His fingers contracted. "I put the rings back on, did you notice?"

"Yes. Thank you. I didn't mean half of what I said. My emotions seem to have gone haywire lately."

His hand freed hers and moved, lightly, reverently, over the soft swell of her stomach. "Does he move yet?" he whispered.

She smiled shyly. "It's too soon. You really don't mind?"

He smiled back. "No. I told you at the very beginning that I'd like to have a baby with you, didn't I?"

"You made some pretty horrible remarks about that," she reminded him.

"Self-defense, Bess," he said quietly. "I told you once that you made me lose control. I'd put a wall between myself and the world, and here you came, knocking out bricks. I didn't understand that at the time, and I liked it even less. So I fought back, with the only weapons I had."

"And now?"

"Now, I'm sorry I didn't start off better with you," he said. "I kept Crystal here thinking that her Frenchman might miss her and come looking. And," he admitted, "that she might make you a little jealous. If I'd realized how tragic the consequences could have been, I'd have sent her packing the first day. If you'd been badly hurt or lost the baby, I couldn't have lived with it."

"You didn't know I was going to start screaming over an innocent kiss," she said ruefully.

"It was that, for what it's worth. She was so excited about being reunited with her man that she had to share it. I'm sorry that I let her, now." He searched her face. "And she was kissing me, not the reverse. I...don't want other women, Bess. Only you."

Her face glowed at his remark, blossomed. His eyes made slow, sensuous love to hers in the silence that followed, and the lean hand across her stomach began to move in whisper soft patterns. His head bent toward her; his eyes glittered with possession. The silence magnified the sound of her unsteady breathing. The moment blazed with promise. His hand started to slide up toward one swollen breast, and her body lifted ardently to meet its ascent while her lips opened to welcome his. His breath caught as his mouth halted, poised just above hers.

At that moment, Dr. Barnes walked in, all smiles, and flopped into a chair to discuss the baby. Ignoring the flustered embarrassment of the parents-to-be, he gave them the name of a good obstetrician, congratulated Jude and gave Bess some high-powered prenatal vitamins to take.

"Eat properly from now on," Dr. Barnes added. "You're much too thin."

"She'll eat if I have to force-feed her," Jude said arrogantly.

She glared at him, and Dr. Barnes laughed. "Good man," the doctor observed. "You get in touch with this obstetrician, young lady, and make an appointment. Prenatal care is important. If you're interested in natural childbirth, by the way, the hospital has classes. Your obstetrician can tell you more about that."

"I'd like that," Bess said.

"So would I," Jude murmured surprisingly, glancing at her. "We'll take them together."

She had to hide her eyes to keep him from seeing the shock of pleasure the words had given her. After the doctor left, the rest of the morning passed in a wild haze, and before she knew it Jude had checked her out and she was home again.

From the minute she walked in the door of Big Mesquite, and Katy hugged and hugged her, she felt different. And things *were* different. Jude strutted around like a proud father, watching her hawklike as if he was constantly searching for something in her expression. And as if his close scrutiny weren't surprise enough, when the women got ready for church the following Sunday, they found Jude in a gray suit waiting for them downstairs.

"You're going to church with us?" Bess asked, astonished.

He glared at her. "Is there anything wrong with a man taking his family to church?"

"No, of course not," she stammered.

"Then shut up and let's go, before you make us late," he said, herding the three of them out the door.

Katy giggled, but she didn't let her father hear her, and Aggie just shook her head with wonder.

The Methodist minister at the church where they attended services looked as if he might faint when he saw Jude sitting in one of the front pews with his family. But he recovered quickly and grinned from ear to ear.

Bess, sitting beside her handsome husband, felt on top of the world. It was a mark of how far they'd come, for Jude to willingly walk into a house of worship. The cold, hard man she'd married so many long months ago wouldn't have been caught dead in one.

He struggled through the songs as if he hadn't sung in a long time, but he had a rich baritone and Bess thought he sounded wonderful. She smiled up at him mischievously. He turned his head, catching it, and grinned back. It was a small invitation, but more than enough for Bess, who was starving for something even closer than the friendly relationship they had shared since her return from the hospital.

That night, Bess tucked Katy into bed and didn't linger as she usually did. Pleading a headache, she excused herself, thinking she hadn't really lied to Katy. Jude did tend to be one, on occasion.

She heard water running as she entered the sanctuary of his bedroom, and had to force her nervous legs to carry her inside it. She locked the door behind her.

Jude's bedroom had dark Mediterranean furniture, with brown and cream accessories and a huge bed. She flushed as she looked at it, because it loomed large in her plans for the rest of the evening. She tugged the powder-blue satin robe she wore closer around her nudity and walked purposefully into the adjoining brown-and-cream bathroom.

He was in the shower, with the glass door closed, just rinsing his hair. She sat down on the stool by the door and watched with rising excitement, because the textured glass was almost transparent and she was getting fascinating glimpses of brown skin and thick black hair that arrowed down chest and stomach and thighs.

Seconds later, the water stopped running and he slid open the door. And froze.

She smiled at him, forcing herself not to back down now. "Hello," she said softly.

"Hello," he mumbled, his hand reaching for a towel.

"You aren't embarrassed?" she asked, staring blatantly at him, her eyes brimming over with appreciation for the sheer muscular power of his tall, hard body.

He considered that for a minute, and his green eyes glittered as they ran over her. "No, not really," he said. "Not with you."

He was thinking about the scars, she knew, one of the tiny insecurities that underlay all that magnificent pride and arrogance. She got up gracefully from the stool and moved to stand in front of him. Her hand took the towel from his.

"Jude..." Her nerve was beginning to fail.

He drew her hands to his body and draped the towel over them. "You've come this far," he whispered. "Don't get cold feet now."

Her lips parted on a shaky rush of breath as she studied his hard, dark face. "I want to make love to you tonight," she whispered. "You said once that when I was ready, I should come and get you."

A corner of his mouth curved, although his chest was rising and falling in shudders. "Is this a seduction?"

"Well, sort of," she admitted, peeking up at him. "You'll have to guide me. I don't really make a habit of this, like some people I could name."

"You're wasting time," he murmured, glancing down. "And we're running out of it."

Her eyes followed his and jerked back up again.

He laughed softly at her flush. "This was your idea. Take off that robe."

"But I haven't dried you off yet," she whispered.

"I've always had this wild fantasy of being toweled dry by a nude pregnant woman," he murmured drily. "Take it off. If I'm not embarrassed, with my flaws, why in hell should you be?"

She reached up and pressed her fingers to his lips. "You aren't flawed," she said quietly. "I love all of you, every inch, and those scars are marks of courage." She dropped her eyes to his mouth and managed to smile. "When I know you better, I'll kiss every one of them."

He laughed delightedly. "When you know me better?"

"Well, we've only slept together twice," she reminded him. "We're practically strangers."

"We'll get acquainted a lot quicker if you'll take off that damned robe."

She sighed. "You'll never get dried off if I do."

"Think so?"

Her hands went to the belt and she untied the robe, watching his face, and let it fall. His breath caught and his eyes went dark. His chest began to heave.

Her hands slid from his waist up to his head and, trembling, they began to make a small effort to dry his thick hair. But meanwhile, her body had touched his, and he cried out.

"Jude!" she whispered, shaken.

His hands drew her against him. He enfolded her, his arms cradled her, his mouth searched urgently for hers.

"I need you," he whispered unsteadily. "I want you, so much!"

Her lips nibbled at his, teasing, playing, until his hand caught in her long hair and pulled, making her mouth open suddenly as his took it. He rocked her against the hardness of his virile body, and she went weak-kneed with hunger for him.

"I can't wait," he bit off, lifting her. "I'm sorry, honey, I can't wait another second!"

"It's all right," she whispered back, arching her back as his lips found her breasts and worshipped their curves, slid down to the slight rise of her belly.

He laid her down on the bed and her arms pulled him over her.

"The baby," he whispered protectively, hesitating.

"Just don't be too rough, darling," she whispered. Her fingers touched his chest, his waistline, his hips. She found his hands and moved them to her own hips. "Hold me like this," she breathed, "the way you did in the woods that day..."

"Bess!" he groaned, and found her lips with his.

"I love you," she whispered into his seeking mouth. "I love you."

"Do you know what you're saying?" he whispered back, shifting his body so that they moved quickly into a devastating intimacy.

"Yes, I know." She lifted, arched, opening her eyes. "Love me back, just a little, darling," she whispered. "Just a little, even if this is all...all you can give... Jude!" She gasped, twisting helplessly as his body began the deep, soft motion she remembered, as his tender hands touched her in more intimate ways.

"It's going to be love this time," he said huskily. "On both sides. For both of us, Bess. You're my life, my heart, my world!"

Warmth flooded her body like fire as the words penetrated, and she saw the truth of them in the loving eyes that looked down into hers. "Darling...!" she cried out, clinging.

His hands went under her. "Move with me," he breathed, bending to her mouth. "Yes, hard, like that... Bess, oh God, Bess, Bess, I love you, I love you...!"

He whispered the words like a litany, until they became a breathless, hoarse chant, until her own voice caught and echoed them, until her body and her soul fused with his in one, explosive burst of color that shattered before her startled eyes like a kaleidoscope of shimmering rainbows.

She was hardly aware of time after that. It seemed that they'd only just finished when the symphony of movement and passion began all over again, with tender, soft kisses growing deeper and bodies kindling each other with brushing, teasing contact. He drew her back into his arms, and then every touch seemed to be more intimate, every kiss longer and deeper, every gasp and sob and moan louder than the one before. And this time he taught her things that made him cry out, ways of touching and tasting that gave her power over him, and she gloried in the pleasure she could see him experiencing. Until he reached a point on the edge of his control and, with a harsh groan, moved over her trembling body and, shivering with frank desire, gave her the satisfaction she pleaded for. Finally, from sheer exhaustion, they pulled up the covers and pressed themselves into each other's arms. And slept until morning.

He woke, and woke her, and as the sun filtered in through the blinds, they made love to the sound of birds rousing in the trees outside the window. And it was just as sweet as the night before. They were filled with shared love, with the wonder of belonging to each other.

"And I thought I liked being a bachelor," he murmured drily, ruffling her hair as she lay damply against his hairy chest in the drowsy aftermath of their loving.

She kissed his skin softly. "I'm going to make sure you like being married from now on."

He caressed her face, turning so that he could see her eyes. "Last night was the first time since Christmas," he observed quietly, "that you've reached out for me. Up until then, I'd done it all. All the chasing. All the taking. I used to hope against hope that one night you'd be starving for me and run the truck through my bedroom door," he added on a dry laugh.

"I kind of hoped the same thing," she confessed. "But I wasn't sure of you. I knew you didn't want to get married. I thought if I let you see how much I cared you'd use it against me. And, too, I was furious about Crystal."

He kissed her forehead gently. "Bess, I did hate the idea of marriage when you first came here. But after the first few weeks, it got to the point that I couldn't think of anything but you." He smiled. "I put up trees I didn't want, I went to unbelievable lengths to get my hands on a painting you'd said you liked, I let you set limits for Katy and watched you get her interested in dresses and parties—all the things I swore I wouldn't do. I saw you with her, how you laughed and played. And I wanted to play, too, but it had been too long, and I didn't know how anymore."

She bit gently at his shoulder. "Katy and I can teach you."

"I tried so hard to make you care," he said, and it all showed in his face, all the pain and hunger and frustration that he'd kept her from seeing. "But I couldn't get near you. And that night when you said you didn't want me…"

She touched his mouth. "I wanted you very much, I always have. I wanted you when I was fifteen years old, Jude," she confessed fervently. "I don't even know when it became love. But I know one thing. I couldn't survive away from you."

He traced her lips with a long finger. "That goes double for me, Mrs. Langston. I don't much like sleeping alone, either. Do you suppose you might sleep with me from now on?"

"We'd like that," she said.

"We?" He lifted an eyebrow.

She snuggled close with a smile. "Your son and I. Katy's ecstatic, did you notice?"

"Yes, and I'm glad." He drew her closer.

She looked up. "Don't you think I'm sexy?"

"God, yes!" he said, laughing. "I'll still love you when you look like a pumpkin. I just hope my arms are going to be long enough to reach around you."

She laughed delightedly. "What stories we'll be able to tell our grandchildren," she murmured. "I can just see their faces when I tell them about how you carried me bodily out of Oakgrove and flew me to Texas to get married."

"If you do," he warned, "I'll tell them how you seduced me on the bridle path."

"Blackmailer."

He grinned, rubbing his nose against hers. "We'll keep our secrets, then. Just for the two of us. And when I'm old, I'll whisper memories into your ear in front of them and watch you blush. And I'll be young, and so will you, all over again."

She brushed her fingers over his stubbled cheek lovingly, searching his eyes. "I'll love you all my life."

He kissed her softly. "I'll love you all of mine. Every minute." He sat up, stretching. "How about breakfast? Then we could go into San Antonio and have lunch at that restaurant on the river walk."

"Only if you promise not to stand up and start insulting me."

"Would I do that to a pregnant lady?" he asked. His eyes wandered slowly over her as he got to his feet and he smiled slowly, seductively. "You're pretty like that, in bed. I could lose my head over you."

She lay back on the pillows with a soft sigh, and moved her legs. "Could you? How exciting. Lie down and let's discuss it."

"You witch," he murmured.

She held out her arms. "It's so lonely here in this enormous bed."

"I've got phone calls to make..."

Her back arched softly. "I have this terrible ache, darling..."

He threw himself down beside her. "To hell with the phone calls. I've got an ache of my own."

Her lips parted and his moved onto them. She smiled, feeling as if there were champagne in her veins, bubbling and bursting with life and joy and delicious flavor. Her hands ran over the smooth, powerful muscles of his back with sweet abandon. Somehow, he didn't feel at all like rawhide anymore.

* * * * *

RELUCTANT FATHER

For Margaret, with love

CHAPTER ONE

BLAKE DONAVAN DIDN'T know which was the bigger shock—the dark-haired, unsmiling little girl at his front door or the news that the child was his daughter by his ex-wife.

Blake's pale green eyes darkened dangerously. It had been a hell of a day altogether, and now this. The lawyer who'd just imparted the information stepped closer to the child.

Blake raked his fingers through his unruly black hair and glared down at the child through thick black lashes. His daughter? The scowl grew and his expression hardened, emphasizing the harsh scar down one lean, tanned cheek. He looked even taller and more formidable than he really was.

"I don't like him," the little girl murmured, glaring at Blake as she spoke for the first time. She thrust her lower lip out and moved closer to the lawyer, clinging to his trouser leg. She had green eyes. That fact registered almost immediately—that and her high cheekbones. Blake had high cheekbones, too.

"Now, now." The tall, bespectacled man cleared his throat. "We mustn't be naughty, Sarah."

"My wife," Blake said coldly, "left me five years ago

to take up residence with an oilman from Louisiana. I haven't seen or heard from her since."

"If I might come in, Mr. Donavan…?"

He ignored the attorney's plea. "We only cohabited for a month—just long enough for her to find out that I was up to my neck in legal battles. She cut her losses and got out quick with her new lover." He smiled crookedly. "She didn't expect me to win. But I did."

The lawyer glanced around at the elegant, columned front porch, the well-kept gardens, the Mercedes in the driveway. He'd heard about the Donavan fortune and the fight Blake Donavan had when his uncle died and left him fending off numerous greedy cousins.

"The problem, you see," the attorney continued, glancing worriedly at the clinging child, "is that your ex-wife died earlier this month in an airplane crash. Understandably her second husband, from whom she was estranged, didn't want to assume responsibility for the child. Sarah has no one else," he added on a weary sigh. "Your wife's parents were middle-aged when she was born, and she had no brothers or sisters. The entire family is dead. And Sarah is your child."

Blake stared down at the little girl half-angrily. He hadn't even kept a photograph of Nina to remind him of the fool he'd been. And now here was her child, and they expected him to want her.

"I don't have room in my life for a child," he said curtly, furious at the curve fate had thrown him. "She can be put in a home somewhere, I suppose…"

And that was when it happened. The child began to cry. There wasn't a sound from her. She went from belligerence to heartrending sorrow in seconds, with great tears rolling from her green eyes down her flushed round cheeks. The effect was all the more poignant because of her silence and the stoic look on her face, as if she hated giving way to tears in front of the enemy.

Blake felt a stirring inside that surprised him. His mother had died soon after he was born. She hadn't been a particularly moral woman, according to his uncle, and all he knew about her was what little he'd been told. His uncle had taken him in and had adopted him. He, like Sarah, had been an extra person in the world, unwanted by just about everyone. He had no idea who his father was. If it hadn't been for his very wealthy uncle, he wouldn't even have a name. That lack of love and security in his young life had turned him hard. It would turn Sarah hard, too, if she had nobody to protect her.

He looked down at the little girl with a headful of angry questions, hating those tears. But the child had grit. She glared at him and abruptly wiped the tears away with a chubby little hand.

Blake lifted his chin pugnaciously. Already the kid was getting to him. But he wasn't going to be taken in by some scam. He trusted no one. "How do I know she's mine?" he demanded to the lawyer.

"She has your blood type," the man replied. "Your ex-wife's second husband has a totally different blood group. As you know, a blood test can only tell who the father wasn't. It wasn't her second husband."

Blake was about to remark that it could have been any one of a dozen other men, but then he remembered that Nina had married him for what she thought was his soon-to-be-realized wealth. He reasoned that Nina was too shrewd to have risked losing him by indulging in a fling. And after she knew what a struggle it was going to be to get that wealth, she hadn't wanted her newest catch to know she was already pregnant.

"Why didn't she tell me?" Blake asked coldly.

"She allowed her second husband to think the child was his," he said quietly. "It wasn't until she died and Sarah's birth certificate was found that he discovered she was yours. Nina had apparently decided that Sarah had a right to her own father's name. By then her second marriage was already on the rocks, from what I was told." He touched the child's dark hair absently. "You have the resources to double-check all this, of course."

"Of course." He stared down his broken nose at the little girl's face. "What's her name again? Sarah?"

"That's right. Sarah Jane."

Blake turned. "Bring her inside. Mrs. Jackson can feed her and I'll engage a nurse for her."

Just that quickly, he made the decision to keep the child. But, then, he'd been making quick decisions for a long time. When his uncle had attempted to link him with Meredith Calhoun, Blake had quickly decided to marry Nina. And as a last effort to force Blake into marrying Meredith, his uncle had left Meredith twenty percent of the stock in the real-estate conglomerate Blake was to inherit.

That had backfired. Blake had laughed at Meredith, in front of the whole family gathered for the reading of the will. And he'd told them all, his arm protectively around a smiling Nina, that he'd rather lose his inheritance and a leg than marry a skinny, plain, repulsive woman like Meredith. He was marrying Nina and Meredith could take her stock and burn it, for all he cared.

His heart lay like lead in his chest as he remembered the harsh words he'd used that day to cut Meredith down. She hadn't even flinched, but he'd watched something die in her soft gray eyes. With a kind of ravished dignity, she'd walked out of the room with every eye on her straight back. That had been bad enough. But later she'd come to offer him the stock and he'd been irritated by the faint hunger in her soft eyes. Because she disturbed him, he'd kissed her roughly, bruising her mouth, and he'd said some things that sent her running from him. He regretted that most of all. He planned to marry Nina, but despite his feeling for her, Meredith had been a tiny thorn in his side for years. He hadn't really meant to hurt her. He'd only wanted to make her go away. Well, he had. And he hadn't seen her since. She'd become internationally famous with her women's novels, one of which had been adapted for television. He saw her books everywhere these days. Like Meredith, they haunted him.

It hadn't been until after Nina had left him that he'd found out the reason for Meredith's haste in getting away. She'd been in love with him, his uncle's attorney had told him ruefully as he handed Blake the documents to sign that would give him full control of the Donavan empire. His uncle had known it and had hoped to make Blake see what a good catch she was.

Blake remembered vividly the day he'd discovered his hunger for Meredith. It had shocked them both. His uncle had come into the stable just in time to break up what might have been a disastrous confrontation between them. Blake had lost control and frightened Meredith, although she'd been so sweetly responsive at first that he hadn't seen her fear until the sound of a car driving up had brought him to his senses. Even a blind man couldn't have missed the faint swell of Meredith's mouth, the color in her cheeks and the way she was trembling. That was probably when the old man got the idea about the stock.

What irony, Blake thought, that what he'd wanted most in life was just a little love. He'd never had his mother's. He'd never known his father. And his uncle, though fond of him, was a manipulative man interested in the survival of his empire through Blake. Blake had actually married Nina because she'd flattered him and played up to him and sworn that she loved him. Now, looking back, he could see that she'd loved his money, not him. Once there was any possibility of the fortune being lost, she'd walked out on him. But Meredith had genuinely loved Blake, and he'd been cruel to her. That had haunted him all these years—that he'd hurt the one human being on earth who'd ever wanted to love him.

Meredith's father had worked for Blake's uncle, but the two men were good friends, as well. Uncle Dan had been at Meredith's christening as her godfather, and when she'd grown into her teens and expressed an interest in writing local history for the school newspaper, Uncle Dan had opened his library to her and spent hours telling her stories he'd heard from his grandfather about the old days. Meredith would sit and listen, her big eyes wide, her mouth faintly smiling. And Blake would brood, because his uncle had never given him that kind of time and affection. Blake was useful, but his uncle loved Meredith. He felt as if she'd usurped the only place in the world he had, and he'd resented her bitterly. And it was more than just that. He'd already learned that he couldn't trust people. He knew that Meredith and her parents were dirt poor, and he often wondered if she might not have some mercenary reason for hanging around the Donavan house. Too late, he discovered that she hung around because of him. Knowing the truth put salt in an old wound.

Plain Meredith, with her stringy dark hair and her pale gray eyes and her heart-shaped face. His uncle had loved her. Blake had almost despised her, especially after what had happened in the stable when he lost control with her. But under the resentment was an obsessive desire for Meredith that angered him, until it reached flash point the day his uncle's will was read. He'd given his word to Nina that he'd marry her and he couldn't honorably go back on it, but he'd wanted Meredith. God, how he'd wanted her, for years!

She'd loved him, he thought wearily as he led the lawyer and child into the study. Nobody else ever had felt that way about him. His uncle had enjoyed their battles; they'd been friends. His death had been a terrible, unexpected blow, made worse by the fact that he'd always felt that his uncle might have cared for him if Meredith hadn't always been underfoot. Not that it was love that had caused his uncle to adopt him. That had been business.

Maybe his mother would have loved him if she'd lived, although his uncle had described her as a pretty, self-centered woman who simply liked men too much.

So it had come as a shock to find out what shy young Meredith had felt for him. It didn't help to remember how he'd cut her to pieces in public and private. Over the years since she'd left for Texas in the middle of the night on a bus, without a goodbye to anyone, he'd agonized over what he'd done to her. Twice, he'd almost gone to see her when her name started cropping up on book covers. But the past was best left in the past, he'd decided finally. And he had nothing to give her, anyway. Nina had destroyed that part of him that was capable of trust. He had no more to give—to anyone.

He dragged his thoughts away from the past and looked at the child, who was staring plaintively and a little apprehensively at the door, because the lawyer had just smiled and was now making his way out, patent relief written all over his thin features. Sarah sat very still on the edge of a blue wing chair, biting her lower lip, her eyes wide and frightened, although she tried to hide her fear from the cold, mean-looking man they said was her father.

Blake sat down across from her in his own big red leather armchair, aware that he looked more like a desperado in his jeans and worn chambray shirt than a man of means. He'd been out in the pasture helping brand cattle, just for the hell of it. At least when he was working with his hands on the small ranch where he ran purebred Hereford cattle, he could let his mind go. It beat the hell out of the trying board meeting he'd had to endure at his company headquarters in Oklahoma City that morning.

"So you're Sarah," he said. Children made him uncomfortable, and he didn't know how he was going to cope with this one. But she had his eyes and he couldn't let her go to strangers. Not if there was one chance in a million that she really was his daughter.

Sarah lifted her eyes to his, then glanced away, shifting restlessly. The lawyer had said she was almost four, but she seemed amazingly mature. She behaved as if she'd never known the company of other children. It was possible that she hadn't. He couldn't picture Nina entertaining children. It was totally out of character, but he hadn't realized that when he'd lost his head and married her. Funny how easy it was to imagine Meredith Calhoun with a lapful of little girls, laughing and playing with them, picking daisies in the meadow...

He had to stop thinking about Meredith, he told himself firmly. He didn't want her, even if there was a chance in hell that she'd ever come back to Jack's Corner, Oklahoma. And he knew without a doubt that she certainly didn't want him.

"I don't like you," Sarah said after a minute. She shifted in the chair and glanced around her. "I don't want to live here." She glared at Blake.

He glared back. "Well, I'm not crazy about the idea, either, but it looks like we're stuck with each other."

Her lower lip jutted, and for an instant she looked just like him. "I'll bet you don't even have a cat."

"God forbid," he grumbled. "I hate cats."

She sighed and looked at her scuffed shoes with

something like resignation and a patience far beyond her years. She appeared tired and worn. "My mommy isn't coming back." She pulled at her dress. "She didn't like me. You don't like me, either," she said, lifting her chin. "I don't care. You're not really my daddy."

"I must be." He sighed heavily. "God knows, you look enough like me."

"You're ugly."

His eyebrows shot up. "You're no petunia yourself, sprout," he returned.

"The ugly duckling turns into a swan," she told him with a faraway look in her eyes.

She twirled her hands in her dress. He noticed then, for the first time, that it was old. The lace was stained and the dress was rumpled. He frowned.

"Where have you been staying?" he asked her.

"Mommy left me with Daddy Brad, but he had to go out a lot, so Mrs. Smathers took care of me." She looked up, and the expression in her green eyes was old for a little girl's. "Mrs. Smathers says that children are horrible," she said dramatically, "and that they belong in cages. I cried when Mommy left, and she locked me up and said she'd leave me there if I didn't hush." Her lower lip trembled, but she didn't cry. "I got out, too, and ran away." She shrugged. "But nobody came to find me, so I went home. Mrs. Smathers was real mad, but Daddy Brad didn't care. He said I wasn't his real child and it didn't matter if I ran away."

Blake could imagine that "Daddy Brad" was upset to find that the child he'd accepted as his own was somebody else's, but taking it out on the child seemed pretty callous.

He leaned back in his chair, wondering what in hell he was going to do with his short houseguest. He didn't know anything about kids. He wasn't sure he even liked them. And this one already looked like a handful. She was outspoken and belligerent and not much to look at. He could see trouble ahead.

Mrs. Jackson came into the room to see if Blake wanted anything, and stopped dead. She was fifty-five, a spinster, graying and thin and faintly intimidating to people who didn't know her. She was used to a bachelor household, and the sight of a child sitting across from her boss was vaguely unnerving.

"Who's that?" she asked, without dressing up the question.

Sarah looked at her and sighed, as if saying, oh, no, here's another sour one. Blake almost laughed out loud at the expression on the child's face.

"This is Amie Jackson, Sarah," Blake said, introducing them. "Mrs. Jackson, Sarah Jane is my daughter."

Mrs. Jackson didn't faint, but she did go a shade redder. "Yes, sir, that's hard to miss," she said, comparing the small, composed child's face with its older male counterpart. "Her mother isn't here?" she added, staring around as if she expected Nina to materialize.

"Nina is dead," Blake said without any particular feeling. Nina had knocked the finer feelings out of him years ago. His own foolish blindness to her real nature had helped her in the task.

"Oh, I'm sorry." Mrs. Jackson rubbed her apron between her thin hands for something to do. "Would she like some milk and cookies?" she asked hesitantly.

"That might be nice. Sarah?" Blake asked more curtly than he'd meant.

Sarah shifted and stared at the carpet. "I'd get crumbs on the floor." She shook her head. "Mrs. Smathers says kids should eat off the kitchen floor 'cause they're messy."

Mrs. Jackson looked uncomfortable, and Blake sighed heavily. "You can get crumbs on the floor. Nobody's going to yell at you."

Sarah glanced up hesitantly.

"I don't mind cleaning up crumbs," Mrs. Jackson said testily. "Do you want cookies?"

"Yes, please."

The older woman nodded curtly and went to get some.

"Nobody smiles here," Sarah murmured. "It's just like home."

Blake felt a twinge of regret for the child, who seemed to have been stuck away in the housekeeper's corner with no thought for her well-being. And not just since her stepfather had found out that she was Blake's child, apparently.

His eyes narrowed and he asked the question that was consuming him. "Didn't your mother stay with you?"

"Mommy was busy," Sarah said. "She said I had to stay with Mrs. Smathers and do what she said."

"Wasn't she home from time to time?"

"She and my daddy—" she faltered and grimaced

"—my *other* daddy yelled at each other mostly. Then she went away and he went away, too."

This was getting them nowhere. He stood and began to pace, his hands in his pockets, his face stormy and hard.

Sarah watched him covertly. "You sure are big," she murmured.

He stopped, glancing down at her curiously. "You sure are little," he returned.

"I'll grow," Sarah promised. "Do you have a horse?"

"Several."

She brightened. "I can ride a horse!"

"Not on my ranch, you can't."

Her green eyes flashed fire. "I can so if I want to. I can ride any horse!"

He knelt in front of her very slowly, and his green eyes met hers levelly and without blinking. "No," he said firmly. "You'll do what you're told, and you won't talk back. This is my place, and I make the rules. Got it?"

She hesitated, but only for a minute. "Okay," she said sulkily.

He touched the tip of her pert nose. "And no sulking. I don't know how this is going to work out," he added curtly. "Hell, I don't know anything about kids!"

"Hell is where you go when you're bad," Sarah replied matter-of-factly. "My mommy's friend used to talk about it all the time, and about damns and sons of—"

"Sarah!" Blake burst out, shocked that a child her age should be so familiar with bad words.

"Do you have any cows?" she added, easily diverted.

"A few," he muttered. "Which one of your mommy's friends used language like that around you?"

"Just Trudy," she said, wide-eyed.

Blake whistled through his teeth and turned just as Mrs. Jackson came in with a tray of milk and cookies for Sarah and coffee for Blake.

"I like coffee," Sarah said. "My mommy let me drink it when she had hers in bed and she wasn't awake good."

"I'll bet," Blake said, "but you aren't drinking it here. Coffee isn't good for kids."

"I can have coffee if I want to," Sarah returned belligerently.

Blake looked at Mrs. Jackson, who was more or less frozen in place, staring at the little girl as she grabbed four cookies and proceeded to stuff them into her mouth as if she hadn't eaten in days.

"You quit, or even try to quit," Blake told the housekeeper, who'd looked after his uncle before him, "and so help me God, I'll track you all the way to Alaska and drag you back here by one foot."

"Me, quit? Just when things are getting interesting?" Mrs. Jackson lifted her chin. "God forbid."

"Sarah, when was the last time you ate?" Blake inquired, watching her grab another handful of cookies.

"I had supper," she said, "and then we came here."

"You haven't had breakfast?" he burst out. "Or lunch?"

She shook her head. "These cookies are good!"

"If you haven't eaten for almost a day, I imagine so." He sighed. "You'd better make us an early dinner tonight," Blake told Mrs. Jackson. "She'll eat herself sick on cookies if we're not careful."

"Yes, sir. I'll go and make up the guest room for her," she said. "But what about clothes? Does she have a suitcase?"

"No, that lawyer didn't bring anything. Let her sleep in her slip tonight. Tomorrow," he added, "you can take her into town to do some shopping."

"Me?" Mrs. Jackson looked horrified.

"Somebody has to be sacrificed," he told her pithily. "And I'm the boss."

Mrs. Jackson's lips formed a thin line. "I don't know beans about little girls' clothes!"

"Well, take her to Mrs. Donaldson's shop," he muttered. "That's where King Roper and Elissa take their little girl to be outfitted. I heard King groan about the prices, but that won't bother us any more than it bothers them."

"Yes, sir." She turned to leave.

"By the way, where's the weekly paper?" he asked, because it always came on Thursday morning. "I wanted to see if our legal ad got in."

Mrs. Jackson shifted uncomfortably and grimaced. "Well, I didn't want to upset you…"

His eyebrows arched. "How could the weekly paper possibly upset me? Get it!"

"All right. If you're sure that's what you want." She reached into the drawer of one of the end tables and pulled it out. "There you go, boss. And I'll leave before the explosion, if you don't mind."

She exited, and Sarah took two more cookies while

Blake stared down at the paper's front page at a face that had haunted him.

"Author Meredith Calhoun to autograph at Baker's Book Nook," read the headline, and underneath it was a recent picture of Meredith.

His eyes searched over it in shock. The plain, skinny woman he'd hurt bore no resemblance to this peacock. Her brown hair was pulled back from her face into an elegant chignon. Her gray eyes were serene in a high-cheekboned face that could have graced the cover of a magazine, and her makeup enhanced the raw material that had always been there. She was wearing a pale suit coat with a pastel blouse, and she looked lovely. More than lovely. She looked soft and warm and totally untouched at the age of twenty-five, which she had to be now.

Blake put the paper down after scanning what he already knew about her skyrocketing career and her latest book, *Choices*, about a man and a woman trying to manage careers, marriage and parenthood all at once. He'd read it, as he secretly read all Meredith's books, looking for traces of the past. Maybe even for a cessation of hostilities. But her feelings for him were buried and there was never a single trait he could recognize in her people that reminded him of himself. It was as if she sensed that he might look at them and had hidden anything that would give her inner feelings away.

Sarah Jane was standing beside him without his knowing it. She looked at the picture in the paper. "That's a pretty lady," Sarah said. She leaned forward and picked out a word in the column below the photograph. "*B...o...o...k*. Book," she said proudly.

"So it is." He pointed to the name. "How about that?"

"*M...e...r*... Merry Christmas," she said.

He smiled faintly. "Meredith," he corrected. "That's her name. She's a writer."

"I had a book about the three bears," Sarah told him. "Did she write that?"

"No. She writes books for big girls. Finish your cookies and you can watch television."

"I like to watch *Mr. Rogers* and *Sesame Street*," she said.

He frowned. "What?"

"They come on television."

"Oh. Well, help yourself."

He moved out of the room, ignoring the coffee. Which was sad, because Sarah Jane discovered it in the big silver pot and proceeded to help herself to the now cool liquid while he was on the telephone in the hall. Her cry caused him to drop the receiver in mid-sentence.

She was drenched in coffee and screaming her head off. She wasn't the only wet thing, either. The carpet and part of the sofa were saturated and the tray was an inch deep with black liquid.

"I told you to stay out of the coffee, didn't I?" Blake said as he knelt to see if she had been burned. Which, thank God, she hadn't; she was more frightened than hurt.

"I wanted some," she murmured tearfully. "I ruined my pretty dress."

"That isn't all that's going to get ruined, either," he said ominously, and abruptly tugged her over his knee and gave her bottom a slap. "When I say no, I mean no. Do you understand me, Sarah Jane Donavan?" he asked firmly.

She was too surprised to cry anymore. She stared at him warily. "Is that my name now?"

"It's always been your name," he replied. "You're a Donavan. This is your home."

"I like coffee," she said hesitantly.

"And I said you weren't to drink it," he reminded her.

She took a deep breath. "Okay." She picked up the coffeepot, only to have it taken from her and put on the table. "I can clean it up," she said. "Mommy always made me clean up my mess."

"This is more than you can cope with, sprout. And God only knows what we're going to put on you while those things are washed."

Mrs. Jackson came in and put both hands to her mouth. "Saints alive!"

"Towels, quick," Blake said.

She went to get them, muttering all the way.

Minutes later the mess was gone, Sarah Jane was bundled up in a makeshift towel dress and her clothes were being washed and dried. Blake went into his study and locked the door, shamelessly leaving Mrs. Jackson to cope with Sarah while he had a few minutes' peace. He had a feeling that it was going to be more and more difficult to find any quiet place in his life from now on.

He wasn't sure he was going to like being a father. It was a whole new kind of responsibility, and his daughter seemed to have inherited his strength of will and stubbornness. She was going to be a handful. Mrs. Jackson knew no more about kids than he did, and that wasn't going to help, either. But he didn't feel right about sending Sarah off to a boarding school. He knew what it was like to be alone and unwanted and not too physically appealing. He felt a kind of kinship with this child, and he was reluctant to push her out of his life. On the other hand, how in hell was he going to live with her?

But over and above that problem was the newest one. Meredith Calhoun was coming to Jack's Corner for a whole month, according to that newspaper. In that length of time he was sure to see her, and he had mixed feelings about opening up the old wounds. He wondered if she felt the same way, or if, in her fame and wealth, she'd left the memories of him in the past. He wanted to see her all the same. Even if she still hated him.

CHAPTER TWO

Blake and Mrs. Jackson usually ate their evening meal with a minimum of conversation. But that was another old custom that was going to change.

Sarah Jane was a walking encyclopedia of questions. One answer led to another why and another, until Blake was ready to get under the table. And just the mention of bedtime brought on a tantrum. Mrs. Jackson tried to cajole the child into obeying, but Sarah Jane only got louder. Blake settled the matter by picking her up and carrying her to her new room.

Mrs. Jackson helped her undress and get into bed and Blake paused at her bedside reluctantly to say good-night.

"You don't like me," Sarah accused.

He almost bristled at her mutinous expression, but she was a proud child, and he didn't want to break her spirit. She'd need it as she grew older.

"I don't know you," he replied reasonably. "Any more than you know me. People don't become friends on the spur of the moment. It takes time, sprout."

She considered that as she lay there, swallowed whole by the size of the bed under her and the thick white coverlet over her. She watched him curiously. "You don't hate little children, do you?" she asked finally.

"I don't hate kids," he said. "I'm just not used to them. I've been by myself for a long time."

"Did you love my mommy?"

That question was harder to answer. His broad shoulders rose and fell. "I thought she was beautiful. I wanted to marry her."

"She didn't like me," Sarah confided. "Can I really stay here? And I don't have to go back to Daddy Brad?"

"No, you don't have to go back. We'll have to do some adjusting, Sarah, but we'll get used to each other."

"I'm scared with the light off," she confessed.

"We'll leave a night-light on."

"What if a monster comes?" she asked.

"I'll kill it, of course," he reassured her with a smile.

She shifted under the covers. "Aren't you scared of monsters?"

"Nope."

She smiled for the first time. "Okay." She stared at him for a minute. "You have a scar on your face," she said, pointing to his right cheek.

His fingers touched it absently. "So I do." He'd long ago given up being sensitive about it, but he didn't like going into the way he'd gotten it. "Good night, sprout."

He didn't offer to read her a story or tell her one. In fact, he didn't know any he could tell a child. And he didn't tuck her in or kiss her. That would have been awkward. But Sarah didn't ask for those things or seem to need them. Perhaps she hadn't had much affection.

She acted very much like a child who'd been turned loose and not bothered with overmuch.

He went back downstairs and into his study, to finish the day's business that had been put on hold while he'd coped with Sarah's arrival. Tomorrow Mrs. Jackson would have to handle things. He couldn't steal time from a board meeting for one small child.

Jack's Corner was a medium-sized Oklahoma city, and Blake's.

office was in a new mall complex that was both modern and spacious. The next day, he and his board were just finalizing the financing for an upcoming project, when his secretary came in, flustered and apprehensive.

"Mr. Donavan, it's your housekeeper on the phone. Could you speak with her, please?"

"I told you not to interrupt me unless it was urgent, Daisy," he told the young blond woman curtly.

She hesitated nervously. "Please, sir?"

He got up and excused himself, striding angrily out into the waiting room to pick up the phone with a hard glare at Daisy.

"Okay, Amie, what's wrong?" he asked shortly.

"I quit."

"Oh, my God, not yet," he shot back. "Not until she starts dating, at least!"

"I can't wait that long, and I want my check today," Mrs. Jackson snorted.

"Why?"

She held out the receiver. "Do you hear that?"

He did. Sarah Jane was screaming her head off.

"Where are you?" he asked with cold patience.

"Meg Donaldson's dress shop downtown," she replied. "This has been going on for five minutes. I wouldn't let her buy the dress she wanted and I can't make her stop."

"Smack her on the bottom," Blake said.

"Hit her in public?" She sounded as if he'd asked her to tie the child to a moving vehicle by her hair. "I won't!"

He said something under his breath. "All right, I'm on my way."

He hung up. "Tell the board to go ahead without me," he told Daisy shortly, grabbing his hat off the hat rack. "I have to go administrate a small problem."

"When will you be back, sir?" Daisy asked.

"God knows."

He closed the door behind him with a jerk, mentally consigning fatherhood and sissy housekeepers to the netherworld.

It took him ten minutes to get to the small children's boutique in town, and as luck would have it, there was one empty space in front that he could slide the Mercedes into. Next to his car was a sporty red Porsche with the top down. He paused for a moment to admire it and wonder about the owner.

"Oh, thank God." Mrs. Jackson almost fell on him when he walked into the shop. "Make her stop."

Sarah was lying on the floor, her face red and tear stained, her hair damp with sweat, her old dress rumpled from her exertions. She looked up at Blake and the tantrum died abruptly. "She won't buy me the frilly one," she moaned, pouting with a demure femininity.

My God, Blake thought absently, they learn how to do it almost before they can walk.

"Why won't you buy her the frilly one?" he asked an astonished Mrs. Jackson, the words slipping out before he could stop them, while Meg Donaldson smothered a smile behind her cupped hands at the counter.

Mrs. Jackson looked taken aback. She cleared her throat. "Well, it's expensive."

"I'm rich," he pointed out.

"Yes, but it's not suitable for playing in the backyard. She needs some jeans and tops and underthings."

"I need a dress to wear to parties," Sarah sobbed. "I never got to go to a party, but you can have one for me, and I can make friends."

He reached down and lifted her to her feet, then knelt in front of her. "I don't like tantrums," he said. "Next time Mrs. Jackson will spank you. In public," he added, glaring at the stoic housekeeper.

She turned beet red, and Mrs. Donaldson bent down beside the counter as if she were going to look for something and burst out laughing.

While Mrs. Jackson was searching for words, the shop door opened and two women came in. Elissa Roper was immediately recognizable. She was married to King Roper, a friend of Blake's.

"Blake!" Elissa smiled. "We haven't seen you lately. What are you and Mrs. Jackson doing in here? And who's this?"

"This is my daughter, Sarah Jane," Blake said, introducing the child. "We've just been having a tantrum."

"Speak for yourself," Mrs. Jackson sniffed. "I don't have tantrums. I just resign from jobs that have gotten too big for me."

"You're resigning, Mrs. Jackson? That would be one for the books, wouldn't it?" a soft, amused voice asked, and Blake's heart jumped.

He got slowly to his feet, oblivious to Sarah's curious stare, to come face to face with a memory.

Meredith Calhoun looked back at him with gray eyes that gave away nothing except faint humor. She was wearing a blue dress with a white jacket, and she looked expensive and sophisticated and lovely. Her figure had filled out over the years, and she was tall and exquisite, with full, high breasts and a narrow waist flaring to hips that were in exact proportion for her body. She had long legs encased in silk hose, and elegant feet in white sandals. And the sight of her made Blake ache in the most inconvenient way.

"Merry!" Mrs. Jackson enthused, and hugged her. "It's been so long!"

And it had been since Mrs. Jackson had made cake and cookies for her while she visited Blake's uncle, who was also her godfather.

She and the housekeeper had grown close. "Long enough, I guess, Amie," Meredith said as they stepped apart. "You haven't aged a day."

"You have," Mrs. Jackson said with a smile. "You're grown up."

"And famous," Elissa put in. "Bess—you remember my sister-in-law—and Meredith were in the same class at school and are still great friends. She's staying with Bess and Bobby."

"They've just bought the house next door to me," Blake replied, for something to say. He couldn't find the words to express what he felt when he looked at Meredith. So many years, so much pain. But whatever she'd felt for him was gone. That fact registered immediately.

"Has Nina come back with your daughter?" Elissa asked, trying not to appear poleaxed, which she was.

"Nina died earlier this year. Sarah Jane is living with me now." He dragged his eyes away from Meredith to turn his attention to his child. "You look terrible. Go to the rest room and wash your face."

"You come, too," Sarah said mutinously.

"No."

"I won't go!"

"I'll take her," Mrs. Jackson said in her best martyred tone.

"No! You won't let me buy the frilly dress!" Sarah turned her attention to the two curious onlookers. "She's in the paper," she said, her eyes on Meredith. "She writes books. My daddy said so."

Meredith managed not to look at Blake. The unexpected sight of him after so much time was enough to knock her speechless. Thank God she'd learned to mask her emotions and hadn't given herself away. The last thing she wanted to do was let Blake Donavan see that she had any vulnerability left.

Sarah walked over to Meredith, staring up at her with rapt fascination. "Can you tell stories?"

"Oh, I guess I can," she said, smiling at the child who was so much like Blake. "You've got red eyes, Sarah. You shouldn't cry."

"I want the frilly dress and a party and other little children to play with. It's very lonely, and they don't like me." She indicated Blake and Mrs. Jackson.

"One day, and she's advertising to the world that we're Jekyll and Hyde." Mrs. Jackson threw up her hands.

"Which one are you?" Blake returned, glaring at her.

"Jekyll, of course. I'm prettier than you are," Mrs. Jackson shot back.

"Just like old times," Elissa said with a sigh, "isn't it, Merry?"

Meredith wasn't listening. Sarah Jane had reached up and taken her hand.

"You can come with me," the little girl told Meredith. "I like her," she said to her father belligerently. "She smiles. I'll let her wash my face."

"Do you mind?" Blake asked Meredith, speaking to her for the first time since she'd entered the shop.

"I don't mind." She didn't look at him fully, then turned and let Sarah lead her into the small bathroom in the back of the shop.

"She's changed," Mrs. Jackson said to Mrs. Donaldson. "I hardly knew her."

"It's been a long time, you know. And she's a famous woman now, not the child who left us."

Blake walked away uncomfortably, staring at the dresses. Elissa moved closer to him while the other two women talked. She'd been a little afraid of Blake when she'd first met him years ago, but she'd gotten to know him better. He and King were friends and visited regularly.

"How long has Sarah been with you?" she asked him.

"Since yesterday afternoon," he replied dryly. "It seems like years. I guess I'll get used to her, but it's hard going right now. She's a handful."

"She's just frightened and alone," Elissa replied. "She'll improve when she has time to settle down and adjust."

"I may be bankrupt by then," he mused. "I had to walk out of a board meeting. And all because Sarah Jane wanted a frilly dress."

"Why don't you buy it for her and she can come to my Danielle's birthday party next week? It will be nice for her to meet children her own age."

"She'll sit on the cake and wreck the house," he groaned.

"No, she won't. She's just a little girl."

"She wrecked my living room in just under ten minutes," he assured her.

"It takes mine five minutes to do that." Elissa grinned. "It's normal."

He stared toward the bathroom. Meredith and Sarah Jane were just coming out. "There are people in the world who have more than one," he murmured. "Do you suppose they're sane?"

Elissa laughed. "Yes. You'll understand it all one day."

"Look what Merry gave me!" Sarah enthused, showing Blake a snowy white handkerchief. "And it's all mine! It has lace!"

Blake shook his head as she turned abruptly and grabbed the dress she'd been screaming about. "It's mine. I want it. Oh, please." She changed tactics, staring up pie eyed at her daddy. "It will go so nicely with my new handkerchief."

Blake laughed and then caught himself. He looked at Mrs. Jackson. "What do you think?"

"I think that if you buy Sarah Jane that dress I'm going to put it on you," the older woman replied in a hunted tone.

"You really shouldn't give in because children have tantrums, Blake," Mrs. Donaldson volunteered. "I know. I raised four."

He stared at Mrs. Jackson. "You started this. Why would you tell her she couldn't have the damned thing in the first place?"

"I told you, it was too expensive for her to play in."

"She'll need a dress to come to Danielle's party," Elissa broke in.

"Now see what you've done," Blake growled at Mrs. Jackson.

"I won't take her shopping ever again. You can just let somebody else run your company and do it yourself," Mrs. Jackson grumbled.

"I don't know what to think of a woman who can't manage to buy a dress for one small child."

"That isn't just one small child, that's one small Donavan, and nobody could say she isn't your daughter!" Mrs. Jackson said.

Blake felt an unexpected surge of pleasure at the words. He looked down at the child who looked so much like him and had to agree that she did have some of his better qualities. Stubborn determination. Not to mention good taste.

"You can have the dress, Sarah," he told her, and was rewarded by a smile so delightful he'd have sold his Mercedes to buy the damned thing for her no matter what it cost.

"Oh, thank you!" Sarah gushed.

"You'll be sorry," Mrs. Jackson said.

"You can shut up," he told her. "It's your fault."

"You said to take her shopping, you didn't say what to buy," she reminded him huffily. "And I'm going home."

"Then go on. And don't burn lunch," he called after her.

"I couldn't burn a bologna sandwich if I tried, and that's all you'll get from me today!"

"I'll fire you!"

"Thank God!"

Blake glared at Mrs. Donaldson and Elissa, who were trying not to smile. This byplay between Blake and Mrs. Jackson was old hat to them, and they found it amusing.

Meredith's expression was less revealing. She was looking at Sarah and Blake wished he could see her eyes.

But she turned away. "We'd better get on," she told Elissa. "Bess will be waiting for us to pick her up at the beauty parlor."

"Okay," Elissa grinned. "Just let me get those socks for Danielle and I'll be ready."

She did, which left Meredith stranded with Blake and his daughter.

"Isn't it pretty?" Sarah sighed, pirouetting with the dress held in front of her. "I look like a fairy princess."

"Not quite," Blake said. "You'll need shoes, and some clothes to play in, too."

"Okay." She ran to the other racks and started looking through them.

"Is it normal for them to be so clothes conscious at this age?" Blake asked, turning his attention to Meredith.

"I don't know," she said uncomfortably. His unblinking green-eyed gaze was making her remember too much pain. "I haven't been around children very much. I must go…"

He touched her arm, and was astonished to find that she jerked away from his touch and stared fully at him with eyes that burned with resentment and pain and anger.

"So, you haven't forgotten," he said under his breath.

"Did you really think I ever would?" she asked on a shaky laugh. "You were the reason I never came back here. I almost didn't come this time, either, but I was tired of hiding."

He didn't know what to say. Her reaction was unexpected. He'd imagined that she might have some bitterness, but not this much. He searched what he could see of her face, looking for something he knew he wasn't going to find anymore.

"You've changed," he said quietly.

Her eyes looked up into his, and there was a flash of cold anger there. "Oh, yes, I've changed. I've grown up. That should reassure you. I won't be chasing after you like a lovesick puppy this time."

The reference stung, and she'd meant it to. He'd accused her of chasing him and more, after the reading of the will.

But being reminded of the past only made him bitter, and he hit back. "Thank God," he said with a mocking smile. "Could I have that in writing?"

"Go to hell," she said under her breath.

That, coming from shy little Meredith, floored him. He didn't even have a comeback.

Sarah came running up with an armload of things. "Look, aren't they pretty! Can I have them all?" she asked the scowling man beside Meredith.

"Sure," he said absently.

Meredith turned away from him, smiling. It was the first time in memory that she'd ever fought back—or for that matter, said anything to him that wasn't respectful and worshipful. What a delightful surprise to find he no longer intimidated her.

"Ready to go?" Meredith asked Elissa.

"Sure am. See you, Blake!"

"But you can't go." Sarah ran to Meredith and caught her skirt. "You're my friend."

The child couldn't know how that hurt—to have Blake's child, the child she might have borne him, cling to her. She knelt in front of Sarah, disengaging the small hand. "I have to go now. But I'll see you again, Sarah. Okay?"

Sarah looked lost. "You're nice. Nobody else smiles at me."

"Mrs. Jackson will smile at you tonight, I promise," Blake told the child. "Or she'll never smile again," he added under his breath.

"You don't smile," Sarah accused him.

"My face would break," he assured her. "Now get your things and we'll go home."

She sighed. "Okay." She looked up at Meredith. "Will you come to see me?"

Meredith went white. Go into that house again, where Blake had humiliated and hurt her? God forbid!

"You can come to see Danielle, Sarah," Elissa interrupted, and Meredith knew then that Elissa had heard the whole story from King. She was running interference, bless her.

"Who's Dan—Danielle?" Sarah asked.

"My daughter. She's four."

"I'm almost four," Sarah said. "Can she say nursery rhymes? I know all of them. 'Humpty Dumpty sat on the wall, Humpty Dumpty—'"

"I'll give your Daddy a call and he can bring you down to Bess's house, where Meredith is staying. Bess is my sister-in-law, and Danielle and I go to see her sometimes."

"I'd like to have a friend," Sarah agreed. "Could we do that?" she asked her father.

Blake was watching Meredith shift uncomfortably. "Sure we can," he said, just to irritate her.

Meredith turned away, her heart going like an over-wound watch, her eyes restless and frightened. The very last thing she wanted was to have to cope with Blake.

"Bye, Merry!" Sarah called.

"Goodbye, Sarah Jane," she murmured, and forced a smile, but she wouldn't look at Blake.

He said the appropriate things as Elissa followed Meredith out the door, but the fact that Meredith wouldn't look at him cut like a knife.

He watched Meredith climb in under the wheel of the red Porsche. It didn't seem like the kind of car she'd drive, but she wasn't the girl she'd been. His eyes narrowed. He wondered if she was still as innocent as before, or if some man had taught her all the sweet ways to make love. His face hardened at the thought. No one had touched her until he had. And he'd frightened her. He hadn't really meant to. The feel and taste of her had knocked him off balance, and at the time he hadn't been experienced himself. Nina had been his first woman, but his first real intimacy, even if it had been relatively chaste, had been with Meredith. Even after all the years in between, he could feel her mouth, taste its sweetness.

He could see the soft alabaster of her breasts when he'd unbuttoned the top of her dress. He groaned silently. That was when he'd lost his senses—seeing her like that. He wondered if she knew how green he'd been in those days, and decided that she was too inexperienced herself to realize it. He'd wanted Meredith to the point of madness, and things had just gotten out of hand. But to a shy young virgin, his ardor must have seemed frightening.

He turned back to his daughter with memories of the past darkening his eyes. It seemed so long ago that the rain had found him in the stable and Meredith had come in looking for his uncle…

CHAPTER THREE

I<small>T HAD BEEN</small> late spring that day five years ago, and Blake had been helping one of the men doctor a sick horse in the stable. Meredith had come along just in time to see the second man leave. Blake was still there. She'd come to ask where his uncle was, but it was a rainy day, and she and Blake had been caught in the barn while it stormed outside.

Blake had hungrily watched Meredith as she stood on her tiptoes to look toward the house. She was wearing a white sundress that buttoned up the front, and as she stretched, every line of her body had been emphasized and her dress had ridden up, displaying most of her long legs.

The sight of those slim, elegant legs and the sensuous curve of her body had caught him in the stomach like a body blow, and he'd stood there staring. It shouldn't have affected him. He had Nina, who was blond and beautiful and who loved him. Meredith was plain and shy and not at all the kind of woman who could attract him. But as he'd looked at her, his body had quickened and the shock of it had moved him helplessly toward where she stood in the wide doorway, just out of the path of the rain.

Meredith had heard him, or perhaps sensed him, because she turned, her eyes faintly covetous before she lowered them. "It's really coming down, isn't it?" she asked hesitantly. "I was just about to go home, but I needed to ask your Uncle Dan some more questions."

"You're always around these days," he'd remarked, half-angry because his body was playing cruel tricks on him.

She'd blushed. "He's helping me with some articles for the school paper, and I'm going to do a book with the same information," she'd begun.

"Book!" He scoffed at that. "You're barely twenty. What makes you think you've learned enough to write books? You haven't even started to live."

Her head came up and there had been a flash of anger in her pale gray eyes, which was instantly disguised. "You make me sound like a toddler."

"You look like one occasionally," he remarked with faint humor, noting the braid of her hair, which she'd tied with a ribbon. "And I'm almost twelve years older than you are." He pushed away from the barn door, noticing the faint hunger in her face as he went toward her.

The hunger was what touched him. It hadn't occurred to him that women besides Nina might find him physically attractive. He had that damned scar down one cheek, thanks to Meredith, and it made him look like a renegade. His arrogance didn't soften the impression.

He looked down his nose at Meredith when he was less than a foot from her, watching the expressions play across her face. It was a pretty good bet that she was innocent, and if she'd been kissed, probably it hadn't

been often or seriously. That, at least, made him feel
confident. She didn't have anyone to compare him with.

His eyes went to her soft bow of a mouth, and with
an impulse he didn't even understand at the time, he
tilted her chin up with a lean hand and bent to brush
his lips over hers.

"Blake…!" she gasped.

He hadn't known if it was fear or shock. The first
contact with her mouth had caused a frightening surge
of desire in his lean body. "Don't back away now," he
bit off against her soft lips. "Come here."

He'd pulled her against him and his mouth had grown
rough and hungry. Even now, five years later, he could
feel the soft yielding of her body in his arms, smell the
scent of her as she strained upward and gave him her
mouth with such warm eagerness. He could hear the
rain beating on the stable roof, and the soft sounds of a
cow settling down in the darkness beyond where they
stood silhouetted against the driving rain.

Blake had been amazed by the tentative response he
got from her lips. That shy nibbling drove him over the
edge. He eased her back against the wall of the barn,
out of sight, with his mouth still covering hers. Then
he let his body slide down against her so that his hips
were pressing feverishly against hers, his chest crushing her soft young breasts.

He felt her quickened breathing, heard the soft "no!"
as he felt for and found one firm breast and touched it
through her clothing. The feel of her made him wild. He
remembered the white-hot flames that had consumed
him with the intimate touch. He'd wanted her with a

shuddering passion and his mouth had grown more and more demanding. She gave in to him all at once, her body relaxing, shivering, her mouth shyly responding. His tongue pushed gently inside her lips and she stiffened, but she didn't try to pull away.

Confident now, his fingers worked at buttons and he lifted his head just fractionally to look down at what they uncovered. Her breasts were bare under the dress and he groaned as he bent to brush his mouth against them. He felt her gasp and her hands gripped his arms hard. The silky taste of her body stripped him of control entirely, the feel of her skin against his face made him wild. His hands grew roughly intimate in passion and his mouth closed hungrily over one firm breast.

What might have happened then was anyone's guess. He hardly heard Meredith's frantic voice. It wasn't until he caught the sound of a car driving up that his sanity returned.

He lifted his head, breathing fiercely, in time to see Meredith's eyes full of fear. He realized belatedly what he'd done. He took a sharp breath and levered himself back up, away from her, his body in torment with unsatisfied desire, his eyes smoldering as they met hers.

She blushed furiously as she fumbled buttons into buttonholes, making herself decent again. And only then did he realize how intimate the embrace had gotten. He didn't know what had possessed him. He'd frightened her and himself, because it was the first time he'd ever lost control like that. But, then, he hadn't been experienced, he realized now. Not until he and Nina were married. His first taste of sensual pleasure had been with Meredith that day in the stable.

He didn't speak—he was too shocked. The sudden arrival of his uncle had been a godsend at the time, but later it dawned on him that his uncle had guessed what had happened between Blake and Meredith and had altered his will to capitalize on it. His favorite godchild and his nephew—he would have considered them a perfect match. But Blake hadn't thought of it at the time. He'd been so drunk on Meredith's soft mouth that he'd almost gone after her when she mumbled some excuse and ran out into the rain as he and his uncle watched her.

Then, within days, his uncle was dead of a heart attack. Blake had been crushed. The sense of loneliness he felt when it happened was almost too great for words. Meredith had been around, with her parents, but he'd hardly noticed with Nina clinging to him, pretending sympathy. And then, suddenly they were reading the will. Blake was engaged to Nina, but still trying to cope with the turbulent emotions Meredith had aroused in him. The will was read, and he learned that Uncle Dan had left twenty percent of the stock in his real estate companies to Meredith. The only way Blake could have it would be by marrying her.

He had forty-nine percent of the stock, but his cousins had thirty-one shares between them. And although one of the cousins down in Texas would have sided with him in a proxy fight if Meredith sided against him, he could lose everything. Nina had laughed. He still remembered the look on her face as she scrutinized Meredith in a manner too contemptuous for words.

Blake had done much worse. The realization that his uncle had tried to control his life even from the grave and the embarrassment of having his haughty cousins snicker at him was just too much.

"Marry her?" he'd said slowly after the will had been read, rising out of his chair to confront Meredith in the dead silence that followed. "My God, marry that plain, dull, shadow of a woman? I'd rather lose the real estate companies, the money and my left leg than marry her!" He'd moved closer to Meredith, watching her cringe and go pale at the humiliation of having him say those things so loudly in front of the family. "No dice, Meredith," he said with venom. "Take the stock and go to hell with it. I don't want you!"

He'd expected her to burst into tears and run out of the room, but she hadn't. Deathly pale, shaking so hard she could barely stand, she lowered her eyes, turned away and walked out with dignity far beyond her twenty years. It had shamed him later to remember her stiff pride and his own loss of control that had prompted the outburst. The cousin from Texas had glared at him with black eyes and walked out without another word, leaving him alone with Nina and the other cousins, who subsequently filed suit to take control of the real estate companies from him.

But Nina had smiled and clung to him and promised heaven, because she was sure he'd get the stock back somehow. She'd advised him to talk to the lawyer.

He had. But the only way to get the stock back, apparently, was to marry Meredith or break the will. Both were equally impossible.

He was still smoldering when he found Meredith coming out the back door. She'd been in the kitchen saying goodbye to Mrs. Jackson.

She was pale and unusually quiet, and she looked as if she didn't want to stop. But he'd gotten in front of her in the deserted, shaded backyard and refused to let her pass.

"I don't want the shares," she said, without looking at him. "I never did. I knew nothing about what your uncle had planned, and I wouldn't have gone through with it if I had."

"Wouldn't you?" he demanded coldly. "Maybe you saw a chance to marry a rich man. Your family is poor."

"There are worse things than being poor," she replied quietly. "And people who marry for money earn it, as you'll find out one day."

"I will?" He caught her arms roughly. "What do you mean?"

"I mean that Nina wants what you have, not what you are," she replied with a sad smile.

"Nina loves me," he said.

"No."

"What does it matter to you, anyway?" he growled. "I haven't been able to turn around without running into you for the past two months. You're always here, getting in the way! What's the matter, did you decide that one kiss wasn't enough, and you're hot for more?"

In fact, it had been the other way around. He'd wanted her so desperately that his mind had gone into hiding, behind the anger he used to disguise the hunger that was driving him mad.

He pulled her into his arms, angry at life and circumstances, ignoring her faint struggles. "God forbid that you should go away with nothing," he added. And he kissed her with all his fury and frustration in his lips. He accused her of chasing him, of wanting his uncle's money. And then he turned around and walked off, leaving her in tears.

His eyes closed as he came back to the present, hating the memory, hating his cruelty. He'd been a different man then, a colder, less feeling man. It had irritated him that Meredith disturbed him physically, that he could be aroused by the sound of her voice, by the sight of her. Because of what he thought he felt for Nina, he'd pushed his growing attraction to Meredith out of his mind. Nina loved him and Meredith just wanted what he had—or so he'd been sure at the time. Now he knew better, and it was too late.

Those few minutes he'd made love to Meredith in the stable that long-ago afternoon had been the sweetest and saddest of his entire life. He'd been cruel after the will was read because he'd felt betrayed by his uncle and by her. But he'd also been sad, because he wanted Meredith far more than Nina. He'd given his word to Nina that he was going to marry her, and honor made him stick to it. So he'd forced Meredith to run away to remove the temptation from his path. He'd known deep inside that he couldn't have resisted Meredith much longer. And he had no right to her.

It struck him as odd that he'd lost control with Meredith. He'd never lost it with Nina, although he'd had a lukewarm kind of feeling for her that had grown out of her adoration and teasing. But what he'd felt with Meredith had been fire and storm. The last time he'd seen her, he'd raged at her that she'd tempted him by following him around like a lovesick puppy, and that had been the last straw. She'd run then, all right, and she hadn't stopped. Not for five years. A week after she left, an attorney brought him the stock, legally signed over to him without a single request for money. Nina had been delighted, and she'd led him right to the altar. He'd been so cut up by his own conscience about what he'd done to Meredith that he hadn't protested, even though his yen for Nina had all but left him.

He went through the motions of making love to Nina, but it wasn't at all satisfying to him. And she always smiled at him so lovingly when they were in bed together. Smiling. Until the day the court battle started, initiated by his cousins, and he was backed into a corner that Nina didn't think he'd get out of. So she left him and divorced him, and he'd had years to regret his own foolishness.

Meredith's attitude toward him in the shop hadn't really come as a surprise. He knew how badly he'd hurt her that day, frightened her. Probably she'd never had a lover or wanted one, because if appearances were anything to go by, he'd left some bad scars. He felt even guiltier about that. But it didn't seem as if he were going to get close enough to tell her the truth about what had happened—even if his pride would allow it.

And anyway, she'd made her feelings about the house clear. She wouldn't voluntarily set foot in it. He sighed heavily. Incredible, he thought, how a man could become his own worst enemy. Looking back, he knew his uncle had been right. If he'd married Meredith, she'd have loved him, and in time he might have been able to love her back. As things stood, that was something he'd never know.

DOWN THE ROAD at Bobby and Bess's house, Meredith Calhoun was halfheartedly watching a movie on Bess's VCR as she tried to come to grips with the unexpected confrontation with Blake.

She felt shaky inside. The sight of Blake, with his jet black hair, green eyes and arrogant, mocking smile, had twisted her heart. Over the years she'd tried to force herself to go out on dates, see other men. But it hadn't worked. She couldn't bear for any man to do more than kiss her, and even the kisses were bitter and unpleasant after Blake's. One part of her was afraid of Blake, but another part remembered the first kiss in the stable, the sweet, slow hunger that had flared between them like summer lightning. And because of that kiss, no other man had ever been able to stir her.

Blake's daughter had come as the biggest surprise. Meredith hadn't known about the child. It seemed, from what Elissa said, that nobody had. Sarah Jane was a quirk of fate, and she wondered if Blake still loved Nina. If he did, Sarah Jane would be a comfort to him. But when he'd said that Nina was dead, it had been without a scrap of emotion in his face or his eyes. He didn't seem to care one way or another. That was strange, because he'd been so adamant about marrying Nina, so certain that she loved him.

Meredith got up, oblivious to the television, and began to wander restlessly around Bess's big living room. She stopped in front of the picture window. Beyond it, on a rise a few hundred yards away, was Blake's house. She sighed, remembering the happy times she'd had there before the will had been read. Blake had always seemed to resent her, but that day in the stable had been full of soft magic. Because of it, she'd actually expected something more from him than anger. She'd dreamed afterward that he'd left Nina and discovered that he loved Meredith and couldn't live without her. Dreams.

She laughed with a new cynicism. That would be the day, when Blake Donavan would feel anything but dislike for her. He hadn't been openly antagonistic today, but he'd verged on it just before she left the store. Sarah liked her and it was going to be difficult to keep the child at bay without hurting her. Meredith had a feeling that Sarah Jane's young life hadn't been a happy one. She didn't act like a contented child, and apparently she'd only been with Blake and Mrs. Jackson for a day or so. Meredith had wondered why, but hadn't dared ask Blake.

Sarah reminded her of herself at that age, a poor little kid from the wrong side of the tracks, with no brothers or sisters and parents who worked themselves into early graves trying to make a living with the sweat of their brows. Bess had been her only friend, and Bess had it even worse than she did at home. The two of them had become close as children and remained close as adults. So when Bess had invited Meredith, with Bobby's blessing, to come and stay for a few weeks, she'd welcomed the rest from work and routine.

She hadn't consciously considered that Blake was going to be a very big part of her visit. She'd actually thought she could come to Jack's Corner without having to see him at all. Which was silly. King and Elissa and Bess and Bobby all knew him, and Blake and King were best friends. She wondered if maybe she'd rationalized things because of Blake, because she'd wanted to see him again, to see if her fears had been real or just manifestations of unrequited love and sorrow. She wanted to see if looking at him could still make her knees go weak and her heart run away.

Well, now she knew. It could. And if she had any sense of self-preservation, she was going to have to keep some distance from him. She couldn't risk letting Blake get close to her heart a second time. Once had been enough—more than enough. She'd just avoid him, she told herself, and everything would be all right.

But avoiding him turned out to be a forlorn hope, because Sarah Jane liked Meredith and contrived to get her father to call Elissa about that visit she'd mentioned.

Blake listened to the request with mixed feelings. Sarah Jane was beginning to settle down a little, although she was still belligerent and not an overly joyful addition to the household. Mrs. Jackson was coping well enough, but she'd vanish the minute Blake came home from work, leaving him to try and talk to his sullen young daughter. He knew that the situation needed a woman's touch, but Mrs. Jackson wasn't the woman. Meredith already liked Sarah, and Sarah was drawn to her. If he could get Meredith to befriend the child, it would make his life easier. But in another way, he was uncertain about trying to force himself and Sarah on Meredith. After having seen how frightened she still was of him, how bitter she was about the past, he might open old wounds and rub salt in them. He didn't want to hurt Meredith, but Sarah Jane was driving him nuts, and he needed help.

"You have to call 'lissa," Sarah Jane said firmly, her mutinous mouth pouting up at him. "She promised I could play with her little girl. I want to see Mer'dith, too. She likes me." She glared at him, her eyes so like his only in her youthful face. "You don't like me."

"I explained that to you," he said with exaggerated patience as he perched on the corner of his desk. "We don't know each other."

"You don't ever come home," she said, sighing. "And Mrs. Jackson doesn't like me, either."

"She's not used to children, Sarah, any more than I am." A corner of his mouth twisted. "Look, sprout, I'll try to spend more time with you. But you've got to understand that I'm a busy man. A lot of people depend on me."

"Can't you call 'lissa?" she persisted. "Please?" she added. "Please?"

He found himself picking up the telephone. Sarah had a knack for getting under his skin. He was beginning to get used to the sound of her voice, the running footsteps in the morning, the sound of cartoons and children's programs coming from the living room. Maybe in time he and Sarah would get along better. They were still in the squaring off and glaring stages right now, and she was every bit as stubborn as he was.

He talked to Elissa, who was delighted to comply with Sarah's request. She promised to set things up for the following morning because it was Saturday and Blake could bring Sarah down to Bess's house. But first she wanted to check with Bess and make sure it was all right.

Blake and Sarah both waited for the phone to ring. Blake wondered how Meredith was going to feel about it, but apparently she didn't mind, because Elissa had called back within five minutes and said that Bess would be expecting the child about ten o'clock. Not only that, Sarah was invited to spend the day.

"I can spend the day?" Sarah asked, brightening.

"We'll see." Blake was noncommittal. "Why don't you find something to play with?"

Sarah shrugged. "I don't have any toys. I had a teddy bear, but he got lost and Daddy Brad wouldn't let me look for him before they brought me here."

His eyes narrowed. "Don't call him that again," he said gruffly. "He isn't your father. I am."

Sarah's eyes widened at his tone, and he felt uncomfortable for having said anything at all.

"Can I call you 'Daddy'?" Sarah asked after a long minute.

Blake's breath caught in his throat. He shifted. "I don't care," he said impassively. In fact, he did care. He cared like hell.

"Okay," she said, and went off to the kitchen to see if Mrs. Jackson had any more cookies.

Blake frowned, thinking about what she'd said about toys. Surely a child of almost four still played with them. He'd have to ask Elissa. She'd know about toys and little girls.

The next morning, Sarah dressed herself in her new frilly dress and her shoes and went downstairs. Blake had to bite his lip to keep from howling. She had the dress on backward and unbuttoned. She had on frilly socks, but one was yellow and one was pink. Her hair was unruly, and the picture she made was of chaos, not femininity.

"Come here, sprout, and let's get the dress on properly," he said.

She glared at him. "It's all right."

"No, it's not." He stood. "Don't argue with me, kid. I'm twice your size."

"I don't have to mind you," she said.

"Yes, you do. Or else."

"Or else what?" she challenged.

He stared down at her. "Or else you'll stay home today."

She grimaced and stared down at the carpet. "Okay."

He helped her turn the dress around and cursed under his breath while he did up buttons that were hard for his big, lean hands to work. He finally got them fixed, then took her upstairs, where he searched until he found matching socks and then brushed her straight hair until it looked soft and shiny.

She turned before he finished, looking small and oddly vulnerable on the vanity stool, and her green eyes met his. "I never had any little children to play with. My mommy said I made her nervous."

He didn't say anything, but he could imagine Nina being uncomfortable around children.

"Can I stay here?" Sarah asked unexpectedly, and there was a flash of real fear in her eyes. "You won't make me go away, will you?"

He had to bite down hard to keep back a harsh curse. "No, I won't make you go away," he said after a minute. "You're my daughter."

"You didn't want me when I was a baby," she accused mutinously.

"I didn't know about you," he said, sitting down and talking to her very seriously, as if she were already an adult. "I didn't know I had a little girl. Now I do. You're a Donavan, and this is your place in the world. Here, with me."

"And I can live here forever?"

"Until you grow up, anyway," he promised. His green eyes narrowed. "You aren't going to start crying or anything, are you?" he asked, because her eyes were glistening.

That snapped her out of it. She glared at him. "I never cry. I'm brave."

"I guess you've had to be, haven't you?" he murmured absently. He stood. "Well, if we're going, let's go. And you be on your best behavior. I'm going to tell Bess to swat you if you don't mind her."

"Mer'dith won't let her hit me," she said smugly. "She's my friend. Do you have any friends?"

"One or two," he said, holding her hand as they went down the long staircase.

"Do they come to play with you?" she asked seriously. "And could they play with me, too?"

He chuckled deep in his throat, trying to imagine King Roper sitting cross-legged on the living room carpet, dressing a doll.

"I don't think so," he replied. "They're grown-ups."

"Oh. Grown-ups are too big to play, I guess. I don't want to grow up. I wish I had a doll."

"What kind of doll?" he asked.

"A pretty one with long golden hair and pretty dresses. I could talk to her. And a teddy bear," she said sadly. "I want a teddy bear just like Mr. Friend. I miss Mr. Friend. He used to sleep with me. I'm ascared of the dark," she added.

"Yes, I know," he murmured, having had to help Mrs. Jackson get her to bed every night and chase out the monsters before she closed her eyes.

"Lots of monsters live in my room," she informed him. "You have to kill them every night, don't you?"

"So far, I'm ahead by one monster," he reassured her.

"You're awful big," she said, eyeing him with an unblinking scrutiny. "I bet you weigh one million pounds."

"Not quite."

"I'm ten feet tall," she said, going on tiptoe.

He led her out the door, calling goodbye to Mrs. Jackson. It seemed natural to hold her hand and smile at her chatter. There was magic in a child, even a hard case like this one. He wondered if security would soften her, and doubted it. She had spirit and inner strength.

Those qualities pleased him. She'd need them if she lived with him.

Bess and Bobby's house was a split-level brick with exquisite landscaping and a small thicket of trees that separated their property from Blake's. In the driveway were Elissa's gray Lincoln, Meredith's red Porsche convertible and the blue Mercedes that Bess drove. Blake parked behind them on the long driveway and helped Sarah out.

She was at the front door before he reached it, excited as the door opened and a little blond girl about her age shyly greeted her.

"This is Danielle, Sarah. She's looked forward to meeting you," Elissa said with a smile. "Hi, Blake. Come on in."

He took off his gray Stetson and stood in the hall while Sarah went into the living room with Danielle, who'd brought a box of toys with her.

Sarah's eyes lit up like a Christmas tree, and she exclaimed over every single one of Danielle's things, as if she'd never seen toys before. She sat down on the carpet and handled each one gingerly, turning it over and examining it and telling Danielle how beautiful the dolls were.

"She doesn't have any toys," Blake told Elissa with a worried frown. "She seems so mature sometimes. I didn't realize…"

"Parenthood takes time," Elissa assured him. "Don't expect to learn everything at once."

"I don't think I've learned anything yet," he confessed. He frowned as he watched his daughter. "I expected her to push Danielle around and try to take her toys away. She isn't the easiest child to get along with."

"She's a frightened child," Elissa replied. "Underneath there are some sweet qualities. You see, she's playing very nicely, and she isn't causing trouble."

"Yet," Blake murmured, waiting for the explosion to come.

His head turned as Meredith came down the hall. She hesitated momentarily, then joined them.

"Bess is getting coffee," she said quietly. She was wearing a pale green sundress that slashed squarely over her high breasts, and her hair was loose, waving around her shoulders. She looked younger this way, and Blake almost sighed with memories.

"Will you stay and have a cup with us?" Elissa asked him.

"I guess so," he agreed. His eyes hadn't left Meredith.

She averted her gaze and started into the living room, too vulnerable to risk letting him see how easily he could get to her with that level, unblinking stare.

"Mer'dith!" Sarah jumped up, all eyes and laughing smile, and ran with her arms open to be picked up and hugged warmly. "Oh, Mer'dith, Daddy brought me to see Dani and he's going to get me another Mr. Friend and he says I can have a doll! Oh, he's just the nicest daddy…!"

Blake looked as if someone had poured ice into his shirt. He stared at the child blankly. She'd just called him 'Daddy' for the first time, and something stirred in the region of his heart, making him feel warm and needed. It was a new feeling, as if he weren't totally alone anymore.

"That's nice, darling," Meredith was telling the child. She let her down and knelt beside her, smiling as she pushed back Sarah's unruly hair. "You look very pretty this morning. I like your new dress."

"It's very pretty," Danielle agreed. She was dressed in slacks and a shirt for playing, but she didn't make fun of Sarah's dress. She was a quiet child and sweet natured.

"I put it on backward, but Daddy fixed it for me." She smiled at Meredith. "Can you stay and play with us? We can play with dolls."

"I wish I could," Meredith said, nervous because Blake was watching her so closely. She was frantic for a way out of the house, away from him. "But I have to go into town to the library and do some research."

"I thought this was supposed to be a holiday," Bess said as she came in with a tray of coffee and cake. "You're here to rest, not to work."

Meredith smiled at her lovely blond friend. "I know. But I'm not comfortable if I don't have something to do. I won't be long."

"I could drive you," Blake volunteered.

She blanched and started to refuse, but Elissa and Bess jumped in and teased and cajoled until they made it impossible for her to turn down his offer.

She wanted to scream. Alone with Blake in his car? What would they say to each other? What could they say to each other that wouldn't involve them in another terrible argument? The past was very much in Meredith's thoughts, and she wasn't about to risk a repeat of it. But she'd allowed herself to be manipulated by him, and it looked as though she wasn't going to be able to get out of going to town with him. Now, she thought, what are you going to do?

CHAPTER FOUR

BLAKE COULD SENSE the nervousness in Meredith as she sat stiffly in the seat beside him while he started the car. In the old days, he might have made some cutting remark about it, but the days were gone when he'd deliberately try to hurt her.

"Fasten your seat belt," he said, noticing that she hadn't.

"Oh." She did it absently. "I usually remember in my own car," she said with faint defensiveness.

"Don't you ever ride with other people?"

"Not if I can help it," she murmured, glancing at his hard profile as he backed the car out of the driveway and pulled onto the highway.

"Are your friends bad drivers," he asked, "or is it that you just don't like being out of control?"

"Who drives you, if we're going to throw stones?" she asked with a pleasantly cool smile.

His mouth twitched. "Nobody."

She toyed with her white leather purse, twisting the thin strap around her fingers while she stared out the window at the green crops and grazing cattle on the way to Jack's Corner. The flat horizon seemed to stretch forever, just as it did back in Texas.

"Sarah engineered this get-together," he remarked. "She damned near drove me crazy until I phoned Elissa to arrange it." His green eyes touched her stiff profile and went back to the road. "She likes you."

"I like her, too," she said quietly. "She's a sweet child."

"'Sweet' isn't exactly the word I'd choose."

"Can't you see what's under the belligerence?" she asked solemnly, and turned in the seat slightly so that she could look at him without having to move her head. "She's frightened."

"Elissa said that, too. What is she frightened of? Me?" he asked.

"I don't know what," she said. "I don't know anything about the situation, and I'm not prying." She stared at the clasp on her purse and unsnapped it. "She doesn't look like a happy child. And the way she enthused over Danielle's things, I'd almost bet she's hardly had a toy in her life."

"I'm a bachelor," he muttered angrily. "I don't know about children and toys and dresses. My God, until a few days ago I didn't even know I was a father."

Meredith wanted to ask why Nina had kept Sarah's existence a secret, but she didn't feel comfortable talking about such personal things with him. She had to remember that he was the enemy, in a very real sense. She couldn't afford to show any interest in his life.

He was already figuring that out by himself. She either didn't care about how he'd found out, or she wasn't going to risk asking him. He wished he smoked. She made him nervous and he didn't have anything to do with his hands except grip the steering wheel as he drove.

"Mrs. Jackson is one of your biggest fans," he said, moving the conversation away from Sarah.

"Is she? I'm glad."

"I guess you make a fair living from what you do, if that Porsche is any indication."

She lifted her eyes to his face, letting them run over his craggy features. The broken nose was prominent, as was that angry scar down his cheek. She felt a surge of warmth remembering how he'd come by that scar. Her eyes fell.

"I make a good living," she replied. "I'm rather well-to-do, in fact. So if you think I came home looking for a rich husband, you're well off the mark. You're perfectly safe, Blake," she added coldly. "I'm the last woman on earth you'll have to ward off these days."

He had to clamp down hard on his teeth to keep from saying what came naturally. The past was dead, but she had every reason for digging it up and throwing it at him. He had to remember that. If she'd done to him what he'd done to her, he'd have wanted a much worse revenge than a few pithy remarks.

"I don't flatter myself that you'd come looking for me without a loaded gun, Meredith," he returned. He glanced at her, noting the surprise on her face.

She looked out the window again, puzzled and confused.

He pulled the Mercedes into the parking lot behind the library and shut off the engine.

"Don't do that. Not yet," he said when she started to open the door. "Let's talk for a minute."

"What do we have to say to each other?" she asked distantly. "We're different people now. Let the past take care of itself. I don't want to remember—" she stopped short when she realized what she'd blurted out.

"I know." He leaned back against his door, his pale green eyes under thick black lashes searching her face. "I guess you think I was rough with you in the stable deliberately. And I said some cruel things, didn't I?"

She flushed and averted her eyes, focusing on his chest. "Yes," she said, taut with embarrassment and vivid memories.

"It wasn't planned," he replied. "And what I said wasn't what I felt." He sighed heavily. "I wanted you, Meredith. Wanted you with a passion that drove me right over the edge. But I'm sorry I hurt you."

"Nothing happened," she said icily. In her nervousness her hands gripped her purse like talons.

"Only because my uncle came driving up at the right moment," he said bitterly. He studied her set features. "You'll never know how it's haunted me all these long years. I was deliberately rough with you the day the will was read because guilt was eating me up. I'd promised to marry Nina, my cousins were talking lawsuits…and on top of all that, I'd just discovered that I wanted you to the point of madness."

"I don't want to talk about it," she said under her breath. Her eyes closed in pain. "I can't…talk about it."

His eyes narrowed. "I thought Nina loved me," he said gently. "She said she did, and all her actions seemed to prove it. I thought you only wanted the inheritance, that I was a stepping stone for you, a way to escape the poverty you'd lived in all your young life." He ran his fingers lightly over the steering wheel. "It wasn't until after…that day, that the lawyer told me why my uncle had wanted me to marry you." His eyes slid to catch hers and hold them. "I didn't know you were in love with me."

Her face lost every vestige of color. She sat and stared at him, her pride in rags, her deepest secret naked to his scrutiny.

"It wouldn't have made the slightest bit of difference," she choked out. "Nothing would have changed. Except that you'd have used the information to humiliate me even more. You and Nina would have laughed yourselves sick over that irony."

The cynicism in her tone made him feel even guiltier. She'd grown a shell, just like the one he'd lived inside most of his life. It kept people from getting too close, from wounding too deeply. Nina hadn't managed to penetrate it, but Meredith very nearly had. He'd pushed her out of his life at exactly the right moment, because it wouldn't have taken much to give her a stranglehold on his heart. He'd known that five years ago, and did everything he could to prevent it.

Now he was seeing the consequences of his reticence. His life had altered, and so had Meredith's. Her fame must have been poor recompense for the home and children she'd always wanted, for a husband to love and take care of and be loved by.

He couldn't answer her accusation without giving

himself away, so he ignored it and let her think what she liked.

"You never used to be sarcastic," he said quietly. "You were quiet and shy—"

"And dull and plain," she added for him with a cold smile. "I still am all those things. But I write books that sell like hotcakes and I've got my own small following of loyal readers. I'm famous and I'm rich. So now it doesn't matter if I'm not a blond bombshell. I've learned to live with what I am."

"Have you?" He searched her eyes for a long moment. "You've learned to hide yourself away from the world so that you won't get hurt. You draw back from emotion, from involvement. Even today you were thinking of ways to keep Sarah from having any time with you. That's the whole point of this trip to the library. Your damned research could have been anytime, but you preferred not to be around while Sarah and I were at Bess's house."

"All right, maybe I did!" she said, goaded into telling the truth. "Sarah is a sweet child, and I could love her, but I don't want to have to look at you, much less be dragged up to that house when you're there. Mars wouldn't be far enough away from you to suit me!"

He was grateful that he'd learned to keep a poker face. She couldn't have known how those words hurt him. She had every reason to want to avoid him, to hate him. But he didn't want to avoid her, and hatred was the last emotion he felt for her now.

"So Sarah's going to have to pay because you don't want to be around me," he replied.

She glared at him. "Oh, no, you don't," she said. "You aren't laying any guilt trips on me. Sarah has you and Mrs. Jackson—"

"Sarah doesn't like me and Mrs. Jackson," he interrupted. "She likes you. She's done nothing but talk about you."

She turned away. "I can't," she said huskily.

"She could have been our child," he said unexpectedly. "Yours and mine. And that's what's eating you alive, isn't it?"

She couldn't believe he'd said that. She looked back at him with tears welling in her gray eyes, blinding her. "Damn you!"

"I saw it in your face this morning when you looked at her," he went on relentlessly, driven to make her admit it. "It isn't fear of me that's stopping you—it's fear of admitting that Sarah reminds you too painfully of what you wanted and couldn't have."

She cried out as if he'd slapped her. She pushed the door open and ran toward the library, almost stumbling in her haste to get away from him. She made it to the lobby and stood there shaking, grateful that the librarian was away from the desk as she tried to get her composure back. She fumbled a handkerchief out of her purse and wiped her eyes. Blake was right. She was avoiding Sarah Jane because of the pain the child caused her. But knowing the truth didn't help. It only made things worse that he should be perceptive enough to sense what she was thinking.

She put the handkerchief away and went back to the reading room to pore over volumes on southwestern history. She didn't know how she was going to get back home. Blake would have gone and she'd just have to call Elissa or Bess.

An hour later, calmer and less flustered, she put the notebook she'd been scribbling in back in her purse, returned the reference books to the shelf and walked outside to find a public telephone.

Blake was there, leaning comfortably against the wall, waiting.

"Are you ready to go?" he asked pleasantly as if nothing at all had happened.

She stared at him. "I thought you'd gone."

His broad shoulders rose and fell. "It's Saturday," he said. "I don't usually work on Saturday unless I have to." His eyes narrowed as he searched her face. "Are you all right?" he added quietly.

She nodded, her eyes avoiding him.

"I won't do that again, Meredith," he said deeply. "I didn't mean to upset you. Let's go."

She sat rigidly beside him on the ride home, afraid that he might start on her again despite what he'd said. But he didn't. He turned on the radio and kept it playing until he pulled into Bess's driveway again.

"You don't have to worry," he said before she got out of the car, and there was a resigned expression on his face. "I won't try to force you into a relationship with Sarah. She's my responsibility, not yours."

And that was that. Meredith went back into the house, and after he'd explained to Elissa and Bess that they could call him when Sarah was ready to come home, he drove off.

He didn't know what he was going to do as he drove away. He hadn't expected Meredith to react like that to his words. What he'd said had only been a shot in the dark, but he'd scored a hit. Sarah disturbed her. The child reminded her of Blake's cruelty, and Meredith was going to keep Sarah at a distance no matter what it took.

That was going to be sad for both of them. Meredith had grown cold and self-contained. She could use a child's magic to bring her back into the sunlight. Sarah likewise would profit from Meredith's tenderness. But it wasn't going to happen and he had to face it. He'd hoped that he might reach Meredith again through Sarah, but she wanted no part of him. She hated him.

He went back to the house and locked himself in his study with his paperwork, forcing his mind not to dwell on Meredith's anger. He had no one to blame but himself. And only time would tell if she could ever forgive him.

LATER THAT AFTERNOON, Meredith sat with Bess and Elissa and watched the little girls play.

"Isn't she the image of Blake?" Elissa smiled as she watched Sarah. "I guess it's hard for him, trying to raise a child on his own."

"He needs to marry again," Bess agreed.

"Well, he's rich enough to attract a wife," Meredith replied with cool disinterest.

"Another Nina would be the end of him," Elissa said. "And think of Sarah. She needs to be loved, not pushed aside. She looks as if she's never really been loved."

"She won't be with Blake," Meredith said. "He isn't a loving man."

Elissa looked at her curiously. "Considering his life so far, is that surprising? He's never been loved, has he? Even his uncle manipulated him, used him for the good of the real estate corporation. Blake has been an outsider looking in. He hasn't known how to love. Maybe Sarah will teach him. She's not the little terror she makes out to be. There's an odd softness about her, especially when she talks to Blake. And have you noticed how unselfish she is?" she added. "She hasn't fought with Dani or tried to take her toys away or break them. She's not what she seems."

"I noticed that, too," Meredith said reluctantly. She looked at the child who was so much like Blake and so little like her beautiful blond mother. Her heart ached at the sight of the little girl who could have been her own. If only Blake could have loved her. She smiled sadly. Oh, if only.

Sarah seemed to feel that scrutiny, because she got up and went to Meredith, her curious eyes searching the woman's. "Can you write a book about a little girl and she can have a daddy and mommy to love her?" she asked. "And it could have a pony in it, and lots of dolls like Dani has."

Meredith touched the small, dark head gently. "I might do that," she said, smiling involuntarily.

Sarah smiled back. "I like you, Merry."

She went back to play with Danielle, leaving a hopelessly touched Meredith staring hungrily at her. Tears stung her eyes.

"Merry, could you watch the girls for a bit while Elissa and I run down to the ice cream shop and get some cones for them?" Bess asked with a quickly concealed conspiratorial wink at Elissa.

"Of course," Meredith agreed.

"We won't be a minute," Bess promised. "Do you want a cone?"

"Yes, please. Chocolate." Meredith grinned.

"I want chocolate, too," Sarah pleaded. "A big one."

"I want vanilla," Danielle said.

"Forty-eight flavors, and we live with purists." Bess sighed, shaking her head. "Okay, chocolate and vanilla it is. Won't be a minute!"

Of course it was more than a minute. They were gone for almost an hour, and when they got back, Meredith was sitting in the middle of the carpet with Sarah and Danielle, helping them dress one of Danielle's dolls. Sarah was sitting as close as she could get to Meredith, and her young face was for once without its customary sulky look. She was laughing, and almost pretty.

The ice cream was passed out and another hour went by before Elissa said reluctantly that she and Danielle would have to go.

"I hate to, but King's bringing one of his business associates home for supper, and I have to get Danielle's bath and have her in bed by the time they get home," Elissa said. "But we'll have to do this again."

"Do you have to go?" Sarah asked Danielle sadly. "I wish you could come live with me, and we could be sisters."

"Me, too," Danielle said.

"I like your toys. I guess your mommy and daddy like you a lot."

"Your daddy likes you, too, Sarah," Meredith said gently, taking the child's hand in hers. "He just didn't know that you wanted toys. He'll buy you some of your own."

"Will he, truly?" Sarah asked her, all eyes.

"Truly," she replied, hoping she was right. The Blake she'd known in the past wouldn't have cared overmuch about a child's needs. Of course, the man she'd glimpsed today might. She could hardly reconcile what she knew about him with what she was learning about him.

"That's right," Bess agreed, smiling down at Sarah. "Your dad's a pretty nice guy. We all like him, don't we, Meredith?"

Meredith glared at her. "Oh, we surely do," she said through her teeth. "He's a prince."

Which was what Sarah Jane told her daddy that very night over the supper table. He'd picked her up at Bess's house, but Meredith's car was gone. She was avoiding him, he supposed wearily, and he listened halfheartedly to Sarah all the way home. Now she was telling him about the wonderful time she'd had playing dolls with Meredith, and he turned his attention from business problems to stare at her blankly as what she was saying began to register.

"She did *what*?" he asked.

"She played dolls with me," she said, "and she says you're a prince. Does that mean you used to be a frog, Daddy?" Sarah added. "Because the princess kisses the frog and he turns into a prince. Did my mommy kiss you?"

"Occasionally, and no, I wasn't a frog. Meredith played dolls with you?" he asked, feeling a tiny glow deep inside himself.

"She really did." Sarah sighed. "I like Mer'dith. I wish she was my mommy. Can't she come to live with us?"

He couldn't explain that very easily. "No," he said simply. "You'd better get ready for bed."

"But, Daddy..." she moaned.

"Go on. No arguments."

"All right," she grumbled. But she went.

He looked after her, smiling faintly. She was a handful, but she was slowly growing on him.

He stayed home on Sunday and took Sarah Jane out to see the horses grazing in the pasture. One of the men, a grizzled old wrangler named Manolo, was working a gelding in the corral, breaking him slowly and gently to the saddle. Blake had complained that Manolo took too long to break horses, especially when he was doing it for the remuda in spring before roundup. The cowhands had to have a string of horses when they started working cattle. But Manolo used his own methods, despite the boss's arguments. No way, he informed Blake, was he going to mistreat a horse just to break it to saddle, and if Blake didn't like that, he could fire him.

Blake hadn't said another word about it. The horses Manolo broke were always gentle and easily managed.

But this horse was giving the old man a lot of trouble. It pranced and reared, and Blake was watching it instead of Sarah Jane when the lacy handkerchief Meredith had given her blew into the corral.

Like a shot, she climbed through the fence to go after it, just as the horse broke away from Manalo and came snorting and bucking in her direction.

Blake saw her and blinked, not believing what his eyes were telling him. All at once he was over the fence, just as Manalo yelled.

Sarah was holding her handkerchief, staring dumbly at the approaching horse.

Blake grabbed her and sent her through the fence, following her with an economy of motion. He thanked God for his own strength as it prevented what would have been a total disaster.

Sarah Jane clung to his neck tightly, crying with great sobs.

He hugged her to him, his eyes closed, a shudder running through his lean, fit body. Another few seconds and it would have been all over. Sarah would have become a tragic memory. It didn't bear thinking about. Worse than that, it brought back an older memory, of another incident with a bronc. He touched his lean cheek where the scar cut across his tan. How many years ago had it been that he'd saved Meredith just as he'd saved Sarah? A long time ago—long before the sight of her began to make him ache.

The fear he'd experienced, added to the unwanted memories, made him furious. He let go of Sarah and held her in front of him, his green eyes glittering with rage.

"Don't you know better than to go into the corral

with a wild animal?" he snapped. "Where's your mind, Sarah?"

She stared at him as if he'd slapped her. Her lower lip trembled. "I had to get my…my hankie, Daddy." She held it up. "See? My pretty hankie that Mer'dith gave me…"

He shook her. "The next time you go near any enclosure with horses or cattle in it, you stay out! Do you understand me?" he asked in a tone that made her small body jerk with a sob. "You could have been killed!"

"I'm so—sorry," she faltered.

"You should be!" he jerked out. "Now get in the house."

She started crying, frightened by the way he looked. "You hate me," she whimpered. "I know you do. You yelled at me. You're mean and ugly…and… I don't like you!"

"I don't like you, either, at the moment," he bit off, glaring down at her, his legs still shaking from the exertion and fear. "Now get going."

"You mean old daddy!" she cried. She turned and ran wildly for the house as Blake stared after her in a blind rage.

"Is she all right, boss?" Manolo asked from the fence. "My God, that was quick! I didn't even see her!"

"Neither did I," Blake confessed. "Not until it was damned near too late." He let out a rough sigh. "I didn't mean to be so hard on her, but she's got to learn that horses and cattle are dangerous. I wanted to make sure she remembered this."

"She'll remember," Manolo said ruefully, and turned

away before the boss could see the look on his face. Poor little kid. She needed hugging, not yelling.

Blake went in the house a few minutes later and looked for Sarah, but she was nowhere in sight. Mrs. Jackson had heard her come in, but she hadn't seen her because she was working in the front of the house.

He checked Sarah's bedroom, but she wasn't there, either. Then he remembered what she'd said about being locked in the closet when she was bad…

He jerked open the closet door and there she sat, her face red and tear stained, sobbing and looking as if she hadn't a friend in the world.

"Go away," she sniffed.

He got down awkwardly on one knee. "You'll suffocate in here."

"I hate you."

"I don't want anything to happen to you," he said. "The horse could have hurt you very badly."

She touched the dusty lace handkerchief to her red eyes. "You yelled at me."

He grimaced. "You scared me," he muttered, averting his gaze. "I never thought I'd get to you in time."

She sniffed and got up on her knees under the hanging dresses and blouses and slacks. "You didn't want me to get hurt?"

"Of course I didn't want you to get hurt," he snapped, green eyes flashing.

"You're yelling at me again," she said, pouting.

He sighed angrily. "Well, I've been doing it for a lot of years, and I won't change. You'll just have to get used to my temper." He stared at her half-angrily. "I thought

I was getting the hang of it, and you had to go crawl in with a bucking bronco and set me back."

"Everybody used to yell at me," she told him solemnly. "But they didn't do it just if I got hurt. They didn't like me."

"I like you. That's why I yelled," he muttered.

She smiled through her tears. "Really and truly?"

He grimaced. "Really and truly." He got up. "Come out of there."

"Are you going to spank me?" she asked.

"No."

"I won't do it again."

"You'd better not." He took her hand and led her downstairs. When Mrs. Jackson found out what had happened, she took a fresh coconut cake out of the pantry, sliced it up and poured Sarah a soft drink. She even smiled. Sarah dried her eyes and smiled back.

On Monday Blake took two hours off at lunch and went to a toy store. He bought an armful of dolls and assorted girlish toys and took them to the house without fully understanding his motives. Maybe it was relief that Sarah was all right or guilt because he'd hurt her.

But she sat down in the living room with her new friends—which included a huge stuffed teddy bear—and the way she handled her toys was enough to bring a tear to the eye. She hugged the teddy bear, then she hugged Blake, who was half delighted and half embarrassed by her exuberance.

"You're just the nicest daddy in the whole world," Sarah Jane said, and she was crying again. She wiped her eyes with her hands. "I have a new Mr. Friend now, and he can help you fight monsters."

"I'll keep that in mind. Behave yourself." He went out the door quickly, more moved than he wanted to admit by his daughter's reception to the impromptu toy surprise.

On the way back to work, he remembered what Sarah had said about Meredith playing dolls with her. Meredith had been trying to keep Sarah at arms' length, so he wondered at her actions. Had he been wrong about Meredith's motives? Had he misjudged what he thought was her reason for avoiding Sarah?

He remembered all too well the feel of Meredith's soft, innocent mouth under his that day in the stable, the wonder in her eyes when he'd lifted his head just briefly to look down at her. And then he'd lost control and frightened her, turning the wonder to panic.

That she'd loved him didn't bear thinking about. At least he and Sarah were closer than ever. But she needed more than a father. Sarah needed a mother. Someone to read her stories, to play with her. Someone like Meredith. It made him feel warm to think of Meredith doing those things with his daughter. In time she might even get over the past and start looking ahead. She might fall in love with him all over again.

His body reacted feverishly to that thought, and as quickly his mind rejected it. He didn't want her to love him. He felt guilt for the way he'd treated her and he still wanted her, but *love* wasn't a word in his vocabulary anymore. It hurt too much.

Letting her get close would be risky. Meredith had

every reason in the world to want to get even with him. He scowled. Would Meredith want revenge if he could bring himself to tell her the truth about why he'd been so rough with her?

Not that *he* needed her, he assured himself. It was only that Sarah liked her and needed her. But Meredith wouldn't come to the house. She wasn't going to let him, or Sarah, get close to her, and that was the big hurdle. How, he wondered, could he overcome it?

He worried the thought for two days and still hadn't figured out a solution, when he had to fly to Dallas on business for the day. But fate was on his side.

While he was gone, Mrs. Jackson's only living sister had a heart attack and a neighbor called asking Amie to come to Wichita, Kansas, and help look after her. That left Mrs. Jackson with nobody to look after Sarah. She couldn't take the child with her while she tried to care for a heart patient. She called Elissa, but she and her husband and child were out of town. Bess wouldn't be able to cope with the angry little girl. That left only one person in Jack's Corner who might be willing to try.

Without hesitation, Mrs. Jackson picked up the phone and called Meredith Calhoun.

CHAPTER FIVE

SARAH JANE WAS almost dancing with pleasure when Meredith came in the door. She ran to her, arms outstretched, and Meredith instinctively picked her up and hugged her warmly. Maternal instincts she hadn't indulged since Blake had sent her running came to the fore, making her soft.

"Now don't you give Meredith any trouble, young lady," Mrs. Jackson cautioned Sarah Jane. "Meredith, this is my sister's phone number, but I'll call as soon as I know something and tell Mr. Blake what's going on. I hope he won't mind."

"You know very well he won't," Meredith said. "I'm sorry about your sister, but I'm sure she'll be all right."

"Well, we can hope, anyway," Mrs. Jackson said, forcing a smile. "There's my cab. I'll be back as soon as I can."

"Bye, Mrs. Jackson," Sarah called.

She turned at the door and smiled at the little girl. "Goodbye, Sarah. I'll miss you. Thanks again, Merry."

"No problem," Meredith said as the housekeeper left.

"We can play dolls now, Merry," Sarah said enthusiastically, repeating the nickname she'd heard for Meredith as she struggled to be put down. She then led

Meredith by the hand into the living room. "Look what my daddy bought me!"

Meredith was pleasantly surprised by the array of dolls. There must have been two dozen of them, surrounding a huge, whimsical tan teddy bear who was wearing one of Blake's Stetsons on his shaggy head.

"He's supposed to be my daddy," Meredith said, pointing to the bear, "since my daddy's away. But actually he's Mr. Friend. My old Mr. Friend got lost, so Daddy bought me a new one."

Meredith sat down on the sofa, smiling as Sarah introduced every one of her new toys to her older friend.

"I dropped the pretty hankie you gave me inside the fence," Sarah explained excitedly, "and a big horse almost ran over me, but my daddy saved me. He yelled at me and I cried and hid in the closet, and he came to find me. He said I mustn't *ever* do it again because he liked me." She laughed. "And then he went to the store and brought me ever so many toys."

Meredith was feeling cold chills at the innocent story. She could imagine how Blake had felt, the fear that had gripped him. She remembered so well the day he'd had to rescue her from a wild horse. She wondered if it had brought back memories for him, too.

Sarah looked up at Meredith. "My daddy has an *awful* temper, Merry."

Meredith knew that already. She remembered his temper very well. A lot of things could spark it, but embarrassment, fear, or any kind of threat were sure to ignite it. She could imagine how frightened Sarah had been of him, but apparently toys could buy forgiveness.

She chided herself for that thought. Blake could be unexpectedly kind. It was just that he seemed so cold and
self-contained. She wondered if Nina had ever really
touched him during their brief marriage, and decided
that it was unlikely.

Meredith got down on the floor with Sarah, grateful,
as they sprawled on the carpet, that she'd worn jeans
and a yellow blouse instead of a dress. She and Sarah
dressed dolls and talked for a long time before Meredith got the small girl ready for bed, tucked her in and
helped her say her prayers.

"Why do I have to say prayers?" Sarah asked.

"To thank God for all the nice things He does for
us." Meredith smiled.

"Daddy talks to God all the time," Sarah said. "Especially when I turn things over or get hurt—"

Meredith fought to keep her expression steady.
"That's not what I meant, darling. Now you settle down
and we'll talk."

"Okay, Merry." She moved her dark head on the pillow. "Merry, do you like me?"

Meredith looked down at the child she might have
had. She smiled sadly, touching Sarah's dark hair gently.
"Yes, I like you very much, Sarah Jane Donavan," she
replied, smiling.

"I like you, too."

Meredith bent and kissed the clean, shiny face.
"Would you like me to read you a story? Have you
any books?"

The small face fell. "No. Daddy forgot."

"That's all right, then. I can think of one or two." She

sat down on Sarah's bed and proceeded to go through several, doing all the parts in different pitches of her voice, while Sarah giggled.

She was just in the middle of "The Three Bears," doing Baby Bear's voice when Sarah sat up, smiling from ear to ear and cried, "Daddy!"

Meredith felt her face burn, her heart start to pound, as he came into the room, dressed in a gray business suit, sparing her a curious glance as he handed something to Sarah.

"Something from Dallas," he told the child. "It's a puppet."

"I love him, Daddy!"

It was a duck puppet, yellow and white, and Sarah wiggled it on her hand while Blake turned to Meredith with a cool smile.

"Where's Amie?" he asked.

She told him, adding that Amie had promised to phone as soon as she knew something. "She couldn't get Elissa, and there wasn't anyone else, so she asked me."

"We had lots of fun, Daddy!" Sarah told him. "Merry and me played dolls and watched TV together!"

"Thank you for taking the time," Blake said, his whole attitude antagonistic. He'd done nothing but think about the irritating woman for days. And there she sat, looking as cool as a cucumber without a hint of warmth in her cold gray eyes, while his body had gone taut and started throbbing at the very sight of her.

Meredith got to her feet, avoiding him. "I didn't mind. Good night, Sarah," she said, running a nervous hand through her loosened dark hair to get it out of her face.

"Good night, Merry. Will you come back to see me again?"

"When I can, darling," she replied absently, without noticing the reaction that endearment had on Blake. "Sleep tight."

"Go to sleep now, young lady," Blake told his daughter.

"But, Daddy, what about the monsters?" Sarah wailed when he started to turn out the light at the door.

He stopped and looked uncomfortable. He wasn't about to start chasing monsters from under the bed and dragging them out of the closet in front of Meredith. Sarah loved the pretend housecleaning and he'd grown used to doing it to amuse her, but a man had to have his secrets. He cleared his throat. "When I walk Meredith to her car, okay?"

That pacified Sarah. She smiled. "Okay, Daddy." She looked at Meredith. "He kills the monsters every night so they won't hurt me. He's very brave and he weighs one million pounds!"

Meredith glanced at Blake and her face went red as she tried to smother laughter. He glared at her, breaking the spell. She rushed out into the hall and kept going.

He caught up with her downstairs and walked her out onto the porch.

"I'm sorry Amie involved you," he said curtly. "Bess would have kept Sarah."

"Bess and Bobby were going out," she replied. "I didn't mind."

"You didn't want to come here, though, even while I was away," he said perceptively. "You don't care for this house very much, do you?"

"Not anymore," she said. "It brings back some painful memories." She moved away from him, but he followed.

"Where's your car?" he asked, searching for it.

"I walked. It was a beautiful night and it's only a short walk."

He glared down at her from his superior height. In his gray suit and pearl-colored Stetson, he looked enormously tall and imposing. He never seemed to smile, she thought, searching his hard features in the light that shone from the windows onto the big, long porch.

"If you're looking for beauty, you won't find it," he said, his mouth twisting into a mocking smile. "The scar only makes it worse."

She gazed at it, the long white line that marred his lean cheek all the way from his high cheekbone to his jaw. "I remember when you got it," she said quietly. "And how."

His expression became grim. "I don't want to talk about it."

"I know." She sighed gently, her eyes searching over his dark face with more poignancy than she knew. "But you were always handsome to me, scar and all," she mused, turning away as the memories came flooding back. "Good night… Blake!"

He'd whipped her around, his lean hands biting into her arms. She was wearing a sleeveless lemon yellow blouse with her jeans, and it made her skin look darker than it was. Where his fingers held her, the flesh went white from the pressure.

"I…" He eased his hold a little, although he didn't release her. "I didn't mean to do that." He drew in a silent breath. "I don't suppose you'll ever get over the fear I caused you in the past, will you?" he added, watching her eyes widen, her body stiffen.

"It was my first intimacy," she whispered, flushing.

"I remember," he replied. His pride fought him when he tried to tell her the truth, although he wanted to. He wanted to make her understand his roughness.

"As you said, it was a long time ago," she added, pulling against his hold gently.

"Not that long. Five years." He searched her eyes. "Meredith, surely you've dated men. There must have been one or two who could stir you."

"I couldn't trust them," she said bitterly. "I was afraid to take a chance with anyone else."

"Most men aren't as rough as I am," he replied coldly.

Her breath was sighing out like a whisper. He made her nervous, and the feel of his hands was affecting her breathing. "Most men aren't as much a man as you are," she breathed, closing her eyes as forgotten sensations worked down her spine and made her ache.

His pride burned with what she'd said. Did she think him masculine, handsome? Or was that all in the past, part of the love he'd killed?

He drew her closer and held her against him warmly but chastely, her legs apart from his. He didn't want her to feel how aroused he already was.

"I'm not much gentler now than I used to be, Meredith," he said deeply, as his head bent toward her. "But I'll try not to frighten you this time…"

She opened her mouth to protest, but his lips met hers. They probed her soft mouth while his lean, strong hands slid up to frame her face.

She stiffened, but only for a minute. The taste of him made her dizzy with pleasure. She liked what he was doing to her too much to protest. After a minute she relaxed, letting his mouth do what it wanted to hers.

"God, it's sweet," he whispered roughly, biting at her lips with more instinct than expertise. His voice was shaking and he didn't care if she heard it. "Oh, God, it's so sweet!"

His mouth ground into hers and his arms slid completely around her. He pulled her body up against his so that his legs touched hers, and he felt her sudden shocked tautness.

He let her move away, his eyes glittering, his breath rustling out of his throat. "I shouldn't have done that," he said gruffly. "I didn't mean to let you feel how aroused I was."

Having him mention it shocked her more than the feel of his body, but she tried not to let him see her reaction. She stepped back, touching her mouth with light fingers. Yes, it had been sweet, as she'd heard him whisper feverishly. Just as it had been five years ago in the stable, when he'd put his mouth on hers and she'd ached to have him touch her.

"I have to get back to Bess's house," she said unsteadily.

"Just a minute." He took her hand and pulled her farther into the light. He held her gaze so that he could see the fear mingled with desire that lingered in her eyes, the swollen softness of her mouth.

"What are you looking for?" she asked huskily.

"You're still afraid of me," he said, his jaw going taut.

"I'm sorry." She lowered her eyes to his chest, to its quick, hard rise and fall. "I can't help it."

"Neither can I," he replied bitterly. He let her go, turning away. "I'm not much good at lovemaking, if you want the truth," he said through his teeth.

That was true. He had the patience, but not the knowledge. Nina had taught him a few things, but she'd been indifferent to his touch and her response to him had always been just lukewarm. She hadn't known he was innocent, but she had known he was inexperienced, and at the end of their relationship she'd taunted him with his lack of expertise. It was one of the things he hated remembering. Better to let Meredith think he was brutal than to have her know how green he was.

Watching him, Meredith was surprised by the admission. She'd always considered him experienced. If he wasn't, it would explain so much.

Suddenly, she understood his fierce pride a little better. She went closer to him, reaching out to lightly touch his sleeve. He jerked a little, as if that impersonal contact went through him like fire.

"It's all right, Blake," she said hesitantly.

He looked down at the slender hand that rested lightly on his sleeve. "I'm like a bull in a china shop," he said unexpectedly, looking into her eyes. "With women."

She felt a surge of emotion at that rough admission.

He'd never been more approachable than he was right now. Part of her was wary of him, but another part wanted once, just once, to give in without a fight.

She went up on her tiptoes and pulled his head down to hers. He stiffened and she stopped dead.

"No!" he whispered huskily when she started to draw back in embarrassment. "Go ahead. Do what you want to."

She couldn't believe that he really wanted her to kiss him, but he was giving every indication that he did. She didn't know a lot about it, either, since all she'd ever done with men was kissing.

She drew her lips lightly over Blake's hard ones, teasing them gently. Her breath shook at his mouth while she held his head within reach, but she didn't relent. Her fingers slid into the thick, cool hair at the nape of his strong neck and her nails slid against his skin while her mouth toyed softly with his.

"I can't take much of that," he whispered roughly. His hands held her hips now, an intimacy that she should have protested, but she was too weak. "Do it properly."

"Not yet," she whispered. Her teeth closed softly on his lower lip, tugging at it sensuously. She felt him tremble as her tongue traced his upper lip.

"Meredith," he bit off, and his hands hurt her for an instant.

"All right." She knew what he wanted, what he needed. She opened her mouth on his and slid her tongue inside it, and the reaction she got from him was electrifying.

He cried out. His arms swallowed her, bruising her

against his hard chest. He was trembling. Meredith felt the soft tremors with exquisite awareness, with pride that she could arouse him that easily after a beauty like Nina.

"Blake," she whispered under his mouth, and closed her eyes as she gave him the weight of her body, the warmth of her mouth.

She felt him move. Her back was suddenly against the wall and he was easing down over her body.

Her eyes flew open and his head lifted fractionally, and all the while his body overwhelmed hers, his hips lying heavy and hard against hers, pressing against her.

She could feel the full strength of his arousal now, and it should have frightened her, but it didn't. He was slow and gentle, not impatient at all as his hands slid to her hips, holding her.

"This should really frighten the hell out of you, shouldn't it?" he asked huskily, searching her eyes. "You can feel what I want, and I'm not quite in control right now."

"You aren't hurting me," she whispered. "And I started it this time."

"So you did." He moved down, letting his mouth repeat the soft, arousing movements hers had made earlier. "Like that, Meredith?" he whispered at her lips. "Is that how you like it?"

"Yes," she whispered back, excitement making her voice husky. Her hands were against his shirt and she could feel the heat from his body under the fabric.

"I want to open my shirt and let you touch me," he whispered roughly. "But that might be the straw that breaks the camel's back, and there's a long, comfortable sofa just a few feet inside the door."

The thought was more than tempting. She could already feel his skin against hers, his body overwhelming hers. She wanted him, and there wasn't really any reason to say no. Except that her pride couldn't take the knowledge that he wanted only her body and nothing else about her.

"I can't sleep with you," she said miserably. She let her head rest against him, drowning in the feel of his body over hers. "Blake, you have to stop," she groaned. "I'm going crazy...!"

"So am I." He pushed himself away from her, breathing roughly. His darkened green eyes looked down into hers. "You wanted me," he said, as if he were only just realizing it.

She flushed and looked up at his hard face. "I don't understand what you want from me."

"Sarah needs a woman's companionship," he said tersely.

"That isn't why you made love to me," she returned, searching his eyes.

He sighed deeply. "No, it isn't." He walked to the edge of the porch and leaned against one of the white columns, looking out over the wide expanse of flat land. The only trees were right around the house, where they'd been planted. Beyond was open land, dotted with a few willows at the creek and a few straggly bushes, but mostly flat and barren all the way to the horizon.

"Why, Blake?" she asked. She had to know what he was after.

"Do you know what an obsession is, Meredith?" he asked a minute later.

"Yes, I think so."

"Well, that's what I feel for you." He shifted so that he could see her. "Obsessed," he repeated, letting his green eyes slide over her sensually. "I don't know why. You aren't beautiful. You aren't even voluptuous. But you arouse me as no other woman ever has or ever will. I couldn't even feel for Nina what I feel for you." He laughed coldly. "After she left me, there wasn't anyone else. I couldn't. I don't want anyone but you."

She didn't know if she was still breathing. The admission knocked the wind out of her, took the strength from her legs. She looked at him helplessly.

"You haven't…seen me in five years," she said, trying to rationalize.

"I've seen you every night," he ground out. "Every time I closed my eyes. My God, don't you remember what I did to you that day in the stable? I stripped you…" He closed his eyes, oblivious to her scarlet face and trembling body. "I looked at you and touched you and put my mouth on you." He bit back a curse and opened his eyes again, tormented. "I see you in my bed every damned night of my life," he breathed. "I want you to the point of madness."

She caught the railing and held on tight. She couldn't believe what she was hearing. It wasn't possible for a man to feel that kind of desire, she told herself. Not when he didn't feel anything emotional for the woman. But Blake was different. As Elissa said, he'd never been loved, so he didn't know what it was. But all men felt desire. A man didn't have to love to want.

"Don't worry—" he laughed mockingly "—I'm not going to force you into anything. I just wanted you to know how I felt. If that sensuous little kiss was some sort of game, you'd better know how dangerous it is. I'm not sane when I touch you. I wouldn't hurt you deliberately for the world, but I want you like hell."

Her swollen lips parted. "I wasn't playing," she said with quiet pride. "It was no game. You…" She hesitated. "You seemed so disturbed because you'd been rough. I wanted to show you that you hadn't made me afraid."

He watched her unblinkingly. "You weren't, were you?" he said then, scowling. "Not even when I brought you close and let you feel what you were doing to me."

She shifted. "You shouldn't have," she murmured evasively.

"Why hide it?" he asked. He moved toward her, encouraged by her response and her lack of bitterness. He was taking a hell of a chance by being honest with her, but it might be his only way of reaching her. "You might as well know it all."

She lifted her face as he stood over her. "Know what?"

"Nina was my first woman," he said bluntly. "And the only woman."

She wanted to sit down, but there was no chair. She leaned against the banister, her eyes searching his hard face. He wasn't kidding. He meant it.

"That's right," he said, nodding when he saw the memories replaying in her eyes. "The day we were in the stable together, I was as inexperienced as you were. That's why I was rough. It wasn't deliberate. I didn't know how to make love."

Her lips opened on a slow breath. "No wonder..." she whispered.

"Yes, no wonder." He brushed a strand of loosened hair from her pale cheek. "Why don't you laugh? Nina did."

She could feel the hurt under that mocking statement. What it must have done to his pride! "Nina was a—" She bit back the word.

He laughed coldly. "She certainly was," he agreed. "She taunted me with it toward the end," he added, his eyes bitter and cynical. "I didn't want to risk that kind of ridicule again, so there weren't any more women."

"Oh, Blake," she whispered, closing her eyes on a wave of pain. "Blake, I'm so sorry!"

"I don't want pity. I wanted you to know the truth. If you're ever tempted to give in to me, you're entitled to know what you'd be up against. My God," he said heavily, moving away, "I don't even know the basics. Books and movies don't make up for experience. And Nina wasn't interested in tutoring me."

"I wish I'd known," she said huskily. "I wish I'd known five years ago."

He looked back at her, his thick eyebrows raised. "Why?"

"I wouldn't have fought you," she said simply. "I thought you were terribly experienced." She lowered her eyes. "I'm sorry. I guess I hurt your ego as much as you frightened me."

He studied her in a tense silence. "You don't have a thing to apologize for. I'm the one who's sorry." He waited until she lifted her head, and he caught her eyes and held them. "You haven't wanted anyone, in all this time?"

"I wanted you," she said frankly. "I...couldn't feel that for anyone else. I'd rather have been frightened by you than pleasured by the greatest lover living." She laughed coldly. "So I guess I'm in the same boat that you are." She clutched her purse. "I really do have to go," she said after a long, quiet moment during which he stared at her without saying anything at all.

He escorted her down the porch steps. "All right. I'll walk you to the woods and watch you through them. Sarah Jane will be all right until I get back, and the house is in full view the whole way."

"Sarah is very much like you," she said.

"Too much like me," he replied. His fingers brushed hers as they walked, accidentally or deliberately she didn't know, making her all too aware of him. "She almost got trampled the other day, climbing into the corral to retrieve a handkerchief."

"She told me. I suppose you were livid."

"Mild word," he said. "I blew up. Scared her. I found her hiding in the closet, and I felt like a dog. I went to town the next day and bought her half a toy store to make up for yelling at her." He sighed. "She scared me blind. I kept thinking what could have happened if my reflexes had been just a bit slower."

"But they weren't." She smiled. "You were always quick in an emergency."

He looked down at her and his fingers lazily entangled themselves in hers. "Luckily for you," he murmured darkly, watching her flush. "I haven't had an easy life," he said then. "I had to be tough to survive. They weren't good days before I came here to live with my uncle. I got in a lot of fights because of my illegitimacy."

"I never heard you talk about that," she said.

"I never could." His fingers tightened in hers as they got to the small wooded area and stopped. "I can't talk about a lot of things, Meredith. Maybe that's why I'm so damned alone."

She glanced toward Bess's house. Bess and Bobby must have come home, because their car was in the driveway next to hers. She hesitated, not eager to leave Blake in this oddly talkative mood. "You've got Sarah now," she reminded him gently.

"Sarah is getting to me," he confessed ruefully. "God, I don't know what I'd do if I could sit down in a chair without crushing a stuffed toy, or go to bed without running monsters out of closets." He smiled mockingly. "It cut me to pieces when she started crying after I raged at her about getting in with the horse."

"She doesn't seem that sensitive at first glance, but she is," she replied. "I noticed it that first day, at the children's shop, and again when she played with Danielle. I gather she was neglected a lot before they sent her to you."

"I got the same feeling. She had a nightmare just after she came here," he recalled quietly. "She woke up in the early hours, screaming her head off, and when I asked what was the matter, she said they wouldn't let her out of the closet." His face hardened, and for an instant he looked relentless. "I've still got half a mind to send my lawyers after that housekeeper."

"A woman that cruel will make her own hell," Meredith said. "Mean people don't get away with anything, Blake. It may seem that they do, but in the end their meanness ricochets back at them."

"The way mine did at me?" he asked with a mirthless laugh. "I scarred you and pushed you out of my life, married Nina, and settled down to what I thought would be wedded bliss. And look where it got me."

"You've got everything," she corrected. "Money, power, position, a sweet little girl."

"I've got nothing except Sarah," he said shortly. His green eyes glittered in the faint light. "I thought I needed money and power to make people accept me. But I'm no more socially acceptable now than I was when I was poor and illegitimate. I've just got more money."

"Acceptance doesn't have anything to do with money." She stared down at the big, warm hand clasping hers. "You're not the world's most sociable man. You keep to yourself and you don't smile very much. You intimidate people." She smiled gently, her eyes almost loving despite her reluctance to give herself away. "That's why you don't get a lot of social invitations. This isn't the Dark Ages. People don't hold the circumstances of their birth against each other anymore. It's a much more open society than it was."

"It stinks," he returned coldly. "Women proposition-ing men, kids neglected and abused and cast off…"

"They don't burn witches anymore, though," she whispered conspiratorially, going up on tiptoe. "And the stocks have been eliminated, too."

His face cracked into a reluctant smile. "Okay. You've got a point."

"Who propositioned you?" she added.

He cocked his head a little to study her. "A woman at the workshop in Dallas I just came back from. I didn't believe she meant it until she put her room key in an ashtray beside my coffee cup."

"What did you do?" she asked, because she had to know.

He smiled faintly. "Took it out and handed it back." He touched her cheek gently, running a lean finger down it. "I told you on the porch. I don't want anyone but you."

She lowered her eyes to his chest. "I can't, Blake."

"I'm not asking you to." He let go of the hand he was holding. "I'm archaic in my notions, in case it's escaped your notice. I don't seduce virgins."

Her body tingled at the thought of making love with Blake. It was exciting and surprising to know how much he wanted her. But her own conscience wasn't going to let her give in, and he knew that, too.

"I guess you'd rather I got my autographing over and left town…" she began.

He tilted her chin up so he could see her face. "Sarah and I are going on a picnic Saturday. You can come."

The suddenness of the invitation made her blink. "Saturday?"

"We'll pick you up at nine. You can wear jeans. I'm going to."

Her eyes lifted to his. "Blake..."

"I like having things out in the open, so there aren't any more misunderstandings," he said simply. "I want you. You want me. But that's as far as it goes, and there won't be any more of what happened on my porch tonight. I'll keep my hands off and we'll give Sarah a good time. Sarah likes you," he added quietly. "I think you like her, too. She could use a few good memories before you go back to the life you left in San Antonio."

So he was going to freeze her out. He wanted her, but he wasn't going to do anything about it. He wanted her for Sarah, not for himself, despite his hunger for her.

She hesitated. "Is it wise letting her get used to me?" she asked, her voice echoing the disappointment she felt.

His hand on her chin became faintly caressing. "Why not?" he asked.

"It will be another upset for her when I leave," she said.

His thumb moved over her lips, brushing them, caressing them. "How long are you going to stay?"

"Until the first of the month," she said. "I do the autographing a week from Saturday."

His hand fell just in time to keep her from throwing herself against him and begging him to kiss her. "Then you can spend some time with Sarah and me until you leave. I won't force you into any corners and we can help Sarah find her feet."

Her eyes searched his night-shadowed face. "Why do you want me around?"

"God knows," he muttered. "But I do."

She sighed audibly, fighting her need to be near him.

"Don't brood," he said. He didn't smile, but there was something new about the way he was looking at her. "Just take things one day at a time and stop analyzing everything I say."

"Was I doing that? Okay, I'll try." She wished there were more light. She managed a smile. "Good night, Blake."

"Go on. I'll watch you."

She left him standing there and went running down to the house, her heart blazing with new hope.

If there was any chance for her to have Blake, she'd take it willingly, no matter what the risk. She now understood the reasons for his actions. And if she went slowly and didn't ask for the impossible, he might even come to love her one day. She went to sleep on that thought, and her dreams were so vivid that she woke up blushing.

CHAPTER SIX

MEREDITH WAS AWAKE, dressed and ready to go by eight on Saturday morning, with an hour to kill before it was time for Blake and Sarah to pick her up.

Bess, an early riser herself these days, made breakfast and smiled wickedly at her friend.

"It must feel strange to have Blake ask you out after all these years."

"It does. But I'm not kidding myself that it's out of any great love for me," she said, neglecting to tell Bess that Blake's main interest in her was sensual. All the same, just remembering the way he'd kissed her Wednesday night made her tingle from head to toe. And he'd shared secrets with her that she knew he'd never tell anyone else. That alone gave her a bit of hope. But she was afraid to trust him too much just yet. She needed time to adjust to the new Blake. She sighed. "I haven't been on a picnic in years. And I'm looking forward to it," she confessed with a smile, "even if he only wants me along because Sarah likes me."

"Sarah's a cute little girl." Bess sighed. "Bobby and I are ready to start a family of our own, but I can't seem to get pregnant. Oh, well, it takes time, I guess. Do you want something to eat?"

"I'm too nervous to eat," Meredith said honestly, her eyes still soft with memories of the night before. "I hope I'm wearing the right thing."

Bess studied her. Jeans, sneakers, a white tank top that showed off her pretty tan and emphasized her full, high breasts, and her dark hair loose around her shoulders: "You look great," she said. "And there's no rain in the forecast, so you should be fine."

"I should have slept longer," Meredith wailed. "I'll be a nervous wreck… Oh!"

The jangling of the telephone startled her, but Bess only smiled.

"If I were a gambling woman," Bess said as she went to answer it, "I'd bet my egg money that Blake's as nervous and impatient as you are." She picked the receiver up, said hello, then glanced amusedly at Meredith, whose heart was doing a marathon race in her chest. "Yes, she's ready, Blake," she said. "You might as well come get her before she wears out my carpet. I'll tell her. See you."

"How could you say that!" Meredith cried. "My best friend, and you sold me out to the enemy!"

"He isn't the enemy, and I think Blake needs all the advantages he can get." Bess's smile faded. "He's such a lonely man, Meredith. He was infatuated with Nina and he let himself be suckered into marriage without realizing she only wanted his money. He's paid for that mistake enough, don't you think?"

"There are some things you don't know," Meredith said.

"I'm sure there are. But if you love him in spite of

those things I don't know, then it's foolish to risk your future out of spite and vengeance."

Meredith smiled wearily. "I don't have the strength for vengeance," she replied. "I wanted to get even for a long time after I left here, but when I saw him again…" She shrugged. "It's just like old times. I can't talk straight or walk without trembling when he gets within a foot of me. I never should have come back. He's going to hurt me again if I give him an opening. After what Nina did to him, he's not going to make it easy for any woman to get close. Least of all me."

"Give it a chance," Bess advised. "Nothing comes to us without some kind of risk. I've learned a lot about compromise since Bobby and I almost split up a few years ago. I've learned that pride is a poor bedfellow."

"I'm glad you two are getting along so well."

"So am I. I went a bit bonkers over my sexy brother-in-law for a while, but Elissa came along and solved all my problems," Bess confessed with a grin. "King Roper has a gunpowder temper, if you remember." Meredith grinned, because she did. "I couldn't stand up to him, but Elissa didn't give an inch. Not that they do much fighting these days, but they had a rocky start."

"She's so sweet," Meredith murmured. "I liked her the minute I met her."

"Most people do. And King would die for her."

Those words kept echoing in Meredith's brain as she sat in the car, with Blake behind the wheel and Sarah chattering away in the back seat. She looked at Blake's taut profile and tried to imagine having him care enough to die for her. It was a forlorn hope that he'd ever love her. His reserved nature and Nina's cruelty wouldn't let him.

He glanced at her and saw that sadness in her eyes. "What is it?" he asked.

"Nothing." She smiled at Sarah, who was looking worried. "I'm just barely awake."

Blake lifted an eyebrow as the powerful car ate up the miles. "That explains why you were up and dressed at eight when I said we'd be at Bess's at nine."

"I couldn't sleep," she muttered.

"Neither could I," he replied. "Sarah was too excited to stay in bed this morning," he added, just when Meredith was breathless at the thought that the memory of the way he'd kissed her had been the reason he didn't sleep.

"I'm so glad you came, Merry," Sarah said, hugging her new Mr. Friend stuffed bear in the back seat. "We'll have lots of fun! Daddy says there's a swing!"

"Several," he returned. "Jack's Corner has added a new park since you were here," he told Meredith. "It has swings and a sandbox and one of those things kids love to climb on. We can sit on a bench and watch her. Then there are plenty of tables. I thought we'd pick up something at one of the fast food stores for lunch, since Amie wasn't around to fix a picnic basket."

"Did she call?"

"Yes. Her sister is recovering very well, but it will be at least two weeks more before Amie comes back."

"How are you managing?"

"Not very well," he confessed. "I'm no cook, and

there are things Amie could do for Sarah that I'm not comfortable doing."

"Daddy won't bathe me," Sarah called out. "He says he doesn't know how."

A flush of color worked its way up Blake's cheekbones and Meredith felt the embarrassment with him. It would be hard for a man to do such things for a daughter when he'd rarely been around a woman and never around little girls.

"I could…" Meredith hesitated at his sharp glance and then plowed ahead. "I could bathe her for you tonight. I wouldn't mind."

"Oh, Merry, could you?" Sarah enthused.

"If your father doesn't mind," she continued with a concerned glance in Blake's direction.

"I wouldn't mind," he said, without taking his eyes from the road.

"And you can tell me some more stories, Merry," Sarah said. "I specially like 'The Ugly Ducking.'"

"Duckling," Blake corrected, and he smiled faintly at his child. "I guess that story fits both of us, sprout."

"Neither of you," Meredith interrupted. "You both have character and stubborn wills. That's worth a lot more than beauty."

"Daddy has a scar," Sarah piped up.

Meredith smiled at the child. "A mark of courage," she corrected. "And your father was always handsome enough that it didn't matter."

Blake felt his chest grow two sizes. His gaze darted to Meredith's face and he searched her eyes long and intently. As she was feeling the effect of that glance, he forced his eyes back to the road barely in time to avoid running the car into a ditch.

"Sorry," Meredith murmured with a grimace.

"No need." He turned the car down the street that led to the city park and pulled it into a vacant parking space.

"It's beautiful," Meredith said, looking at the expanse of wooded land with a children's playground and a gazebo. There was even a fountain. At this time of the day, though, the area was fairly deserted. Dew was still on the grass, and as they walked to the benches overlooking the playground, Meredith laughed as her sneakers quickly became soaked.

"Your feet are getting wet," Sarah said, laughing, too. "But I have my cowgirl boots on!"

"I think I can spare your feet," Blake murmured.

Before she realized what he intended, Blake bent and whipped Meredith off the ground, carrying her close to his chest without any sign of strain.

"Gosh, you're strong, Daddy," Sarah remarked.

"He always was," Meredith said involuntarily, and her eyes looked up into Blake's, full of memories, full of helpless vulnerability.

His arms contracted a fraction, but he didn't look at her. He didn't dare. He could already feel the effect that rapt stare had on his body. If he gazed at Meredith's soft, yielding face, he would start kissing her despite the small audience of one watching them so closely.

He put her down on the sidewalk without a word and moved to the bench to sit down, leaning back and crossing one booted foot over his jeans-clad knee. "Well, sit down," he said impatiently. "Sarah, play while you can. This place probably fills up in an hour or so."

"Yes, Daddy!" Sarah said and she ran for the swings. Meredith sat down beside Blake, still glowing and warm from the feel of his arms and savoring the warm, cologne-scented fragrance of his lean body. "She's already a different child," she commented, watching Sarah laugh as she pumped her little legs to make the swing go higher.

"She's less wild," Blake agreed. He took off his hat and put it next to him on the bench, pausing to run his hand through his thick black hair. "But she isn't quite secure yet. The nightmares haven't stopped completely. And I've had less time to spend with her lately. Business goes on. A lot of jobs depend on the decisions I make. I can't throw up my hands and stay home every day."

"Sarah likes Amie, doesn't she?" Meredith asked.

"Amie won't be here for several weeks, Meredith," he said impatiently. "That's what I'm worried about. Monday morning I've got a board meeting. What do I do with Sarah, take her along?"

"I see your problem." Meredith sighed, fingering the face of her watch. "Well… I could keep her for you."

He didn't dare let himself react to that offer, even if it was the second time in a day that she'd volunteered to spend time with Sarah. It wouldn't do to get his hopes up too high.

"Could you?" he asked, and turned his head so that his green eyes pinned her gray ones.

"All I have to do is the autographing," she said. "And that's next Saturday. The rest of my time is vacation."

"You'd need to be at the house," he said with apparent unconcern. He pursed his lips, watching Sarah. "And considering how late I get home some nights, it's hardly worth rousing Bobby and Bess to let you in just for a few hours. Is it?"

She colored. "Blake, I don't care if this is the nineteen eighties, I can't move into your house…"

He glanced at her and saw the rose-red blush. "I won't seduce you. I told you that Wednesday, and I meant it."

The blush deepened. She averted her gaze to Sarah and her heart shook her with its mad beat. "I know you won't go back on your word, Blake," she whispered. "But it's what people would think."

"And you're a famous author," he said, his eyes narrowing. "God forbid that I should tarnish your reputation."

"Don't start on me." She sighed miserably and got up. "This isn't a good idea. I shouldn't have come…!"

He got up, too, and caught her by the waist, holding her in front of him. "I'm sorry," he bit off. "I've never given a damn what people thought, but I guess when you aren't looked down on to begin with, reputations matter."

She looked up at him with soft, compassionate eyes. "I never looked down on you."

His jaw clenched. "Don't you think I know that now?" he asked huskily. He pulled her hand to his chest and smoothed over the neat pink nails, his eyes on her long fingers. "You were always defending me."

"And you hated it," she recalled with a sad smile. "I always seemed to make you mad—"

"I told you," he interrupted. "I wanted you, and I didn't know how to handle it. I knew it was impossible to seduce you, and I'd given my word that I was going to marry Nina." His shoulders lifted and fell. "It wasn't conscious, but afterward when I thought about what I did to you that day, I thought maybe it would be easier for you if I made you hate me." He looked up into her gray eyes with quiet sincerity.

Her face felt hot. She searched his hard expression for a long moment. "I suppose in a way it was," she said finally. "But it undermined my confidence. I couldn't believe any man would want me."

"Which worked to my advantage," he whispered, smiling faintly. "Because you weren't tempted to experiment with anyone else." The smile faded. "You're still a virgin. And your first man, Meredith, is going to be me."

Her heart stopped and then ran wild. "That's the most chauvinistic—"

He stopped her by simply lowering his head until his lips were almost touching hers. She could taste his coffee-flavored breath and the intimacy of it made her knees feel rubbery. "I am chauvinistic," he whispered. "And possessive. And hard as nails. I can't help those traits. Life hasn't been kind to me. Not until just recently."

His hands were on her shoulders, holding her in place, and his eyes were on her mouth in a way that made her breath rustle in her throat.

"Sa-Sarah Jane…" she stammered.

"Is facing the opposite direction and doesn't have eyes in the back of her head," he murmured. "So just give me your mouth, little one, and I'll show you how gentle I can be when I try."

He felt her mouth accept his with the first touch, felt her body give when he drew her against his hard chest. She sighed into his mouth, and his brows drew together tightly over his closed eyes with the sheer pleasure of holding her.

She reached up under his arms to hold him and her body melted without a vestige of fear. Even when she felt the inevitable effect of her closeness on his powerful body, she didn't flinch or try to move away. He was her heart. Despite the pain and the anguish of years ago, he was all she knew or wanted of love.

His hands smoothed her hair as his hard mouth moved slowly on hers. She'd dreamed of this for so many years, dreamed of his mouth taking hers with exquisite tenderness, giving as much as he took. But the dreams paled beside the sweet reality. Her nails scraped against his back, loving the way the muscles rippled under her fingers.

His mouth lifted a fraction of an inch, and his breath was audible. "Who taught you to do that?" he whispered huskily.

"Nobody. I…guess it comes naturally," she whispered back.

His hands slid up her back to her hair and tangled gently in it. "Your mouth is very soft," he said unsteadily. "And it tastes of coffee and mint."

"I had Irish mocha mint coffee," she said.

"Did you?" He searched her eyes slowly. "Your legs are trembling," he remarked.

She laughed nervously. "I'm not surprised," she confessed. "My knees are wobbly."

He smiled, and the smile echoed in his eyes. "Are they?"

"Daddy, watch how high I can go!" a small voice called out.

Blake reluctantly loosened his hold on Meredith. "I'm watching," he called back.

Sarah Jane was swinging high and laughing. "I can almost touch the sky!" she said.

"Funny, so can I," Blake murmured. He glanced at Meredith, and he wasn't smiling.

She looked back, her heart threatening to burst. He took her hand in his, threading his fingers through hers so that he had them pressed in an almost intimate hold.

"To hell with your reputation," he said huskily. "Move in with us for a couple of weeks. Nobody will know except Bess and Bobby, and they're not judgmental."

She wanted to. Her worried eyes searched his. "Your company is an old and very conservative one. Your board of directors wouldn't like it at all."

"My board of directors doesn't dictate my private life," he replied. "We could sit close on the couch and watch television at night with Sarah. We could have breakfast together in the kitchen. If Sarah had nightmares, she could climb in with you. You could read her stories and I could listen." He smiled crookedly.

"I don't remember anybody ever reading me a story, Meredith," he added. "My uncle wasn't the type. I grew up in a world without fairy tales and happy endings. Maybe that's why I'm so bitter. I don't want Sarah to end up like me."

"Don't run yourself down," she said softly. Her eyes searched over his face warmly. "I think you turned out pretty well."

He touched her hair with a big, lean hand. "I never meant to be as cruel to you as I was." He sighed wearily. "And I guess if it hadn't been for Sarah, you wouldn't have come near me again, would you?" he asked.

She lowered her eyes to his chest. "I don't know," she said honestly. "I was still bitter, and a little afraid of you when I came back. But when I saw you with Sarah…" Her eyes lifted. "You might not realize it, but you're different when she's around. She takes some of the rough edges off you."

"She's pretty special. No thanks to Nina," he added curtly. "God knows why she kept the child when she so obviously didn't want her."

"Maybe her husband did."

"If he did, he sure changed his tune when he found out she was mine. He turned his back on her completely. I'm damned if I could have done that to a child," he said coldly. "Whether or not we shared the same blood, there are bonds equally strong."

"Not everyone has a sense of honor," Meredith reminded him. "Your sense of honor was always one of your strongest traits."

"It still is." He sat down on the bench again, tug-

ging her down beside him and drawing her closer while
Sarah stopped the swing and ran to the sandbox. "She'll
carry half that sand home with us," he murmured ruefully.

"Sand brushes off," Meredith reminded him.

He smiled. "So it does." He leaned back and his hand
contracted on her shoulder. "She's crazy about you."

"I like her, too. She's a wonderful little girl."

"I hope you'll still think so after she's treated you to
one of her tantrums."

"Most children have those," she reminded him. She
leaned back against his arm and looked up at him. Impulsively she reached up and touched the white line of
scar tissue on his face, noticing the way he flinched and
grabbed her hand. "It's not unsightly," she said softly,
and she smiled. "I told Sarah it was a mark of courage,
and it is. You got it because of me. It was my fault."

His fingers curled around hers and pressed before he
led them back to the scar and let her touch it. "Saving
you from a wild bronc," he recalled, smiling because it
was a lot like what had happened to Sarah in the corral.
"You weren't after a lacy white handkerchief. Instead
it was a kitten that had run into the corral. I got to you
in the nick of time, but I ran face first into a piece of
tin on the way out."

"You used words I'd never heard before or since,"
she murmured sheepishly. "And I deserved every one
of them. But you let me patch you up, anyway. That
was sweet," she said unthinkingly, and then lowered
her eyes.

"'Sweet.'" His hard lips pursed as he studied her

face. "You'll never know what I felt. The atmosphere was electric that day. I gritted my teeth and forced myself to glare at you. It kept me from doing what I really wanted to do."

"Which was?" she asked, curious, because she remembered too well the cold fury in his face and voice as she'd doctored him.

"I wanted to pull you into my lap and kiss the breath out of you," he said huskily. "You were wearing a cotton blouse with nothing, not a damned thing, under it. I could see the outline of your breasts under the blouse and I wanted to touch them so badly that I shook with longing. It wasn't more than a day later that I did just that, in the stable. You didn't know," he guessed, watching the expressions play across her face.

"No," she admitted breathlessly. "I had no idea. Of course, I was shaking a little myself, and trying so hard to hide my reaction from you that I didn't notice what you might be feeling."

"I lay awake all night, remembering the way you looked and sounded and smelled." He glanced at Sarah, watching her make a pointed castle in the sand and stack twigs around it for doors and windows. "I woke up aching. And then, days later, they read the will, and I went wild. Nina was clinging to me, I was confused about what I felt for you and for her." He shrugged. "I went crazy. That's why I said such cruel things to you. I wanted you so badly. When I saw you later, I couldn't resist one last chance to hold you, to taste you. So I kissed you. It took every last ounce of willpower I had to pull back."

"I really hated you for that," she said, remembering. "I knew you were getting even for the will, for what your uncle tried to do. I never realized that you really wanted me." She smiled self-consciously.

His lips twisted. "Do you think a man can fake desire?" he asked with a level stare.

She flushed and avoided his gaze. "No."

"At least I know now that I'm still capable of feeling it," he said heavily, his eyes going again to Sarah. "It's been a long dry spell. I couldn't bear the thought of having some other woman cut up my pride the way Nina did. And no one knows better than I do that I'm not much good in bed."

"I think that depends on who you're in bed with," she said, staring at his shirt. "When two people care about each other, it's supposed to be magic, even if neither of them has any experience."

"It wasn't magic for us, and we both fit into that category the day the will was read," he murmured softly.

"That's true. But I fought you. I didn't understand what was happening," she confessed.

He studied her down-bent head. "Do you think it might be different now that we've both had five years to mature?"

"I don't know," she said.

His lean hand touched her hair hesitantly and trailed down her cheek to her soft mouth. "I haven't learned a lot," he said, his voice quiet and deep. He drew in a slow breath. "And you knock me off balance pretty bad. I might frighten you if things got out of hand."

He sounded as if the thought tormented him. She

lifted her eyes and looked up at him. "Oh, no," she said softly. "You wouldn't hurt me."

His heart stampeded in his chest when she looked at him that way. "Would you go that far with me?" he whispered.

She couldn't sustain that piercing green-eyed gaze. Her eyes fell to his hard mouth. "Don't ask me, Blake," she pleaded. "I would, but I'd hate both of us. All those years of strict upbringing don't just go away because we want them to. I'm not made for a permissive life. Not even with you."

She made it sound as if he were the exception to the rule, and he felt a sting of pure unadulterated masculine pride at her words. She wanted to. He smiled slowly. That made things a little easier. Of course, the walls were all still up. The smile faded when he realized that those scruples of hers were going to stop him, because his own conscience and sense of honor wouldn't let him seduce her. Not even if she wanted him to.

"I guess I'm not either, if you want the truth." He sighed. "You and I are a dying breed, honey."

She heard the endearment with a sense of awe. It was the first time he'd used one with her, the very first time. She was aware of a new warmth deep inside her as she savored it in her mind.

"Daddy, look at my sand castle!" Sarah Jane called. "Isn't it pretty? But I'm hungry. And I want to go to the bathroom."

Blake smiled involuntarily. "Okay, sprout. Come on." He moved slightly away from Meredith. "She doesn't settle for long. Her mind is like a grasshopper."

"I think it's the age." Meredith smiled. She knelt and held out her arms for Sarah to run into, and she lifted the child, hugging her close. "You smell nice," she said. "What do you have on?"

"It's Daddy's," Sarah said, and Blake's eyebrows shot up. "It was on his table and I got me some. Isn't it nice? Daddy always smells good."

"Yes, he does." Meredith was fighting a losing battle with the giggles. She looked at Blake's astounded face and burst out laughing.

"So that's where it went," he murmured, sniffing Sarah and wrinkling his nose. "Sprout, that stuff's for me. It's not for little girls."

"I want to be like you, Daddy," Sarah said simply, and there was the sweetest, warmest light in her green eyes.

Blake smiled at her fully for the first time, his white teeth flashing against his dark tan. "Well, well. I guess I'll have to teach you how to ride and rope, then."

"Oh, yes!" Sarah agreed. "I can ride a horse now. And I can rope anything. Can't I, Merry?"

Meredith almost agreed, but Blake's eyes were making veiled threats.

"You'd better wait a bit, until your daddy can teach you properly," Meredith said carefully, and Blake nodded in approval.

"I hate to wait," Sarah muttered.

"Don't we all," Blake murmured, but he didn't look at Meredith as he started toward the car. "Let's find someplace that sells food."

They found a small convenience store with rest

rooms just a little way down the road, where they bought coffee and soft drinks and the fixings for sand-wiches, along with pickles and chips. Blake drove them back to the park, which was beginning to fill up.

"I know a better place than this," he remarked. "Sarah, how would you like to wade in the river?"

"Oh, boy!" she exclaimed.

He smiled at Meredith, who smiled back. "Then let's go. We're between the Canadian and the North Cana-dian rivers. Take your pick."

"The North Canadian, then," Meredith said.

He turned the car and shot off in the opposite di-rection, while Sarah Jane asked a hundred questions about Oklahoma, the rivers, the Indians and why the sky was blue.

Meredith just sat quietly beside Blake as he drove, admiring his lean hands on the wheel, the ease with which he maneuvered through Jack's Corner and out onto the plains. He didn't try to talk while he drove, which was good, because Sarah wouldn't have let him get a word in edgewise, anyway.

Sarah's chatter gave Meredith a breathing space and she used it to worry over Blake's unexpected proposal. He wanted her to move in with him and Sarah, and she was more tempted than he knew. She had to keep re-minding herself that she had a lot to lose—and it was more than just a question of her reputation and his. It was a question of her own will and whether she could trust herself to say no to Blake if he decided to turn on the heat.

He wasn't a terribly experienced man, but that

wouldn't matter if he started kissing her. She still loved him. If he wanted her, she wasn't sure that all her scruples would keep her out of his bed.

And being the old-fashioned man he was, she didn't know what would happen if she gave in. He'd probably feel obliged to offer to marry her. That would ruin everything. She didn't want a marriage based on obligation. If he grew to care about her, and wanted her for his own sake and not Sarah's...

She forced her mind back to the present. It didn't do to anticipate fate. Regardless of how she felt, it was Blake's feelings that mattered now. He had to want more than just her body before she could feel comfortable about the future.

CHAPTER SEVEN

BLAKE DROVE OVER the bridge that straddled the Canadian River, but he didn't stop on its banks. He kept driving until finally he turned off on a dirt road and they went still another short distance. He stopped the car under an oak tree and helped Meredith and Sarah Jane out into the shade.

"Where are we?" Meredith asked, disoriented.

He smiled. "Come and see." He took Sarah's hand and led them through the trees to a huge body of water. "Know where you are now?" he asked.

Meredith laughed. "Lake Thunderbird!" she burst out. "But this isn't the way to get to it! And this isn't the North Canadian or the Canadian. It's in between!"

"Don't confuse the issue with a lot of facts," he said with dry humor. "Isn't this a nice place for a picnic?" he went on. "We have shade and peace and quiet."

"Who owns this land?"

He pursed his lips. "Well, actually, it's part of what I inherited from my uncle. It's only fifteen acres, but I like it here." He looked around the wooded area with eyes that appreciated its natural beauty. "When I need to think out something, I come here. I guess that's why I've never built on it. I like it this way."

"Yes, I can see why," Meredith agreed. Birds were singing nearby, and the wind brushed leafy branches together with soft whispers of sound. She closed her eyes and let the breeze lift her hair, and she thought that with Sarah and Blake beside her, she'd never been closer to heaven.

"Sarah, don't go too near the edge," Blake cautioned.

"But you said I could go wading," the child protested, and began to look mutinous.

"So I did," he agreed. "But not here. After we eat, there's a nice place farther down the road where you can wade. Okay?"

For several long seconds, she matched her small will against his. But in the end she gave in. "Okay," she said.

Blake got out the cold cuts and bread, and a heavy cloth to spread on the grass. They ate in contented silence as Sarah offered crumbs to ants and other insects, fascinated with the variety of tiny life.

"Haven't you ever seen a bug before, Sarah?" Meredith asked.

"Not really," the little girl replied. "Mama said they're nasty and she killed them. But the man on TV says that bugs are bene…bene…"

"Beneficial," Blake said. "And I could argue that with the man on TV, especially when they get into the hides of my cattle."

Meredith smiled at him. He smiled back. Then the smiles faded and they were looking at each other openly, with a blistering kind of attraction that made Meredith's body go hot. She'd never experienced that electricity with anyone except Blake. Probably she never would, but she had to get a grip on herself before it was too late.

She forced her eyes down to the cloth. "How about another sandwich?" she offered with forced cheer.

After they finished the makeshift meal, Blake drove them down to the small stream. It ran across the dirt road, and Sarah tugged off her cowgirl boots in a fever to get to the clear, rippling water. Butterflies drifted down on the wet sand, and Blake smiled at the picture the child made walking barefoot through the water.

"I used to do that when I was a boy," Blake said, hands in his pockets as he leaned against the trunk of the car and watched her. "Kids who live in cities miss a hell of a lot."

"Yes, they do. I can remember playing like this, too. We used to get water from streams occasionally in oil drums, when the well went dry." Her eyes had a wistful, faraway look. "We were so poor in those days. I never realized how poor until I went to a birthday party in grammar school and saw how other kids lived." She sighed. "I never told my parents how devastating it was. But I realized then what a difference money makes."

"It doesn't seem to have changed you all that much, Meredith," he said, studying her quietly. "You're a little more confident than you used to be, but you're no snob."

"Thank you." She twisted the small gold-braid ring on her finger nervously. "But I'm not in your class yet. I get by and that's all."

"A Porsche convertible is more than just getting by," he mused.

"I felt reckless the day I bought it. I was thinking

about coming back here and facing the past," she confessed. "I bought it to give me confidence."

"We all need confidence boosters from time to time," Blake replied quietly, his eyes on Sarah. "She's slowly coming out of the past. I like seeing her laugh. She didn't in those first few days with me."

"I guess she was afraid to," Meredith said. "She hasn't really had much security in her young life."

"She's got it now. As long as I live, I'll take care of her."

The pride and faint possessiveness in his deep voice touched Meredith. She wondered how it would feel to have him say the same thing about her, and she blushed. Blake might allow himself to become vulnerable with a small child, but she had serious doubts about his ability to really love a woman. Nina had hurt him too badly.

They stayed another few minutes, and then Sarah announced that she needed to find a bathroom again. With an amused smile, Blake loaded them into the car and set out for a gas station.

They drove around looking at the countryside until almost dark. Then they went home and Meredith helped Sarah get a bath. After that, she settled down by the child's bedside to tell her some stories before she fell asleep.

She was halfway through "Sleeping Beauty," when Blake came into the room and sat down, legs crossed, in the chair by the window to listen. He was a little intimidating, but Sarah laughed and encouraged Meredith, and in no time she was lost in the fantasy herself.

She told the child two more stories and Sarah's eyelids grew heavier by the second. By the time Meredith had started on "Snow White," Sarah Jane was sound asleep.

Meredith got up, tucked the covers around the tired little body and bent impulsively to kiss Sarah good-night.

"That's another thing she's missed," Blake remarked as he joined her by the bed. "Being kissed good-night." He shifted, his hands in his pockets as he looked down at his daughter. "Showing affection is difficult for me." He glanced at Meredith. "My uncle wasn't the kissing sort." He smiled a little. "And I guess you know that."

She laughed. "Yes. I remember. He was a sweet man, but he hated touching or being touched."

"So do I," Blake replied. His eyes slid over Meredith's soft oval face. "Except by you," he added quietly. "I used to love to get cut up when you were here because you always patched me up. I loved the feel of your hands on my skin. I remember how soft and caring they were." He sighed heavily and turned away. "We'd better get out of here before we wake her up."

It was obviously embarrassing to him to admit how much he'd enjoyed her doctoring. That was surprising. She hadn't realized until he'd said it just how many minor accidents he seemed to have had in the old days, when she was around. She smiled to herself. That was one more tiny secret to cherish in the years ahead, when these sweet days were just a memory and Blake was far out of her reach.

"Why are you smiling?" he asked curtly.

She looked across at him as she closed Sarah's door.

"I was thinking how ironic it is. I loved it when you needed patching up because it gave me an excuse to get close to you." She colored a little as she averted her eyes.

"Isn't it amazing how green we both were?" he asked. "Considering our ages. We weren't kids."

"No."

The atmosphere was getting tenser by the second. She could almost feel the hard pressure of his mouth on her lips, and the way he was watching her, with that single-minded level stare, made her knees feel weak under her.

"How do you remember all those fairy tales?" Blake asked to relieve the tension that he was feeling.

"I don't know. It's a knack, I guess. Blake, you really do need to get her some storybooks," she said.

"You'll have to pick them out," he replied. "I don't know beans about what kids her age read."

"All right. I'll see if Mrs. Donaldson has any in her shop. I noticed some books in the back, but I didn't take time to look at them."

"I appreciate your help tonight," he said. "Some facets of being a parent are difficult. Especially dealing with frilly underwear and baths." He leaned against the wall, in no hurry to go downstairs, and his green eyes wandered slowly over Meredith's exquisite figure in the revealing button-up white tank top and well-fitting blue jeans. His eyes narrowed on that top because he didn't think there was anything under it and her breasts were hard tipped when they hadn't been a minute ago. "You're very maternal."

"I like children. Shouldn't we go downstairs?" she added nervously, because she felt the impact of his eyes on her breasts.

"Why? Do you suspect that I'm going to drag you into my bedroom and lock the door?"

"Of course not," she said too quickly.

"Pity," he remarked, shouldering away from the wall. "Because that's exactly what I'm going to do."

And he did, quickly, smoothly and with deadly efficiency. Before Meredith had time to say anything, he had her in his room. He paused to lock the door and then lowered her onto the middle of the king-size bed.

She lay there breathless, staring up at him, as he bent over her, one lean hand on either side of her head, his green eyes biting into hers.

"How afraid of me are you, Meredith?" he asked quietly. "If I start making love to you, are you going to kick and scream for help?"

Her lips parted as she looked up at him. She wasn't afraid of him at all. During the day, something had happened to both of them. The time they'd spent together had acted to bring them close. She knew more about him now than she ever had, and the thought uppermost in her mind was how much she loved him. Her eyes fell to his hard mouth, and she wanted it, and him, almost shockingly.

"No, I'm not frightened," she said. "Because I know you won't hurt me or force me to do anything I don't want to. You said so."

He seemed to relax a little. "That's true. I meant it, too." His eyes slid down her body, lingering on the thrust of her breasts against the tank top and the way her jeans clung to her rounded hips and long legs. "You can't imagine the effect you've had on me all day in that getup. Do you know how sexy you are?"

"Me?" she asked with a faint, delighted smile.

"You." He lifted his gaze back to collide with hers. "And you aren't getting out of here yet."

She felt tiny tremors shooting up and down her spine at the delicious threat. "I'm not?" she asked huskily.

He lowered himself down over her so that his chest was almost touching her breasts and his mouth was within an inch of hers. "No," he breathed. "You're not."

Her hands slid up around his neck and her eyes dropped to his mouth. He smelled of cologne and she loved the feel of his shoulders and back under her hands, the hard muscles under the thin shirt. Her breath jerked out of her throat as she felt the warm threat of his body and tasted his coffee-scented breath on her lips.

"Just relax," he whispered as his mouth brushed hers. "I won't hurt you."

Her hands slid into his thick hair and she let her body sink under the warm weight of his chest as it pressed against hers. His mouth was slow and hungry, and she didn't mind when it began to probe inside her own. She'd never kissed anyone except Blake this way, and she loved the sensuality of it. She let his tongue enter her mouth and her hands clung as the new sensations ran like fire along her nerves and made her weak.

She kissed him back, savoring the warm hungry mouth on hers. One of his hands supported her neck, but the other slid over her shoulder and suddenly covered her soft breast.

She took an audible breath and he lifted his head, but he didn't remove his hand.

"You're a woman now," he whispered. "And we've done this together once before. Except that this time, I'm not so green."

"Yes." She touched his fingers, lightly brushing them, while her eyes looked into his glittering ones with building excitement. Her swollen lips parted. "You could…unbutton it," she whispered shakily. "I'm not wearing anything under it."

She colored as she said it, and he realized how much courage it took for her to make him such an offer. Was she trying to prove that she trusted him, or could she feel the same hunger he did?

His fingers slid to the buttons and slowly began to slip them out of the buttonholes. And all the while, he searched her eyes, held them. "Why aren't you wearing anything underneath?" he asked when he'd finished and the edges were still touching.

"Don't you know, Blake?" she whispered with aching hunger. She arched just a fraction of an inch.

The invitation was as blatant as if she'd shouted it. He slowly peeled the edges of the tank top away from her full, firm breasts and let his eyes fall to them. They were as beautiful as they had been five years ago. A little fuller now, firmer. The color of seashells and rose petals, he thought dizzily as his eyes lingered on the hard tips that signaled her desire.

"Have you ever let any other man see you like this?" he whispered, because it was suddenly important.

"Only you," she replied, and her eyes were warm and soft, almost loving as they met his. "How could I let anyone else…?" she asked huskily.

"Meredith, you're exquisite," he bit off. His fingers brushed over one perfect breast lightly, barely touching it, and she cried out.

The sound startled him. He stopped at once, scowling at her in open concern. "Did I hurt you?" he asked softly. "I knew you were delicate there. I didn't mean to be rough with you."

She stared at him curiously, biting her lower lip as she tried to control the tremors he'd set off. "Blake…it didn't hurt," she said hesitantly.

"You cried out," he said, his eyes steady and honestly worried.

She colored furiously. "Yes."

The scowl stayed as his hand moved again. His green eyes held hers the whole time while he stroked her gently, smoothed the hard tip between his fingers and cupped her in his lean, rough hand. And she whimpered softly and cried out again, her body shivering and lifting up to him.

"Damn Nina!" he whispered roughly.

Meredith was too drugged to understand what he'd said at first. Her whirling thoughts barely registered in her mind. "What?"

"Never mind," he whispered huskily. "Oh, God, Meredith…!" His mouth went down against her breast, and she moaned, arching under him. The sound and her trembling drove him crazy.

He kissed every soft inch of her above her hips, savoring both breasts, nibbling at her creamy skin, dragging the edge of his teeth with exquisite tenderness over her stomach and rib cage. And all the while his hands caressed her, adored her. He made a meal of her, and long before he lifted his head, she was crying and pleading with him for something more than he was giving her.

He dragged air into his lungs, his eyes wild, his chest rising and falling raggedly as he looked down into her abandoned eyes.

Her face fascinated him. She looked as if he was torturing her, but her hands were pulling at his head, her soft voice was begging for his mouth. She moaned, but not in pain. And the most exquisite sensations racked his lean body as he poised over her. "You want me," he whispered huskily.

"Yes."

"Badly," he continued.

"Yes!"

His hands smoothed over her breasts and she shuddered. His breath caught. "I never dreamed a woman could sound like that. I never knew…" He bent to her mouth and kissed it softly. "My God, she was suffering me, and I didn't even have the experience to realize it."

"What?"

He dragged himself into a sitting position, and when she made a halfhearted effort to cover herself he pulled her wrist away. "Don't do that," he said quietly. "You're the most beautiful thing I've ever seen in my life. I won't hurt you."

"I know that. I'm just…embarrassed," she faltered, flushing.

"You shouldn't be," he said firmly. "The first intimacy I ever shared with a woman was with you. And your first one was with me. I know what you look like. I've seen you every night in my dreams."

She relaxed a little, sighing as she sank back on the bed. "It's just new," she tried to explain.

"Yes, I know." He brushed his fingertips over a firm breast and watched her shiver with pleasure. "That's sweet," he breathed. "That's so damned sweet, Meredith."

Her breath sighed out. "Blake…"

"What do you want?" he asked, reading the hesitant curiosity in her eyes. "Tell me. I'll do anything you want."

"Could you…unbutton your shirt and let me look at you?" she whispered.

His blood surged in his veins. He flicked buttons open with a hand that was deftly efficient even as he trembled inside with the hunger she aroused. He moved the fabric aside, and when he saw the sheer delight in her eyes at the thick mat of hair over impressive muscle, arrowing down to his jeans, he stripped the whole damned shirt off and threw it on the floor to give her an unobstructed view.

She held out her arms, and he groaned as he went into them, shuddering when he felt her nipples press against his chest as he crushed her into the mattress.

"Blake," she moaned. Her arms clung and her lips searched blindly for his. She found them and kissed him with all her heart, feeling his mouth tremble as it increased its hungry pressure.

He slid over her. His hands found her hips and urged them up against his, moving them against his rhythmically, letting her experience the full surge of his arousal.

She was whimpering, and he felt his control giving. It would only take another few seconds...

"No!" he bit off. He jerked himself away from her and rolled over, but he couldn't get to his feet. He lay there doubled up, while Meredith managed to get her trembling arms to support her. But she didn't touch him. He was shivering and she wanted to cry because she knew it was hurting him that he'd had to stop.

"I'm sorry," she wept. "It's all my fault."

"No, it isn't," he said through his teeth. He drew in sharp breaths until he could get himself under control. His body relaxed and he lay there for a long moment, fighting the need to roll over and strip her and submerge himself in her soft warm body.

"I wouldn't have stopped you," she breathed.

"I know that, too." He finally dragged himself up and ran his hands through his damp hair. His eyes darted to her half-clad body, softening as they swept over her full breasts. "Button your top," he said gently. "Or I'm going to start screaming my head off."

She managed a shaky smile as she pulled her top together and buttoned it with trembling fingers. "You make me feel beautiful," she whispered.

"My God, you are," he returned. His darkened green

eyes held hers. "I can't begin to tell you what those sweet little noises you were making did for my ego. I didn't know women made noise or looked like that when they made love."

She searched his eyes. "I don't understand."

"Meredith," he began heavily, "Nina smiled. All through it, all the time. She smiled."

It took a minute for that to get through to her. When it did, she went scarlet. "Oh!"

"I hurt you, that first time," he continued. "So I didn't get any passionate response. I didn't have any other experience when I married Nina, so I thought women were supposed to smile." A corner of his hard mouth lifted ruefully. "But now I know, don't I?"

Her face felt as if she might fry eggs on it. "I couldn't help it," she confessed self-consciously. "I never dreamed there was such pleasure in being touched by a man."

He caught one of her hands and pressed its soft palm hungrily to his mouth. "The pleasure was mutual," he said, his glittering gaze holding hers. "I almost lost it. You let me hold your hips against mine, and I went crazy."

"I'm sorry," she said softly. "I should have pulled away."

"Are you supposed to be superhuman?" he asked reasonably. "I couldn't stop, either. Together we start fires. I wanted nothing more in life than to feel you under me and around me, skin on skin, mouth on mouth, absorbing me into you."

She caught her breath and trembled at the words,

seeing the quiet pride in his eyes when he realized the effect they had on her.

"I want to make love to you," he whispered roughly. "Here. Now. On my bed."

"I can't." She closed her eyes. "Please don't ask me."

"It isn't lack of desire. What, then? Scruples?"

She nodded miserably. "You know how I was raised, Blake. It's hard to forget the teachings of a lifetime overnight, even when you want someone very, very much."

"Then suppose you marry me, Meredith."

Her eyes opened wide. "What?"

"We get along well together. You like Sarah. You want me. You've got a career, so I know you don't need my money, and you know I don't need yours. We could build a good life together." He searched her shocked face. "I know I'm not the best matrimonial prospect going. I'm short-tempered and impatient, and I can be ruthless. But you know the worst of me already. There won't be any terrible surprises after the vows."

"I don't know..." she argued.

"You want hearts and flowers and bells ringing." He nodded. "Well, that doesn't always happen. Sometimes you have to settle for practicalities. Tell me you don't want to live with me, Meredith," he challenged with a faintly mocking smile.

"That would be a lie," she said, sighing, "so I won't bother. Yes, I want to live with you. And I'm very fond of Sarah Jane. Taking care of her wouldn't be any trial to me. But you're still not going to let your emotions get in the way of a good business deal, are you, Blake?" she returned. "You want me, but that's all you have to offer."

"For a man, lovemaking is one big part of a relationship," he said, choosing his words. "I don't know much about love. I've never had any." He lifted his eyes back to hers. "If it can be taught, you can teach me. I've never been in love, so you've got a good shot at it already."

She sighed at his summing-up of the situation, despite the ache in her heart for something he might never be able to give her. He was locked up emotionally, and nobody had a key.

He leaned down, his face poised just above hers. "Stop thinking, Meredith," he whispered. His mouth nibbled at her lower lip, smoothing over its delicate swell. His hands cupped her breasts, hot even through the fabric of her tank top and sensual as they caressed her. One long leg insinuated itself between both of hers and she felt it begin to move lazily.

"This isn't fair," she whispered shakily.

"I know. Unbutton your top again," he whispered, and proceeded to tell her exactly why he wanted her to and what he intended to do when she unfastened it.

Her body tingled with heat. She wanted him. Her moan was pure surrender, and he knew it. His heart leaped as he felt her fingers working at the buttons. And then she was all silky warmth under him, her breasts soft and yielding under his searching hands, his hungry mouth.

"You aren't…going to stop…this time, are you?" she whimpered as his mouth grew even bolder.

"That depends on you," he said in a strange, thick tone. "I'd never force you."

"I know." Her mind tumbled while she tried to decide what to do. Part of her knew it was a mistake. But it had been so many years, and she'd done little else but dream of him, of lying in his arms and loving him.

His hand slid to the fastening of her jeans and he lifted himself so that he could see her eyes. "If I start this, I'll have to finish it," he said gently. "I'll go all the way. You have to decide."

Her fingers lingered on his. "I don't know," she moaned. "Blake, I'm afraid. It's going to hurt…!"

"Only a little," he whispered solemnly. "I'll be as slow and tender as I can. I'll do anything you want me to do to make it easier for you." He bent to her mouth, touching it lightly with his. "Meredith, don't you want to know all the secrets?" he asked huskily. "Don't you want to see how much pleasure we can give each other? My God, just kissing you makes my blood run like fire. Having you…" He groaned as he kissed her. "Having you…would be unbearably sweet."

"For me, too." Her arms tightened around his neck, and she buried her face in his hair-roughened chest, savoring the smell and feel of him in her arms.

His hands smoothed down her hips and his weight settled over her, gently, so that he wouldn't frighten her. His mouth trembled as it found hers, and he kissed her with exquisite warmth and tenderness.

"This is how much I want you," he whispered as he moved sensuously against her.

She felt his need, and an answering hunger made her tremble. "Blake…what about…precautions?" she choked out. "I don't know how."

His lips lifted just above hers. "I'm going to marry

you," he told her roughly. "But if precautions are important to you, I can use something."

Heat shot through her. She felt her nails digging into his back, heard her own wild cry as she lifted to him. His face hardened and she saw his eyes darken as his mouth came slowly back down to cover hers.

"We should…" she whimpered.

"Yes," he whispered. But his mouth grew demanding, and his last sane thought was that creating babies with Meredith was as natural as wading in country streams and walking in the park. He closed his eyes, shaking with the need to join his aching body to hers and give her the same sweet pleasure he felt when he touched her.

CHAPTER EIGHT

MEREDITH TREMBLED, HALF BLIND with pleasure as Blake's mouth became more demanding. It was almost enough just to kiss him, to feel the exquisite weight of his body on hers as his hand worked at the fastenings of her clothes.

"The light," she whispered huskily.

He touched her mouth tenderly. "I know," he said deeply, reaching for it. "You might not believe it, little one, but I've got more hang-ups than you have."

The room was in darkness then, except for the faint moonlight seeping in through the white curtains. His hands smoothed down her breasts, savoring their warm fullness. She gasped and he searched for her mouth in the darkness.

"Meredith," he whispered huskily.

"What?" she breathed.

"One of us needs to do something if you don't want me to make you pregnant. You haven't really answered me."

She felt the heat in her cheeks. He was right, it was something they had to consider. She swallowed. "I'm not on the pill," she confessed.

"Do you want me to take care of it?"

Her fingers touched his face, involuntarily running

down the scar, while visions of his son in her arms made her tremble with hunger. "I... I don't mind, either way," she said unsteadily.

"God!" He buried his face in her throat and shuddered. It was so profound to hear her say that. It would be all of heaven to see her grow big with his child, to share the sweetness of raising it.

"Blake?" she whispered, uncertain.

"I don't mind, either," he said roughly. "Come here."

He pulled her closer still and she melted against him with blinding hope as he began to tease her breasts with his hands. He trailed his fingers around the outer edges, feeling the tension in her body, the heat of her skin as he drew his caresses out, making her wait, building the need, until she caught his wrists and tried to make him touch her.

And he did, finally, so that it was like a tiny fulfillment, and she shuddered and arched into his warm, lean hands. He liked her reactions, delighted in her responses. She had to care about him, he thought dizzily as his hands smoothed away her clothing, to let him do these things to her and to feel such pleasure when he did.

He was slow. Deliberately slow. More patient than he'd ever dreamed of being. He loved the soft sounds that came whispering out of her throat, the way her hands were clinging to him. He loved the very texture of her skin, the sound of her quick breathing like a rustle in the darkness as he touched her more intimately.

He should be out of his mind with the need to have her, he thought in the back of his mind. But stronger

than passion was the need for her to feel the same exquisite sensations that were rippling through his powerful body and making him tremble with each new touch,
each soft kiss. He wanted much, much more than quick
fulfillment. He wanted to touch all that was Meredith,
to join his body to hers and feel the oneness that he'd
read was possible between two people who cared for
each other.

His lips smoothed over hers, barely touching, while
his hands found her where she was untouched and
gently, tenderly probed. She gasped under his mouth.
Thank God for books, he thought while he could. He
hadn't known anything about virgins until he'd done
some reading the other night.

"It's all right," he whispered tenderly. "I'm going to
be very gentle, Meredith. I just want to make sure that
what we do won't be any more painful than it has to be."

"I don't mind," she told him softly, clinging.
"Blake… I'd give you anything…!"

"Yes." His mouth whispered against hers. "I'd give
you anything, too, Meredith. I'd do anything to please
you, even forgo my own pleasure."

That didn't sound like lust. Neither did the exquisitely slow movements of his hands, the gentle crush
of his body. He was hungry, she could feel his need,
but he wouldn't take his pleasure at her expense. That
consideration, incredible given the length of abstinence
for him, made her want to cry. He had to care a little
to be so…!

Her mind went crazy as his hand moved and she

felt a stab of pleasure so sweet that it lifted her and she cried out.

She clung to him, telling him without words that it was pleasure, not pain, she was feeling. He warmed, remembering his own earlier withdrawal when she moaned or gasped, because he'd never known how a woman responded when giving herself to pleasure.

He opened his mouth on hers and let his tongue gently stab inside her lips, aching at the implied intimacy, delighting in the way her soft, slender body turned in his hands when he did that. She was loving this, he thought dizzily. Loving every second of it, reveling in his mouth, his touch. He could feel her pleasure even as his built and built until he couldn't contain it any longer.

She was trembling now, and tiny whispers of excitement were moaning past her lips as she lay waiting for him, her body twisting sensually with mindless abandon.

He was heady with pride at his own latent abilities. He hadn't dreamed that with his inexperience he could bring her to this frenzy.

He stripped with quick, deft movements and slid onto the coverlet beside her, his hands moving on her body, holding her while he kissed her with whispery tenderness.

"Pl…ease." She managed the one word, and her voice broke on it.

"I want you, too, little one," he breathed against her mouth. "I want you so much."

He balanced his weight on his forearms and slid over

her, trembling at the soft warmth of her legs tangling with his. She moved, helping him, and he let his hips ease down.

She felt the first hesitant probing and shuddered, but she didn't tense. She forced her body to relax, not to fight him.

He could feel that, and his mouth smoothed over her lips in silent reassurance.

His hands went to her face, holding it while he kissed her, and he felt her soft cry go into his mouth as he pushed gently against the veil of her womanhood.

And it was easy then. He felt the faint tension go out of her body, felt her sigh feather against his lips.

"I won't ever have to hurt you again," he murmured unsteadily. "I'm sorry it has to be this way for a virgin."

"But it wasn't bad," she whispered back. Her fingers slid into his cool, thick hair. "Oh, Blake…" she whimpered. She kissed him softly. "Blake, it's…incredible!"

"Yes." He touched her eyes, closing them; he touched her nose, cheeks and forehead with lips that were breathlessly tender. And all the while his body moved with equal tenderness, drowning her in the exquisite sensation of oneness. She pulled his mouth to hers as his movements began to lengthen and deepen with shuddering pleasure, her breath filling him, her tiny cries making him feverish with contained passion.

His hands slid under her, savoring the warm, soft skin of her back and hips, holding her to him.

"Meredith—" His voice broke on her name. His eyes closed. He felt the tension growing in his powerful body with each torturously slow movement, felt the control he had beginning to slip. But her control was going, too. She was trembling, clinging, her mouth ardent and hungry. He lifted her up and overwhelmed her with desperate tenderness, and when the spasms came, they were white hot, blinding, but with a gentleness that he couldn't have imagined.

She bit him in her passion, but he was riding waves of completion and he hardly felt her teeth. His hands contracted. He cried her name against her damp throat and the tide washed over him in pulsating shudders.

He heard her crying an eternity later and he managed to lift his head and search her face. "Meredith?" he whispered huskily. "Oh, God, I didn't hurt you, did I?"

"No!" She buried her face against his chest, kissing him there, kissing his throat, his face, everywhere she could reach, with lips that worshipped him. "Blake!" she moaned, her arms contracting around his neck. "Blake...!" She shuddered again and again, and when he realized why, he put his mouth gently against hers and began to move.

The second time was every bit as sweet, but slower, more achingly drawn out. He hadn't dreamed a man could hold out as long as he was managing to. But he adored her with his mouth, his hands, and finally, when she was crying with the tension he'd aroused, he adored her with the slow, worshipping motion of his body in one long, sweet pinnacle of fulfillment.

She couldn't seem to stop crying. She lay in his arms with her wet face pillowed on his chest where the thick hair was damp with sweat. She couldn't let go of him, either, and he seemed to understand that, because he held her even closer and gently brushed her hair away from her face while he kissed her tenderly and soothed her.

"I thought…passion was uncontrollable and…and quick…and men couldn't…men were rough," she told him.

"How could I be rough with you?" His mouth touched hers, brushing softly over her trembling lips. "Or make something that beautiful into raw sex?"

Her breath sighed out, making little chills against his damp skin. "I'm so glad I waited for you," she said simply, shaken by the experience. "I'm so glad I didn't give in to some man I didn't even like out of curiosity or because everybody else was doing it." She nuzzled her face against him. "You are so wonderful."

He drew her mouth up to his and kissed her possessively. "So are you," he whispered. "I didn't know what lovemaking was until tonight. I didn't know that there could be such pleasure in it," he murmured against her mouth.

"I thought men felt the pleasure with anyone," she replied.

"Apparently it's an individual thing," he said quietly. "Because I never felt anything approaching this before." He heard the words without realizing their importance, until it suddenly came to him that he'd hardly felt anything with Nina. But Meredith's soft young body had sent him spinning into oblivion and he'd done things with her and to her that had come naturally. Perhaps it was instinct. But what if it was something stronger?

He'd called it lovemaking, and it had been. Not sex,

or the satisfaction of a need. And he couldn't imagine doing that with anyone except Meredith. Not that way. Not with such staggering tenderness. He hadn't even known he was capable of it.

"I wasn't sure I could wait for you," he confessed, nuzzling her face. "Was it enough?"

Her body burned with the memory, and she kissed his throat with breathless tenderness. "Yes. And...was it for you?" she asked, worried.

"Yes." Only the one word, but there was a wealth of unspoken pleasure in it.

She was beginning to feel self-conscious, and he seemed distant all of a sudden, as if he were withdrawing. Had he satisfied his hunger for her and now he was looking for a way out of what could become an embarrassing situation? Did he regret what they'd done? He had old-fashioned ideas about sex, after all. In fact, so did she, but they hadn't helped once he'd started kissing her. Her love for him had betrayed her into his bed.

"Blake, you don't... I mean, you don't think I'm easy...?" she asked suddenly.

"My God!" he exclaimed. He reached over and turned on the light, blinding her with stark illumination and embarrassment.

She fumbled for the cover, scarlet faced, but he stayed her hand.

"No," he said quietly, his eyes as solemn as his face. "Look at me, Meredith. Let me look at you."

Her eyes darted over him and she looked away quickly as the heat grew in her face, but he turned her eyes back gently.

"I'm not a monster," he said softly. "I'm just a man. Flesh and blood, like you. There's nothing to be frightened of."

She managed not to look away this time, and after the first shock, she found him beautiful, in a very masculine sense. He was looking, too, his eyes reconciling sweet memories of her five years ago with the reality of today.

"You've blossomed," he said after a minute, and there was no masculine mockery or teasing in his tone. It was deep and soft as he searched over her swollen breasts, her flat stomach, the curve of her hips, the elegant sweep of her long legs. "You're much more pleasing to my eyes than the Venus, Meredith," he said huskily. "The sight of you knocks the breath right out of me."

Her breath caught at the emotion in his voice. "You make it sound so natural," she said with faint curiosity.

"Isn't it?" he asked. His green eyes searched her soft gray ones. "We made love. I know your body as well as I know my own. We touched in more than just the conventional way, and you're part of me now. Isn't it natural that I should want to see the lovely body I've known so intimately?"

She colored, but she smiled. "Yes."

"And to answer your other question, Meredith, no, I don't think you're easy." He smoothed back her dark hair and his eyes slid over her face. "We both knew it wasn't going to be a casual encounter. I knew you were a virgin." He brought her hand to his lips and kissed the palm tenderly. "We're going to get married and spend the rest of our lives together. That's the only reason I didn't pull away from you. If sex had been all I wanted,

I could have had it long before now, and I wouldn't have seduced you in cold blood for my own pleasure."

She searched his darkened eyes. "It isn't just because of Sarah that you want to marry me, is it? Or just because you wanted me—"

He stopped the words with his mouth. "You talk too much. And worry too much. I want to marry you." He lifted his head. "Don't you want to marry me?"

Her eyes softened. "Oh, yes."

"Then stop brooding." He got up, stretching lazily while she watched him with shy fascination. He dug in his chest of drawers and pulled out a set of navy silk pajamas. He tugged the bottoms up over his hard-muscled legs and snapped them before he carried the pajama top to the bed, lifted Meredith into a sitting position and eased her arms into the sleeves.

"It's economical to share these," he murmured dryly when her eyes asked him why. "I used to sleep raw, but I have to wear something now that Sarah's here. Except that I never wear the tops." He looked down at the soft thrust of her breasts, swollen and dark tipped in the aftermath of passion. He bent slowly and brushed his lips over them, tautening as the tips went hard involuntarily. "I've never felt more like a man than I feel when I touch you," he said roughly, his eyes closing, his brows knitting in the most exquisite pleasure.

She held his dark head against her, loving the feel of his warm mouth. "Are we going to sleep together?" she asked.

"We have to," he murmured, sliding his lips slowly over her breast. "I can't let you go."

She slid her arms around his neck as he lifted his head. "But, Sarah…"

"Sarah will be the first to find out we're going to be married," he murmured. "I'll get the license. We can have a blood test on Monday morning and the service two days later. Will that give you enough time to close out your apartment in San Antonio and change your mailing address?"

"Yes." She was breathless with his impatience, but not irritated. She wanted to live with him, and the sooner the better, before he woke up to what he was doing and changed his mind. She couldn't bear it if he'd only proposed in the heat of the moment.

He read that fear in her eyes. "I'm not going to change my mind. I'm not going to back out at the last minute or decide that I've satisfied my hunger for you and I don't need you anymore. I want you, Meredith," he emphasized. "I want to live with you, and not in some modern way with no ties and no legal status. To me, living with someone involves a thing called honor. It's a lost word in this society, but it still means a hell of a lot to me. I care enough to give you my name."

"I'll try to be a good wife," she said solemnly. "You won't mind if I just sit and stare at you sometimes, will you?"

He searched her eyes quietly. "Do you love me?"

Her lips trembled and she averted her gaze, focusing on his bare chest.

"All right. I won't force it out of you." He brought her forehead to his lips, his chest swelling with the knowledge that she did love him, even if she wouldn't admit it. He could see it in her eyes, feel it in her body. Apparently love could survive the cruelest blows, because God knows he'd hurt her enough to kill anything less. He closed his eyes and nuzzled his cheek against her soft dark hair. "I'll take care of you all my life," he promised. "Don't be afraid."

She trembled a little, because she was. Afraid that he didn't care enough, that he might regret his decision. He might fall in love again someday with someone else like Nina, and what would she do? She'd have to let him go…

It was happening so fast. Almost too fast. She hesitated. "Blake, maybe we should just get engaged…" she began worriedly.

He lifted his head and searched her eyes. "No."

"But—"

He put a long finger over her lips. "Do you remember what we said to each other when we came in here? About precautions?"

She colored. "Yes."

"Marriage and children are synonymous to me," he said quietly. "I think they are to you, too. I'm illegitimate, Meredith. I won't let my child be called what I was."

She sighed. "Does it really bother you so much?"

"I'd like to know who my father was at least," he replied. "Half my heritage is lost forever, because I have no idea who he was or what his background is. I can't tell Sarah anything about him. She'll ask someday."

"She'll understand, too," she replied. "She's a very special little girl. She's so much like you."

His green eyes searched hers. "We could have another daughter," he said. "Or a son."

She held her breath while he touched her flat stomach under the long open pajama top. Her heart went crazy when he looked down, watching the tips of her bare breasts harden helplessly.

She tried to pull the fabric together, but he caught her hands and held them gently.

"No," he said. "You can't imagine the pleasure it gives me just to see you like that."

Her breath sighed past her parted lips. "It's hard."

"I know." He lifted his eyes back to hers, searching them in a long, static silence. "It was for me, too, believe it or not. But I let you look at me, and I wasn't embarrassed." He smiled faintly. "I couldn't let Nina."

She reached up and touched her lips to his. "I'm glad," she said huskily.

He pulled her against him, nudging the pajama top out of the way so that her breasts brushed slowly against his hair-roughened chest, and she caught her breath with pleasure at the exquisite friction.

"We've got a lot to learn about this," he said softly. "We can learn it together."

"Yes." She touched her mouth to his throat, his collarbone. He took her head and guided her lips to his own nipples, groaning at the pleasure that shot through him when he felt the moist suction of her mouth.

"God, that feels good!" he ground out, forcing her mouth closer.

"Let's take our clothes off and experiment some

more," she suggested brazenly, teasing him for the first time.

It delighted him. "You hussy!" he accused, and tugged her head up. His eyes were playful, and his face had never looked less hard.

"You started it," she pointed out, smiling back.

"But I can't finish it," he said ruefully. He sighed over her breasts before he buttoned them out of sight. "It's too soon," he said, answering the question in her eyes. "I don't want to rush you. You're much too new to this for any more experimenting."

She studied his face quietly. "How do you know?"

"Simple logic." He touched her lips. "And a book I read," he confessed, brushing his mouth over them. "In case I ever got this far with you, I wanted to make sure I knew enough so that I wouldn't make you afraid of me again."

"Oh, Blake." She hugged him hard, nestling her face against him. "Blake, I adore you."

His heart skipped when she said it. He smiled, aglow with satiation and the knowledge that she cared. "Lie down with me. We'll sleep in each others' arms."

She tingled all over as he pulled back the cover and tucked her in, turning out the light before he climbed in beside her. He drew her to him with a long, warm sigh and kissed her.

"Good night, little one," he whispered.

"Good night, Blake."

He closed his eyes, sure that he'd never been happier in his entire life. He pulled her closer and sighed when he felt her arms go around him. For a beginning, it was perfect.

But the next morning, when he awoke and found Meredith lying asleep in his bed, the perfection waned. His body surged at the sight of her, and he realized belatedly that the hunger he'd thought assuaged last night had only grown with feeding. He wanted her more now than ever, with a fever that actually made him shake as he looked at her sleeping body.

The realization terrified him. He'd never been vulnerable. Even Nina hadn't really knocked him off balance very far, or tested his control over his emotions. But Meredith did. She was the very air he breathed, the sun in his sky. He felt a rush of possessiveness when he looked at her, a desperate need to keep her, to protect her. He got out of bed and stared at her as if he'd gone mad. He'd sworn that he would never let her get to his heart, but last night he'd given her a lien on it. This morning, she owned him lock, stock and barrel.

He swallowed down a wave of nausea. The tender loving of the night faded into cold fear with the dawn. He didn't trust women, and now that distrust had extended itself to Meredith all over again. As long as he could persuade himself that it was only physical, marriage hadn't bothered him. But what he was feeling this morning gave new meaning to the situation. He could care for her. He could go crazy over her after a few more nights like last night. He could be so enamored of her that he'd do anything she wanted just to feel her arms around him. And that realization was what caught him by the throat—that he might not be able to keep his pride, his independence. He was afraid of her because he might love her, and he couldn't trust her enough to give in to her. She might be just like Nina. How could he know before it was too late?

Like a trapped animal, he felt the need to run, to get away, to think it through.

He got up and got dressed, taking one long, hungry look at Meredith before he forced himself to jerk open the door and go out. Last night everything had been so simple, until he'd touched her for the first time. And now he was mired up to his neck in quicksand. He didn't know what to do. He had the most ridiculous urge to go out and get Meredith an armload of roses. God knows, it must be the first stages of insanity, he thought as he went down the stairs and out the back door.

CHAPTER NINE

MEREDITH WOKE UP SLOWLY, aware of new surroundings and light coming into her room from the wrong direction. Then she moved, and her body told her that the light wasn't the only difference.

She sat up. She was in Blake's bedroom, in Blake's bed, wearing Blake's pajama top. Her face burned. The night before came back with startling clarity. She'd given in. More than given in. She'd participated wildly in what she and Blake had done together.

Her breath came unsteadily as wave after wave of re-membered pleasure tingled in her sore body. She looked around, wondering if Blake was in the bathroom. But she spotted his pajama bottoms laid across the foot of the bed, and his boots were missing. They'd been sitting beside the armchair last night.

She got out of bed slowly, a little disoriented. "Bess!" she exclaimed, then remembered that she'd called Bess just after they'd gotten home last night to tell her that she was spending the night to help Blake with Sarah. Wouldn't Bess be grinning when she got back home this morning, she moaned to herself.

She put back on the clothes she'd taken off—the clothes that Blake had taken off for her, she corrected—

and pulled on her socks and sneakers before she combed her hair.

In the mirror she could see the imprint of her head and Blake's on the pillows, and she blushed. Well, it was too late now for regrets. He'd said that they were getting married, so she might as well reconcile herself to her new status in his life. At least they were physically compatible and she loved him desperately. Perhaps someday he might learn to love her back. He was already different, mostly due, she was sure, to Sarah's gentle influence.

She opened the door and went to Sarah's room, but the little girl was nowhere in sight.

"If you're awake, breakfast is ready," Blake called from the foot of the staircase.

She looked down, thrilling to the sight of him, tall and dark headed, dressed in gray slacks and shirt with a lightweight tan sport coat and brown striped tie. He looked very elegant, and just a little somber.

That didn't bode well. She almost missed a step on her way down, nervous and shy with him after the night before. Her face was wildly colored and she couldn't look at him.

She paused two steps above him because his hand shot out and kept her there. His green eyes forced her to look at him, and he searched her face quietly.

"Come here," he said gently. "I've got something for you."

His big, lean hand curved possessively over hers and his fingers tangled in her cold ones as he led her into the hall and stopped her at the chair, which was covered with waxed paper that held dozens of small pink roses, their fragrance like perfume.

"For me?" she whispered, breathless.

"For you. I went out into the field and cut them early this morning."

She lifted them, burying her nose in their beautiful scent. "Oh, Blake," she moaned with pleasure, and looked up with her heart in her eyes.

He was glad then that he'd followed the crazy impulse in spite of his disturbing thoughts after waking. He bent and brushed his mouth over her forehead, his mood light. "I hoped you might like them," he murmured. "They looked as virginal as you did last night."

Her face felt like fire. "I'm not anymore," she said hesitantly.

He smiled slowly. "I'll carry last night in my heart until I die, Meredith Anne," he told her huskily. "It was everything it should have been. Magic."

She smiled into her roses, feeling all womanly and soft when he said things like that.

"Are you sorry that I took the choice away from you?" he asked unexpectedly, and his eyes were serious. "I carried you into my room without asking if it was what you wanted, and I didn't give you much chance to get away."

"Don't you think I could have gotten away if I'd really wanted to?" she asked honestly.

He smiled back at her. "No."

She traced rose petals. "Well, I could have. You didn't force me."

"In a way I did," he replied worriedly. "I didn't try

to protect you. I don't want to force you into marriage with the threat of pregnancy."

Her eyebrows lifted. "Threat?" she picked up on the word. "Oh, no, it isn't that. A baby is…" Her breath caught as she searched his eyes and felt the hunger for a child. "Blake, a baby would be the sweetest thing in the world."

His heart began to race as he looked at her. "That's what I thought, too," he said. "That's why I didn't try to hold back." He smiled ruefully. "And the fact is, I don't think I could have. Years of abstinence makes it pretty hard for a man to keep his head."

Her eyes widened. "You meant it?" she exclaimed. "It was actually that long?"

He nodded. "Now I'm glad," he confessed. "It made it that much more intense with you." He framed her face with his lean hands and bent to savor her lips with his warm, moist ones. "So intense," he whispered roughly, "that I want it again and again and again. Every time I look at you, my body burns."

His mouth became demanding, and she felt the quick, violent response of his body to the feel of hers.

"So does mine," she whispered back, reaching up with her free hand to cling to his neck. "Blake," she moaned as his hands dropped to her hips and pulled her hard against him.

"God!" he groaned, and his mouth covered hers urgently.

Somewhere in the fever they were sharing, a door opened.

"Daddy? Meredith? Where are you?"

They broke apart with heated faces, trembling bodies and faintly crushed roses. "We're here," Blake said, recovering quickly. "We'll be there in a minute, Sarah. I was just giving Meredith her roses."

"Okay, Daddy. Aren't they nice, Merry?"

"Yes, darling," she murmured absently, but her eyes were on Blake as the child went back through to the kitchen.

"You aren't going home tonight," he said huskily. "I've got you and I'm keeping you, and to hell with gossip. I'll get the license tomorrow and arrange for blood tests with my doctor. I'll phone you from my office in the morning with the time. Meanwhile—" he smiled slowly "—you can go over to Bess's and get a change of clothes."

"What will I tell her?" she groaned.

"That we're getting married and you're taking care of Sarah while Mrs. Jackson's away," he said simply. He pulled her hand to his lips and kissed it warmly. "Sarah and I will even go with you to make things respectable. But first we'll have breakfast. Okay?"

She sighed with pure delight. "Okay. But I'll have to go to my apartment in San Antonio this week," she added.

"I'll take time off to go with you Tuesday. Sarah can come, too." He bent, half lifting her against his lean, hard body. "I'm not letting you out of my sight any more than I have to. You might decide to run for it."

"If you think that, you underestimate yourself," she murmured, and buried her face in his throat. "I don't have the strength to get away."

His hands contracted. "How sore are you?" he asked intimately.

She burrowed closer. "Blake...!"

"Is it bad?"

She grimaced and looked up at him, hesitating.

"Tell me the truth," he said. "It will spare us a lot of frustration later—if I start making love to you and have to stop."

"It's uncomfortable," she confessed finally, averting her eyes.

But he tilted her chin and forced her to look at him. "No secrets between us," he said. "Not ever. I want the truth, no matter how much it hurts, and you'll always get it from me."

"All right," she said. "I want it that way, too."

His eyes brushed over her soft features with lazy warmth. "You look very pretty without makeup," he remarked. "As pretty as these roses." He glanced at them and frowned. "We've bruised them a bit."

"They'll forgive us," she said. She reached up to kiss him softly. "Will your board of directors understand your taking two days off in one week?" she asked. "For a blood test and a license and then to go with me to Texas?"

"I haven't taken two days off in five years, so they'd better." He let her go. "Let's get breakfast. Then we'll go see Bess and Bobby."

She curled under his arm and, carrying her precious roses, let him guide her to the table.

It was cozy in the kitchen. Blake kept watching her and Meredith could hardly keep from bursting into song with the sheer joy of having him look at her that way. He might not love her, but he was already very, very possessive. And in time, love might come.

"Meredith and I are going to get married, Sarah," Blake said. "She's going to live with us and take care of you and write books."

Sarah's eyes lit up and the expression on the small face was humbling. "Are you, Merry? Are you going to be my mommy?" she asked, as if they were offering her the earth.

"Yes." Meredith smiled. "I'm going to be your mommy and hug and kiss you and tell you stories and— oh!"

Sarah ran to her like a whirlwind, almost knocking the breath out of her as she climbed onto her lap and clung, crying and mumbling things that Meredith couldn't understand.

"What is it, honey?" Blake asked, torn out of his normal calm by the child's totally unexpected reaction. He touched Sarah's dark hair gently. "What is it?" he repeated.

"I can stay now, can't I, Daddy?" Sarah asked him with wet red eyes. "I don't have to go. Merry is going to live with us and I'll be her little girl, too."

"Of course you can stay," Blake said shortly. "There was never any question of that."

"When I first came," she reminded him, "you said I could go to a…a home!"

"Damn my vicious tongue," Blake burst out. He got up, lifting Sarah out of Meredith's arms and into his own. He held her close, his green eyes steady on hers.

"You'll never live in any home but mine," he said huskily. "You're my own flesh and blood, my own little girl. I…" He choked on the words. His jaw worked. "I…care for you—very much," he bit off finally.

Even at her age, Sarah seemed to realize what a difficult thing it was for him to say. She lowered her cheek to his shoulder with a sigh and smiled through her tears. "I love you, too, Daddy," she said.

Blake didn't know how he managed not to break down and cry. His arms contracted around her and he turned so that Meredith couldn't see his face. In all his life he'd never been so shaken.

"How about some more coffee?" Meredith asked gently. "I'll get it, okay?" She went to the stove to pour coffee from the percolator into the carafe, and her eyes were wet. She felt stunned by Blake's brief display of vulnerability, his hope for the future. If he could love Sarah, he could love others. She dabbed at her eyes and filled the carafe. Miracles did happen, after all.

When she turned back to the table, Sarah was sitting on Blake's lap. And she stayed there for the rest of breakfast, her small face full of love and wonder. Blake just looked smug.

"What about your work?" Blake asked when they'd finished breakfast and Sarah had excused herself to go and watch her eternal cartoons in the living room.

"I just need a place to set up my computer," she said.

His eyebrows arched. "What have you got?"

"An IBM compatible," she said. "Twin disk drives, over 600K memory, word processing software, a big daisy wheel printer and a modem."

"Come and look over my setup."

She let him take her hand and lead her into the study. "It's just like mine!" she exclaimed when she saw what he had on his desk.

He smiled at her. "A good omen?"

"Wonderful! Now we'll both have a spare," she said with a dancing glance.

"You can work here when I'm not home. And if you want to set up your equipment in the corner, we'll order another desk and some filing cabinets."

"It won't bother you?" she asked hesitantly. "I work odd hours. Sometimes, if I get on a streak, I may work into the small hours of the morning."

"I'm marrying you," he said. "That includes your job, your eccentricities, your bad habits and your temper. I don't mind what you do. You're entitled to a life that allows you the right to be your own person, to make your own dreams come true in business."

"I thought you were a chauvinist," she said. "That's the wrong attitude. You're supposed to refuse to let me work outside the home and say that no job is going to come before you."

He arched an eyebrow. "Okay, if that's what you want."

She hit his chest playfully. "Never mind. I like you better this way." She reached up and slid her arms around his neck. "Sarah says she won't mind if I hug and kiss her. So can I hug and kiss you, too?" she asked daringly.

His mouth quirked a little. "I guess so."

"You might show more enthusiasm," she said.

He bent his head and whispered, "I can't. You're sore."

She blushed and opened her mouth to protest just as his came down and settled over her lips. He kissed her gently, swinging her lightly in his arms from side to side as he held her mouth under his.

"That was nice," she told him huskily.

"I thought so, too." he let her go abruptly, the hardness back in his face. "I'll line up a charter flight to San Antonio for Tuesday. We can have your furniture sent out."

"It's a furnished apartment." She smiled. "All I have is my clothes, a few manuscripts and my computer stuff."

"Okay. We'll have that sent out."

"Blake, you're sure, aren't you?" she asked seriously.

"As sure as you are," he replied. "Now stop brooding over it. I'll get the license and set up the blood test for you tomorrow. Sarah can go with you to the doctor, because it will only take a minute."

"All right. It sounds like a nice day." She sighed.

"Every day is nice with you, Meredith," he said unexpectedly and with a wry smile.

But just as they started to go down to Bess's, a friend of Blake's arrived out of the blue, and Meredith went by herself, letting Sarah stay with her dad and his friend while she told Bess what was going on.

Bess was overwhelmed when she heard the news. "Congratulations!" She laughed. "It's the best thing that could have happened to both of you. You'll make a good marriage."

"Oh, I hope so." Meredith sighed. "I'll do my best, and at least Blake likes me."

"At least," Bess said, and laughed. "If you need witnesses, Bobby and I will be glad to volunteer. Elissa and King, too."

"You can all come," Meredith promised. "I'll need as much moral support as I can get." She shook her head. "It seems like a beautiful dream. I hope I don't wake up. Well, I'd better get my things and get back up to his place. I hope you don't mind, but he, uh, doesn't want me out of his sight until the ceremony Wednesday."

"Fast mover, isn't he?" Bess grinned and hugged her friend warmly. "I'm so happy for you, Merry. And for Blake and Sarah. You'll make a lovely family."

Meredith thought so, too. She carried her single suitcase out to the Porsche and drove up in front of Blake's house. Sarah Jane met her at the door as she set her case down, and Blake came out of the living room smiling.

"Well, what did she say?" he asked. He answered her silent glance into the living room. "He's gone. What did Bess say?"

"She said congratulations." Meredith laughed. "And that we'll make a lovely family."

"Indeed we will," Blake murmured gently.

"Merry, can I be a flower girl?" Sarah asked from behind her.

"You certainly can," Meredith promised, kneeling beside the child to hug her. "You can carry an armload of roses."

"But, Merry, they're all crushed."

"Daddy will cut some more," Meredith said, warming when she remembered how the roses had gotten crushed. She glanced at Blake and the look in his eyes made her blush.

The next two days went by in an unreal rush. The blood tests were done, the license obtained, and a minister was lined up to perform the ceremony at the local Baptist church where Meredith's parents had worshipped when she was a child. For reasons that Meredith still didn't understand, Blake had given her a guest room to sleep in until the wedding, and although he'd been friendly enough, he hadn't really attempted to make love to her. She preferred to think it was because she was still uncomfortable from their first time rather than because he had any regrets.

The ceremony was held late Wednesday afternoon, with King and Elissa Roper and Bess and Bobby for witnesses. Meredith said her vows with tears in her eyes, so happy that her heart felt like it would overflow.

She'd bought a white linen suit to be married in, with a tiny pillbox hat covered in lace. It was so sweet when Blake put the ring on her finger and lifted the veil to kiss her. She felt like Sleeping Beauty, as if she'd been asleep for years and years and now was waking to the most wonderful reality.

The reception was held at the Ropers' sprawling white frame house outside Jack's Corner, and Danielle and Sarah Jane played quietly while the adults enjoyed champagne punch and a lavish catered buffet.

"You didn't have to go to this kind of expense, for God's sake," Blake muttered to big King Roper.

King pursed his lips and his dark eyes sparkled.

"Yes, I did. Having you get close enough to a woman to marry again deserved something spectacular." He glanced at Meredith, who was talking animatedly to Elissa and Bess a few feet away while Bobby, the exact opposite in coloring to his half-brother, King, was watching the kids play.

"She's a dish," King remarked. "And we all know how she felt about you when she left here." His dark eyes caught Blake's green ones. "It's not a good thing to live alone. A wife and children make all the difference. I know mine do."

"Sarah likes her," Blake replied, sipping punch as his eyes slid over Meredith's exquisite figure like a paintbrush. "She's a born mother."

King smiled. "Thinking of a large family, are you?"

Blake glared at him. "I've only just got married."

"Speaking of which, why aren't you two going on a honeymoon?"

"I'd like that," Blake confessed. "But neither Meredith nor I like the idea of leaving Sarah behind while we have one. She's had enough insecurity for one month. Anyway," he added, "Meredith's got that autographing in town Saturday, and she doesn't want to disappoint the bookstore."

"She always was a sweet woman," King remarked. "I remember her ragged and barefoot as a child, helping her mother carry eggs to sell at Mackelroy's Grocery. She never minded hard work. In that," he added with a glance at his friend, "she's a lot like you."

Blake smiled faintly. "I didn't have a choice. It was

work or starve in my case. Now that I'm in the habit, I can't quit."

King eyed him solemnly. "Don't ever let work come before Meredith and Sarah," he cautioned. "Bobby had to find that out the hard way, and he barely realized it in time."

Blake was looking at Meredith with faint hunger in his narrow eyes. "It would take more than a job to overshadow Meredith," he said without thinking. He finished his punch. "And we'd better get going. I've got reservations at the Sun Room for six o'clock. You're sure you and Elissa don't mind having Sarah for the night?"

"Not at all. And she loves the idea of sleeping in Danielle's room," King assured him. "If she needs you, I promise we'll call, even if it's two in the morning. Fair enough?" he added when he saw the worry in Blake's eyes.

"Fair enough," Blake said with a sigh.

A few minutes later, Blake and Meredith said their goodbyes, kissed Sarah good-night and went to the Sun Room for an expensive wedding supper.

"I still can't quite believe it," Meredith confessed with a smile as she looked at her husband across the table. "That we're married," she added.

"I know what you mean," he said quietly. His eyes caressed her face. "I swore when Nina left that I'd never marry again. But it seemed the most natural thing in the world with you."

She smiled. "I hope I don't disappoint you. I can cook and clean, but I'm not terribly domestic, and when

I'm writing, sometimes I pour coffee over ice and put mashed potatoes in the icebox and make coffee without putting a filter in it. I'm sort of absentminded."

"As long as you remember me once in a while, I won't complain," he promised. "Eat your dessert before it melts."

She picked up a spoon to start on her baked alaska. "Sarah was so happy." She sighed.

"You'll be good for her." He sipped his coffee and watched Meredith closely. "You'll be good for both of us."

Meredith felt as if she were riding on a cloud for the rest of the evening. The Sun Room had a dance band as well as a wonderful restaurant. They danced until late, and Meredith was concealing a yawn when they got home.

"Thank you for my honeymoon," she said with a mischievous smile when they were standing together in the hall. "It was wonderful."

"Later on I'll give you a proper one," he promised. "We'll go away for several days. To Europe or the Caribbean."

"Let's go to Australia and stay on a cattle station," she suggested. "I wrote about one of those in my last book, and it sounded like a great place to visit."

"Haven't you traveled?" he asked.

"Just to the Bahamas and Mexico," she said. "It was great, but no place is really exciting when you have to see it alone."

"I know what you mean." He pulled her against him

and bent to kiss her. "You still taste of ice cream," he murmured, and kissed her again.

"You taste of coffee." She linked her arms around his neck and smiled at him. "I want to ask you something."

"Be my guest."

"Do you have any deeply buried scruples about intimacy after marriage?" she asked somberly. "I mean, I wouldn't want to cause you any trauma."

He smiled in spite of himself. "No," he replied. "I don't think I have any buried scruples about it. Why? Were you thinking of seducing me?"

"I would if I knew how," she assured him. She smiled impishly. "Could you give me a few pointers?"

He reached down and picked her up in his arms. "I think I might be able to help you out," he said. He started for the staircase with his lips brushing hers. "It might take a while," he added under his breath. "You don't mind, do you? You don't have any pressing appointments in the next few hours…?"

"Only one. With you," she whispered, and pressed her open mouth hungrily to his, shivering with delight as his tongue pushed softly inside it and tasted her. She moaned with the aching pleasure.

His lips drew back a little. "I like that," he whispered huskily. "Make a lot of noise. Tonight there's no one to hear you except me."

Her teeth tugged at his lower lip and she obliged him with a slow, sultry moan that caused his mouth to grow rough with desire. She smiled under the heat of the kiss, and when he lifted his head and saw her expression, for just an instant he wondered if, like Nina, she was pretending pleasure that she didn't feel. And then he saw her eyes. And all his doubts fell away as his mouth bit hungrily into hers. He thought that in all his life he'd never seen such a fierce passion in a woman's soft eyes...

This time he left the lights on. He undressed her slowly, drawing it out, making her dizzy with pleasure as he kissed every inch of her as he uncovered her body. When the clothes were off, his mouth smoothed over her adoringly, lingering on her soft, warm breasts. He'd never realized how infallible instinct was until now. Apparently it didn't matter how skilled he was. She cared for him, and that made her delightfully receptive to anything he wanted. His heart swelled with the knowledge.

By the time he'd undressed, she was trembling, her body waiting, her eyes so full of warm adoration that he felt like a lonely traveler finally coming home. This was nothing like the indifference Nina had shown when he'd touched her. He looked at Meredith's lovely face and wanted nothing more in life than her arms around him.

She raised her feverish eyes to his, drowning in their green glitter. His lips parted and she trembled, because he wasn't in any hurry.

His hard mouth brushed at hers while his hands touched her with reverence. His wife. Meredith was his wife, and she wanted him. He groaned softly. "Merry, love me," he whispered as his mouth bit hungrily into hers. "Love me."

She felt her body trembling with delight as she heard the soft words and wondered dizzily if he even realized what he was saying. Poor, lonely man...

Her arms went around him hungrily and she kissed him back, willing to give him anything as tenderness and love welled up within her.

"You're…killing me," she bit off minutes later, when his slow, exquisitely tender caresses were making her shudder with need for him.

"Liar," he told her, smiling gently at her even through his own trembling need. He moved suddenly, and watched her eyes dilate, felt her body react. "That's it. Help me," he coaxed. "Show me what you want, little one. Let me…love you," he groaned when she lifted her body up into his.

Blinded with the passion they were sharing, she pulled his head down to her mouth and kissed him with all the lonely years and all her smothered love in her lips. She felt his powerful body tremble until it gave way under his hunger for her and he overwhelmed her with exquisite tenderness.

Her cry was echoed in his as unbearable pleasure bound them, lifted them together in a fierce buffeting embrace, and they clung to each other as the wave of fulfillment hit them together.

Meredith could barely breathe when she felt the full weight of Blake's body against her. He was shivering, and her arms contracted around him.

"Darling," she whispered. Her lips touched his cheek, his mouth, his throat, damp with sweat. "Darling, darling…!"

The endearment went through his weary body like an electric current. He returned her tender kisses, smoothing her bare body against his and loving the soft curves caressing him. His hands felt almost too rough to be touching her. He savored the warm silk of her skin, the cologne scent of her, the pleasure of just being close to her.

Somewhere in the back of his mind, he remembered whispering to her to love him. He buried his mouth in her throat, kissing it hungrily as his need broke through his reserve and made him just temporarily vulnerable.

He pulled her into the hair-roughened curve of his chest and thighs, holding her with a new kind of possessiveness. His mouth brushed her forehead and her closed eyes with breathless tenderness. He felt the tension of pleasure slowly relax in her soft body, as it had in his own.

"I've been alone all my life until now," he said quietly, his face solemn. "I never realized how cold it was until you warmed me."

Tears formed in her eyes. "I'll warm you all my life if you'll let me," she assured him huskily.

He searched her soft face and bent to take her mouth under his. "Warm me now," he breathed against her lips, and his hands slid to her hips. As he pulled her close, he heard her voice, heard the soft endearment that broke from her lips, and his heart almost burst with delight that she cared too much to be capable of hiding it.

Later, curled up together with the lights out, Blake lay awake long after Meredith was enveloped in contented sleep. He couldn't quite believe what had happened so quickly in his life. He'd been alone, and now he had a daughter and a loving wife, and the way it was affecting him made him nervous.

Something had happened tonight with Meredith. Something incredible. It hadn't been just the satisfying of a physical desire anymore. It went much deeper than that. There was something reverent about the way they made love, about the tenderness they gave to each other. He was being taken over by Meredith and he had cold feet. Could he really trust her not to walk out on him as Nina had? If he let himself fall in love with her, would she betray him? He looked down at her sleeping face, and even in the darkness he could see its warm glow. The distrust relaxed out of him. He could trust her.

Of course he could, he told himself firmly. After all, he could live with her profession and she'd have Sarah to keep her busy. Her writing wasn't going to interfere in their lives. He'd make sure of it.

CHAPTER TEN

BUT MEREDITH'S JOB did interfere with their marriage. Her autographing session was the first indication of it. Blake and Sarah had gone to the bookstore Saturday to watch, and Blake had been fascinated by the number of people who'd come to have her sign their books. Dressed in a very sexy green-and-white ensemble, with a big white hat to match, Meredith looked very much the successful, urbane author. And she was suddenly speaking a language he didn't understand. Her instant rapport with people fascinated and disturbed him. He didn't get along well with people, and he certainly didn't seek them out. If she was really as gregarious as she seemed and started to expect to throw lavish parties and have weekend guests, things were going to get sticky pretty fast.

As it happened, she wasn't a party girl. But she did have to do a lot of traveling in connection with the release of her latest book.

Blake went through the ceiling when she announced her third out-of-state trip in less than three weeks.

"I won't have it," he said coldly, bracing her in the study.

"*You* won't have it?" Meredith replied with equal

hauteur. "You told me when we married that you didn't mind if I worked."

"And I don't, but this isn't working. It's jet-setting," he argued. "My God, you're never here! Amie's spending most of her time baby-sitting Sarah because you're forever getting on some damned airplane!"

"I know," Meredith said miserably. "And I'm sorry. But I made this commitment to promote the book before I married you. You of all people wouldn't want me to go back on my word."

"Wouldn't I?" he demanded, and he looked like the old Blake, all bristling masculinity and outraged pride. "Stay home, Meredith."

"Or what?" she challenged, refusing to be ordered about like a child of Sarah's age. "What did you have in mind, tying me to a tree out in the backyard? Or moving to your club in town? You can't, you know, you don't have a club in town."

"I could use one," he muttered darkly. "Okay, honey. If you want the job that much, go do it. But until you come to grips with the fact that this is a marriage, not a limited social engagement, I'm sleeping in the guest room."

"Go ahead," she said recklessly. "I don't care. I won't be here!"

"Isn't that the gospel truth," he said, glaring at her.

She turned on her heel and went to pack.

From then on, everything went downhill between them. She felt an occasional twinge of guilt as Blake reverted to his old, cold self. He was polite to her, but nothing more. He didn't touch her or talk to her. He acted as if she were a houseguest and treated her accordingly. It was a nightmarish change from the first days of their marriage, when every night had been a new and exciting adventure, when their closeness in bed had fostered an even deeper closeness the rest of the time. She'd been sure that he was halfway in love with her. And then her traveling had started to irritate him. Now he was like a stranger, and Meredith tossed and turned in the big bed every night, all alone. In the back of her mind, the knowledge that she had failed to conceive ate away at her confidence. As the days went on, Blake was becoming colder and colder.

Only with Sarah was he different. That was amusing, and Meredith laughed at the spectacle of Blake being followed relentlessly every step he took by Sarah Jane. She was right behind him all weekend, watching him talk to the men, sitting with him while he did the books, riding with him when he went out over the fields in the pickup truck to see about fences and cattle and feed. Sarah Jane was his shadow, and he smiled tolerantly at her attempts to imitate his long strides and his habit of ramming his hands in his pockets and rocking back on his heels when he talked. Sarah was sublimely happy. Meredith was sublimely miserable.

She tried once to talk to Blake, to make him understand that it wouldn't always be this way. But he walked off even as she began.

"Put it in your memoirs, Mrs. Donavan," he said with a mocking smile. "Your readers might find it interesting."

In other words, he didn't. Meredith choked back tears

and went to her computer to work on her next book. It was taking much longer than she'd expected, and the tense emotional climate in the house wasn't helping things along. It was hard to feel romantic enough to write a love scene when her own husband refused to touch her or spend five minutes in a room with her when eating wasn't involved, or watching the news on television.

"You're losing weight," Bess commented one day at lunch when Meredith had escaped to her house to avoid the cold silence at home.

"I'm not surprised." Meredith sighed. "It's an ordeal to eat over there. Blake glares at me or ignores me, depending on his mood. I tried to explain that it wasn't going to be like this every time a book came out, but he refuses to listen."

"Maybe he's afraid to listen," Bess said sagely. "Blake's been alone a long time, and he doesn't really trust women. Maybe he's trying to withdraw before he gets in over his head. In which case—" she grinned "—it could be a good omen. What if he's falling in love with you and trying to fight it? Wouldn't he act just that way?"

"No normal man would," Meredith grumbled.

"Bobby did. So did King, according to Elissa. Men are really strange creatures when their emotions get stirred up." She cocked her blond head and stared at Meredith. "You might put on your sexiest negligee and give him hell."

"There's a thought. But he'd probably toss me out the window if I dared."

"You underestimate yourself."

"All the same, it's his heart I want to reach. I can't really do that in bed," Meredith said with sad eyes. "He's always wanted me. But I want more. I'm greedy. I want him to love me."

"Give it time. He'll come around eventually."

"Meanwhile I'm miserable," Meredith said. "At least he and Sarah are getting along like a house on fire. They're inseparable."

"Camouflage," Bess said. "He's using her to keep you at bay."

"He wouldn't."

"You greenhorn." Bess sighed. "I wish I could make you listen."

"Me, too." Meredith got up. "I've got to go. I have to fly to Boston for a signing in the morning. And I haven't told Blake yet." She grimaced. "He's been in an explosive mood for two weeks. This will sure light the fuse, I'm afraid."

"Do you have to go?"

She nodded. "It's the very last trip, but I did promise, and the bookseller is a friend of mine. I can't let her down."

Bess searched Meredith's face. "Better Blake than her?" she asked quietly. "It seems to me, from an objective standpoint, that you're running as hard from this relationship as he is. Do you really have to make these trips, or are you doing it to spite him, to prove your independence?"

"I can't let him own me," Meredith said stubbornly.

"Good for you. But a man like that isn't going to be

owned, either. You're going to have to compromise if you want to keep him."

Meredith felt herself going pale. "What do you mean, if I want to keep him?"

"Just that you could drive him away. He isn't like other men. He's been kicked around too much already. His pride won't take much more abuse. You see these trips as simple tours," she explained. "Blake sees that you prefer your work to him."

Meredith felt sick. "No. He couldn't think…"

"I did with Bobby," Bess said simply. "I was sure that he would walk over my dying body to get to the office. I very nearly left him because of it. I couldn't bear being second best." Her eyes narrowed. "Neither can Blake. So look out."

"I've been blind," Meredith groaned. She wrapped her arms around herself. "I thought it was important not to be led around like a dumb animal, so I was fighting for my independence." She closed her eyes. "I never dreamed he'd think I considered him less important than writing."

"If you want some expert advice, tell him while there's still time," Bess suggested.

Meredith hugged the blond-haired woman. "Thanks," she said huskily. "I love him so much, you know, and it was like a dream come true when he married me. Maybe I was afraid to let myself be happy with him, afraid of being hurt, of losing him again. I guess I just lost my perspective."

"Blake probably lost his for the same reason. Get over there and fight for what you have."

"Ever thought about joining the army?" Meredith murmured on her way out the door. "You'd make a dandy drill sergeant."

"The marines offered, but then I found out they expected me to take showers with the men." Bess grinned. "Bobby would never approve of that!"

Meredith laughed and waved as she got into her car and sped back up to the house. Bless Bess for making things so clear. It was going to be all right now. She'd tell Blake the real reason she'd insisted on the tours, and it would smooth over the tension.

She got out of the car and ran into the house, but there was no sound. Odd. She was sure Sarah had been playing in the living room.

She wandered into the kitchen, but there was no one there except Amie.

"Where is everybody?" Meredith asked, excitement shining in her eyes as she savored speaking to Blake.

Amie looked at her worriedly. "Surely Blake told you, Merry," she said hesitantly.

Meredith blinked. "Told me what?"

"Why, that he was taking Sarah to the Bahamas for a few days," Amie said, dropping the bombshell.

Meredith knew her face was like rice paper, but she managed to smile. "Oh. Yes. Of course. It slipped my mind."

"You're crying!" Amie put down her dishcloth and hugged Meredith. "Poor little thing," she mumbled, patting the weeping woman. "He didn't tell you, did he?"

"No."

"I'm sorry."

Meredith reached into her pocket for a tissue and wiped her red eyes. "I've given him a hard time lately," she said. "It's no more than I deserve." She took a deep breath. "I have to fly to Boston in the morning, but when I come back, that's the end of my traveling. I won't go on tour again. Not ever."

Amie searched her white face. "Don't do that," she said unexpectedly.

"What?"

"Don't do it. If you let him get the upper hand now, if you ever let him start ordering your life, you'll never be your own person again," she said simply. "He's a good man in many ways, but he has a domineering streak a mile wide. If you let him, he'll tell you how to breathe. I know you want peace with him, but don't sacrifice your freedom for it."

Meredith felt torn. Bess had said give in, Amie was saying don't. She didn't know what to do anymore. Who was right? And what should she do?

Her heart shattered, she went upstairs to pack. What had begun as a beautiful marriage had turned sour. It was partly her fault, but Blake was as much to blame. She wondered if he was able to admit fault. Somehow she didn't think so.

Boston was lovely. She did her autographing and stayed an extra day to enjoy the historic places and spend a little time in the local library. But her heart was broken. Blake had gone away without her, without even asking if she wanted to go with him. She didn't know if she even wanted to go home again.

She did go home again, of course—to an empty

house. She and Amie ate together and Meredith worked on her newest book because there was nothing else to do. And all the while she wondered what Blake and Sarah were doing. Most of all, she wondered if his eye was wandering to a more domestic kind of woman, one who would be content to stay at home and have his babies.

She stopped writing and sat with her head in her hands, daydreaming about having Blake's child. Even though they hadn't taken precautions she hadn't conceived. In a way that was a shame. A baby might have helped bring them together. On the other hand, if Blake decided to leave her, it would be better for both of them if there were no blood ties.

Leave her. She closed her eyes. *If Blake should leave her...* She couldn't bear even to think of it. She loved him so, missed him so. Tears ran down her cheeks, blinding her. If only he could love her back...

BLAKE, MEANWHILE, WAS riding around New Providence in a jitney with Sarah at his side, smiling as she enthused over the beautiful flowers and the unbelievable colors of the ocean and the whiteness of the sand. If Meredith had been with them, it would truly have been paradise.

His eyes darkened at the thought. Meredith. He hadn't really given her a chance, he supposed. Her traveling made him mad and he'd pushed her out of his life because she refused to stop. In a way he was glad she had the spirit to stand up to him. But in another, he felt miserable because she was telling him he was nothing compared to her career. It hurt far more than Nina's betrayal. Because he hadn't loved Nina. And he...cared... for Meredith.

He couldn't bear to think about her. He'd come down here with Sarah to hurt her. Probably she was in tears when Amie told her they had gone. His face hardened. She was going to take a long time to forgive him for that slap in the face. He was sorry he'd done it. He'd been hurting and wanted to strike back, but now it all seemed so petty and unnecessary. Being cruel wasn't going to win Meredith back. He sighed. He didn't quite have the hang of marriage yet. But he was going to work at learning how when he got back. He had to. He couldn't bear to lose Meredith. These past few cold weeks had made his life hell, especially at night. He missed her soft body, her quiet breathing next to him. He missed her laughter and the lazy talks they'd had late at night. He missed a lot. He only hoped he hadn't left things too late.

"Sarah," he said, "how would you like to go home tomorrow?"

"I'd like that, Daddy," she said. "I miss Merry something awful!"

"Yes, so do I," he murmured under his breath.

MEREDITH WAS SITTING at the computer with her reading glasses on when she heard the front door open.

"Merry!" Sarah Jane cried, and flung herself at Meredith to hug her convulsively. "Merry, why didn't you come with us? We had such fun, but it was lonely without you!"

"It was lonely without you, too, baby." Meredith sighed, hugging Sarah close.

She heard Blake's step in the hall, and her heart ran away. Her body quivered. She didn't look up because she didn't dare. He'd hurt her enough. She wasn't giving him any more openings.

"Hello, Meredith," he said quietly.

She lifted cool gray eyes to his. "Hello, Blake. I hope you had a pleasant time."

He shifted. He had a faint sunburn, but he looked almost gaunt. She realized that he'd honed down a little, too, during their cold war, and guilt made her throat constrict.

"It was all right," he said coolly. "How have you been?"

"Oh, I've had a ball," she said nervously, hiding her lack of confidence from him. She smiled at Sarah. "I went to autograph in Boston and researched a new book while I was there."

Blake's expression closed up. He'd imagined her sitting home crying, and she'd been in Boston working on another damned book. He turned on his heel without another word and left her sitting there.

"And I'm going to have a party and everything, Merry, 'cause Daddy said so!" Sarah was chattering excitedly. She looked pretty. Her hair was neatly combed and she had on a soft, lightweight cotton dress with red and beige patterns on it, obviously bought for her in the Bahamas. Blake had even put a bow in her hair.

"A party?" Meredith echoed. She hadn't been listening, because the cold look on Blake's face had hit her hard. She'd put her foot in it again by raving about her trip.

"My birthday, Merry!" Sarah said with forced patience.

"That's right," Meredith said. "It's coming up."

"And we have to have a party," Sarah said. "Dani can come, and you and Daddy, and we can have cake."

"And ice cream," Meredith said, smiling at the child's obvious excitement. "We might even have balloons and a clown. Would you like that?"

"Oh, yes!"

"When are we having the party?" Meredith asked.

"Next Saturday," Sarah said.

"Well, I'll see what I can do." She took off her reading glasses and Sarah picked them up and tried to look through them, making a face when everything was blurry.

Mrs. Jackson fixed the birthday cake with a favorite cartoon character of Sarah's on the top and Meredith arranged for a local clown to come to the party to entertain the children. She invited Dani and some of Dani's friends, anticipating bedlam. Maybe if they ate in the kitchen, it would be less messy.

"Why should they eat in the kitchen?" Blake asked icily when Meredith got up her nerve the day of the party to approach him about it. "They're children, not animals. They can eat in the dining room."

Meredith curtsied and smiled. "Yes, my lord," she said. "Anything you say, sir."

"That isn't funny," he said. He stalked out of the room and Meredith stuck out her tongue at him.

"Reverting to childhood?" Mrs. Jackson asked with a gleam in her eye as she opened the hutch to get out plates and glasses, since the party was less than two hours away.

"I guess so. He infuriates me!" She sighed. "He says we have to have it in here. Doesn't he know that cake and ice cream are terrible on carpet?"

"Not yet," Amie said with her tongue in her cheek. "But he will."

Meredith smiled conspiratorially at her. "Yes, he certainly will."

They had the party in the dining room. There were seven four-year-olds. In the middle of the cake and ice cream, they had a food fight. By the time Meredith and Elissa, who'd volunteered to help out, got them stopped, the room looked like a child's attempt at camouflage. There was ice cream on the carpet, the hutch, the tablecloth, and even tiny splatters on Blake's elegant crystal chandelier. Waterford crystal, too, Meredith mused as she studied the chocolate spots there. The chairs were smeared with vanilla cake and white frosting, and underfoot there was enough cake to feed several hungry mice.

"Isn't this fun, Merry?" Sarah Jane exclaimed with a chocolate ring around her mouth and frosting in her hair.

"Yes, darling," Meredith agreed wholeheartedly. "It's fun, indeed. I can hardly wait until your daddy gets here."

Just as she said that, Sarah Jane's daddy walked in the door and stopped as if he'd been hit in the knee with a bat. His lower lip fell a fraction of an inch and he stared at the table and children as if he'd never seen either before.

He lifted a finger and turned to Meredith to say something.

"Isn't it just such fun?" Meredith asked brightly. "We had a food fight. And then we had chocolate warfare. I'm afraid your chandelier became a casualty, but, then, you'll have *such* fun hosing it down…"

Blake's face was getting redder by the instant. He glared at Meredith and went straight through to the kitchen.

Seconds later, Meredith could hear his deep, slow voice giving Amie hell on the half-shell, and then the back door slammed hard enough to shake the room.

Elissa's twinkling blue eyes met Meredith's gray ones. "My, my, and he insisted on the dining room? Where do you think he's gone?"

"To get a hose, I expect," Meredith commented, and then broke into laughter.

"I wouldn't laugh too loud," Elissa cautioned as she helped mop Dani's face.

The clown arrived just after the children were tidied, and he kept them occupied in the living room with Elissa while Meredith and Amie began the monumental task of cleaning the dining room.

Meredith was on the floor with a wet sponge and carpet cleaner when Blake came in, followed by two rugged looking men wearing uniforms. Without a word, he tugged Meredith up by the arm, took the sponge from her hand, tossed it to one of the men and guided her into the living room.

He left her there without a word. Belatedly she realized that he'd gone to get some cleaning men to take care of the mess. Oddly, it made her want to cry. His thoughtfulness had surprised her. Or maybe it was his conscience. Either way, she thought, it had been kind of him to do that for Amie and her.

Seconds later, Amie was pulled into the living room. She stared at Meredith and shrugged. Then she smiled and sat down to enjoy the clown with the children.

It was, Sarah Jane said after the guests had gone, the best party in the whole world.

"I made five new friends, Merry," she told Meredith gaily. "And they liked me!"

"Most everyone likes you, darling," Meredith said, kneeling to hug her. Her white-and-pink dress was liberally stained with chocolate and candy, but that's what parties were for, Meredith told herself. "Especially me," she added with a big kiss.

Sarah Jane hugged her tight. "I love you, Merry." She sighed. "I just wish…"

"Wish what, pet?"

"I wish my daddy loved you," she said, and her big green eyes looked sadly at Meredith.

Meredith hadn't realized until then how perceptive Sarah was. Her face lost its glow. She forced a smile. "It's hard to explain about grown-ups, Sarah," she said finally. "Your daddy and I have disagreed about some things, that's all."

"Why not tell her the truth?" Blake demanded coldly

from the doorway. "Why not tell her that your writing comes before she does, and before I do, and that you just don't care enough to stay home?"

"That's not true!" Meredith got to her feet, her eyes flashing. "You won't even listen to my side of it, Blake!"

"Why bother?" He laughed mockingly. "Your side isn't worth hearing."

"And yours is?"

Neither of them noticed Sarah Jane's soft gasp, or the sudden paleness of her little face. Neither of them saw the tears gather in her green eyes and start to flow down her cheeks. Neither of them knew the traumatic effect the argument was having on her, bringing back memories of fights between her mother and stepfather and the violence that had highlighted most of her young life.

She sobbed silently and suddenly turned and slipped from the room, hurrying up the staircase.

"Your pride is going to destroy our marriage," Meredith raged at Blake. "You just can't stand the idea of letting me work, or giving me any freedom at all. You want me to stay home and look after Sarah and have babies—"

"Writers don't have babies," he said curtly. "It's too demeaning and limiting."

She felt her face go pale. "I never said that, Blake," she said. "I haven't done anything to prevent a baby." She lowered her eyes to the carpet and hoped the glitter of her tears wouldn't show. "I just can't...can't seem to get pregnant."

His breath sighed out roughly. He hadn't meant to say such a cruel thing. It was cruel, too, judging by the look on her face. She seemed to really want a child, and that warmed him.

He moved forward a little, his hand going out to touch her hair. "I didn't mean that," he said awkwardly.

She looked up. There were tears in her eyes. "Blake," she whispered achingly, and lifted her arms.

He cursed his own vulnerability even as he reached for her, lifting her hard against him, holding her close. "Don't cry, little one," he said against her ear as she sobbed out the frustration and loneliness and fear of the past few weeks against his broad shoulder.

"There's something…something *wrong* with me," she wailed.

"No, there isn't." He nuzzled his cheek against hers. "Unless you count a husband with an overdose of pride. You're right. It was just feeling second best, that's all. You can't stay home all the time."

"I promised I'd go on tour," she said huskily. "I didn't want to. But then, when I kept not getting pregnant, I hated having so much time to sit and worry about it." Her arms tightened around his neck. "I wanted to give you a son…"

His arms contracted. He'd never considered that as a reason for her wandering. He'd never dreamed she wanted a child so much.

"We've been married only a few weeks," he whispered at her ear. "And the past several, I've been sleeping in another room." He smiled faintly in spite of himself. "It takes a man and a woman to make babies. You can't do it by yourself."

She laughed softly, and he felt warm all over at the sound, because she hadn't laughed in a long time.

"If you want to get pregnant, Mrs. Donavan, you'll have to have a little help."

She drew in a breath and looked into his soft green eyes. "Could you do that for me?" she whispered playfully. "I mean, I know it would be a sacrifice and all, but I'd be *sooo* grateful."

He laughed, too. The joy came back into his life again. She was beautiful, he thought, studying her face. And he cared so damned much. His eyes darkened and the smile faded. Cared. No. It was more. Far more than that. He...loved.

"Kiss me," he said, bending to her soft mouth. "It's been so long, honey. So long!"

His mouth covered hers hungrily, and she felt her body melting into him, aching for his touch, for the crush of his mouth on her soft lips. She moaned, and his kiss became suddenly ardent and demanding.

"Merry?" Mrs. Jackson called suddenly from the hall.

Blake and Meredith broke apart with breathless reluctance, but there was a strange note in Amie's usually calm voice.

Meredith moved to the closed door and opened it. "Amie, what is it?" she asked, wondering at the closed door, because it had been open when Sarah was in the room with them—"Where's Sarah!" Meredith asked suddenly.

Blake felt himself pale when he remembered the argument. Sarah Jane had heard.

Amie grimaced. "I don't know where she is. I can't find her," she said. "She isn't in her room. And it's raining outside."

It was thundering, too. And it was almost dark. Meredith and Blake didn't waste time on words. They rushed down the hall and out the back door, forgoing rain gear in their haste to find the child they'd unknowingly sent running out into the stormy night.

CHAPTER ELEVEN

BLAKE WANTED TO throw things. He searched the stable, every nook and cranny of it, and every one of the outbuildings, with Meredith quiet and worried beside him. The rain was coming down heavier now, and the last bit of light had left the sky, except for the occasional lightning.

"Where can she be?" Meredith groaned as they stood in the doorway of the barn and looked out into the night.

"I don't know," Blake said heavily. "God, I could kick myself!"

She slid her hand into his big one and held on tight. "I'm every bit as responsible as you are, Blake," she said gently. "I was being stubborn and proud, too." She went close to him, nuzzling her cheek against his broad chest. "I'm sorry for all of it. I never looked at things from your point of view."

"That goes double for me." He bent and kissed her forehead. "I wish we'd remembered that Sarah was in the room. She's had nightmares about arguments her mother and stepfather used to have. Violence upsets her. Any kind of violence. When I yelled at her about getting in the corral with the horse she—" He stopped dead, remembering. He straightened. "No," he said to himself. "No, she couldn't be. That would be too easy, wouldn't it?"

"What would?" Meredith asked as she tried to follow his train of thought.

"Come on!"

He ran toward the house, tugging her along behind him. They were both soaked. Meredith's blouse was plastered to her skin, and her hair hung in wet tangles over her face. Blake didn't look much better. His tan shirt was so wet that she could see right through it to the thick tangle of black hair on his chest.

"Did you find her?" Amie asked worriedly from the sink, where she was washing dishes.

"I'm almost sure I have," Blake said. He dragged Meredith with him and shot up the staircase.

He opened the door to Sarah's room, went straight to the closet and, with a silent prayer, opened it.

And there was Sarah Jane, sobbing silently in the very far corner of the closet floor, under all her pretty things.

"You…hate each other," Sarah sobbed, "just like my mommy and Daddy Brad. I'll have to go away…!" she wailed.

Blake eased into the closet and caught her up in his arms. He held her and hugged her and walked the floor with her while she cried. His shirt was soaked, but Sarah didn't seem to mind. She held on with all her might.

"I love you, baby girl," he whispered in her ear. "You'll never have to go away."

"But you fought!" Sarah said.

"Not the bad kind of fighting," Meredith said,

smoothing the child's soft hair as she rested against Blake's wet shoulder. She smiled. "Sarah Jane, how would you like to have a brother or sister?"

Sarah stopped crying and her eyes widened. "A real live baby brother or sister?"

"A real live one," Meredith assured her. She looked up into Blake's soft, quiet eyes. "Because we're going to have one, aren't we, Blake?"

"Just as soon as we can," he agreed huskily, his eyes full of warmth and faint hunger.

"Oh, that would be so nice." Sarah sighed. "I could help you, Merry. We could make clothes for her. I can sew. I can make anything."

"Yes, darling," Meredith said with an indulgent smile.

"And Meredith isn't going anywhere," Blake added. "Neither are you, young lady." He chuckled as he put her down. "I can't do without my biggest helper. Who'll go out with me to feed the horses on weekends and help me talk to the men if you leave?"

Sarah nodded. "Yes, Daddy."

"And who'll help me eat the vanilla ice cream that Mrs. Jackson has in the freezer?" he added in a whisper.

Sarah's eyes brightened. "Vanilla?"

"That's right," he said. "Left over from your birthday party. Would you like some?"

"Blake, it's too late…" Meredith began.

"It is not," he said. "It's her birthday, and she can have more if she wants it."

"Thank you, Daddy." Sarah grinned.

"I guess birthdays do only come once a year," Meredith said, relenting. "I'll go and get it. And some cake."

"Amie will get it," Blake said, eyeing Meredith's clothes. "You and I have to change before we can join the party. We got soaked on your account, young lady," he told Sarah with a faint smile. "We thought you'd run out into the fields."

"Oh, I couldn't have done that, Daddy," Sarah said matter-of-factly. "I would have gotten my lovely party dress wet."

Blake laughed with pure delight. "I should have thought of that."

Mrs. Jackson had followed them upstairs and was sighing with relief. "Sarah, I'm so glad you're all right," she said, and smiled. "I was worried."

"You're nice, Mrs. Jackson," Sarah said.

"So are you, pet. Want to come and help me dish up some ice cream and cake while your mommy and daddy change clothes? And we could even make some cookies if you want to. It's not at all late. If your daddy doesn't mind," she added, glancing at Blake.

"Please, Daddy!" Sarah asked.

"All right," he said, relenting. "Go ahead. Your mommy and I will expect some when we get showered and changed. And they'd better be good," he added.

Sarah laughed. "Me and Mrs. Jackson will make lots," she promised. She took Mrs. Jackson's hand and went with her.

"We are a mess," Meredith said, looking down at her clothes.

"Speak for yourself," he returned. "I look great soaking wet.".

She eyed him mischievously, her gaze running possessively over his hard muscles. "I'll drink to that."

He took her hand. "Well, come on. We'll get cleaned up together."

She went with him, expecting that he'd leave her at the door to the master bedroom, but he didn't. He pulled her into the bathroom with him and closed the door, locking it as an afterthought.

Meredith's heart went wild. "What are you doing?" she asked.

"We have to shower, don't we?" he said softly. His hands went to her blouse. "Don't panic," he whispered, bending to touch his mouth gently to hers. "We've seen each other before."

"Yes, but…"

"Hush, sweetheart," he breathed into her open mouth.

She was hungry for him. It had been so long. Too long. She gave a harsh moan, and the blood went to his head when he heard it.

"Do that again," he whispered roughly.

"Do…what?"

"Moan like that," he bit off against her mouth. "It drives me crazy!"

She felt his hands on her breasts when he pushed the blouse out of his way, and she did moan, not because he'd said to, but because the pleasure was so exquisite.

He reached out to turn on the shower and adjust the water, and then, his jaw set, his eyes glittering with desire, he stripped her and then himself and lifted her into the shower.

In between kisses, he soaped her and himself, and

it was an adventure in exploration for Meredith, who'd never dreamed of touching and being touched so intimately. The soap made her skin like silk and the feel of his hands against her most secret places was unbearable delight.

He rinsed Meredith off, and himself, then turned off the water and reached for a towel. But he didn't dry them with it. Holding her eyes, he spread the towel on the tiles of the big bathroom floor, and catching her waist, he lifted her against him and kissed her with probing intimacy.

"We're going to make love. Here," he whispered, "on the floor."

She shuddered at the images that flashed through her mind. "Yes," she groaned, pressing hard against him so that her soft breasts flattened against the thick pelt of hair on his muscular chest.

He spread her trembling body on the thick towel and himself over her, his mouth demanding and slow, his body making the sweetest kind of contacts as he moved sensually over her.

She felt his hands on her and she shivered, but he kept on, evoking sensations she hadn't dreamed existed. She opened her eyes and looked at him and cried out, her nails digging into his shoulders as she lifted against his hand.

"I've never wanted you this badly," he whispered as he poised above her. "I don't want to hold back anything this time."

"Neither do I." She lifted her hands to his face. "I

love you," she said, parting her lips as they brushed his with open sensuality. "I love you, Blake."

His hands contracted on her hips as he moved down, very slowly, his eyes holding hers so that he could see them while his body began to merge with hers. "I love you, too, honey," he whispered shakenly, jerking a little with each deepening movement. She started to lift up, but his hands held her still. "No," he murmured breathlessly, his eyes still on hers. "No, don't…move. Don't rush it… God!" His eyes closed suddenly and he shuddered.

She felt him, breathed him, tasted him. Her body shook with what he was doing to it, with the exquisite slowness of his movements, the depth… She clenched her teeth and cried out in protest, her hips twisting helplessly.

"Blake…if you don't…hurry!" she wailed in anguish.

"Ride it out," he whispered at her ear. His body flowed against hers like the tide, lazy and deliberate, despite the sudden hot urgency that was burning them both. "It's going to be good," he groaned. "Good…so good… Meredith!" His body clenched. "Merry, now!"

She felt his control slip and she let go of her own, yielding totally, trusting him. And the tension all but tore her to pieces before she felt the heat blinding her, burning her, and she fell into it headfirst with tears streaming down her cheeks.

His hands were in her hair, soothing her, smoothing the wet strands away from her rosy cheeks. He was kissing her, sipping the tears from her eyes, kissing away the faint sorrow, the fatigue, the trembling muscles.

She opened her eyes and his face came into focus. She couldn't breathe properly. Her body felt as if it had fallen from a great height. His eyes held hers, and there was adoration in them now, openly.

"The bed would have been better," he said, brushing her mouth lazily with his. "But this was safer."

"She's making cookies," she told him wearily.

"She's unpredictable." He nuzzled her nose with his. "I love you," he breathed, his eyes mirroring the statement. "I couldn't admit it until today, but, oh, God, I feel it, Meredith," he said huskily, his face taut with emotion that made her heart jump with excitement. "I feel it when I look at you, when I'm with you. I didn't know what it was to love, but now I do."

"I've always felt that way about you," she whispered, smiling adoringly. "Since I was eighteen. Maybe even longer. You were the moon, and I wanted you so much."

"I wanted you, too. But I didn't understand why I wanted you so badly." He kissed her again. "You complete me," he breathed. "You make me whole."

Her arms linked around his neck, she buried her face in his throat. "I feel like that, too. Was it necessary to torture me to death?" She laughed shyly.

"It was good, though, wasn't it?" he said. "So intense that I thought I might pass out just at the last. I like losing control with you. I fly up into the sun and explode."

"Yes, so do I." She cuddled closer. "The floor is hard."

"The bed is unprotected."

She sighed. "Well, there's always tonight." She drew back a little. "Are you going to sleep with me?"

"No, I thought I'd sack out with one of the horses—oof!"

She withdrew her fist from his stomach. "Sarah Jane wants a brother or sister."

"At the rate we're going, that won't take long. There's nothing wrong with you," he added, emphasizing it. "And meanwhile, Sarah's going to have time to adjust to us and feel secure. Okay?"

"Okay. I'll stop worrying," she promised.

"Good. Now let's go get some ice cream," he said, moving away to get to his feet and pull her up with him. "I'm starving!"

She wanted to make a comment about men and their strange appetites, but she was too hungry to argue. Her eyes adored him. So much had come out of such a stormy, terrible night, she thought as he wrapped a towel around his lean hips and tossed an extra one to her. He loved her. He actually loved her. She smiled, tingling all over with the newness of hearing the words, of having the freedom to say them. It was like a dream come true. Or it would be, she thought, if she could ever give him a child. She had to force herself not to think about it. Anyway, Blake had said there was plenty of time.

EPILOGUE

EIGHT MONTHS LATER, little Carson Anthony Blake Donavan was born in Jack's Corner Hospital. Looking down at the small head with its thick crown of black hair, Meredith could have jumped for joy. A son, she thought, and so much like his father.

Sitting by her bed, Blake was quiet and fascinated as his first son gripped his thumb. He smiled down at the tiny child. "He's a miracle," he said softly. "Part of us. The best of us."

She smiled up at him tiredly and her hand touched the finger that was caught in the baby's grasp. "He's going to look like you," she said.

"I hope so, considering that he's a boy," he replied dryly.

She laughed. Her eyes made soft, slow love to his. "I'm so happy, Blake," she whispered. "He's the end of the rainbow. And I was so afraid that I couldn't give you a child."

"I knew you could," he said simply. "We love each other too much not to have a child together." He bent and kissed her soft mouth. "Sarah wanted to come, too. I explained that they wouldn't let her in here, but you're getting out tomorrow and she can see her brother all she wants to. She's coloring a pretty picture for him."

"She's been almost as excited as we have," Meredith said. "She'll love not being an only child. And it will give her some security. She still doesn't quite believe that she's safe and loved."

"It will take time," he said. "But she's coming around nicely."

"Yes." She smoothed her fingers lovingly over the baby's downy soft hair. "Isn't he just perfect, Blake?"

"Just perfect," he said, smiling. "Like his mother."

She searched his eyes. "No regrets?"

He shook his head. "Nobody ever loved me until you and Sarah Jane came along," he said quietly. "I can't quite get over it. I'm like Sarah—happiness takes some adjusting to. You've given me the world, Meredith."

"Only my heart, darling," she said softly. "But maybe it was enough."

He bent to kiss her again. "It was more than enough," he replied. The light in his eyes was so full of love for Meredith and his child that it was almost blinding. He smiled suddenly. "I meant to tell you—I met Elissa and Danielle in town just before I came here. They're bringing over a surprise for you." His eyes twinkled. "The store was a little crowded, full of people. I walked in, and do you know what Danielle said?"

Meredith smiled lazily. "No, what?"

"She pointed to me and said, 'Look, Mama, there's Sarah Jane's daddy!'" He grinned. "And do you know what, Merry? I think I'd rather be Daddy than president."

Meredith reached up and touched his mouth lovingly. "I'm sure Sarah Jane and little Carson will agree with that." She took his hand in hers and held it. "And so do I."

He looked down at his son, and foresaw long days ahead of playing baseball in the backyard and board games at the kitchen table. Of drying Sarah's tears and helping Meredith patch up Carson's cuts and bruises. Together, he and Meredith would raise their children and make memories to share in the autumn days. He brought Meredith's hand to his mouth and lifted his gaze to her quiet face. There, in her gray eyes, was the beginning and end of his whole world.

* * * * *

*Molly Orton has loved Zeke Dawson since middle
school. Except Zeke wants Molly to set him up with
her best friend! Molly knows if Zeke spends more time
with her and her adorable baby, he'll see what love
really looks like. All this plain Jane needs is a little
Cinderella magic…*

Read on for a sneak peek at
Wyoming Cinderella,
*the next book in the Dawson Family Ranch series
by* Melissa Senate.

"So the reason you won't kiss me again, the only reason,
is because you're my boss?" She held her breath and
waited.

He stared at her for a second, his grip getting tighter on
the stroller handles. He glanced away, looking up toward
the path. "No. Not the only reason. For another, you're a
parent, and you know my take on having a family of my
own, so getting involved would be wrong."

"I thought you said the right woman could turn you
around, change your mind," she countered, her stomach
churning. She was going to lose in this back-and-forth.

"You're not the right woman, Molly. You can't be.
Because you're my administrative assistant. End of story.

Shall we go?" he added tensely.

"In a second. I just want to understand. You kissed me last night because…?"

He let out a breath and looked down at the ground… well, Lucy's pink-hatted head. "A little crush, I guess. I like you, clearly we have a great rapport and you're lovely, Molly. I acted without thinking and I had no right."

She was swooning. Lovely. Lovely. Lovely.

"And for the reasons I stated," he added, "that kiss, our rapport, any of it, can't be explored further. But it's all right because I've already figured out a solution."

She almost puckered up. *Go ahead, kiss me passionately. If you're thinking that'll get me out of your system, you're so wrong, bucko.*

Don't miss
Wyoming Cinderella *by Melissa Senate,*
available February 2021 wherever
Harlequin Special Edition books and ebooks are sold.

Harlequin.com

⬡ HARLEQUIN
SPECIAL EDITION

**Believe in love. Overcome obstacles.
Find happiness.**

Save **$1.00**

off the purchase of ANY
Harlequin Special Edition book.

Available wherever books are sold,
including most bookstores, supermarkets,
drugstores and discount stores.

✂ -

Save **$1.00**

the purchase of ANY Harlequin Special Edition book.

Coupon valid until June 30, 2021.
Redeemable at participating outlets in the U.S. and Canada only.
Limit one coupon per customer.

2616987

65373 00076 2 (8100)0 12492

Harlequin Enterprises ULC

DPCOUP0121

If you love

DIANA PALMER

then you'll love...

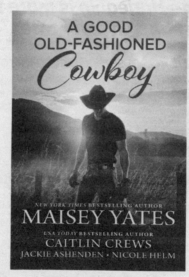

Available February 2021

ROMANCE WHEN
YOU NEED IT

HARLEQUIN

Heartfelt or thrilling, passionate or uplifting—Harlequin is more than just happily-ever-after.

With twelve different series to choose from and new books available every month, you are sure to find stories that will move you, uplift you, inspire and delight you.

SIGN UP FOR THE HARLEQUIN NEWSLETTER

Be the first to hear about great new reads and exciting offers!

Harlequin.com/newsletters

Love Harlequin romance?

DISCOVER.

Be the first to find out about promotions, news and exclusive content!

 Facebook.com/HarlequinBooks

 Twitter.com/HarlequinBooks

 Instagram.com/HarlequinBooks

 Pinterest.com/HarlequinBooks

 YouTube.com/HarlequinBooks

ReaderService.com

EXPLORE.

Sign up for the Harlequin e-newsletter and download a free book from any series at
TryHarlequin.com

CONNECT.

Join our Harlequin community to share your thoughts and connect with other romance readers!
Facebook.com/groups/HarlequinConnection

HSOCIAL2021

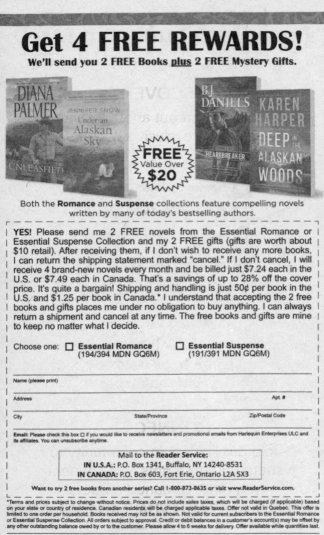